RED GOLD

A Hard Science Fiction Novel

IDO SHARON

Producer & International Distributor
eBookPro Publishing
www.ebook-pro.com

RED GOLD

IDO SHARON

Translation: Dr. Jonathan Boxman
Contact: ido@pitaron.info

ISBN 9798852726827

Dedication

*Dedicated to Moshe Weiss, my Physics teacher, and Yekutiel Fekete,
my electricity teacher at Bezeq High-School.
To Mario Livio, who taught me astrophysics, and also about the
smile of the Cheshire Cat, at the Technion.
To Lany (Ilan) my brother, who taught me history and prehistory.
To Ada my wife, who taught me about myself.
To all the teachers of truth, wherever they may be.*

Table of contents

Global warming and Christopher Columbus

When we were children, we were taught that, until Columbus, humanity assumed the world was flat. Reality is somewhat different.

By 1490, the roundness of the world was widespread, and almost consensual. The Church, its priests and the literate all knew the world was round — it was only the ignorant commoners, who were mostly illiterate 550 years ago, who believed otherwise.

By the same measure, there are those who currently claim that global warming is a "theory" only accepted by some scientists. In reality, it is hard scientific fact. Unlike the commoners of the 15th century, those who are willfully ignorant and deny this fact, cannot offer illiteracy as a defense for their error.

Nonetheless, a genuine dispute between Columbus and mainstream opinion did exist back in the 15th century, just as one exists today. But the past dispute was not between flat earthers and round earthers, just as the present one is not between global warming proponents and deniers.

Rather, mainstream educated opinion in the 15th century held (correctly) that the circumference of the globe was around 40,000 kilometers. As China's eastern seaboard was known to lie some 10,000 to the East of Iberia, it followed that to reach China by voyaging westwards across the Atlantic, as Columbus proposed, would involve sailing over 30,000 kilometers of trackless ocean. This was clearly impossible, as no ship, not even Portugal's ingenious caravels, could carry provisions for a voyage greater than 5,000 kilometers. The crew of any ship that passed that line condemned itself to death.

Columbus, however, insisted — wrongly — that the circumference of the globe was a mere 15,000 kilometers. Hence, he confidently predicted he would make landfall after less than 5,000 kilometers. In the event, he did indeed make landfall, albeit 6,000 kilometers from his port of embarkation in the Canaries, far beyond what anyone thought possible. He landed, however, on the previously unknown continent of America, discovering an entirely new world.

So, it is with global warming. Everyone who is not willfully ignorant knows that our planet periodically undergoes massive cycles in the global temperature, leading to ice ages interspersed with warm periods. It is also well known that this great cycle also contains smaller cycles, so that even in the midst of global warming there will be cold, even very cold, years.

The only question is *how* the fluctuations of these cycles will impact the clear and present trend of global warming. Are we facing a point of no return, to extinction within fifty years, or do we have one hundred and fifty years to find a technological solution to global warming?

Let us return to Columbus. When he approached King John II of Portugal to sponsor his intended westwards voyage around the globe, he was knocking on a locked door. King John, you see, was in possession of a secret with profound significance. Previous explorers, sent south and east around the African coast to find a passage to the Indian Ocean (which Vasco de Gama would finally achieve a decade after Columbus's momentous discovery of the New World) had crossed the Tropic of Capricorn. The celestial charts of the southern hemisphere enabled

Portuguese cartographers to precisely calculate the circumference of the Earth. King John therefore knew, with absolute certainty, that the circumference of the Earth was, in fact, 40,000 kilometers, and hence Columbus's vision of reaching China by sailing westwards was utterly impossible. So, he made what seemed to him the shrewdest move — sending Columbus to the court of his rival for the African and future Indian trade routes, the King of Spain. Hopefully, he would be foolish enough to fund Columbus's expedition and squander his treasury and the lives of his sailors.

Of course, things did not work out quite that way. Columbus discovered a New World, ascribing his success to divine providence. And don't we all like to believe that the Good Lord is looking out for us? But just as it seems unlikely God desired Spain's subsequent rampage across the Western Hemisphere, and the mass slaughter of tens of millions of his Native American children by the sword and Old-World diseases, so it would behoove not to attribute God with a propensity to actively interfere in his creation and save us from the consequences of our own bad decisions. I invite you, if you are skeptical of the prospects of divine salvation as a cure-all for global warming, to continue reading.

Part A: Big Oaks and Little Oaks

1.

Nadav Ben Harush was born in Berkley, the son of a university professor and a Hebrew teacher. When he was four years old, his mother secured a permanent teaching position in the Technion, the Israeli Technology Institute, and the family moved to Haifa in northern Israel.

Nadav seemed, at first glance, to possess a typically Israeli appearance. Cropped, straight black hair, of average height, with tanned skin. He spoke little, but when he did, like many Israelis, he used his hands as much as his mouth.

Nadav had struggled with stage fright from a young age. In first grade, when the teacher asked him a question, he would blush and fall silent. In the second grade, a new teacher asked Nadav to solve a simple math question to which he knew the answer — but shame, stage fright and fear prevented him from speaking. The teacher asked him to stand in front of the class, with Nadav behind her, and asked the question again.

Nadav saw the class laid out before him, lines of children all seated at their tiny desks. Nadav felt the desks fade away — all he could see was the intent faces of his classmates watching him, testing him. Then, he felt a warm trickle run down his legs. The entire class, apart from the teacher, saw what was happening. Some of the children laughed, while others tried to direct the teacher's attention to Nadav. Nadav's friend, who sat in one of the front rows, stood up and took Nadav by the hand, leading him out of the classroom while the teacher remained occupied with the pandemonium. They slipped out of school through a hole in the fence, where Nadav, adding insult to injury, sliced his leg on the torn-up chain links. By the time they reached Nadav's house, he was limping so badly that he could barely walk, collapsing on the front stoop. Nadav's mother rushed out and drove him to the hospital. The doctor who stitched up his leg said he hoped Nadav would recover without a limp. Nadav stayed home for a week to recuperate, his friend was punished for sneaking him out of school, and no one remembered the question that was asked of him in mathematics class that day.

When Nadav returned to school, he found out he was simply unable to speak in the classroom. It was not that he did not want to speak, but even when he tried, his mouth refused to produce any sound. Nadav tried to overcome this on several occasions. He would try to speak quietly, to himself, without anyone noticing. He activated the same throat muscles when he used at home but to no avail — he was simply unable to produce any sound. After a while, he decided that this situation did not perturb him in the slightest. While there were certain disadvantages to his condition, there were also benefits. For example, when he was asked a question in class, he did not even blush. His classmates would shout at the teacher that Nadav was a mute, and all was resolved. Nadav never again felt an urge to pee in his pants.

When he was older, Nadav learned that his condition was a recognized one and was known as "elective muteness." He suffered from social anxiety in high school as well, but not as badly. Still, Nadav remained silent in class, not even attempting to speak.

In the Israeli army, Nadav did well enough. He served as a tank commander instructor in Brigade 460. But when he was offered the chance to undertake an officer's course, Nadav turned it down. Back then, exceptional soldiers were not pressured to become officers, and so he remained a tank commander in the reserves as well. Nadav was highly appreciated for his extraordinary technical abilities. Thus, in the Second Lebanon War, when the tread of the company commander's tank uncoupled, it was Nadav, whose tank was at the rear of the convoy, who was called forward to repair the busted tread. It was a complex engineering operation, for the tread had uncoupled when the tank was tilted on a side slope. There was no textbook solution for this situation, and the fallback option was to blow the tread off — not an ideal fix given the combat environment. Nadav proved his company commander right — he resolved the situation without blowing up the tread, utilizing superlative improvisational engineering skills.

Nadav was an avid cyclist and watched his nutrition. Something about his gait seemed off, sort of a limp but not quite. Like his parents, he was academically inclined, with a PhD in chemistry from the University of Samaria. His alma mater was not exactly by choice: when he completed his term of service in the IDF, he applied to the Technion and various other universities, but his SAT equivalent scores, even after three repeat tests, was only 1022.

Nadav knew the material, of course, but the rapid, automatic thinking tested in the standardized tests was not his forte. Nadav's thinking was slow, methodical, and purposeful.[1] With only mediocre SAT scores, he was persona non grata to his initial choices. Fortunately, the newly established Chemistry Fac-

1. Brain studies have now revealed that the "slow mode of thought" is the more essential one. This thought generates physical effort which burns calories and activates high gamma frequencies (250Hz-70Hz). This mode of thought is more difficult to practice, measure and diagnose. Hence universities continue to cling to what they know and are familiar with – psycho-technical tests which maintain established occupations.

ulty in the University of Samaria was eager to take in new students and so he managed, barely, to get accepted.

Following his PhD studies in the non-prestigious University of Samaria, Nadav moved on to teach in the equally non-prestigious North Galilee College. Nadav was also the laboratory supervisor. Every year, 300 bachelor's degree students entered the lab. Every student had to perform several experiments. To purchase the experimental materials and to perform the upkeep of the laboratory, the college allocated Nadav 200 dollars per student. The budget was calculated according to listed cost of the materials in the "Beit Dekel Marketing Ltd" price list.

Nadav, rather than purchasing the laboratory materials from the industry leading but pricey company, purchased them instead from "Abu Maruf Ltd.," a small company in Jenin in the northern West Bank. Someone once told him that Abu Maruf purchased the chemicals in Jordan, where they were subsidized by the United States. Whatever the real story behind Abu Maruf's low prices, Nadav ended up paying the man only $85 American dollars per student, putting aside the remaining $115, to the sum of $34,500 per year. With this money he would purchase materials for his own private research. Not that the North Galilee College supported research, let alone research in chemistry, but Nadav set up a little corner for himself in the lab and used the $34,500 to build his own personal black-ops lab. Nadav, thereby, sought to carry on his PhD research. The $34,500 was not nearly enough, nor was the $6,000 he put in from his own funds, but he refused to abandon his research.

Early on in his second year of college, Nadav pled with his favorite boss to allow him to leave for a conference on complicated quantic formulas in Windsor, England.

"This is my field, after all," Nadav emphasized.

"I will try to set up time off for you then," his boss answered, skeptically. "While the conference is on the summer break, you are also supposed, as you no doubt know, to teach the summer semester as well."

Nadav ended up travelling at his own expense. The college would not even pay the entry fee to the conference and deducted his days of absence from his sick days. Nonetheless, Nadav wrote "North Galilee College" on his name tag. Not that anyone in the prestigious conference had ever heard of the backwater institution.

Adam Mansour was almost diametrically opposite in every possible way from Nadav. He was a tall man who spoke quickly and thought even faster. In high school, Adam played basketball, though his movements seemed graceless to external observers. He did not care how he was perceived, however — the game suited his both his height and his rapid thinking. Despite his lankiness, when he stood, he was a very handsome man. Adam was also very sociable — unlike Nadav.

Adam initially wanted to study computers but was not accepted into any university in Israel. Since he did not want to study for the SAT, he went on to study mathematics at the Hebrew University in Jerusalem. The mathematics faculty there was prepared to accept anyone with a pulse — but you were unlikely to retain one, let alone graduate, if you did not know your stuff.

Adam knew his stuff.

He graduated *summa cum laude*. With this achievement under his belt, all the universities were prepared to roll out the red carpet for him to study computer science, or physics, or medicine, or any field of his choice, medieval literature included. But by this point, Adam was no longer fixated on computers as his life path, and he began studying for a second degree in physics under Professor Yoel Meir of the Hebrew University. Only then did he learn about energy state equations — the Schrodinger equations. That is how he chose to specialize in surface physics.

His thesis topic was a sub-field of energy states in contact with the surface of various materials in different materials in various lattices.

Hadas was a cat. She always fell on her feet and easily connected to all living things; cats included. Like cats, she too found it difficult to delay gratification when unsupervised, including picking the cherry from the top of a cake or snatching grapes from the bunch at the supermarket when no one was looking. Hadas was Adam's girlfriend back in high school. She enlisted in the IDF shortly after he did and tried for acceptance in the female combat infantry unit Caracal, but was rejected, instead becoming a Company Clerk in the 71st Armor Battalion. As mistress of her domain, she made sure Adam be assigned to her company.

Since Adam did not want to leave her side, he turned down the tank commander course. In this way, Adam served most of his term in the military with Hadas, his girlfriend. Hadas completed her service only a few months before him and she began studying literature at the Hebrew University. As soon as he was discharged and out of uniform, they got married, and once Hadas completed her studies, she began working as a literature teacher at the Boyar High School in Jerusalem.

Meanwhile, Adam's laboratory in the Hebrew University was plagued with complaints over lacking the budget to perform experiments.

"We, with an annual budget of around one million dollars, get nearly as much done as in MIT, where our counterparts enjoy an annual budget of over twenty million dollars," they would say. In practice, it was one of the best funded research labs in Israel.

Adam had heard that one of the lectures at the Windsor conference may be of interest to him, so he registered to the conference at the last moment. His laboratory paid, of course, for the cost of the conference, including flights, hotel and living expenses. Not that the bill was too hefty, given that the conference only lasted three days, or that the bill would have been particularly onerous for him, given the affluence of his family. Nonetheless, he felt a certain satisfaction at being recognized by his institution, a recognition he did not take for granted, given that his parents, born in Iraq and in the retail trade, were not considered part of the Israeli elite which dominated academia.

As soon as he reached the meticulously trimmed grass outside the 15th century building, he met someone he knew from the United States. Adam greeted him heartily and a circle of chatter immediately formed around them. When Adam entered the sumptuous lobby, he saw a shamefaced looking man in a suit standing next to the refreshments. Something about his body language immediately identified him as an Israeli. When he approached the refreshments himself, he also noticed that the nametag on his lapel included the word "Israel" on it. When he drew closer, he realized that he knew the man, but from being in uniform, not dressed in suit. It was Nadav, a tank commander from another company in his battalion. Nadav was renowned in the battalion as a walking technical solution to any problem. Computerized stabilizing system bugs, engine troubles, the ever-decoupling treads — all ended up with Nadav. Whenever the battalion technical team gave up — they would call up Nadav. Adam was a tank driver in H company, and he too would often end up getting technical support from Nadav.

"Ben Harush,"[2] Adam greeted Nadav, "what brings you here?" Nadav stared at Adam, clearly not recognizing him. Adam smiled, "I'm Mansour. From H company." Nadav took another moment to collect himself and figure out who he was.

---

2. In the IDF, as in many armies, comrades generally address each other by their family name, as it is a rare platoon that does not have several individuals with the same given name, and no one wants the wrong fellow (or no one. Or both) to respond when an urgent operational need arises.

"How about it! You're Adam," he said. He had never known, until that moment, that any of his army buddies had ended up in a similar field as he.

The conference turned out to be rather boring. Most of the time they chatted together about the upcoming reserve duty, slated for November in the Golan Heights, on the Syrian border.

"It will be cold in November, there will probably already be snow in the Hermon," said Nadav.

"The problem with wintertime reserve duty, is that the quartermaster never has any warm clothes. You need to bring them from home," said Adam.

"Yeah, and when winter ends, there are only warm clothes — just when you don't need them," Nadav agreed, and they both laughed.

"So, what do you actually do?" asked Adam.

"Among other things, I grow an interesting crystalline substrate in the lab, with very unusual surface energy properties. In fact, if there was some other material I could grow on my lattice, with very specific properties, it might be that at a temperature of under fifty degrees Celsius, the contact area between the two materials might develop superconductor properties.[3] But no such substance has yet to be found or invented."

Adam found his project to be quite fascinating. Although Adam had yet to publish his results, he was growing just such a substance in his lab. Adam's lab specialized in building one layer on top of another, just as electronic components were overlain on a silicon chip. Labs and electronic factories were capable of placing millions of electronic components on a coin sized sili-

---

3. A superconductor is a substance that in deep cooling, at a low temperature, has no electric resistance. Utilizing superconductors, super-powerful magnets can be produced. Superconductors are currently widely used in MRI machines, superfast trains (particularly in China), particle accelerators, and many other uses.

con chip. Electronic components, such as transistors, also operated on the basis of quantic energy level principles.

"I think I might have a substance suitable for the layer you need," Adam said in a low voice. "We could look it over together with my laboratory's new electronic microscope."

On the British Airways flight back to Israel, they sat next to each other on both sides of the aisle and talked shop incessantly. They agreed that Nadav would send Adam a small piece of his substrate, around half a square centimeter in area, and Adam would grow a layer of his substance on it and examine it under a microscope.

When they returned to Israel, they both forgot all about it, but when they met back up during their reserve duty in November, they reminded each other of their agreement, and Nadav promised once again to send Adam the material. Though Nadav returned to teaching immediately after his reserve duty, he took the time to send a piece of substrate to Adam. Though the Israeli Postal Service insists that 99% of all letters sent via their services reach their destination within a week, Nadav's package only arrived at the Hebrew University in Jerusalem two months later. The Hebrew University once had several employees who handled internal mail. But because of the cutbacks, there was only one employee left, and he had knee injuries. Hence, he would cycle through all the buildings once a week, and it took the entire week for the package to arrive at Adam's lab. As luck would have, it, this was precisely when Adam took paternity leave, relieving Hadas, his wife, of her six-week-long vigil. It would take another six weeks for him to return to the lab and get near the substrate.

Adam had a tiny room in the department which was defined as the "surface properties lab." In practice everyone called it "Professor Joel's Lab." When Adam returned to work in "Professor Joel's Lab," there were several urgent matters requiring his attention, and then the COVID-19 pandemic started. So it was, that by the time he returned to work in the lab regularly, it was nearly the end of the year. But eventually, Adam did reach Nadav's substrate.

Adam layered Nadav's substrate with his own substance and examined it under the microscope. Indeed, the results seemed excellent. True, even should the substance transform into a superconductor under low temperatures, Adam thought, it would not be a scientific breakthrough because there were already superconductor materials in higher temperatures, but nonetheless, it may well be worthy of an article in Science or Nature. Adam called Nadav, joked about the lateness of his reply, informed him of the results and suggested they perform the superconductivity experiment under low temperatures together. And indeed, a week later, Nadav arrived in Jerusalem.

It only took them a few hours to set up the devices for the experiment. Nadav was unfamiliar with the lab, and everything was new for him. The lab was located in a room with a window that overlooked the road lawns of the Racah Institute. Nadav, gazing out of the window, admired the view, both of the lawn and of the Jerusalem skyline.

Usually, the lab was filled with people, but it was Thursday evening, and they were all alone in the lab.

They began cooling the material, anticipating seeing what would happen once they reached the requisite cold.

Once they realized that, at minus 52 degrees Celsius, the material transformed into a superconductor, Adam's hands began to tremble. This result, and the article which would follow, could jumpstart their careers. But something was wrong. The thickness of the substance Adam had layered on Nadav's substrate was under three microns. At such a thickness, the maximal possible superconductor current could not exceed a few milliamperes. But Adam's trembling hand accidentally pushed the current upwards to several amperes — and the superconductivity remained.

After the initial euphoria, upon realizing they had developed a new superconductor, they realized there was some kind of error and felt disappointed. Clearly, there was some superconductivity, but their experiment must be insufficiently rigorous. They needed to plan a new experiment which would definitively determine whether superconductivity did or did not exist. The grass in the laboratory window no longer seemed so green. They decided to meet again on Sunday morning and reexamine their results.

2.

Neither Nadav nor Adam got much sleep over the weekend. Each ruminated continuously about the experiment, trying to figure out what could have gone wrong.

By Saturday morning, Hadas, Adam's wife, had had enough. They were lying on their comfortable, functional bed, surrounded by the chaos of their messy bedroom. Neither of them could muster the time and effort to tidy up their small house on Palmach Street. Usually, both found it all too easy to fall asleep and rest deep into the early afternoon on weekends. But on this weekend, Adam tossed and turned and generally made a nuisance of himself, disturbing Hadas's sleep.

"What's going on, Adam?" Hadas asked, determined to uncover what was troubling her husband.

"I had a breakthrough at the University," Adam replied, "together with Nadav."

"Nadav? Who's Nadav?" asked Hadas.

"A reserve duty buddy. Until recently, I had no idea Nadav was in my field. But I am not sure if it is really a breakthrough, or just a mistake in a laboratory experiment."

"Well, what does it mean?" asked Hadas.

"I am not at all sure. If it is an absolute mistake in the experiment, then it means nothing. Frankly, that is the most likely option."

"But why do you think it is a mistake?" she asked.

"During the experiment, we accidentally ran a current a thousand times higher than what we intended — and it still worked!"

Adam did not want to admit, not even to himself, that it was his own excitement which was the cause of the error.

"It is... well, exceedingly unlikely to work under such conditions. No one in the world ever approached such a result." Hadas stared at him, clearly uncomprehending, and Adam elaborated.

"In a running competition, the world record is improved every few years by a few fractions of a second. The world record in running the Marathon is two hours and change. Say we were the world's marathon race champions. If we were measured to have completed the 42-kilometer course in under three minutes, exceeding the speed of a jet plane, then what would be more likely: that we had a good day, that we had really great running shoes, or that the measurements were wrong?"

"So, what are you doing in bed? Go to the lab and run the experiment again!" said Hadas.

"Nadav lives in Haifa, and I don't want to repeat the experiment on my own without a second pair of eyes to double check the setup and the results" Adam replied curtly.

Hadas turned in bed and pushed herself up on her elbows.

"But what if it isn't a mistake?" she asked.

"That is why I can't sleep," replied Adam in exasperation." "I've gone over every step of the experiment repeatedly, and I can't see what we did wrong. Understand this. If this is true, even without any significant improvement to existing superconductivity, it means a prestigious article in a high impact journal. This means a direct tenure track. If we show greater superconductivity, even by 10%, than the most powerful known superconductor, this means a Nobel prize. And if the results are real, then this is a world changing discovery."

Hadas thought Adam was exaggerating.

"Why would a new superconductor change the world?" she asked.

"Do you remember how I once explained to you that global warming was a far more severe problem than most people thought that it was so serious it constituted a clear and present danger to humanity's very existence?"

Hadas smiled and said nothing. Yes, Adam had shared his alarm at global warming with her once, or maybe twenty or thirty times. She did not think he was wrong — but it was too big, too depressing and too unproductive to spend time and energy worrying about. It wasn't like they could do anything about it. Or could they?

"In any event, this discovery, if implemented correctly, could solve, among many other problems, global warming as well. But we aren't there yet. At the moment, this looks like an experimental error."

Hadas shook her head, kissed Adam, and whispered in his ear, "then it sounds like you will just have to wait till tomorrow to save the world. In the meantime, why not come back to bed?"

Adam sighed, "I can't sleep" he admitted.

Hadas rolled her eyes. Her brilliant husband could be quite dense sometimes. "Who said anything about sleeping?"

On Sunday morning, Nadav and Adam met in Adam's lab. Nadav had left Haifa at dawn break and arrived at the Hebrew University at 7:00 am sharp. Usually, only Professor Joel was present there so early in the morning. Morning dew could still be seen on the grass outside. When their eyes met, they both knew the other was running the same three scenarios through his mind:

Scenario one — a complete and total error. No scientific interest.

Scenario two — a small measurement error in the current amplitude. Eventually - a career changing article.

Scenario three — no error — a global game changer in every possible way. And on the personal level — a Nobel prize.

"So, let's examine option three," Nadav cut to the chase. "If this is true then this will change the world! Do you realize the ramifications?"

"Absolutely," Adam replied.

"Look, if we don't want to be a tiny cog in this change, if we want to manage the change instead of letting the universities run us, we should publish absolutely nothing. Let's take our materials to a private external lab and run the experiment there. This way the university will have no claim to our intellectual property. Each of us will invest 1,500 dollars for this external validation. Moreover, we should not share the context of what we are testing with the external lab."

"I have no problem putting up the funds," said Adam. "I will explain to you precisely how my substrate is composed and…"

"Absolutely not!" Nadav flinched back in horror. "You tell me nothing about your material and I will tell you nothing about mine. This way each of us will hold half the key and none of us will have the entire solution. If this is truly a world-changing development, we will come under enormous pressure from multiple directions. So long as there is no single individual in possession of the technology, our ability to withstand the pressure will be far greater."

"You are right," Adam reluctantly agreed.

That very week they arrived at a private laboratory in Tel Aviv which could perform the basic experiment. The lab thought it was an experiment for a new MRI component. They thought that the interior of the component was filled with a superconductor with a very large cross section, when, in practice, Nadav's substrate, coated with Adam's lattice, was only a few microns across. The laboratory confirmed that at a temperature of minus 51 degrees Celsius the component became a superconductor capable of transmitting a current of 1.5 ampere. Adam and Nadav did not want to run current larger than the one they accidentally tried in the university, because they were afraid of burning out the only component in their possession.

"Last week in the laboratory," Adam confessed to Nadav, "my hand shook with excitement. That was why the current was so jumpy. I'm even more excited now. I hope it is not quite as obvious." Adam was as white as a sheet. He thought about how he had just submitted his PhD thesis. This discovery was a guaranteed Nobel prize. But Adam accepted Nadav's way was better. In fact, Adam greatly admired Nadav. He was, after all, "the ultimate technological solution."

True, that was in reserve duty, not in the academic world, but the solutions Nadav provided him with, for situations Adam could not solve on his own, were no less than brilliant, and Adam knew this.

They decided to manufacture a dozen more superconductor chips identical to their prototype so that they could perform several experiments on them. In this way, they would be able to both ensure they could reliably produce such components as well as test their limitations.

Adam went home early that day. Hadas had made herself a sandwich for lunch before the children returned from school, and she munched on it as Adam gripped their dining room table until his knuckles went white.

"The external lab test revealed our initial results were not an experimental error, or a fluke," he said with no preambles.

Hadas choked on her sandwich. She sputtered, spat out a piece of bread and took a deep drink of water.

"So, this means a Nobel prize?" she asked, "Are we going to be rich? What does this mean?"

"I don't really know" Adam replied pensively, "right now this is all very much a secret. Nadav and I aren't gunning for a Nobel prize — we want to change the world."

Hadas did not like this answer. She didn't really believe her husband would be the one to change the world. Her husband was a very smart physicist, and she loved him more than words could say, but he wasn't Einstein. Besides, her motto was "there is no more loyal friend than cold hard cash," as her lecturer in her "Introduction to Accounting" class once told her.

In the nights following that conversation, sleep eluded Hadas as well. So it was that their nights were spent discussing the various possibilities to use the properties of the new superconductor.

Nadav and Adam returned to their respective work but maintained daily, and sometimes hourly, contact, sometimes for several hours every day, mostly via Zoom. Discussing the potential of their discoveries, they soon realized that they had more in common than their military and academic background — they both viewed global warming as a clear and present danger to human survival, and to all life on Earth. Adam came to recognize that Nadav's technical and mathematical solutions were nothing less than genius, whereas Nadav grew to appreciate Adam's deep commitment to his family, a commitment which he realized underlay Adam's equally determined commitment to the environment. Wistfully, he wished he too had someone special with whom he could share his life and start a family with, someone who could motivate him the way Hadas motivated Adam. Regretfully, he concluded that this was not on the cards for him.

They covertly created another ten identical components and examined them. It turned out they could easily run a twenty-ampere current through a cross section of only a few microns — about 2,000 times higher than the best superconductor hitherto known to science.

Moreover, the cross section required for them to reach this achievement was about fifty times smaller. Nadav's substrate could be processed with technologies identical to those used on the silicon computer chips. A single centimeter was enough to manufacture an electronic coil with millions of loops. In other words, using this technology it was possible to produce magnets 100,000 times stronger than anything previously seen.

They clearly needed a manufacturing facility with a clean room.[4] There were quite a few such factories equipped with clean rooms in Israel, but you needed over $10,000 to rent such facilities for any extended period of time, and they would be facing a $100,000-sized hole in their non-existent slush fund very soon if they went down this road.

They wanted to coat a two-meter diameter ring with 1.5-centimeter sized chips. Constructing two such rings would cost them in the ballpark of $150,000. Furthermore, they required a frame capable of holding the ring which could withstand pressures of up to fifty tons, and it had to encase a very precisely cut hollow ring of glass containing vacuum in which the protons could move. They would need around a million dollars to prepare everything required.

Well, that was that then. They needed an investor — that was the only way forward. Vision and innovation could take them this far and no further — it was time for infusion of cold, hard cash.

---

4. A clean room is a room that is completely free of dust and other particulates. The growth of crystals from Atoms layering on top of each of each other would be severely impaired by dust settling on the surface. This would mar the perfection of the lattice and render it worthless. Therefore, a clean room needed to be immeasurably more sterile than a surgery room in a hospital. And such a room was a minimum threshold requirement for a factory manufacturing micron thin silicon chips.

3.

Shlomo Grossman was the CEO of Gilboa Ventures, one of the leading venture capital funds in Israel, and with a powerful international reputation. Shlomo, unlike Nadav and Adam, was the darling of the Israeli establishment. He was the favored son and grandson of the traditional Israeli elite. An 8200[5] graduate with proven managerial abilities in various international companies, leading Israeli high-tech companies, and several startups and governmental committees.

Shlomo had a massive presence in every room he entered thanks to his unkempt beard and massive dimensions, both in height and girth. But it was more than that — people wanted to hear what he had to say, but Shlomo was careful to speak only after everyone was done, both in meetings and in social events. He was a warm individual who smiled a great deal, in accordance with the stereotype of large, fat people.

"We will have to act in secrecy, versus the entire world," Nadav explained to Adam, "and to do that we need someone who understands intelligence, and who has intelligence contacts."

Shlomo Grossman was precisely the man they needed. Nadav and Adam's problem was how to reach Shlomo without spilling the beans to all of the experts and assistants he kept precisely to screen applicants such as themselves. When one approaches a venture capital firm such as Gilboa, you are first directed to one of the junior partners. Only after they hear you out and interrogate you thoroughly are you directed to a senior partner. And only after you persuade that senior partner, or if you are asking for a particularly large investment, will the CEO, Shlomo Grossman himself, get involved. Nadav and Adam did their research

---

5. 8200 is an elite Israeli intelligence unit, whose graduates are disproportionately represented in Israel's high-tech sector, and particularly among startup founders (translator).

and found out that Shlomo once ran a medical imaging company. They talked with Professor Joel, who knew Shlomo through a friend, and asked him to introduce them as seeking to consult with him concerning a potential improvement in superconductors for medical imaging.

And so it was. They arrived for a short half hour consultation concerning "medical imaging." They understood in advance that a half hour appointment meant Grossman would arrive ten minutes late, followed by ten minutes of small talk, leaving them with ten minutes at best to explain what they wanted. So, they planned the conversation thoroughly, without any reliance on PowerPoint presentations.

Venture capital firms all over the world always maintain very sumptuous offices, as in Israel as well. The purpose of the sumptuousness is to signal to the capital-seeking entrepreneur visiting the offices that there is plenty of money there. Hence, even the poorest venture capital fund offices are more luxurious than even the richest law firms.

Usually, original art pieces by famous artists hang from the walls. The floor is mahogany wood, covered with Persian carpets, and the tables are made from heavy African wood. The Gilboa fund was, of course, no exception. The largest table in the "Kinneret" room was made of finely polished tropical wooden railway rails. The wood from which these rails had been constructed over a century ago had been imported to the Ottoman Empire from Africa, since, by then, the Land of Israel, like much of the Middle East, had been denuded of trees by heedless logging and grazing. This wood was very heavy and difficult to process. It needed to be sliced into two-centimeter strips utilizing a band saw — and the band needed to be replaced every two or three rails. Despite being over a century old, the wood had been preserved by the engine oil that had dripped on them from the locomotives. The strips were lacquered to prevent the toxic oil fumes from being released after the wood dried, polished, and the process was repeated several times. The end result was beautiful but also very expensive and artificial — symbolic, Adam moodily mused, of the sorry state of human civilization.

And indeed, Grossman entered five minutes late, and as soon as he entered, he began to small talk in which he explained that he had not dealt with medical applications for over thirty years and hence his medical sciences expert, Amir, would enter in a moment, and he, Shlomo, would have to bid them farewell, since he was late for another meeting that was unfortunately scheduled for almost the exact same time in Jerusalem. And he had already risen up to leave.

"Our subject is not medical imaging," blurted out Nadav, who was not exactly a great speaker. "We are physics and chemistry researchers, and our subject is superconductors." Adam removed their superconductor chip from his pocket and presented it to Shlomo.

"The strongest magnet in the world was built this year" he said. "It produces a 34 Tesla magnetic field.[6] This chip, which includes our "ultimate superconductor," costs less than fifty dollars to produce — and easily generates 100 Tesla. The technological implications are massive, and we can demonstrate it, should it suit you, next week."

Shlomo took in Nadav's hurried words as he was already approaching the door. He paused in place and turned around. His massive figure stood in the entryway, facing Nadav and Adam, who remained seated. He stood there for a second or two. Shlomo understood immediately that if their claims were correct then this was something extraordinary, far from a common occurrence, even for Gilboa Venture Capital.

"All right," Shlomo nodded and said, "I will ask Kinneret, the

---

6. Tesla is a magnetism measurement unit, named (as is the electric car) after the inventor Nikola Tesla.

Gilboa secretary to schedule two hours for a demonstration next week. She will call you."

"We will demonstrate it at the Piskel Laboratories on Ahad Ha'am Street in Tel Aviv," said Adam.

"That's fine," replied Shlomo and strode out the door.

The meeting itself ended up lasting less than thirty seconds, but Nadav and Adam were quite pleased.

On the way to Jerusalem, Shlomo considered what Nadav had told him. If his claims were true, he mulled, then the cost of MRI production would be reduced at least twofold, representing a global market value of three billion dollars a year. The fast train sector would leap on the new magnets as well, representing another billion dollars a year. In fact, if it were so inexpensive, wheeled trains might finally be facing their end. Even the simplest trains would use Maglevs, representing a market that would breach the ten billion threshold.

But Shlomo was not born yesterday, and he had already seen and heard everything possible in startup companies, technology ventures, and Israel's dream market. Shlomo knew that the chances of what he had heard being true were less than 1 in 100. Nonetheless, he told himself, that chance was worth two hours of his time.

Nadav and Adam left the sumptuous offices in Herzliya and ambled off to the parking lot.

"Why did you tell Shlomo our chip could manage 100 Tesla?" Asked Nadav, "We can easily demonstrate 3,000 Tesla."

"Aside from the minor technical problem of the magnet ripping out the iron from the concrete mold of the laboratory floor at 3,000 Tesla," Adam replied drily, "Shlomo would have stopped listening if I claimed anything over 100 Tesla. Even so, this claim is extraordinary, and Shlomo likely doesn't really believe us. That is why we need to keep the demonstration simple, clear — and modest. 100 Tesla is enough. Shlomo is not a physicist, but he is sharp as a whip and understands the implications. I suggest we send him the explanation of the demonstration by the weekend to make sure he arrives at the demonstration fully prepared."

Fifteen minutes after they left the parking lot, Kinneret, the secretary, called and asked if Monday at 2:30 pm worked for them. After they confirmed, she asked for the precise address of the Piskel Labs.

"Shlomo wants to bring Professor Joel with him and asks if that is all right," she added.

They exchanged a look and put their phone on mute as they consulted, then finally agreed. While including Joel would expand the number of individuals who knew about their secret, it was clear that Shlomo would not be able to rely solely on his own impressions and would want an expert opinion. Although the fund managed the capital of its investors, it still owed them an accounting for its investment decisions.

They had five days to prepare.

They decided to use the chip that Adam showed Shlomo in the meeting. They built this chip with 10 million coils in the spool. They had already performed such an experiment with over 300 Tesla, but not for demonstration and display. In that experiment, the magnet was only activated for brief, five millisecond intervals — not long enough for the iron rods in the concrete walls and floor to be sufficiently affected by the super magnet to pose a problem.

They proceeded to divvy up the work to be done for Monday: "Adam, you order the lab for Monday from 12:00 pm until the end of the day."

"There goes another $650 up in smoke," Adam said, resignedly. "You need to design an iron sheath which will prevent the magnetic forces from escaping, because 100 Tesla demonstrated over several seconds will wreak havoc on the lab. Every iron particle in the lab will be pulled towards the magnet by massive forces and will puncture a hole in whatever stands in its way, human beings included."

"No problem, I will order in the metalworker. He's already fulfilled several orders for us in a very satisfactory manner. This frame needs to be made from six-centimeter-thick iron plates. It needs to be an armor that can stop a 0.5 mm bullet. It needs to be a sort of iron box with an interior space of 20 X 20 X 10 centimeters. Despite its small size, it is going to weigh over 250 kilos, because the entire sheathe is one big iron lump."

"So, we also need to order transportation," said Adam.

"Constructing the sheathe, transporting it to the lab, and hiring movers to lug this iron lump up to the lab — all this will cost us another $1500, and this is only the beginning of the costs we will face."

"I will prepare a document," added Adam, "which will describe and explain the experimental plan, including all the calculations which will show that if the measurements are correct — what will be demonstrated absolutely must be above 100 Tesla. I will send this document to Professor Joel as well as Shlomo."

"Agreed," said Nadav.

The next day, Kinneret called again and informed them that Professor Joel would arrive on Monday for the demonstration and that he had signed a non-disclosure-agreement with the Gilboa foundation, which also covered them, as the entrepreneurs. Yes, Shlomo had signed an NDA which covers any entrepreneur who contacts him. The NDAs had been emailed to them, Kinneret added.

On Thursday, Professor Joel met with Adam at his lab in the Hebrew University.

"You know," Joel said, "until now I thought that you turned down the research assistant position because your family is wealthy, but now I realize that you have another job outside the university and that we are supposed to meet in Tel Aviv on Monday, correct?"

"That's right," said Adam, and handed over the details of the experiment.

"Magnetism is not my specialty," said Joel apologetically, "But all that is required here is basic physics calculations, and I do believe I can still handle that." Joel thought the experiment was meant to demonstrate several thousandths of a Tesla, still a very powerful magnet. Joel could not conceive that the two young researchers were intending to demonstrate 100 Tesla.

By Sunday morning the Haifa metalworker had the sheathe ready. Adam and Nadav drove to Haifa with the chip, liquid nitrogen to keep the chip cool, and all else that was required to generate the superconductivity necessary for the basic experiment. They found out that the metalworker had "taken initiative" and painted the metal sheathe from withing and without. They had not considered this possibility, but it turned out that the base paint contained trace quantities of iron.

When the experiment was activated, the inner coat of paint, even though it was already dry, pulled with massive force towards the chip — and destroyed it. Fortunately, Nadav had two more chips at home.

While Nadav drove home to bring the additional chips, Adam and the metalworker cleaned and polished the internal metal frame.

"I don't understand what I did wrong," said the metalworker, "I merely painted the sheathe."

Adam didn't even try to explain.

When Nadav returned, they reinitialized the system, and demonstrated 250 Tesla over five seconds.

"By the way, what did Hadas have to say about us giving up on a Nobel Prize in order to save the world?" Nadav asked.

"She's fine with it," laughed Adam, "provided we do actually save the world." In practice Hadas and he had a long-running argument about this decision, but Adam had no intention of opening it up with Nadav.

4.

In the morning, Nadav and two of the metal worker's employees loaded the small metal sheath into the van and drove to Tel Aviv. When they reached Ahad Ha'am Street in Tel Aviv, it turned out that there were no available parking facing the Piskel Lab. The most significant difficulty was that there was no way to transfer the metal sheath, even though it was small, past the row of cars parked in front of the entrance to the labs. Adam thought at least one of the parked cars must belong to a Piskel employee and that it might be possible to ask this employee to move his vehicle for five minutes. But none of the employees admitted that their car was parked there — everyone was too concerned with losing their parking space, a precious commodity in crowded Tel Aviv.

"There is no choice," Adam said, "I am calling up a truck with a crane."

The truck only arrived after two hours, not within the promised half an hour. It was already 2:00 pm when the truck blocked the street, and the operator sedately lowered the crane legs to stabilize the truck on the street. The traffic jam it created blocked the entire road, and back flowed to plug up Rothschild Boulevard as well.

They lowered the sheath from the van directly to the cart awaiting it on the sidewalk, beyond the line of parking cars. As they manhandled the cart into the Piskel Labs, they could see the truck driver arguing with a policeman over the traffic ticket he insisted on giving him, heedless of the desperate honking horns behind him.

When Nadav and Adam entered the labs, they understood they would not be able to start the experiment on schedule. But then Shlomo called to apologize for his delay — they were on the way, but stuck in a traffic jam on Rothchild Boulevard, about a kilometer from the lab. Nadav exchanged a grin with Adam.

The obstinacy of the truck driver had won them the time they needed to set up the experiment, it seemed.

Finally, Joel and Shlomo entered the lab. It was located on the second floor of a restored Bauhaus building. The interior was very basic, and the lab itself was functional. They began chit-chatting sedately, with Adam introducing himself to Shlomo at length, telling him how he and Nadav knew each other from reserve duty and how they happened to run into each other at the Windsor conference nearly a year ago. Meantime, in the other room, Nadav was hectically completing the experimental setup they had originally reserved two hours to perform. Now he had ten minutes, maybe fifteen, before Adam's delaying tactics wore thin.

This was not a challenge one would expect Nadav, a slow thinking and speaking person, to do well in. His slow thoughts often led people to think he was not particularly smart. That was also why he had such a hard time in the SAT, where success was predicated on speed and efficient time management. If he had unlimited time, Nadav would have surely gotten every question right. His slow thoughts, after all, enabled him to understand every issue from every aspect, including aspects others did not even see. On the other hand, Nadav was not easily pressured. As he had plenty of time to review all the experimental preparations in his head. Nadav simply performed everything like a robot, and all was ready in under ten minutes.

When Shlomo and Joel entered the experiment room, everything was ready. Adam was surprised at the speed. Nadav briefly reviewed the sequence of the experiment again, and they then cooled the chip with liquid nitrogen, placed it into its iron sheath, and turned on the magnet for a single second.

"The devices must not be calibrated," said Joel after flanking at the results. "I haven't performed the exact calculation, but it seems there is over a Tesla here, and we know there cannot be more than a few thousandths of a Tesla at most."

"All the devices are calibrated," said Adam, showing Joel their calibration labels. "Please — perform the exact calculation."

Joel took out his pocket calculator and punched in his calculations pensively. Absent mindedly, he wiped his forehead before raising his eyes.

"My calculation shows around 110 Tesla, but that is utter nonsense, because no such powerful magnet exists on Earth."

Nadav and Adam exchanged meaningful glances. They deliberately shot short of the 250 Tesla they measured in Haifa, because they did not want anything they hadn't thought of to go wrong in the demonstration.

Nadav invited Shlomo and Joel in the stark meeting room, adorned with nothing more than a simple Formica table in its center. Now, over a cup of coffee, they tried to explain.

"This is indeed a much more powerful magnet than known to date," said Nadav. "That is the reason for the veil of secrecy under which we are operating."

"If this is true — then it is a guaranteed Nobel Prize," said Joel.

"Perhaps, but we have grander aims," said Nadav, "which is why we don't want to publish. The Nobel Prize will have to wait," he added with a smile.

At this point Joel was showing signs of stress, with Shlomo, in contrast, appearing increasingly excited at the implications.

"In truth I was not expecting this," said Joel, "I am no longer sure of myself, perhaps I should double check the calculations and consult with magnetics experts."

"Yes, we assumed you would need time and would want to consult with others," said Nadav, "But we do ask that you do not expose this secret. So, you can describe the experiment and ask if your calculations are correct. You can also ask what would happen should the measurements indicate a magnetic field 1,000 times as powerful than that planned for the experiment — just don't let on that this experiment actually took place or what the results were."

They agreed to meet come Thursday at the Gilboa offices, after Joel has had a chance to double check his calculations.

On his way back to the office, Shlomo ran the numbers again in his head. If this was all true, he mulled, this would be the greatest thing the Gliboa Fund had ever been involved in. Nadav and Adam may well represent the most significant start-up company Israel has ever seen. But on the other hand, Shlomo knew from experience, the chance they would crash and burn was well over 90 percent.

Joel Meir was a Jerusalemite by both character and residence ever since he returned from completing his post doctorate at Yale. Joel realized he was facing one of the most momentous physics discoveries of the decade, if not the century. On the drive back to Jerusalem, he tried to understand where the measurement error occurred, but could find none, for the experiment was very simple and very clear. It was something that even a freshman could perform with one hand tied behind his back. But if this was really true, and Adam, his student, had discovered a Nobel Prize worthy phenomenon, then this was truly grand. It would certainly boost the Racah Institute's ability to secure funding and publish papers. On the other hand, the secrecy they insisted upon was not clear to him. Secrecy was, in principle, alien to his academic world. Obviously, prior to publishing an article, one must maintain a certain level of confidentiality over experimental results to avoid scooping. But once the results are published, the need for privacy is eliminated. Here, in the commercial world, things seem to be very different.

5.

Nadav arrived first, and Kinneret the secretary ushered him into the small conference room. From the window they could see the beachfront of Herzliya Pituah, where most of the companies he knew were headquartered. Nadav felt calm, relaxed, despite the importance of the upcoming meeting. He took his time, studying the water lily painting by Monet that was hanging on the wall. At first, he thought it was a reproduction, but now, upon closer examination, he was not at all sure. The brushwork bore the unmistakable print of Monet, he thought.

A short while later the others entered, and coffee was served.

"Well," Joel began, "the calculations I performed so far confirm that what we saw on Monday afternoon; that the result was indeed 110 Tesla."

Shlomo was about to launch into his usual speech, in which he would explain the facts of life to the eager young entrepreneurs, and return them back to Earth, but Adam beat him to it.

"We have a few additional bits of information which may surprise you. The first is that last week, we generated 250 Tesla in the device used in the demonstration. According to our theoretical calculations, we can also reach — and quite easily — 3,000 Tesla. But that will not be possible in the current configuration for its mechanical properties won't tolerate the strain."

Joel's jaw dropped, flummoxed, and Shlomo's response was not very different.

"As you will no doubt agree, this is a global game changer," Adam added.

Nadav, who usually found it difficult to speak before an audience, even a small audience such as this one, found himself strangely serene, just as he had been when he entered the office.

"We have been sitting on this discovery for several months, and we have had time to sleep on it, digest the ramifications, and fantasize about them. Our fantasies include the 'big oaks plan' and the 'small oaks plan,' if you will forgive the military reference. We aren't interested in founding a start-up company only to make a massively profitable exit. We want to solve the great problems of the world, the greatest of which is global warming."

At this point, Shlomo's suspension of disbelief was sorely challenged, and he began to entertain the possibility that he was dealing with people who had lost connection with reality. But Nadav, completely focused on Shlomo to the exclusion of everyone and everything else in the room, persevered.

"It is clear to us that you have heard many fantasies aired in the Gilboa Fund, Shlomo, which is why I must beg your forbearance, so we can outline the details of our plan. Let us start with the fact that particle accelerators are currently primarily research devices. It requires a ring like structure several kilometers in length. We are planning to construct a 2-meter diameter particle accelerator. With the electromagnets utilizing our superconductor, this is possible. Moreover, it will be able to accelerate protons to very near the speed of light."

At this point, Adam turned on the PowerPoint presentation and displayed the calculation supporting his claims. The calculation included consideration of both the general and special theory of relativity, necessary when dealing with such great speeds and massive energy.

"Once they reach the desired speed, our hydrogen atoms will be discharged from the ring and encounter hydrogen atoms in a state of rest," Adam continued, and once again displayed on the PowerPoint presentation the energetic calculation which demonstrated this was sufficient to result in nuclear fusion.[7] "The nuclear fusion will generate massive energy and two processes," he continued, "most of the protons will be boosted with energy and perform another revolution of the ring. But at the same time, a stream of helium atoms[8] will leave the ring and generate thrust, just as in a rocket engine. But instead of rocket thrust generated by a large mass of fuel and oxygen combusting and being repelled backwards, the thrust in this case will be generated by a relatively small mass of Helium atoms which are propelled backwards, but at an enormous speed; a speed of 80% of the speed of light. We call this initial stage of the fusion 'ignition.' After the ignition, the electricity flowing in the ring will serve as an electric generator to continue generating the electricity required for the activity of the accelerator and will serve as an energy source for all the systems we require." Adam moved to the next slide in the presentation and displayed the relevant calculations.

"As you can see, we generate a rocket-like thrust which in the minimal ignition stage is a five-ton thrust, and in this ring can reach up to fifty tons of thrust. The limitations are the mechanical limitations of the forces operating within the chips fixed within the ring."

---

7. There are two types of atomic energy. The first is nuclear fission, in which the nucleus of an element containing many protons is split into two separate elements with fewer protons. This is a highly polluting process that generates harmful radiation and fallout. This is the process used in contemporary nuclear reactors – and atomic bombs. The second type is nuclear fusion. This is a totally green process (and how the sun generates its radiance and heat). In this process, two elements fuse into a single atom with a larger number of protons. This process is unfeasible with contemporary technology, generating an unstable element for a few seconds, for we lack powerful enough magnets to concentrate the process over time.

8. In the nuclear fusion of two hydrogen atoms with a single proton, helium is formed. The nucleus of helium contains two protons.

Adam quipped: "This is where we need Joel." Quantum mechanics was not part of their specialty. "We have the general concept, but we are missing a few pieces of the puzzle," he added.

At this point, Shlomo began to pay close attention, for he began to understand where the two wild eyed young men were going.

"Our plan" continued Nadav, "is to build two such rings and install them in the wings of a regular jet plane, such as the Boeing 767. Unlike space flights to date, this will be very similar to a regular flight. Contemporary space shuttles need to reach an escape velocity of 11 kilometers per second within the first few minutes of flight, and in fact, most of the fuel is burned up during takeoff. In this way, no fuel is left to slow down the spaceship on reentry to the atmosphere. What slows the spaceship down on re-entry is friction with the atmosphere during the descent back to planet Earth. The heat generated on re-entry is the cause of most spaceflight accidents."

Adam knew Nadav well enough to know that Nadav could sometimes suffer from paralysis when speaking to an audience, so he continued the presentation on his own.

"In our case, as you will see, fuel is almost no problem, and hence re-entry into the atmosphere will take place at a much lower speed, and with very little risk. Furthermore, we don't need to reach escape velocity within the first few minutes. We will, of course, eventually far exceed escape velocity, but we have enough thrust to generate this speed sedately after an hour or more of flight. Our goal is to reach the moon and construct a permanent base there. On that basis we will mine the Helium 3 isotope[9] and bring it back to Earth."

Only at this point did all the chips fall for Shlomo and Joel. They were both rather stunned.

Shlomo halted Nadav. "I see all sorts of problems," he said. "But before we continue sailing off into the fantasy world, I want to make two clarifications in terrestrial reality. First of all, why attach the engine to a plane? Why not to a bus? A spacecraft and an airplane are two entirely different things, so why use a plane as the chassis for your spaceship?

Adam smiled. "Yes, that is a good question, because it will enable us to explain why there is no great difference, in our case, between an airplane and a spaceship, and your example of the bus is excellent." Adam glanced at Nadav, who picked up the explanation.

"A spaceship carrying human passengers needs to maintain internal air pressure equivalent to the atmospheric pressure of Earth, while being surrounded by a vacuum — an atmospheric pressure of 0. If we were to launch a bus into space, its windows would almost immediately shatter outwards from the internal air pressure. In a plane, by contrast, the small windows are designed to withstand this pressure — and there is no great difference between the negligible air pressure at 10-kilometer altitude to the absolute absence of air in outer space. That said, there are many airplane systems which will have to be adapted

---

9. The Helium Atom nucleus has two protons. A nucleus containing an additional neutron will contain three particles, and hence will be called "Helium 3 isotope" or Helium 3, for short. If it has two neutrons, then it will contain four particles and be called Helium 4. The Helium 4 isotope is the most common isotope on planet Earth, with almost no Helium 3 in existence.

Utilizing early 21st-century technology, one can relatively easily perform a nuclear fusion of Helium 3 to generate clean electricity. The only problem is that the only known large-scale deposits of Helium 3 are on the moon. NASA has plans of mining them – but none have yet been realized.

to be compatible with spaceflight. The three central ones are: first, unlike the airplane which pumps in air from outside the plane, heats it, and circulates it to refresh oxygen content for the passengers, the spaceship has no outside source of air — it must recycle its internal stores, supplemented with oxygen from the engine. Second, solar rays, unfiltered by the atmosphere, can heat the external fuselage of the plane to temperatures of hundreds of degrees, melting the aluminum from which the spaceship is constructed. To solve this problem the plane needs to be coated with a substance that will reflect solar radiation back into space, without heating the fuselage of the plane. We will use gold paint to achieve this effect, as is also used in satellites. This color requires actual gold, but not in huge quantities. Finally, the control and navigation systems of a plane will not work in space and will require extensive redesign."

Nadav sat up as Shlomo asked: "My second question is as follows. If we have an engine capable of nuclear fusion, why not use it to generate energy? Why go to all the trouble of importing Helium 3 from the moon?"

It was now Joel who chuckled and answered. "Let me try to field this question and let us see if my answer matches yours."

Nadav and Adam gladly deferred, and Joel continued: "The green fusion energy is transformed into heat and motion in their engine. Then, as in any electricity generating reactor, the heat is used to transform water into steam which drives turbines connected to the generator. Every such transition of energy wastes some of the energy which becomes waste heat that contributes to global warming. In contrast, the Helium 3 fusion reactors transform all the fusion energy into electric energy directly, without all of these superfluous transitory stages."

Kinneret entered with sandwiches for lunch, and reminded Shlomo that he had another meeting in an hour. Shlomo asked her to reschedule the meeting and clear his afternoon. The secretary was so stunned that she stayed standing in place, tray in hand. This had never happened before, and she had been working with Shlomo for over twenty years.

Adam carried on heedlessly: "In order to get all this done, we need you, Shlomo. This is not a start-up company. We need to hook it up with the massive systems of the Israel Aerospace Industries, NASA and various governments. They each have their own interests, which do not necessarily align with saving humanity. Even when they do, they will not necessarily agree about how to go about it."

"This is the little oak? Then what exactly did you have in mind for big oaks? Terraforming the solar system? A generation starship? Conquering the galaxy?" Shlomo asked, only half-ironically as he took a big bite out of his sandwich.

"Only Earth... at first. Big Oaks requires the cooperation of the Great Powers. Water needs to be desalinated in order to feed the world. Some solar radiation must also be diverted in order to stop global warming before it reaches the point of no return. Only a very small portion of the radiation needs to be diverted, but to do so we require a very specific element — gold. We need gold because it is the only heat reflective substance we know how to layer at a sufficiently low thickness, to make the heat shield a viable option. But even at the thinnest layer possible we will still need massive amounts of gold, more gold than can be found on Earth. But Mars has plenty. Our aim in Big Oaks is to reach Mars and then Europa, the Jovian Moon, and colonize them," Nadav responded. "But we are not planning to implement Big Oaks in the upcoming years, so there is no point discussing it today — there is plenty on our plate right now."

Joel glanced wistfully at the luncheon plate — unfortunately, there was not much on it, as Shlomo had absentmindedly demolished half a dozen sandwiches as Adam spoke.

"Financially speaking, I am sure that Shlomo has already calculated that the global energy market has an annually 100 trillion-dollar turnover," Adam continued, once again worried Nadav would suffer paralysis. "Our technology may reduce energy consumer costs to 10% of its current prices. That's still ten trillion dollars per year. Even if we only capture 10% of the market, this is a trillion dollars every year."

To Adam's considerable surprise, Nadav interjected and took over the presentation.

"We don't think the Israel Space Agency could possibly launch such a global project, and so we will need the help of NASA — which means the involvement of the United States Government. Moreover, we think this technology is such a global game changer that no major player can afford to stay out of this race. Staying out means missing out and being relegated to the ranks of the inconsequential. That is why it will be necessary to involve China, India and Japan, Russia and the European Union, at a relatively early stage."

After giving Joel and Shlomo a moment to process the information, Nadav continued: "As you must understand, this chip," he said, taking the chip out of his pocket, "has two layers of two separate materials. The intersection between their surfaces displays energy level behavior — that electron behavior there is modelled via the quantum level transition equations. That is what generates the miracle we saw earlier this week. I developed one substance, and Adam has no idea what it is or what its properties are. Likewise, Adam developed the second substance and I too have no idea of its origin or properties. Each of us holds one half of the key to this miracle. We have deliberately avoided sharing the secret with each other, to ensure there are two keys to this technology, to avoid the possibility of any single individual controlling this all too powerful technology. I and Adam will be the 0 level gatekeepers. To ensure the death or incapacitation of one of us by mishap will not spell the end of our endeavor, we have prepared a black box mechanism to safeguard the various secrets. Not a physical box, but a virtual system which in the event one of us is out of the picture, will pass on the secret to an individual we have designated — and whose identity will remain secret until the time comes.

Adam interjected, "We, or more accurately, Nadav, developed the ring's resonance equations in the ring. I think Nadav's solution is nothing less than brilliant. Joel will also, once he completes his calculations, keep those pieces of the puzzle to himself."

"Solving these equations," Nadav wove in, "is required to manufacture the helium rocket engine. People who understand these secrets and understand what we told you just now will be level 1 gatekeepers. We want you to be these level 1 gatekeepers. We want you, Joel, to be the CTO, and you, Shlomo, to be the CEO of this company. We don't expect you to answer right now, of course."

"The operations of this business," he continued, "will require recognition and understanding of physics that is not accessible to the public. People who possess this knowledge will be level 2 gatekeepers."

"And why do we want all this secrecy? Because if any state; Israel for example, or the United States, should gain full knowledge of all of the secrets I just enumerated, then the politicians will control the process. This technology can certainly be weaponized and that is what will happen, as happens to every technology, if we do not control it. By keeping the technological knowledge scattered, it will be hard for a state, or a terror organization, or any organization, to assume control of our technology."

Joel had lived his entire adult life in academia. True, he had fantasized once or twice of descending from the ivory tower and joining or founding a start-up company, but never actually went through with it. On the other hand, this venture was ground-breaking, even in pure research terms. It was like taking part in the Manhattan Project,[10] but instead of designing the ultimate weapon, he would be developing the ultimate energy generation technology. At this point, he had yet to internalize that the true goal of the project was nothing less than the salvation of mankind.

10. The American WWII-era atomic bomb project.

6.

"Well, you certainly seem to have it all figured out," Shlomo said, a bit less than half seriously, after wolfing down another sandwich. "So, how about problems? Do you foresee any?"

Nadav sat down to grab a sandwich from the rapidly diminishing tray, and Adam answered in his stead.

"I'll start with a problem you probably do not see as a problem, but it matters to us, and we have no solution for it. By transferring humanity to all-green energy, we are trying to solve a whole array of problems. The first of them is global warming, but it is far from the only problem. We have come to realize that even if we make the transition, global population growth coupled by the growing hunger of civilization for more and more energy will eventually lead to the exhaustion of even this seemingly inexhaustible font," Adam said, but then immediately added, "still, this is not what you meant by your question, which I will now try to answer. The first problem we see is that in a normal rocket engine the stream of burning fuel is indeed polluting, but over a cross section of several dozen square meters. In out envisioned helium rocket, the helium atoms will be expelled very precisely over only a few square microns who do not, according to our calculations, 'want' to scatter. Supposedly, this makes them an environmentally friendly gas- but not to anyone or anything caught in the path of this micron thin helium stream. They would be sliced in twain as by a science fiction death beam. According to our calculations the safe distance behind the engine is over 10 kilometers within the atmosphere."

"But particles usually scatter," Joel said.

"Not in this case," Nadav said, leaning forward.

"At such high speed, a Venturi effect is formed between the particles. In space, the situation is similar, but it is gravitational forces, rather than the Venturi effect, which operate on the particles. Our solution to this issue is for the helium jet planes to take off with a normal jet engine system. Only after about half an hour, when the plane reaches a cruising height of 13 kilometers, or 40,000 feet, and once the pilot confirms on radar that no plane is flying behind him, will he ignite the helium jet engine. The regular jet engines of the plane generate about thirty tons of thrust. The two helium rockets will generate a minimum of eight tons of thrust each, so another ten tons of thrust. If the pilot ignites the helium and normal jet engines together, then the resulting forty tons of thrust will outstrip the tolerance of the plane. In the void of outer space, that is not an issue, but within the atmosphere we must take the aerodynamic properties of the plane into account. Hence, the pilot will have to turn off, or at least close the throttle completely when he ignites the helium rocket engines."

"And we have another, rather curious, problem. The plane itself weighs a bit over one hundred tons when empty. So, on the moon, the plane will weigh a bit over sixteen tons. This means that even when the two rocket engines are in minimum thrust, they will prevent the plane from landing on the moon. Hence, the plane will have to carry a fifty-ton ballast — otherwise it will simply be too light to land on the moon, like a hot air balloon with a basket that is too small. Since the moon has no air, the plane will not be able to slide down for a landing. It will have to operate the helium rocket engines to land. Otherwise, it will crash on the moon."

They took a slight recess to connect to their cellphones — a must in the early 21st century, where being disconnected for more than an hour or two was cause for panic.

Nadav opened up once the recess was done.

"I want to review the technical milestones, as we see them. Clearly it is all much more complicated when you add the economic and political components which Shlomo is responsible for, not to mention the missing pieces of the puzzle which Joel still needs to complete," he said.

"In the first stage, we will construct a single helium rocket engine for proof of concept and initial tests. This should take us around three months and half a million dollars. The breakdown of these expenses is presented here on the slide. By the conclusion of this stage, I hope that Shlomo will agree to become the CEO, and Joel will agree to become the CTO. Completing this stage will enable us to approach the Israel Aerospace Industry.

The second stage will be to share the general plan with the Israel Aerospace industry and install two helium rocket engines within a broad bodied old jet plane. The old 767 has been retired from the fleets of most airlines, and today they generally purchase its new version, the 787. The Israel Aerospace Industry is in the business of converting the old 767s into cargo planes, so refitting them to our specifications will not be completely unfamiliar to them.[11] This stage will take another six months.

The third stage will focus on performing a test space flight. We must take into account that NASA and other space agencies might identify the flight as a rocket leaving Earth and it will be necessary to coordinate the flight with them.

The fourth stage will be to bring NASA into the project, in parallel to performing a circumlunar flight. Up to this stage it will be possible to perform everything here in Israel. The fifth stage will be to land on the moon. The Israel Aerospace Industry can certainly "upgrade" the Boeing 767 and add our helium rocket engines to it, but a moon landing requires detailed meticulous planning — and experience. The first is something that the Israeli character, so good in thinking outside the box

11. Since the rocket engine will be installed on the wing it will generate forces on the plane from the same direction as the regular engines generate so there is no need for structural changes. The internal pressure our space shuttle fuselage needs to withstand is around one atmosphere or one kilo per square centimeter. This is a rather high pressure, but the fuselage of a passenger plane is already designed to withstand it because the external pressure at a cruising height of a passenger plane is negligible – the void of outer space is not qualitatively lower.

and coming up with new inventions, is less suited for. The second requires more time than we, or humanity, have to spare."

"Humanity?" asked Joel, "do you really think the situation is so dire that we can't afford a little trial and error?"

Adam shook his head. "We are already living on borrowed time — and that time is up. We are like a man sitting on a gunpowder barrel — after the fuse has already been lit. Global warming will kill millions in this very decade, mostly in Africa. Africa is the poorest continent and contributes little to global warming, but it is also the continent most vulnerable to increased desertification, as the Sahara expands into the Sahel and the Maghreb. Millions will die from famine, tens of millions will flee the famine and try to cross the Mediterranean, no matter how many perish in their journey. In another decade, by the 2030s, tens of millions more will perish in the West, and elsewhere in the world, as well. We cannot stop that. It is too late. But maybe, just maybe, we will be able to prevent the calamities of the 2040s from coming to pass. Our goal is saving the tens of millions who are condemned to die if nothing changes."

Nadav, anxious, interjected: "If we had the time to review some basic sustainability studies, we could show you that even completely halting fossil fuel burning would not suffice to restore things. We are facing a wide variety of problems — climatic instability, for instance, will substantially reduce agricultural production over the upcoming decades. So, there won't be enough food to feed the global population, which is still expanding, particularly where religious fundamentalism still holds sway, both in the West and the Global South. Beyond an energy solution, the world requires food security, which means massive desalination. We can provide the energy for that, but energy is only a small part of desalinization and agriculture. For that, we need involvement of the Great Powers. But even if we achieve energy and food security, we will only be staving off the end, so long as global warming is not halted. To stabilize, perhaps even turn back global warming, it will be necessary to divert some of the sun's radiation. But that is not a project we can even plan for today. Hence, any delay in the more realizable projects will cost many, many human lives. And on this optimistic note I suggest we conclude our business for today. Can we meet tomorrow?"

"If all of your plans really will be realized," said Shlomo, the responsible yet still skeptical, adult. "And to be honest I still think there is no more than a 1 in 10 chance we won't crash and burn, then we are facing a very pressured time down the line. If we start working weekends this early in the game, we will collapse later on. I therefore suggest we meet here again, in the Gilboa office, on Sunday at 11:00 am. We should discuss the financial and company structure we need to establish."

Part B: Rakefet

1.

The meeting on Sunday began half an hour late. Adam and Joel, who arrived together from Jerusalem, were delayed by traffic at the entrance to Tel Aviv, whereas Shlomo was held up in a previous meeting. Nadav, who arrived on time, poured himself a cup of coffee in the conference room.

While sipping the coffee, Nadav calculated the amount of material he would have to purchase from Abu Maruf in Jenin in order to construct the first engine. He planned to have the material delivered to him next Sunday, but then recalled that the next Sunday was Tisha B'Av, the holy day commemorating the destruction of the Temple by the Roman Legions. On that day, as on other Jewish holidays, passage between the West Bank and Israel was barred to Palestinians, so Abu Maruf would not be able to make the delivery. It struck Nadav that he had never actually met Abu Maruf. Three years ago, when he began working in the North Galilee College, Nadav visited his parents, and had to purchase several screws and screw anchors in order to hang up shelves. Nadav drove with his father to the hardware store of Abu Snein in downtown Haifa, an Arab neighborhood where such products were far cheaper. While waiting in the store, he discussed the chemical material he needed. Abu Snein overheard the conversation and said that his cousin had just gotten married and moved to Jenin in the West Bank, and that he was importing chemical materials at dirt bottom prices. Nadav took the number but never considered calling. Only when he saw the incredibly high prices of "Beit Dekel Marketing Ltd," did he call Abu Maruf.

Shlomo was well known for his sedate management style. Usually, he spent entire meetings without expressing his own opinion, but let everyone say their piece and then aimed towards consensual decisions. This time, when he entered the meeting, he deviated from his custom.

"I want us to try to examine two issues today," Shlomo opened with, "the organizational structure of the company, and its financial structure. I think I understand your intentions, Adam and Nadav, but I want to propose a framework in which to achieve it. Once I present it, if you find this is not the direction you want, we will discuss alternatives suggested by others. But if it is the right direction, then we shall discuss concerns and steps to implement it. Does this sound acceptable?"

Nadav and Adam nodded in agreement, as did Joel.

"I'll start out by noting that I presented the detailed expenses you provided me with on Thursday to Danny Cohen, one of my partners in Gilboa and a fellow who understands such expenses. Don't worry, I did not explain to him what we were doing or what type of chip we were constructing. I told him to take a look and tell me if it made sense. Danny said that at first glance the plan seemed well thought out and highly detailed, including price quotes from several suppliers for each of the proposed activities. So, without committing prior to more detailed examination, it seemed to him to be a fine job. Danny also added that if we raise half a million dollars, there will probably be some change left over from the initial stage of constructing the first engine."

"Regarding the structure — as seems to me right now, this project will include a lot of unusual, even crazy, stuff, and I don't use such superlatives lightly when speaking to entrepreneurs.

So, it is best to do things as simply and conservatively as we can, when we can. Accordingly, I think it is best to establish the project as a regular Israeli company. Nadav and Adam will be the founders, and should Joel and I join, it will be as co-founders. A third category will be the initial group of investors, those who will fund the first half million dollars required by the plan. By the way, I suggest we aim at recruiting one million dollars rather than half a million. This capital raising round will be defined as the "seed investment," and the investors will be titled as 'first round investors.' I do believe we will eventually have a first, second and third round."

"If the seed will raise one million dollars," interjected Adam, "Then I do not think any further investment will be required. The project, at that point, will pay for itself."

Shlomo nodded with a smile. He had heard this music before from many other entrepreneurs.

"But you intend to bring in IAI as partners, right? They will put in their resources and receive a certain partnership, right? Under what conditions will they receive it? Under first round conditions. That is the standard way these things work. As I said, it is best to make this as simple as possible, because it will be much more complicated later on. The same applies to NASA. If you are planning on making them partners, they will enter on second round conditions. The upcoming stages, as I understand them, are as follows: Stage one — building the helium rocket engine. That is the first half million." Nadav and Adam nodded in agreement.

"Stage two — to bring the helium rocket engine to IAI and convince them it can be assembled on a plane, transforming it into a space shuttle, following additional modifications." Nadav and Adam nodded again.

"The third stage — getting our shuttle into orbit, outside Earth's atmosphere. At this point NASA will begin to notice us and we therefore must, as you noted, inform them and other space agencies, to ensure no one thinks it is a warlike ballistic missile. As part of this stage, we will also have to ensure our plane, or rather space shuttle, lands back safely in Ben Gurion Airport, and remains capable of repeating this stunt several times."

"Accurate," Adam replied.

"The fourth stage," Shlomo continued, "is to take the shuttle from orbit around the Earth and move it to an orbit around the moon. This is the stage in which we bring NASA in as partners and let them begin running the development. Other than the development of the helium rocket, of course," he added with a smile.

"The fifth stage — land on the moon under NASA management."

"The sixth stage — bring together the Chinese, Europeans, Japanese, Indians and Russians as partners and establish a lunar colony."

"Stage seven — begin to import Helium 3 from the moon to the Earth."

"Quite right," agreed Nadav.

"And this is how we end Small Oaks," Shlomo continued. "Big Oaks begins by repeating the same steps of Small Oaks, but on Mars. Do I understand your direction correctly?"

"Perfectly," responded Nadav.

"Have you thought of a name for the company?" Shlomo asked.

"I suggest *Rakefet*;[12] that being, Rakefet Ltd," Adam said. Nadav turned towards Adam in surprise. This was the first time he had heard this name.

"Why Rakefet?" he asked instinctively.

_____

12. Rakefet is the Hebrew name for the Cyclamen – a delicate pink flower that grows beneath sheltering rocks mostly in Mediterranean climates.

"Rakefet is a plant with absolutely no value to anyone other than for its beauty," responded Adam, "and it is also Israel's national flower. But the beautiful thing about it is in the initial vision of the Rakefet Ltd Company; to grow a rakefet on the moon, and later — on Mars, and so on. In other words, one can say that our vision is to generate beauty, and the benefit to mankind is a side benefit — such as in the story about the monk with two pennies, who used one to purchase bread and the second to buy a flower. Bread to live, and the flower so he may have something to live for."

"Alright," Shlomo said. "Are there any other name suggestions?" Since no one suggested any other name, Rakefet Ltd it was.

"Guys," Shlomo turned to Nadav and Adam, "what do you want as entrepreneurs? In other words, what are your conditions?"

"We have already thought about this," Nadav said. "We both come from affluent families. We will take an unpaid vacation for a year. We hope that in a year the project will take off and then we can draw a fine salary from it. Beyond this, in terms of stocks or options, our desire is as follows: if the company does not reach a value of one hundred million dollars within three years, then we want nothing. We will return to academia. We want, during those initial three years, to have the right to veto any change to the company structure. We believe that within three years the company will return all the investment, and that it will achieve financial independence."

"Very few companies return their investment within three years," Shlomo cut him off.

"Yes, I know," said Nadav, "perhaps we are really naïve, but we believe that this is not just any company. And if we fail to return the investment within three years — we will go home."

"However, if the company does take off, we want the founder group, which includes you two, to receive 51% of the options, with the other 49% to be distributed between the Seed investors, first, second and third round, according to the distribution you, Shlomo, decide upon. Of the 51% portion of the founders, we, Adam and I want 5% each for the invention of the Helium rocket engine. The CEO, you, Shlomo — should you take on the position — will receive 1%, and the remaining 40% will be split equally between the founders. If the founders are limited to the four of us, Adam and I will therefore get 15% each, you will receive 11% and Joel, 10%."

Shlomo mulled this over. "If we do secure a seed investment for one million dollars, and a second round of $20 million, once a partnership is formed with IAI, then another 60 million once we begin collaborating with NASA, we will reach a sum of investments over three years approaching $100 million. For the value of the company to be higher than $100 million, investors need to believe that we can sell the company for a sum significantly greater than that $100 million — all that in around three years. In such a case the numbers do add up, but the odds seem unlikely to me." Shlomo said, thoughtfully.

"Well, I understand what you want," he finally said. "I am not sure this will be the final agreement. We may get better terms in some respects and worse terms in others. But in any event, we will secure everyone's agreement before we close the contract and define the company's articles of incorporation."

Adam raised his hand like a dutiful pupil. "Until we secure the initial investment," he said, "we need to progress, and progress quickly. Nadav and I already decided to lend 100,000 shekels each to this future company. We will be happy if you could contribute your own money as well."

"I can lend 200,000 shekels," said Shlomo.

"I need a week to decide from where, how and if, I can spare the funds," Joel said.

"The Piskel Laboratories can generate the necessary materials once I transfer them the raw materials from Abou Maruf," said Nadav. "Beyond this, in order to manufacture the engine, we need a company that has a clean room with the ability to construct layers of material, as in silicon. One such company is the Tower Company in Migdal HaEmek. But given that they have suffered a cyber-attack in the past, I am somewhat concerned."

"Being the victim of a cyber-attack is actually an advantage," said Shlomo, "because they will be all the more careful now. Besides, I know their CFO. I will talk to him, see if it is an option."

"And then," continued Nadav, "we need to build up the mechanical aspect of our operations, and that requires a chip processing company. We also need to design the control system of the engine, and this requires..."

"The general outline of your stages," Shlomo interrupted him, "the company structure and the investment structure you are proposing, are clear to me." Shlomo turned to the window and took a deep breath of fresh, unconditioned air. He felt he needed it. "What concerns me is the urgency," he continued. "It is well known that little good comes from haste. A less hectic pace is most beneficial to raising investments, greatly increasing the company's chances to grow." Shlomo remembered how Adam and Nadav described any delays in their plan as costing human lives, but it ran against his grain to rush headlong into this interplanetary adventure with yet unproven technology. "Why are we in such a rush?" he asked plaintively.

2.

"This is a long explanation," said Adam, "so let's have another coffee before we continue."

"I don't understand all the cutting-edge technologies we raise capital for in Gilboa," said Shlomo as he stood up, "but I certainly understand this highly advanced coffee machine in the corner. Hence my domain in Gilboa is the warm beverages." Shlomo explained how to operate the machine and poured himself a simple Wissotzky tea.

Nadav asked to speak and stood up. He was tense, for even speaking before this small group was stressful to him. He had no clear idea how he would explain an entire world of concepts and terms, let alone the formula governing them, in a way that would be both clear and succinct.

"The full explanation," began Nadav, "requires quite a bit of chemistry, ecology and physics. That is why we do not want the full explanation. We will start off with summing up our goal in two words: "Saving humanity." Making haste will not only save human lives, but it may also, if we are successful, save humanity from stumbling off the brink of extinction. I will try to explain why without too many formulas."

"From the dawn of modern man," began Nadav, "over 300,000 years ago, say, at the peak of Ice Age some 22,000 years ago, the concentration of carbon dioxide particles in the air was roughly 250 molecules per million of other molecules, primarily nitrogen and oxygen. These levels oscillate, but never greatly — not until we started burning up fossil fuels such as gas, oil and coal."

"Volcanic eruptions also release abnormal levels of CO_2 into the atmosphere," added Joel.

Nadav, who found it easier to speak once he got started, nodded in agreement. "Yes, volcanic eruptions raise atmospheric CO_2 levels. But over time, vegetation absorbs the excess and breaks it into oxygen that is released back into the atmosphere, and carbon plants incorporate into their own mass, which is eventually deposited in the soil and is transformed into coal, oil and gas. The history of CO_2 concentrations can be measured precisely in our polar icecaps. These icecaps reach down hundreds of meters deep, each layer representing earlier eras. The age of the ever-frozen polar ice can be precisely dated via C_{14} measurement. The ice also contains bubbles of air — they are sampled to determine the concentration of carbon dioxide in those years."

"There is irrefutable evidence," Adam interjected, "that over the past millions of years — not only during the 300,000 year reign of modern man — temperature has also closely followed the carbon dioxide concentrations in the atmosphere, with a 20-to-35-year delay. Carbon dioxide concentration did not remain stationary throughout these millions of years. Still, this relatively stable concentration — around 250 particles per million over the past 300,000 years, enabled relatively stable atmospheric and temperature conditions, and that is what enabled humanity to evolve from prehistoric man to who we are now. CO_2 particles you see, prevent solar radiation from escaping back into space, thereby trapping their heat in our atmosphere, much as greenhouses do. So, the more CO_2 molecules there are in our atmosphere, the more the Earth heats up. That is why we see a consistent correlation over millions of years between CO_2 particles in the atmosphere and Atmospheric temperature. That is what the media calls "global warming.""

"Yes, yes. Al Gore, the former American Vice President, has already said all that before," Shlomo interjected, wanting to get to the point — the pace of planned expansion and activities of their company.

"Yes," Nadav, who had no intention of being rushed, said. "I just want to remind us all of this salient point before we move on. We discovered fire over 100,000 years ago and made increasing use of coal over more than a thousand years, but it was only a little over a hundred years ago, during the latter stages of the industrial revolution, that man began massively utilizing fossil fuel burning machines which belched out CO_2. Between 1890 to 1990, the concentration of CO_2 in the atmosphere grew to levels unseen over hundreds of thousands of years, reaching 350 parts per million. By 2020 it was already 420 parts per million (PPM), representing a 70 PPM rise in only 30 years — more than double the rate of the preceding century, which itself displayed a completely unprecedented rise in CO_2 concentration. Even if we could halt this rise, and we can't, the climatic impact of 420 PPM will only hit us 30 years down the line, in 2050. All the natural disasters we are witnessing right now are only the tip of the iceberg — the result of having passed the 350 PPM point 30 years ago."

Nadav sipped his coffee and continued his explanation.

"We will reach 450 PPM, a point considered by many experts as the point of no return, in only a few years. The point of no return means the earth will never recover. Ice in the poles will not disappear in the 2030s, but it will be gone by the 2060s or 2070s, a generation later. It will not return for thousands of years."

Nadav paused, gathering his thoughts, and continued: "Media coverage of polar ice is sometimes confused and confusing, so let me clarify. First, ice, like any natural phenomena, is cyclical. Small cycles lasting several decades, medium cycles such as the 14th-19th century Little Ice Age, lasting several centuries, and great cycles, such as the Ice Ages, lasting over 100,000 years. Contrary to what is presented in the media, ice coverage has actually grown since 2017. However, this increase is far lower than what this stage in the current small cycle calls for. Indeed, the increase is so mild, that we will likely face reduction by the mid-2020s.

When ice floes in the Antarctic Sea or arctic seas melt, this makes no difference to the sea level. That is most of the ice affected to date by global warming. However, when landbound ice in Antarctica or Greenland melts, the sea level rises, for this, unlike rivers — which merely recycle vaporized water which return to the sea as rain — represents a new addition of water into the sea; one that will not be recycled. So far, most of the ice that has melted has come from the fringes of the polar regions, primarily from ice floes. But should all of the ice in Greenland and Antarctica vanish, the sea level shall rise by more than 70 meters. Many people imagine that since global warming has not had much effect on sea-level so far, the process will continue sedately, at a linear pace, a centimeter here and there, with plenty of time to adjust. Indeed, most scientists are projecting a rise of no more than 50 centimeters by the end of the century. But a more realistic calculation, taking into account exponential developments, show that we are facing a 10-15-meter rise during that time frame. There will be no time to relocate and adjust."

"Why is this process exponential? Because as the polar ice-caps melt, they will no longer reflect solar radiation into space. The faster they melt, the faster the world will heat up, leading to ever faster polar icecap melting. This is a positive feedback loop, the very definition of an exponential process. This is what we experienced in the recent COVID-19 outbreak, but this time we have no vaccine!"

"Let us return to cycles. There are small cycles and there are large cycles. The Ice Ages constitute a relatively large cycle. The last Ice Age began about 100,000 years ago and ended around 15,000 years ago. Prior to the last Ice Age, the world was very different. There was very little ice in the poles and the sea level was tens of meters higher than it is today. For example, our distant ancestors lived in the Carmel Caves in the warm period, prior to the previous Ice Age. During this period, the sea-level was several dozen meters higher than it is today, and the Carmel Mountain touched upon the Mediterranean. At that time, the area now covered by the Sahara Desert was a well-watered verdant savannah. Pre-historic archaeological sites testifying to this are scattered throughout its broad expanse. In contrast, at the height of the last Ice Age, 22,000 years ago, Northern Europe, much of North America, as well as the southern tip of Africa were all covered by glaciers towering three kilometers high. The sea level was a hundred meters lower than today. And all this occurred with an average global temperature only five degrees lower than present times. Back then, the shoreline was dozens of kilometers seaward in comparison to today. If the polar caps melt completely, it will be dozens of kilometers inland in comparison with the current situation."

"Do you ever wonder what this will do to our coastal cities in Israel and throughout the world? Consider Tel Aviv. The highest point in Tel Aviv is 62 meters above sea level. Should the sea rise by 60 meters, the entire city would be underwater! But even should the sea rise by only 15 meters, Tel Aviv will become an archipelago, with hilltops such as the upper portion of the Old City of Jaffa, its wishing bridge and St Peter's cathedral included, just peeking over the sea, with the nearest island over a kilometer away. Even a "modest" ten-meter rise would leave most of Tel Aviv swamped. The same applies to New York, London, Shanghai, and almost every other great city in the world. Humanity has erected its greatest cities along the coast, and on the banks of great rivers and lakes. Hence, civilization is massively endangered by any shift in the sea level."

"But rising seas are the least of our concern. I said that a CO_2 level of 450 PPM is considered to be the first point of no return. The second point of no return is a CO_2 level of 500 PPM — a point to which we are rather close and will very likely reach before the end of this century. If we do, then this will be the last century of human civilization."

Joel and Shlomo shifted uncomfortably in their chairs. It was not that they were not aware of the global crisis, but, like most people, each was focused on his own field, and they found the contemplation of the end of humanity off-putting, even when they had no rational counter to the apocalyptic scenario being described to them. Shlomo rose, opened the window and loosened his collar, wiping the sweat beads off his brow.

"Go on," he said curtly, as he sat back in his seat.

"The reason most of humanity will not survive is that the food crops we depend on will not survive. Rice, wheat, potatoes, and maize will no longer be cultivatable and so there will not be enough food to feed mankind — whose numbers, I remind you, are still multiplying. Consider the drought plaguing much of Africa, causing massive famine and mortality, even though the world is supplying the continent with what is seemingly enough wheat to stave off disaster. Now try to imagine the situation should drought afflict the entire world, with no one being able to export a surplus. And don't even think the shortfall can be made good with meat; cattle, poultry and fish cultivation requires roughly ten times as much water and land to produce the same amount of grain calories."

Adam wove in, his tone more casual.

"Sometimes we hear on the news that global temperatures will rise by a single degree over twenty years. Usually, when I hear this, I tell myself: 'one degree? That is not terrible, I can barely feel one degree.' Do you know how much energy a single global degree represents?" Adam asked, answering his own question after a brief pause. "That energy is equivalent to

400 million atomic bombs[13] such as the one the United States dropped on Hiroshima. Not one bomb, not a thousand bombs, not a million bombs and not one hundred million bombs — four hundred million atomic bombs."

"We humans," added Nadav, "can't really grasp such huge numbers. It is perhaps easier to understand this figure in a different way: a single degree rise in global temperature is like dropping an atomic bomb for every twenty people living in the world today."

Neither Shlomo nor Joel had ever thought about it that way. By this point, they were both a bit pale. But Nadav and Adam were not done.

"The problem is not merely the rising temperature, but the increased energy in the atmosphere," continued Adam. "This excess energy will result in thunderstorms and deluges alternating with droughts, alternating with freezing cold fronts. We will have to endure worse alterations of cold with drought than humanity has ever had to contend with over the past 300,000 years. This is not a well-disciplined, cozy energy which will merely heat us up by only one degree. As aforementioned, this is the wild energy of 400 million atomic bombs."

"There are also other significant aspects of the upcoming crisis, but they are more complicated to explain. First, even a minor

---

13. "Little Boy," the atomic bomb dropped on Hiroshima, released 13,000 TNT tons worth of energy. Each kilo of TNT is capable of heating one ton of mass by a single degree. In other words, this bomb contained energy capable of heating 13×10^9 kilos of mass by a single degree. We will examine the mass of atmosphere on the planet: the pressure on the sea level (weight) on every square centimeter is one kilo. In other words, a pillar of a square centimeter of atmosphere stretching from the sea surface to outer space, has a mass of around one kilo. The surface of the Earth is 5×10^{18} square centimeters, hence the mass of the atmosphere is 5×10^{18} kilos of mass. If we divide the mass of the atmosphere (5×10^{18} kilos) with the number of kilos a single atomic bomb can heat by a single Celsius degree (13×10^9), we will get the number of bombs required to heat the atmosphere by a single degree – 400 million.

temperature rise will disrupt the oceanic conveyor belt.[14] Such a disruption will release toxic gases that have been trapped on the ocean floor since the age of the dinosaurs, poisoning the plants and animals. And that will affect each and every one of us. The four of us will, in any event, not live to see the end of the century. But our grandchildren could be middle aged by then, raising their own children and even their grandchildren — except civilization, and most of mankind at large, will not survive the effects of global warming. We are robbing them of their future, of their lives."

Though Joel and Shlomo were aware of most of what they were being told, Nadav and Adam's blunt presentation left them shocked to the core and despondent. Unlike Nadav and Adam, they did in fact have grandchildren. And as the two young researchers reviewed the bleak numbers and points of no return, an uncomfortable truth became clear to them. It was their generation who had doomed the planet, who had missed the chance to halt the slide towards environmental catastrophe before it was too late. Nadav and Adam's grandiose plans were, at the end of the day, nothing more than damage control.

"We and the grand majority of the scientific community," continued Adam, "cognitively understand the ramifications of what we just discussed. But given that Nadav and I had no solution we had no choice but to join the lotus eaters, content to drift down the current and over the waterfall into the abyss."

"Let me review the problem again, but from an energy perspective," Nadav added, ignoring the despondent atmosphere in the room. "Man is an energy consumer. Energy is generated from burning fuel and releasing CO_2. Western man consumes more per capita than those living in the third world. But, given

---

14. Warm water currents flow to the poles on the surface of the oceans, as in the Gulf Stream, whereas cold water currents flow towards the equator on the bottom of the oceans.

both demographic growth and the narrowing of the economic gap between the West and the rest, even were the West to adopt radical energy conservation policies, growing energy demands from the rest of the world would soon overtake it. Humans demand gasoline consuming cars, air-conditioned homes and offices, and products shipped across the world on gasoline guzzling cargo ships. Even the bread we eat is made from wheat planted and reaped by oil burning tractors. Humanity's addiction to fossil fuels to sustain an ever more affluent lifestyle and the demographic growth of humanity is the main, but not the only, problem. Even those who understand the problem, fear the solution. The only solution available currently to the essential problem of global warming is nuclear energy, notwithstanding the dangers of uranium fission reactors. Current green sustainable energy solutions, however, might contribute, but are not enough on their own. We need an alternative primary and stable source of energy, as population growth outpaces all existing sources of energy."

"In fact," added Adam, "the root problem we are dealing with is population growth. If only a fifty million people lived in the world, rather than eight billion, as was the case 3,000 years ago, then there would be no global warming, for the fossil fuel consumption of those million would be negligible. Our vast numbers, and addiction to fossil fuels, is choking the planet with toxic pollutants and CO_2 that are released when we burn these fossil fuels. Historically, there are only three developments that can reverse population growth.

"The first is Malthusian pressure - when population growth outpaces food supply, or when food supply collapses, then mortality, including infant mortality, rises, and new births decline. The higher the population peak, the harder the fall. And the unfolding environmental crisis will hit us at our greatest historic peak population.

"The second development is shifting lifestyle and norms. When the material and time demands required to maintain an acceptable lifestyle and social status outpace earning power, then people have less children. This is what has happened in the West, Japan, and other first world countries. The only problem is that these increased material demands also contribute to energy consumption and hence global warming.

"The third development is government fiat — this is what happened in Communist China. The central government decided to limit births to one child per family, deciding this was the only way to enable China to advance and become a world power. This policy, unlike almost every other communist policy, worked. Reducing population growth enabled China to become a superpower, one that is vying with the United States for global dominance. Today, illiteracy is nearly eradicated in China, and poverty and hunger is vastly reduced.

"Ignorance, which contributes to blind pursuit of maximal reproduction is strongly associated with religious fundamentalism. And this fundamentalism is likewise associated with refutation of scientific facts, be it that the Earth is round, that the solar system was generated about five billion years ago, that man is evolutionarily descended from primate ancestors — or that the greenhouse effect, and global warming are a real and present danger."

Nadav took a sip of water and Adam picked up.

"I want to emphasize a point that is not politically correct — but the danger we face is too dire, and too imminent to be concerned with political correctness. The central problem is fundamentalist religion and ignorance which feed upon another globally. Fundamentalists in the United States object to teaching evolution, and the lessons it teaches us, all the while the US defunds global family planning programs in Africa, resulting in greater poverty and misery, while their Muslim counterparts in the Middle East violently oppose secular education, especially for women. In Israel, we have the Ultra-Orthodox sect who deliberately abstain from any work or secular education, while having families far larger than they can afford, relying on secular taxpayers to support them.

"The solution to this willful ignorance must come from politicians, not science. For our purposes, those politicians belong to one of two types. The first type of politicians are themselves ignorant. Not necessarily stupid, but ignoramuses who do not believe in science and of course do not understand the cataclysmic ramifications of global warming. They think global warming is not cause by man, that it is either an act of God or nature running its course."

Adam paused. He felt like he was giving a speech at a political rally, except he was not pro-choice or anti-abortion, progressive or conservative. He was just ranting against everyone. Because really, everybody was responsible for creating and then ignoring the problem.

Nadav did not want to end the discussion on this note, so he wrapped up by saying: "The moment I realized Adam and I had even the smallest chance at a solution to this unfolding catastrophe, it became clear that there was absolutely nothing more urgent and worthwhile for me to do for humanity than to move forward with the projects we outlined at full speed ahead. If we can bring back Helium 3 from the moon and begin generating green energy, the crisis might be ameliorated, and perhaps your grandchildren's grandchildren will have a chance at life."

"Yet at the same time, it is clear to us that population growth, and a demand for rising standards of living, will simply eat up any energy this new technology may produce. That is why it is so important for us to control the invention. The general model, which will obviously need to be adapted to evolving conditions, is to provide each country with the Helium 3 nuclear fusion capacity to provide them with as much annual energy consumption as they use **today**, rather than increasing it over the years."

"A weakness of this approach is that countries with rapidly growing populations or rising living standards might consume our Helium 3 but at the same time use oil and other fossil fuels to bankroll their population growth and rising standard of living."

"However, you must keep in mind that these countries will not need to use oil initially, for Helium 3 will provide all of their energy needs. Switching back to oil as their population grows or their living standards increases will prove difficult given how much more expensive it will be, especially given the collapse of the industry and its infrastructure once we introduce nuclear fusion. There will therefore be a strong economic incentive to remain on clean energy, which we hope will work to counteract fundamentalist pressure.

"That is why secrecy is so essential. Should this technology fall into the hands of a government, any government, they will find it impossible not to give in to fundamentalist pressure, be it Christian, Muslim, Jewish, Hindu or Buddhist, to continue procreating excessively and dooming our planet, and ourselves, to oblivion."

Nadav looked over Shlomo and Joel and took a deep breath.

"That is the short explanation. I think it suffices."

3.

"Today," Shlomo looked around the conference room grimly, "we are going to talk about operational security." Nadav, Adam and Joel looked at each other in confusion. Adam said, part-sarcastically: "Nadav and I only just got back from reserve duty. Can we hold off on the military jargon until our next call-up?"

Shlomo smiled. "You really are babes in the wood, aren't you?" he laughed. "The moment you two made your discovery you became an intelligence gathering target — and so did everyone else in the room. Listen and learn, grasshopper."

Shlomo, a graduate of the elite 8200 intelligence unit, was no stranger to the world of intelligence. He knew full well that intelligence organizations around the world were concerned with technology just as much as they were with military and terrorism. This was nothing new, especially for a state such as Israel, which depended on technological superiority to counter the numerical disparity it suffered versus its foes.

World War Two ended in 1945, and surplus military material initially filled the arsenals of both Israel and its Arab enemies. The 1948 war was fought with these weapons on both sides, though with the Arab armies initially enjoying overwhelming quantitative advantages in material. Though eventually victorious, Israel suffered the death of nearly one percent of its population. But by 1956, Israel, a small and insignificant country, had acquired the French Mystere planes. These jet planes were four times faster than the WWII era planes, equipped with precise munitions and onboard radar capable of detecting enemy planes from afar. Had France possessed such planes during WWII, it never would have fallen, and had the Germans possessed such planes at the time, the Battle of Britain would surely have been lost.

The rate of technological innovation has consistently doubled every forty years since the outbreak of the industrial revolution. Eighty years has passed since 1940; a decade worth of technological innovation would, in 2020, be expected to occur within two and a half years. Every intelligence agency on the globe understood that any country who missed out on two years of technological development in any essential area would cease to be a relevant actor. A superpower who fell behind technologically would lose in any conflict.

Technological and industrial espionage was therefore the primary intelligence effort of the great powers.

The primary powers contending on the world scene were the United States and the European Union on the one hand, and China and Russia on the other. The European Union however, in spite of its economic strength, lacked a unified intelligence service and tended to rely on the intelligence gathering of the United States. Russia, though still contending for global relevance, had fallen too far behind technologically, economically and demographically to truly contest American hegemony. One edge was the optical capabilities of the Russian satellites — those satellites enabled Russian intelligence services to read, on a cloudless and sunny day, a 14-font article lying on a Tel Aviv porch.

The Americans and the Chinese, however, were the main global players, and both had frightfully powerful intelligence capabilities. Their intelligence services could track the location of any individual with a cell phone, listening to any conversation; landline or cell phone. They could track any individual or vehicle wandering outdoors, day or night. Agents could listen in on conversations taking place in the open air, anything they had a line of sight on, so long as they were within a mile of their position, while their satellites could do the same for conversations taking place indoors, provided they could aim dedicated lasers at a window in the room where the conversation was occurring. The interference pattern of the laser bouncing off the window reflected the sound waves impacting the window from within, and analysts in Washington or Beijing could reconstruct the conversation. Still, they could not listen to every indoor conversation at the same time, for the number of such systems in every spy satellite was limited, and every such system could only track one window at a time. Nonetheless, Shlomo knew it was only a matter of time before one of these intelligence organizations would wise up to Rakefet's possession of global, game changer technology. That was, after all, exactly what they were on the prowl for. Given that these organizations also spied on each other, the moment one of them found them out, within a few weeks, all three would know. The moment that happened, every conversation among Rakefet employees and anyone associated with Rakefet would be closely monitored and analyzed. Every movement by the executives would be tracked, and any gathering, social or work related, would be photographed.

Patiently, Shlomo explained all this to the others.

"We need to behave as if these organizations are already aware of Rakefet and act accordingly, in order to prevent the specifics of the technological secrets from being uncovered by the superpower's intelligence agencies. If at all possible, we should also conceal our projects ultimate destination."

As Shlomo spoke, Nadav looked around the room. It suddenly dawned upon him why Shlomo had insisted on meeting in Gilboa's Kinneret conference hall. It was a central room, without any exterior walls or windows.

Shlomo noticed Nadav's wandering gaze and nodded. "From now on we only hold these meetings here, in the Kinneret hall," Shlomo declared. Adam smiled, as he suddenly realized that the hall shared the same name as Shlomo's secretary and wondered about the internal politics.

Adam and Joel seemed confused for a moment, but then they too realized they were sitting in a windowless interior room. They exchanged glances and slowly nodded.

Shlomo was well familiar with the intersection of intelligence and politics. This was not the first time he had worked with sensitive technology as a potential espionage target. But that night, after he left the office, Shlomo developed stomach pains which he suspected were psychological, rather than bacterial. Shlomo began to consider the ramifications of Rakefet Ltd. It was not merely a company, but a company with global human significance. Such meaning raised complex moral and philosophical issues.

Shlomo had never thought of himself as being responsible for the State of Israel, let alone humanity or the planet. What made him or Joel or Adam or Nadav qualified to decide what was in the best interests of humanity? On the contrary, in a representative democracy citizens elected their leaders, and it was them who were qualified to understand and determine what was good for the state. Concealing such an essential development from the state's decision makers was inconsistent with everything Shlomo believed about democracy. On the other hand, there was nothing illegal in what they were contemplating. A company such as Rakefet Ltd was certainly entitled, according to every law and norm, to act in accordance with the plan of action they discussed.

"Yes," Shlomo mused, "it was legal — but the technology on our hands was so significant to the world, and to our own state, should the Israeli Prime Minister be made aware of this capability he never would permit us to act as we intended. They would want Israel to gain far more advantages and power over the technology. So, on the philosophical level we are operating contrary to the democratic process.

On the other hand, on a philosophical level, Socrates and Plato thought that a good rule was not the democratic rule of the people, but the reign of philosopher kings. And here we are, appointing ourselves philosophical kings of the entire world.

Shlomo knew Professor Asaf Carmel from a committee they were both members of. Whenever he consulted with him on moral issues, without going into details, he would recommend Professor Galit Cohen, the Deputy Dean of the Philosophy Faculty at the Tel Aviv University. His long conversation with Professor Cohen, an opinionated woman in her 60s, left Shlomo with great admiration for her. He decided that he wanted Galit to serve as his moral-ideological conscience, and, should the others agree, of the Rakefet Ltd Company as well.

The only thing that bothered Shlomo about Professor Cohen was that she had never served in the military. Galit spoke fluent Persian, as her parents had fled Iran following the Islamic revolution, but she would have been in Israel when she turned eighteen and it troubled him to think that she might have somehow shirked service in the IDF, which was mandatory for women as well as men. What Shlomo did not know was that when Galit was 18, she was recruited directly into the Mossad, Israel's CIA equivalent, where she served in various roles intermittently over a cumulative period of 25 years. Though they discussed her personal history over the course of their conversation, Galit was practiced in speaking only of her covers in various countries, as well as her employment for several years as a stewardess for El-Al, Israel's national airline.

4.

Over the next month, many things happened. First of all, Rakefet Ltd was formally founded. Shlomo explained his moral qualms to the other founders and asked to appoint Professor Galit Cohen of the Tel Aviv University's Philosophy Department to be Chair of the Board of Directors.

"Galit is an expert in ethics and all the other issues underlying my stomach-ache," he said. "This way I can be CEO and take charge of the company while Galit can take charge of our stomach pains."

Nadav and Adam were so enthused by Shlomo's agreement to be CEO, that they immediately agreed to the new appointment. Joel didn't really care and so raised no objection.

Rakefet was able to raise the entire Seed investment of two million dollars that very month. After investors heard that Shlomo put in $400,000 of his own money into the company, as well as assuming the position of CEO, they lined up to put their own money in. The only problem now was how to turn the others down without offending them.

"Don't get too excited," said Shlomo, "the very same investors who are so nice right now will be the first to raise all sorts of outlandish demands the moment things get rough."

The materials needed to construct the superconductor chip arrived at the Piskel Labs and they began assembling them. They closed a contract with Tower Semiconductor Ltd. in Migdal HaEmek, to dedicate one of their facilities to manufacturing Rakefet's chips for two weeks. The chip processing institute had completed the base ring of the engine, a steel circle two meters in diameter, fifteen centimeters wide, and six centimeters thick. This time they knew better than to paint the interior side. Furthermore, the glass tube ring was already installed within the steel ring. The chassis component which was still missing was the steel cover, which had to be at least five centimeters thick in order to prevent magnetism from leaking outside the engine ring. The total engine weight was therefore 11 tons. Another two weeks were required to complete the electronic control system. Even though Nadav was not an electrical engineer by training, he still undertook to manage the control system development. To see it through, he hired an electronic engineer and computer engineer, who became the first non-founder employees of Rakefet Ltd. It turned out that the cost of constructing the engine would be around $400,000, not the half million that was originally estimated.

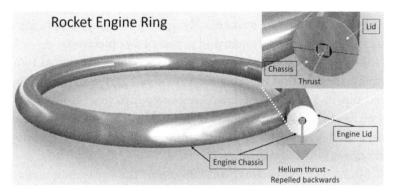

Schematic of the rocket engine ring, all engine connections are on the back and are not seen in this picture.
In appendix B "Ismail technical lecture" there is a computerized image of a cross section of the engine affording a view of its internal systems.

Now they had to think about how to operate the engine and inspect it.

"Obviously, the ejected helium needs to be aimed towards the earth," said Nadav. "If we aim skywards, and a plane happens to pass over us, we will simply slice it in two — or at the very least kill everyone on the plane."

"Clearly, we can't aim it horizontally," added Adam. "So, it seems that we should aim it downwards."

"If the engine begins vibrating this could be dangerous," said Joel after performing many calculations. "My calculations indicate that the control room for this experiment should be at least a kilometer away from the engine."

Given these constraints, they decided to locate an experimental site in the Negev, Israel's southern desert. Shlomo found a farm founded by a New Age spiritual couple about fifteen kilometers away from the crater of Mitzpe Ramon and leased a large area from them for six months, with an option to extend the lease for an additional five years.

"There is a location near ancient Nabatean terraces where we can install the engine," Shlomo explained. "There is also a good site to set up the control room a little less than a kilometer away. Both will be surrounded by closed military areas, so we will have plenty of privacy. We will be able to reach the experimental site via a relatively comfortable dirt road, which a truck with a crane should be able to navigate."

They also needed to construct a very large concrete cube. The cube had to be drilled with a hole facing the ground. The engine would be anchored to the cube to keep the helium emission downwards, towards the hole. Beneath the hole would be a tiny room where they could enter to examine the influence of the helium emission on the room floor. Their assumption was that the helium would penetrate about forty meters in a narrow beam.

Kinneret, Shlomo's talented secretary, was now Rakefet's de-facto secretary as well. She was well suited to the job because of her efficiency and multi-tasking capabilities. She secured the services of the Hashomer Company to guard the area and prevent guests and curious Bedouin from approaching. She explained to the security company that they were being hired to guard a "facility" in the Negev, where only a few employees would have access to the site. The security company guarded several stations in the Negev: some cellular company installations, some belonging to the Mekorot water corporation and others to the electric company. Usually, a patrol arrived at the above secured facilities once every two or three days. Here, in contrast, 24/7 patrols were required. The company sent three security guards with a jeep and a trailer home where they could rest. The security guards, or "security officers" as they insisted on calling themselves, in practice, ran the site. They explained to the contractor where to construct the fence and the gate, and shortly thereafter they made sure they ran the project.

By September, everything was ready. The engine reached Mitzpe Ramon and from there, by dirt road, to the farm and to the concrete cube where it was installed. During the installation, the engine was covered with tarp in order to prevent the curious from observing what was going on. A small room, constructed out of a shipping container was placed over the engine. Another container was brought in to serve as the control room, placed about a kilometer away. The farm itself had a significant power supply via the adjacent powerline, and the Rakefet Company ordered a triphasic 6,000 Volt connection to the engine site. The Electric company at first refused to make the connection, and only the judicious calling in of political favors by Shlomo persuaded them to perform the odd connection in the middle of the desert.

By hook and by crook, by noon on the 1st of September everything was ready. Joel, Nadav, Shlomo, Adam and the three security officers manned the control station. The security officers did not understand why they were forbidden to stand by the engine.

"Our orders are to guard the engine," they stridently argued.

Only after a loud disagreement did they agree to relocate to the control room. Joel reexamined the ignition circuits of the engine.

"All is in order," Joel announced, "Nadav, you can start the ignition sequence."

Nadav started the sequence, and all seemed in order. The engine ignited. As planned, the engine began to work on its own, supplying its own power and no longer requiring the external power line. The thrust measured surpassed their calculations: ten tons worth, rather than eight. However, the resulting vibrations seemed within the parameters. Everyone in the room sighed in relief.

Yet, a mere thirty seconds later, Nadav began to grow concerned.

"I think the engine turned off," he said. At that moment, the security officer standing outside the control room rushed in. "There is a huge cloud of smoke over the facility!" the security officer cried out hysterically, "I don't know what you are doing here, but I think you should stop."

"According to all the parameters I see," said Adam, "the engine ceased working about half a minute after ignition." They hurried out to see the smoke.

It was humbling. A massive mushroom cloud, several hundred meters tall, towered over the site of the engine.

Joel was the first to recover.

"It is not a smoke cloud, it is a cloud of dirt," he said. They stayed rooted in place and silently observed as the cloud dissipated. It took half an hour before it was, mostly, gone.

When they cautiously approached the engine, they saw a hillock of dirt five meters tall where the container-room housing the engine had been located. The container itself was nowhere to be seen. Two days later, the container was found some three kilometers away in the Israeli Air Force training area, after aerial photography picked up an odd object.

The disappointment was crushing.

Nadav and Adam brought in four Bedouin workers who, over the course of a week, helped them clear the dirt until they discovered the engine standing precisely where it was when they started the experiment, as if nothing had happened.

When Joel arrived at the site, Ismail, one of the Bedouin workers, stared at him with interest.

"Hi, Joel," he said, startling Nadav and Adam. They didn't even realize Ismail spoke Hebrew.

Joel did not recognize Ismail.

"I am studying for my Master's degree at the Hebrew University, with Dr. Yonit," said Ismail.

"So, what are you doing here?" asked Adam, gesturing self-consciously at the pile of dirt.

"It's the semester break now, and I am helping my uncle," Ismail replied.

Joel suddenly remembered that he had seen Ismail with Dr. Yonit at the University, but until Ismail brought it up, his mind had not made the connection. Joel decided to kill two birds with one stone and called Yonit to ask after her impression of Ismail. When Yonit assured him that Ismail was solid, he raised the idea of hiring him as a Rakefet employee. Bringing Ismail in would give them a skilled worker with relevant academic qualifications, and, since Ismail had already seen the engine and linked it to Professor Joel, the damage in terms of compromised secrets was already done. Better to bring Ismail into the fold and get him to sign an NDA.

But Adam and Shlomo opposed the idea.

"Look, Ismail may be skilled, but this technology has national and global security implications which our own government will be concerned about. Bringing in an Arab employee at this early stage is not going to help alleviate these concerns once they become aware of what is going on."

"We may be intending to keep this technology strictly civilian," added Adam, "but I think this experiment has amply demonstrated how easy it would be to weaponize."

"Don't forget," Nadav countered, "that our goal is to save all of humanity. Arabs included. Hence, he has as much interest to maintain secrecy as any Israeli Jew has."

The argument went downhill from there, as is the wont of political arguments between the Left and Right in Israel.

"Where is your Zionism?" asked Shlomo, "we need to put the security of the State of Israel first."

"Oh, come on. We are no less Zionist than you are," Joel and Nadav retorted heatedly. "We show up for reserve duty on time, every time."

"Enough already with this progressive leftist posturing," Adam shouted.

And then, as is the wont of Israeli political arguments, everybody calmed down. They decided to submit the matter to Galit, who had stepped into her role as Chair of the Board of Directors of Rakefet Ltd.

Galit decided that Ismail would be cleared for Level 2 secrecy — he would know all the technical secrets in broad terms but would not be told that the critical components of the two substances were held by Nadav and Adam separately. He would henceforth be tasked with orienting and training new employees. In the meantime, Ismail began to work with Adam and Nadav to learn things in the field. On the rides with Joel to Jerusalem, he was given the theoretical explanations.

So, what actually happened during the initial activation of the engine? It turned out that when the helium stream penetrated the ground, it generated a counter steam of dirt which — in the absence of any outlet — burst upwards, tossing aside the walls and roof of the engine room. The engine itself, ensconced within the steel ring, was as armored as a tank, but the system operating the engine was thrown aside with the structure. Once the engine ceased receiving commands, it shut itself down, precisely according to specifications. Now Nadav and Adam wanted to open up the engine lid in order to see what was inside. But the five-centimeter-thick steel would not open and there was no way to see what was happening inside the engine without getting the lid open.

After two days of repeated attempts, Joel located the problem. The massive magnetic forces within the ring had effectively welded the lid to the base of the engine. So, there was no hope whatsoever of opening it up.

Nonetheless, they decided to try to operate it once again, for a single second, just in case it was still operational.

Amazingly, the engine worked! Once more, a mushroom cloud of dust rose into the air. But since the engine had only been operated for a second, there was no damage to the structure, and Ismail and the Bedouin workers had everything cleaned up in less than an hour. Fortunately, everyone around them, including the farm owners and relevant military authorities, assumed the dust mushroom clouds were just part of the regular bombing exercises of the Israeli Air Force.

"You know," Nadav told Adam, "Doesn't Ismail remind you of the Battalion tracker, Muhamad Huzail? The one who was with us on our last tour of duty in the Golan Heights? He has the same last name, not that that means much — there are probably more than 10,000 Huzail's in the Negev."

Nadav was at the company commander's side during that tour of duty. The tracker, Muhamad, would lie in the back of his jeep like a sack of potatoes. Muhamad would only exit the vehicle to scout the route of their advance in the morning. Nadav and the tracker would cover their sector of the buffer zone with Syria, searching for tracks formed during the night, and the company commander would drive — or occasionally switch, with Nadav. The tracker would show Nadav the tracks of boars, porcupines, rabbits and other animals that had walked through the buffer zone. Nadav once asked Muhamad what he did outside the army. Muhamad's answer stunned him.

"I am finishing my medical studies in the Technion and starting up my surgery internship at Rambam Hospital," said Muhammad.

"So why are you here?" Nadav asked him, flummoxed.

"Look," Muhamad told him, "I had to fund myself over all seven years of medical studies, because I got into a stupid fight with my affluent parents. I was a tracker during my regular service, and now I take up this occupation, for pay, during the semester breaks. It is two months a year, and the salary is high enough to pay my bills and tuition for the rest of the year. Now, when I begin my residency, my mother will support me."

"You know, you are right," Adam told Nadav. "Ismail does have an uncanny resemblance to Muhamad."

"Ismail," Nadav asked him directly, "do you maybe know Muhamad Huzail?"

Ismail smiled.

"Yes" he replied, "Muhamad the tracker is my elder brother, older by a year. I guess you know him from the army? I did not serve."

"You know," Ismail said, surveying the experiment site, "Me and the guys don't mind cleaning up after the dust clouds. But don't you think our neighbors," he jerked his chin in the direction of the air force training zone, "are going to start asking questions if we blow up the desert every few days?"

Given the complications caused by the previous experiment, they had to think how to proceed. They decided to perform the experiments at night, so the mushroom clouds would not be quite as easily observed or conspicuous. They also decided to bring in two massive 300 horsepower fans. They would suck out the air from the chamber under the engine before scattering all the dust backflow from the hole dug by the helium jet outwards. It would still generate a massive mushroom cloud, but it would no longer cover the engine with dust — or fling the control unit away. Ismail and the other Bedouin workers reinstalled the engine room, which they brought with a tractor from the air force firing zone. Although the chamber was completely bent out of shape, several hours of pounding it with the tractor and five kilo hammers bent it back into a rough square shape that fit over the engine.

Adam and Nadav decided to try to operate the engine for an entire night.

At 3:00 am, the security officer burst in to the control room again.

"There are very strange noises coming from the facility," he said. "You had best come."

Nadav deactivated the engine and they headed off to see it. By the time they arrived, it was nearly 4:00am. The scene before them was surreal. A massive steaming stream of water was bursting out of the doorway of the concrete cube below the engine.

"Where is this coming from?" Nadav and Adam were stunned.

At dawn, the water flow began to weaken, and by 8:00 am it had almost completely ceased. The water filled the Nabatean terraces along the stream below them completely, giving them the appearance of Vietnamese rice paddies. These terraces had not received such an amount of water since Nabatean times — and perhaps not even then.

Fortunately, a light drizzle had occurred the previous day, so claiming that they had been under a localized cloudburst was a semi-plausible alibi to anyone, including the hippie farmers from whom they were leasing the experimental site, who might enquire as to the source of all this water.

But more pressing was discovering the source of the water. They sent the water to a laboratory in Tel Aviv, where the water was found to be fresh, potable and of excellent quality. Once again, Joel offered an explanation.

"Few non-geologists are aware of this, but a massive aquifer underlies much of the Negev. It is over 300,000 years old. The only problem is that it is four kilometers deep — too deep to be financially viable for drilling and pumping. Hence the aquifer remains unutilized."

"But how did our engine get to the aquifer?" asked Adam, "The helium jet is powerful, but it doesn't penetrate four kilometers into the earth!"

"True, the helium jet only penetrates a few dozen meters in the initial seconds of its operation," explained Joel, "but due to the vibrations of the engine, the jet shifts its direction slightly, and the hole widens over time. Hence, when the helium particles are flung into the hole, they fling earth upwards, as you have seen. We have seen this earlier and overcome this with the giant fans. The helium current has slowly carved out a hole a few millimeters wide in the earth and rock underlying the engine, and our fans cleared the earth away. At some point the helium jet reached the amazing depth of four kilometers. At that point, the helium jet heated the water, resulting in a massive pressure of steam — which led to their eruption outwards." Joel locked his gaze with theirs, trying to make them understand the significance of what he was saying.

"My preliminary calculations indicate that every second the engine is active, about one hundred cubic meters of water will be released. That is five times the flow of the Jordan River when it flows into the Kinneret in wintertime," Joel smiled and added, "of course, explaining the appearance of so much water will be very difficult, and without a good explanation, the entire world will know all about our engine before we are ready to go public."

"But the water of the ancient reservoirs is somewhat saline," said Shlomo, who knew some geology. "It may be good for certain types of agriculture, but it is not potable."

"True," said Joel, "but we heated them into steam, which is pure water, without any salts. These steam vapors condensed into the water you see exiting our 'spring,'" Joel continued. "In fact, every second we operate the engine, in this location, we are sending jets of energy into the reservoir."

The thought that passed through everyone's mind was that this was a serious problem. While making the Negev Desert bloom was a value they were all raised on, it was probably less important than saving the world.

"We need to find some kind of cover story for this water without revealing the true source to everybody," Shlomo said. "Either that or reduce the experiments to the minimum necessary."

And indeed, at that point they decided to limit each engine operation experiment to three seconds per night, and hope for abundant rainfall to explain the copious quantity of water all around them.

5.

Ismail's mother, Maira Salman, was not born in a hospital delivery room. Maira was born in a Bedouin camp on Mount Sinai near the Santa Catherina Monastery, in the aftermath of the Suez War in 1957, shortly before the Israeli withdrawal to the 1949 ceasefire lines. Her father used the opportunity to visit, with her mother, the camp of the mountain Bedouin who had served since medieval times as the guardians of the Christian Monastery. The thirty-six monks in the monastery, a fixed number for centuries, had always preferred to employ Muslim Bedouins from this tribe over the local Arab Christians. On Maira's birth certificate, her place of birth read "Mount Sinai."

Maira was a member of the Al-Huzail Tribe. Their territory lay north of Beer Sheva, including the land on which the Bedouin town of Rahat was established. She was the granddaughter of Salman Al-Huzail, from whom she derived her middle name. Maira was the only daughter of the eldest son (out of seventy-six children). This lineage was highly significant, for Salman al Huzail was the most powerful sheikh in the Negev and northern Sinai. He was titled by the British as the Sheikh of Sheikhs and they granted him extensive authority. Nonetheless, the Al Huzail tribe faced a constant problem.

It was well known that the Al-Huzail were descended from a Jewish clan who lived in Northern Arabia and the Sinai prior to their conquest by the Muslims and their subsequent conversion. Genetic tests performed in the late 1990s confirmed this historical memory. Moreover, some of the tribe members maintained certain Jewish traditions over the centuries, much like the *conversos* in Spain.

When Prophet Muhammad was active in Arabia, some 1400 years ago, some Arab tribes worshipped the traditional Arab Gods, while others had converted to Christianity. Others, particularly in Northern Arabia and in the Sinai, adjacent to the Jewish homeland, had converted to Judaism, or were descended from those Jews who fled the defeat of the anti-Roman rebellions. All were forced to convert to Islam — and were forced, like the Huzail's, to constantly prove their loyalty to Islam and Bedouin traditions. Thus, safeguarding 'family honor' was all the more significant for them than for other Bedouin, who are known to place utmost importance on such a value.

'Family honor' often involved violent intimidation, or even murder of women who did not follow the rules and overstepped accepted gender roles. Thus, when Maira began to study medicine in Ben Gurion University, she was very careful not to be seen to overstep her inferior station as a woman in any way.

For Maira, or as the Jews called her — Mira, this was particularly difficult. Maira was an opinionated, tough and strong woman. To keep herself away from temptation, she threw herself into her studies above and beyond the efforts of other students, and graduated *cum laude*, going on to intern in mouth and jaw surgery at the Soroka Hospital. When she met Amir at university, it was clear to that any straying from the rigid gender relations protocol would result in her immediate slaughter. Thus, Maira never glanced at Amir, not during their common lessons and not without them. She used a Jewish friend, Hagar, who lived next door in the dorms, to approach Amir. Maira explained to Hagar the danger she was in, and though Hagar never really understood the urgency and thought Maira was exaggerating, Hagar respected her need for secrecy.

Given Maira's lineage, over a dozen other Bedouin students assumed the role of her minders, making sure she did not stray. Indeed, since all the Bedouin students in Ben Gurion University knew who she was, any one of them could become an informant.

Amir was a member of the Tarabin Tribe, with no distinctive lineage. When Hagar approached him on Maira's behalf, his jaw literally dropped. How was it that the princess was even aware of his existence?

He would occasionally sneak a peek at her during classes, and he was well aware that she had never even glanced in his direction. During their studies they never met physically, only circumspectly via notes they hid around the campus and burned after reading. Once they completed their studies and began their residency, Maira in oral surgery and Amir in dermatology, they decided, still via notes, to get married. Amir asked his parents to approach hers. They laughed and said Maira's station was far out of reach for him. However, Maira's father was actually quite desperate. Not only had his daughter crossed the threshold of being 25 years old, beyond which almost no one would propose marriage in Bedouin society, but she also had an academic education and profession, which severely impaired her value on the marriage market. Accordingly, when Amir's parents approached him, he did not toss them out on their ear. Instead, he said, albeit with distinct repugnance, that he would discuss this with his wife and Maira herself. To his surprise, Maira told him she knew who Amir was, and that she was ready to marry him.

Ismail was born in Mount Sinai Hospital in New York City. During those years, his mother began working parttime in the hospital, continuing the research she had begun at Soroka Hospital in Israel — looking into a virus which homed in on oral cancer cells and marking them with a fluorescent substance. Soroka, unfortunately, lacked the budget to fully support her research. When she registered for work in Mount Sinai Hospital, the clerk checking her in remarked that her birth certificate showed that she was coming home, for she had been born on Mount Sinai. When she corrected him, insisting she had been born in the Israeli, now Egyptian, Sinai, he showed her the documentation and she burst out laughing.

"Yes," she said, "but I was born on the real Mount Sinai, in the Sinai Desert. The hospital was named after where I was born."

"There is a hospital in the Sinai Desert?" the confused clerk asked.

"No," she responded, "I was born in a tent on the mountain slope."

The clerk, a devout Christian, would not let the matter drop, and soon spread the word to much of the hospital staff that the famous oral cancer researcher had been born in a tent on the holy Mount Sinai, after which the hospital was named.

Ismail was Maira's sixth child, and in addition to his four older brothers he also had a big sister. His mother was known as Professor Maira Salman (everyone though Salman was her family name, although it was actually her second given name), Soroka's premier cancer researcher. Some experts claimed Maira was a viable Nobel Prize candidate, and should she become a laureate, that would make her the first Arab Muslim woman to receive a scientific Nobel Prize. Both mother and baby were treated like VIPs.

At school, however, Ismail was only a mediocre student. His father did not mind, but his mother took it hard. His older brothers commiserated and consoled him that his mother was more patient with him than she was with them — and that had they gotten such grades, they would have preferred to run away from home than face her wrath. His father, in contrast, was forgiving and loving. When he began his physics studies in the provincial Ben Gurion University, unlike his older siblings who studied medicine in the world's leading universities, his mother's disappointment was palpable.

"Well then," his mother told him, "during your vacation you will help your uncle who lives near Mitzpe Ramon."

6.

Shlomo knew Amit Schwartz, deputy director of development at IAI, from high school. As a teenager, she had had a crush on him. Amit now handled various startup companies that IAI was grooming, but it was important to Shlomo that Amit will not classify Rakefet Ltd. as a startup, as the massive conglomerate would thereby presume they could set the pace and future direction of Rakefet — derailing all their well-laid plans.

Accordingly, Shlomo first e-mailed Amit, telling her that, prior to closing a deal with Boeing in Seattle, he wanted to contact IAI concerning a large project of several hundred million dollars which would unfold over the next two years. In the e-mail, he also noted that the project was highly secret, and that Amit was more than welcome to contact him for more details.

Amit immediately called him back.

"What is all this about?" she asked.

"I would be happy to meet you this week," he responded, "the issue is essential adaptations to Boeing 767, which will transform it into an extremely attractive plane, even more than the 787, the Dreamliner. But this is a very secret project, and so I first want to make sure IAI is both interested and capable of taking it up."

"All right," replied Amit.

"I want to first of all meet up with you alone, so that the issue only leaks to a minimum number of people, should it eventually not deem suitable for IAI."

"That's fine," she responded.

The meeting with Amit took place in Shlomo's office in Gilboa. After serving coffee, Shlomo opened up.

"Well, to be frank, I was not being entirely truthful on the phone."

"What do you mean?" Amit asked.

"The goal of Rakefet Ltd. is not to upgrade the 767 into an

improved version superior to the 787. The goal is to transform it into a space shuttle."

Amit was shocked. She undertook every effort to conceal her excitement from Shlomo, but the old fox sniffed her out without too much trouble.

"Rakefet Ltd manufactures super-advanced rocket technologies utilizing top secret technology," Shlomo continued. "Rakefet's rocket engine is capable of generating thrust sufficient to push a 767 plane into orbit outside the Earth's atmosphere. Unlike rocket engines intended to push rockets out of the atmosphere by burning fiercely for only a few minutes, our engine only generates forty ton's worth of thrust, but it can maintain its strength for hours."

"Hold on now!" said Amit, "Just one second. Normal jet engines reach this thrust, so how do you intend to reach an escape velocity of 11 kilometers per second with this engine? And with such a heavy plane no less? If this is possible, why isn't this done with a regular jet engine?"

"This is a question that I can answer, but should you have more technical questions, then we will have to invite our scientists and technicians to explain. To return to your question, the big difference is that a jet engine requires air to generate thrust, whereas a rocket engine does not require air to generate thrust. Jet engines can only generate thrust up to a ten-kilometer ceiling. Special engines used by stealth planes can do so at twenty kilometers, but that is pretty much the hard ceiling. We generate thrust regardless of the height, even in vacuum. So, our engine can accelerate the plane endlessly. So long as it is in atmosphere, the plane will use aerodynamic lift to continue rising. That is good up to about eighty kilometers. At that height, the plane will accelerate to a high enough speed for the centrifugal force to counteract gravity. As we continue to accelerate, the centrifugal force will increase, too. Thus, we will continue to rise higher and higher until one hundred kilometers is reached. A hundred-kilometer height is considered to be the boundary between the atmosphere and space and is called the Kármán Line. In truth, the atmosphere stretches out for seven hundred kilometers, and is surrounded by the ecosphere. But past the Kármán Line, there is insufficient atmosphere to generate lift, which means the aerodynamic structure of the plane is of no use. Temperature at these heights are extremely variable, rising very high on the sunwards side of Earth and declining in the outfacing side.

"Well, we both know IAI wants in," Shlomo continued, changing tact, "the big question is whether IAI is capable of performing the required changes to the 767 at such short notice, as per the Rakefet Company's needs and timeline. The primary changes are first of all in the fuel tanks in the wings. We need the 63-ton tanks to be replaced with much smaller, 4-ton tanks. We want to install the rocket engine within the wings, one in each. Since each engine weighs 11 tons, that makes 22 tons and 4 tons regular jet fuel. That leaves 37 tons for our rocket fuel."

"This does not add up for me," Amit said. "A space shuttle requires fuel which weighs ten times as much as the shuttle, if not more. You are talking about fuel which will weight only 20% of the weight of your plane, or space shuttle. How does this work out?"

"Our fuel is water — not ordinary rocket fuel," Shlomo responded. After saying that, he watched Amit with a slight smile on his lips as she processed the ramifications of the bombshell he had just dropped.

"By water, you surely mean oxygen and hydrogen. When hydrogen burns, the water generates as much thrust as any other fuel, but that is only about an eighth of the mass of water. That doesn't add up. Unless this is a nuclear engine," Amit said, staring at Shlomo before the penny dropped: "Hold on," she said, "is this what I think it is?"

"Yes," Shlomo retorted, "this is exactly what you think. And this is part of the reason everything is so secret."

At this point Amit could no longer curb her enthusiastic expression.

"Before you get too excited, you need to understand our requirements," said Shlomo. "We need two shuttles. The first needs to be flight capable within six months, and the second two months later. In other words, the first test flight, where everything already needs to work, needs to be ready by April next year, six months from now."

"This timeline don't make sense," said Amit.

"That's right," said Shlomo. "That means, first of all, we can't waste any time right now. This is another reason we need to see if IAI is capable of taking this project on. On the 'no wasting time' front, I want you to come and see the engine in action this week, together with an engineer who understands rocket engines. One engineer of your choice, who knows how to keep his mouth shut and not blab to his mates. Other than this rocket engineer, we don't want anyone from any division, except for the Flight Division. We will provide a ready-to-use rocket engine."

"I expect that in the following week, Barry, your CEO, will come see our engine," Shlomo continued. "I know Barry is planning a trip to Paris at that time. He will have to cancel it and be here on the date when we can present the engine in action. For reasons of field security, we can only do the demonstration on cloudy — preferably rainy— days in Mitzpe Ramon. In this way we can disguise the effects the engine generates around it."

"The bottom line," Shlomo continued, "is that since the test flight needs to take part in April, getting everything in place for it to occur will require you to clear your schedules and obligations and focus solely on this project. If you can't do that, then we will close with Boeing in Seattle next week. But if you can undertake this obligation then this will be the most significant thing IAI has done since it was established. In addition, since this is top secret, there can be only three people who can hear about the project: you, your engineer of choice, and Barry. None of your executives, employees, directors, let alone unions and various ministries associated with IAI can receive any updates from you. Any deviation from this policy of secrecy will lead us to transfer the project to Boeing."

"I cannot commit IAI to such tight schedules," Amit hedged.

"Yes, this is clear to me," Shlomo replied. "That is precisely why I want the CEO here on the weekend, Friday or Saturday, after your engineer has looked into our engine's capabilities. Next week Barry will also see the engine himself."

IAI's Flight Division was active in the business-civil sector. In 2020, the division was IAI's weak link. True, it was building a small executive jet, its own original design, but that did not represent outstanding success. The central activity of the Flight Division was the conversion of Boeing 767 planes into cargo planes. While the financial scope of this activity was huge, every old plane cost over a hundred million dollars, so the profit margins on the conversion were extremely narrow.

Should this project be taken up by IAI, Barry, the CEO, would be considered to be the man who saved the Flight Division. The activity with Rakefet would transform the Flight Division into the most profitable division of the company and its primary growth engine. That would be a dream come true for him.

"So, the way I see it," said Shlomo, "is that currently, you have four 767 planes undergoing conversion into cargo planes. The clients for two of them ditched you because of ongoing problems in this field. We want those two planes — and we want them tomorrow morning."

"I see you are more informed than I am about what is happening in the Flight Division," said Amit. "Can I talk to my CEO first? I will talk to him first thing today when I return to the office."

"All right, but make sure Barry understands the confidentiality required here." Said Shlomo.

"If these are the timetables you are talking about, I need to return to the office and talk with the CEO right now," said Amit. "Grabbing the CEO for an hour-long conversation on a moment's notice is not quite acceptable in our company culture. We go about things more calmly."

"Yes, tell me about it," said Shlomo, "ever since I entered this project," he added, "I live in a parallel universe where the clock spins forward twice as fast than the ordinary world."

"Why the rush?" Asked Amit, "Who is chasing us? These are truly impossible timetables."

"It's complicated," replied Shlomo, "but there is a reason for the rapid pace, and it is not merely a commercial reason. Should IAI join the project, we will describe to you, as our partners in crime, the reasons for the insane pace this project requires."

Part C: The first plane

1.

In the business world, there is considerable importance to status symbols, such as who arrives at whose office. That is how the alpha male, or female, is marked out. The common executives make pilgrimage and pay homage to the office of the sublime senior executive. Shlomo was supposed to arrive at the offices of IAI and wait patiently for the secretary to call him in. Moreover, the CEO of a startup company would never usually meet the CEO of IAI. It was positively unnatural for Barry, the illustrious CEO of IAI, a company with a 1.3 billion dollars sale cycle per annum, to pay homage to Shlomo's offices. On the other hand, while Shlomo's current position was now that of a CEO of a small, unknown company, Shlomo was also a reputable senior executive and near celebrity in the rarified circles of the high-tech industry and venture capital funds. Barry admired Shlomo's large, sumptuous office, which surpassed his own in size alone — not to mention the view! Barry avidly looked down on the Herzliya beachfront. He was an excellent professional and manager, but his political skills had been neglected. Barry had grown up in IAI ever since he finished his studies at the Technion. His career had not developed as quickly as it could have — primarily due to his lack of understanding of organizational politics.

Barry had been informed by the deputy director of development Amit, and by Suzan from the Rocket Engine Department, that the Rakefet Company possessed a nuclear fusion-based rocket engine, which was built on the fusion of hydrogen into helium and the emission of helium at near light speed. Barry was no fool — he immediately understood that collaboration in order to manufacture a space shuttle would be the biggest project IAI ever undertook. Moreover, this project would be a lifesaver for the Flight Division and take IAI to an entirely new level.

The meeting began, with Barry opening: "IAI will do everything to meet the impossible timetables you present us with."

Shlomo responded: "I want Yossi, the Flight Division Manager, to come here tomorrow, in the morning, for a detailed, three hour briefing of all that entails. He will need the briefing in order to select ten engineers who will come here on Monday at 8:00 am. These engineers will receive three days of training, so that they understand what they are supposed to design. In addition, since it seems it will be cloudy tomorrow, you will be able to see the engine in action tomorrow night."

Shlomo was surprised to hear Barry had no need to see the engine himself and that he trusted the impressions of Amit and Suzan, who had examined the engine themselves.

"Frankly, I do not have the know-how to assess what I see. I do, however, want to accompany Yossi tomorrow, so that I will get a better grasp of what is required."

"That's fine," Shlomo replied.

"Who in the government has been informed of the project" Barry asked.

No-one in the Israeli government knew about this project, and Shlomo wanted to keep it that way — but he also did not want to share this information, so as to avoid complications.

He paused before answering: "This is a completely civil commercial project. The necessary secrecy is not security related, but industrial. Accordingly, the minister of defense, who is the state's supervisor of IAI, is out of the loop at this stage. Only those whose inclusion is essential are even aware of the Rakefet Company. As you no doubt realize, in this project the required secrecy is far more severe and complicated to maintain than any military project you have ever been involved in before. It is of the utmost importance to ensure that the people who will be exposed to the project know how to keep a secret. We in Rakefet will take care of all of the state institution connections — you will, in this project, act solely as a subcontractor.

Once various portions of this project are revealed to the public, you will all get due credit for your own contributions. But until then, we are operating on a need-to-know basis — which means no unions, no board of directors, and no ministers either. The contract we will sign will explicitly note the required confidentiality constraints, and should you violate it, then we will be entitled to transfer the subcontracting to Boeing."

Barry was flummoxed. "Are you saying I cannot update my own board of directors about this project?" he asked.

"That's right," responded Shlomo, "and I understand this is a problem. You will have to be creative to make this maneuver."

Barry did not think Shlomo fully understood just how problematic maintaining secrecy would be. He knew the individuals involved, and knew that the board, with all due respect, was like a flock of chickens who would show up in the very next morning's news program if only given the chance.

Out loud, Barry said: "I will mislead them and explain that Rakefet is taking us on as a subcontractor to convert a 767 into a new configuration, matching Rakefet's special and secret need. On the other hand, I must, at the end of the day, answer to the defense minister."

"Before you report to the defense minister, you must notify me," Shlomo said. "We need to maneuver in such a way that the prime minister, his deputy and the defense minister will be appraised of the technology in a way that will not result in crises in the coalition." This explanation seemed plausible to Barry. Shlomo knew, however, that he had to consult with Galit on this issue.

Shlomo understood that legal issues might occur, should the planned spaceplanes be built to completion. The defense minister had the authority to pass an ordinance against the removal of the technology from Israel. However, so long as the technology remained unbeknown to him, clearly no injunction could be issued forbidding its removal from the country. Galit's solution was to transfer the technology (but not the knowledge underpinning it) to other countries before there could be any concern the defense minister may issue such an ordinance.

"I think we should first transfer the technology to China, and only then to the United States," Galit suggested.

"The United States won't sit by and let Israel transfer technology to China," Shlomo said. "Why China before the United States?"

"Because if a situation develops in which the United States has both knowledge and possession of the technology," responded Galit, "then they will pressure Israel to exclude other countries — especially China. In this way, the United States would eventually be able to gain control of the technology."

Shlomo was persuaded Galit was right, and he was happy to let her handle these issues. Shlomo knew that analyzing the power plays between the superpowers were beyond his knowledge and abilities.

2.

The serendipitous life story of Noa Dagan, a.k.a. 'The Eagle,' seemed almost legendary. Her father worked as a development manager at Bell Labs in New Jersey. Noa's mother was on one of her frequent walks in New York City when she began undergoing contractions, before laying, writhing in pain, on the sidewalk. The passersby literally stepped over her, as they would do with a homeless person. A pair of El-Al stewardesses who happened to pass by noticed Hebrew writing on her trousers. They addressed her in Hebrew, asking what was wrong, and she told them she was going into labor. They immediately called an ambulance which evacuated her to Mount Sinai hospital, where Noa was born — quite possibly in the room next door to Ismail. Little Ismail, however, was in the royal suite, and she was born in a standard maternity wardroom. Either way, both were American citizens by birth.

Noa was one of the first combat pilots to graduate from flight school. She truly was the salt of the earth type — an honor's student from Ra'anana, with a teacher for a mother and an engineer for a father. Noa had few inhibitions or obstacles in her life — everything seemed to flow naturally — studies, friends, boyfriends. Only later in her life did Noa understand that she was queen of denial and repression. Early on, when she was in elementary school, her father was murdered in a terror attack in Jerusalem. His death hurt her just the right amount — not too little, but also not too much. When her mother re-married, she received the news gladly and treated her stepfather lovingly. Her stepfather was, like her father, an engineer, and invested great effort in Noa's studies, particularly during her flight school, pushing her to study electric engineering and computers at the Technion. This was not exactly common in flight school, and for the first time, Noa ended up walking her own path, different from those of her fellow cadets. Some incorporated a bachelor's degree in computers at Ben-Gurion University, situated near the air force base where the flight school was based. This track incorporated studies with the needs of the course. Noa, however, used her stepfather's connections to be given permission to attend the Technion courses. As she could not drive all the way north to the Technion on most days, she watched the classes on YouTube (this was before the era of Zoom) and completed other courses via Google and the Open University. Her stepfather also served as her personal mentor, but even so, she was not able to complete her studies within the framework of the flight school, but only a year after she graduated.

As a combat pilot she was considered a rising star. Despite opposition from the political echelon, she was assigned to conduct many of the airstrikes on Syria — strikes the Israeli air force denied ever performing. Noa also outperformed everyone else in air combat training, whether on simulators or live planes. The engineers who operated the computerized system that monitored pilot performance, both in combat strikes in Syria and in training, showed that she was off the charts. Some claimed she was half-avian.

By that time, Noa was already a divorcée. She had married her high school boyfriend, Oded, after graduating from flight school. They had been friends for many years before becoming lovers. Two months after their marriage, she flirted with a pilot from her wing during a social event. Her husband was furious, and by the time they returned home together he had lost control of his tongue, shouting and screaming that he would not allow her to continue screwing everything that moved as she did in high school. Noa remained icy cold during the argument, even when Oded slapped her. Noa, uncharacteristically, did not respond or say anything. Oded, upset, immediately apologized and left the house to calm down. After leaving, Noa collected her belongings, drove to her parents and never talked to him again. The divorce was swift and civilized.

After her divorce she took a long trip in India, where she fell and severely injured her leg, rib and arm. The leg injury required a long process of recuperation which rendered her unfit to fly as a combat pilot. In the meantime, she carried on in the air force as a transport pilot and became a major following her second term of service in the professional army. Noa was selected the Prime Minister's pilot for his personal airplane. Policymakers thought a female combat pilot would be a "good look."

Rotem Carmel was the first transport plane pilot in the Israeli Air Force. There were female helicopter and even fighter plane pilots before her, but Rotem was the first female pilot to participate in combat operations. When she began serving in the air base, her unit was tasked with a mission to transfer equipment to a Mossad unit in Sudan. It turned out that all the base's pilots were in training in the UK. The base commander did not want to pass up on the mission, so Rotem flew copilot to a reserve duty colonel. Before they landed in Sudan, the senior pilot suffered a heart attack, forcing Carmel to land a Hercules on her very first operational mission. Not on the tarmac of an airfield, but in the desert sands, on a moonless night, without lighting, in total darkness. Rotem was awarded a citation of merit from the chief of the Mossad.

On her base, Rotem was considered to be a prodigy. She possessed a deep understanding of the aircraft's capabilities. Operational flights only left following her technical confirmation, and usually led by her. A brief glimpse at flight plans enabled Rotem to diagnose hidden problems and defects. Rotem managed all of the investigations of malfunctions in transport planes on her base — and in practice in all serious cases in the Air Force. By 2020, she was entering into her third professional army service extension and had herself reached the rank of colonel, having three children along the way.

Rotem decided to stay in the Air Force, as she was promised that after two more years, she would be able to secure a high-paying position in El-Al. After receiving a call from IAI's CEO Barry, Rotem's squadron commander contacted her and told her that a representative of Rakefet would be in touch, and that she should consider his offer.

And indeed, that very day, a man who identified himself as a Rakefet representative arrived at her home. Rotem had never heard of the company, but the offer the representative made her was fascinating.

"The Rakefet company is interested in employing your services on a top-secret project for a salary of $24,000 per month, on a five-year contract, as the captain of a 767 plane," the representative told her. Rotem looked him over and said nothing.

True, the pay of an El-Al captain could be higher, but Rotem had not even begun her career track in El-Al. That was two years in the future, and it would take her another decade to make captain. The offer being made to her was a tempting short cut. A salary three times that of her current pay, and a highly desired job right now — not over a decade in the distant future.

"You don't need to decide right now, only after the job in question will be presented to you," the representative assured her and continued with his explanation. "In the framework of this position, you will work and learn together with IAI engineers for around three months, of course with full pay. If this is of interest to you, you will need to sign a harsh non-disclosure agreement, both regarding your own position and the Rakefet Company in general. This NDA emphasizes you can share nothing regarding either your job or your employer with anyone, your husband included. You can tell him you were offered a position as a civilian pilot of a 767 plane. You can also tell him the salary, and that the job falls under the auspices of IAI. Should you be interested, you will sign the NDA, and from there we will proceed."

As the terms were being outlined to Rotem, another Rakefet representative was holding the exact same conversation with Noa.

The next day, both pilots arrived in Gilboa's offices to sign the NDA.

Shlomo was on the prowl for outstanding transportation aviators. Shlomo was of the opinion that experience and seniority was always an advantage in every possible field — every field except for aviation. He well recalled how, during the Israeli strike on Saddam Hussein's nuclear reactor near Baghdad, the only pilot to miss was the most experienced one, the commander of the Ramat David Air Base. Shlomo wanted Rakefet's pilots to be at their professional peak.

When IAI presented him with two female pilots as their leading candidates, Shlomo was delighted. He favored female pilots for several reasons. First, his experience in the 8200-intelligence unit led him to believe that women kept secrets better than men. Women, he believed, compartmentalized their information management. They found it difficult not to gossip about personal matters and relationships — but professional matters were kept under lock and key. The second was the political appeal of the project — female pilots were simply a better, more newsworthy, look. Finally, there were studies that showed women functioned better under professional pressure — of which Rakefet's projects were sure to provide plentiful quantities. Noa and Rotem, therefore, seemed perfect to him.

"On Sunday at 10:00 am, you must show up for a meeting in the Kinneret Hall, right here, at the end of the corridor," Kinneret told them once they signed the NDA.

"That is a bit of a problem, because I am still on duty at the squadron," Noa said.

"I'll handle that," Rotem said. "We will both be here at 10:00 am next Sunday, sharp."

"Tell me, what do you know about the project?" they both tried to fish for information from the secretary.

"I have no idea what it is all about," said the secretary truthfully, and carried on with her work.

3.

Come Sunday morning, everyone sat down together in Kinneret Hall: Barry, Yossi Turgeman, Director of the Flight Division, Rotem and Noa. Everyone duly deposited their cellphones with the secretary. Other than Barry, who had visited the offices before, everyone was awestruck with their opulence. On one side of the table was a tray with coffee, tea, mini sandwiches, and cookies. When the secretary noticed that everyone was too tense to drink coffee, she served each of them personally and admonished them to load up.

At precisely 10:00 am, Shlomo entered the hall. It was clear to him his audience were tense and restless, so he decided to wade right in.

"I suppose that, with the exception of Barry, you do not know why you are here and who is here with you," he began. "I will make the introductions in order to save time, and then I will present the general outline of the project."

Neither Noa, Rotem and Yossi thought that this man, whom they had never seen before, had any idea who they were, and were taken aback when he went on to introduce them.

"I will start with Barry, CEO of IAI. Besides him is Yossi, the Flight Division Director at IAI." Noa and Rotem had heard of Yossi before, because all of the Airforce 767s had gone through the Flight Division, both for upgrades and for regular maintenance. But it was clear to both of them that sitting down for a meeting with the CEO of IAI was not a run-of-the-mill occurrence for a pilot.

"And this is Noa and Rotem," Shlomo continued. "They will be the first pilots to fly our upgraded plane. We are now beginning to upgrade two planes. When they are both ready, Rotem will fly one, and Noa will fly the other. Later on, two co-pilots will be coupled to each of our pilots. And last but not least," he added with a smile, "I am Shlomo, CEO of the Rakefet Company."

Yossi remembered that he had run into Shlomo before. Shlomo had showed up in the media on several occasions in all sorts of contexts. Yossi understood that this was an upgrade of some sort for the 767 — and this was something he understood back to front. Yossi did not understand why Barry was in such a hurry and why so much secrecy was required, but he felt calmer now that he was on familiar territory and leaned back in his chair. Shlomo picked up on Yossi's body language out of the corner of his eye and focused on him, mimicking his body language, and leaning back himself.

"Rakefet Company, together with IAI," he said in a clear, secure tone, "is set to upgrade two 767-200 planes... into space shuttles. The first shuttle will take off in April."

His words landed like a bomb. So, Yossi thought he misheard. He knew that only NASA had space shuttles. Israel and IAI were generations behind the necessary abilities and technology. The 767 was too heavy, borderline obsolescent, and those were only the obvious issues with this crazy idea. He nonetheless tried to focus on Shlomo's next words.

Shlomo stroked the wooden table with his large hand.

"From here on out, we will not use the term 'space shuttle.' We will only say 'plane.' This way, if someone overhears us, it won't trigger any inconvenient questions. Our 'plane' will take off for its first test flight in April. By May, the plane will have to achieve several hours of flight on the Kármán Line, one hundred kilometers above sea-level. By June, we want to reach six-hundred-kilometer flights, and by July we want to reach 36,000-kilometer-high flight, where geostationary satellites orbit the planet."

The tension in the room was so high that it felt like the air had congealed. Barry had never heard about the July 36,000-kilometer milestone — this was news to him. Yossi was beginning to assimilate to the idea that he had heard and understood correctly. He was actually being tasked with designing a space shuttle — and realized that Shlomo was examining his reaction to the bombshell. Yossi was no rube in the woods and knew a thing or two about organizational politics and reading people. He realized that he had just become a key player in a major, perhaps unprecedented, project. Noa and Rotem, in contrast, were completely shellshocked. Their constant refrain from the moment they entered the Airforce was that they were there to shatter the glass ceiling — but now Shlomo was talking about breaking through the stratosphere!

"I invite you now to listen to two technical presentations," Shlomo continued. "Both will be delivered by Ismail, who is responsible for training and orientation in Rakefet. The first presentation, which will last for about two hours, will explain the principle which will enable our upgraded plane to operate. After the presentation, I will be happy to speak with both Noa and Rotem. Yossi, you need to select, right now, ten engineers who will begin working, starting tomorrow, on designing the upgrade. The entire week has been allotted to lecturing the engineers and the pilots. The second presentation will be in the questions and answers format, and is particularly pertinent for you, Yossi, so you will be able to pick the engineers best qualified to carry the project through." Yossi now understood why Shlomo had so studiously examined his reactions.

Shlomo left; Ismail entered. He immediately noticed the shellshocked faces of his audience.

"Maybe we should take a coffee and refreshment break before we start talking about technology," he said, deliberately emphasizing his Arab accent. "May as well get past all the surprises at once," he thought.

Everyone was relieved at the idea of a break, especially given Ismail's extra surprise — it was not every day that Israeli Air

Force pilots were presented with top secret technology by an Arab.

"Tell me, do you understand what they are talking about here?" Yossi asked Barry.

"In broad strokes," Barry responded, "I admit — on the one hand I am just as confused and excited as you are. I am terrified we won't be up to the task. On the other hand — you do realize this is the biggest project IAI ever undertook, right?"

"But the timetable! How the hell are we going to meet that?" Yossi asked.

"We still do not understand what is required," Barry replied, "but when they tell us to jump, the only thing we need ask is — 'how high?'"

"I don't understand why there is no one here from the Aerospace Division," Yossi said.

"It is their call. They said they only want the Flight Division," Barry replied. "Moreover, they know IAI better than we do, I have no idea how, but as I told you — their wish is our command."

On the other side of the room Noa was asking Rotem precisely the same question.

"Did you know what this was about?"

"No," Rotem replied, "I am just as shocked as you are. I don't know what to think."

"Neither do I," Noa said, "except that I definitely need to visit the Ladies room."

Noa left the room and glanced left and right. She was trained for perfect situational awareness, but she was damned if she remembered where the restroom was.

"Can I help?" Nadav, who walked by with Ismail asked.

Noa was not used to being confused and needing help.

"Restroom?" she asked, embarrassed.

Nadav pointed at the door to the right.

"They are still stunned," Nadav told Ismail and continued walking.

Noa was somewhat confused. She was not usually treated this way.

The break was over, and Ismail returned to the room. He presented them with two brief lectures. The first overviewed the rocket engine, and the low quantity, but near-light-speed helium jet it emitted. The second was a general explanation on how the plane would reach space.

"Do we know where the great powers such as the United States, the European Union, China and Russia — not to mention corporations such as SpaceX, Virgin Galactic and Blue Origin — stand in regard to this technology?" Barry asked.

"That is the beautiful thing," Ismail responded. "As far as we can tell, we are several years ahead of all of them thanks to several technological breakthroughs we made. We are truly the beneficiaries of several outliers which came together serendipitously. That is why secrecy is of such paramount concern — we need to preserve our unique technological advantage for as long as we can. As far as SpaceX and Elon Musk, we intend to offer him a seat on the advisory board, so that our relative advantages can be combined. The chairman of our advisory board is Professor Joel Meir, from the Hebrew University, who is also Rakefet's CTO.

"Regarding maintenance of secrecy, you will get the full lecture about safeguards and information compartmentalization structures tomorrow. For now, keep in mind that we need to always be aware that this project will, at some point, be monitored by superpowers who have extraordinarily powerful espionage capabilities, including listening in on every single phone conversation we make, as well as listening in on any conversation we hold in any room with a window or exterior wall — and that is only scratching the surface of what the Great Powers are capable of."

Only now did everyone notice that 'Kinneret Hall' was an interior, windowless room, with lighting designed to create the illusion of being open to the air.

"From this moment on, you need to assume, and this is probably true, that all of your phone conversations are being deciphered and analyzed, not only by some AI server, but also by a human intelligence agent in Moscow, Washington and Beijing. Beyond that, you should assume you are being photographed from satellites and from the ground 24/7. On the bright side," Ismail added with a grin, "if you ever get mugged, there will be photographs of the event from at least three separate angles."

Later, Ismail explained that since the plane had sufficient fuel to both reach escape velocity and slow down while re-entering the atmosphere, all of the problems generated from atmospheric friction-based slowing down on re-entry were not something they need to worry about. This was a safe flight, not fundamentally different from a regular flight by plane. By the end of the lecture, it was clear to everyone they were going to make history.

Following the lecture, Noa and Rotem came knocking on Shlomo's office door.

"Come on in," he greeted them, "take a seat."

"Well," he said, once they were seated, "you understand that you are the only pilots, right? Everyone else, including myself, are only engineers and mechanics sitting in the industry offices and hangers going about their daily routine. You, on the other hand, will need a cover story you will be able to sell to your social circles, families included, about the upcoming change in your lives. This cover story will also enable you to confer with your families about whether you even want to take the job — without exposing any confidential information, of course.

"According to this cover story, you will become test pilots for IAI on upgraded 767 planes. The advantage of this cover story is that it is completely true. In addition, this will enable you to explain to your family that this is a job with various risk factors. In any event, I need your final answer on whether you want the job or not, by the end of the week."

"I'm in," Rotem said immediately "I want the job."

"I do as well," replied Noa, "but I feel I should discuss this with my parents and sister."

Shlomo nodded. "You have until the end of the week, but I remind you to stick to the cover story. The real project is not to be hinted at."

"Clear," Noa tersely replied.

The next morning, ten engineers showed up in the Gilboa offices. All signed the NDAs and heard the initial presentation. After a short recess, Barry, Yossi, Noa and Rotem joined them. The engineers were rather surprised to find their Division Director and CEO in the classroom with them. This only added to their excitement at the grand scope of the project. Ismail informed them that the next lecture would be primarily a technical explanation.[15]

Following the technical lecture they took another recess, drank coffee and visited the lavatories. Noa once again ran into Nadav. "Well," she laughed, "I am still stunned, but at least this time I know where the restroom is." Nadav blushed, realizing she had overheard him when he commented on her confusion to Ismail, and ruefully reminded himself to be more careful with his words in the future — social interactions were hard enough for him as it was.

---

15. Those interested in the technical specifications of the helium rocket space plane are invited to read Ismail's full lecture in the appendix.

119

4.

Israel's 8200 intelligence unit constantly monitors Russian, American and Chinse satellites. So, when those satellites suddenly began to focus their attention on IAI complex in Lod, an immediate red flag was raised, and the information was transferred to the Mossad.

The deputy commander of the Mossad, who was headed towards a meeting at the Ministry of Defense, was walking down the corridor leading to the ministerial offices flanked by the pictures of his predecessors since the founding of the state. Seemingly by happenstance, he ran into Barry, CEO of IAI, who was also headed there for a meeting. Barry had just left another of Ismail's nuclear fusion lesson at the Gilboa headquarters in Herzliya.

"Say, are you aware of the interest the United States is directing at your installation in Lod?" the deputy director asked Barry, seemingly casually.

Barry assumed that the deputy director was aware of Rakefet, and so answered, just as casually, while he walked: "Yes, they must be interested in Rakefet."

"Rakefet? What is Rakefet?" the blindsided deputy director asked.

Barry did not know quite what to answer to the spy chief. He paused for a moment, before finally saying: "It's a top-secret project we are collaborating on."

As far as the deputy director was concerned, this was apparently a sufficient answer and took a mental note to look into the project in the future.

Shortly before that conversation took place, both American and Chinese satellites picked up an electromagnetic pulse being emitted from the Mitzpe Ramon area. It was one of the rocket engines tests. They decided to refocus their attention on the area. While the Russians lacked the instrumentation to identify the electromagnetic burst, their surveillance of the Americans clued them onto the fact that something was going on in the Israeli desert, somewhere on the lonely farm next between the Israeli Air Force and Central Training Compound fire zones. The next day they saw Ismail's uncle's tractor towing a crushed container on the site grounds. They focused their lens onto the tractor, identifying the yellow license plate and cross referencing it with their database. Based on the motions of the driver, they decided he was too young to be Ismail's uncle, and after a few more eliminations, zeroed in on Ismail.

The Americans and the Chinese, who were also of course tracking the Russians, soon became aware that the driver of the tractor was a Bedouin from the Mitzpe Ramon area.

The Americans, well aware of Israeli politics and society, lost interest as soon as they realized a Bedouin was involved in whatever was going on in the site. The Israelis, they well knew, would not rely on Arab-Muslim workers on anything involving the development of cutting-edge technology, certainly not systems with military applications.

The Chinese, however, who were not familiar with local politics to such an extent, continued to follow Ismail. They identified Ismail as a student at the Racah Institute in the Hebrew University, and then discovered Ismail frequently visited the Gilboa Venture Capital Fund as well as IAI. Once the Americans realized the Chinese were still following Ismail, they too resumed monitoring him. Soon, the intelligence agencies of all three zeroed in on Rakefet and began monitoring everyone involved with it, from Rotem and Noa to Shlomo, just as Shlomo predicted they would.

In addition, the NSA decided to ask the CIA to take over the operation of one of their agents, sharing any information she collected. The agent had already retired from the CIA after 20 years of service. After retiring, she made many changes in her life, including getting a divorce, changing her name from Danielle to Daniela and moving to Israel, securing a teaching position at the Hebrew University of Jerusalem as a lecturer in Geology. The CIA agreed to loan out their ex-agent and convinced Daniella to return to service, while the NSA used their influence network to bring Daniela in as a guest lecturer for atmospheric layers into IAI.

They also followed the electromagnetic pulses in the experimental engine in Mitzpe Ramon generated during the ten-second engine ignition trials. The Israeli 8200 Unit, which was tracking the activities of the satellites of the three superpowers in its own backyard, passed on the information to the Mossad — where a report was duly filed for review in the next quarterly meeting. Unfortunately, the deputy chief, who had already looked into the matter with IAI, could not attend due to his daughter's wedding, and so the dots were never connected.

5.

Six months passed, and April arrived, but the two IAI 767 planes were still grounded in the hanger. Several critical components for their conversion to space planes were still missing. The most problematic component, in terms of time needed to develop it, was the hydraulic system necessary to change the direction in which the helium jet was emitted by shifting the angle of rocket engine relative to the wing. The precision required was 0.065 degrees, which meant that all of the bearings had to be highly precise, with very little degree of freedom, and the control of the hydraulic system had to be tight. This precision was necessary as the two nuclear fusion engines fixed in the wings were far more powerful than the regular, hydrogen-oxygen combustion engine installed just behind the plane's front wheel. That engine's role was merely to fine tune flight direction in space — most of the balancing would have to be performed via the hydraulic system of the nuclear fusion engines in the wings. The front engine could only generate a thrust of one hundred and fifty kilos and could not be active for long without burning up all of the oxygen and hydrogen generated from the water, leaving no hydrogen for the nuclear fusion engines, or oxygen for the crew to breathe — which would be a shame.

In other words, they needed less than twenty kilos of thrust, on average, from the front of the plane. This almost negligible force needed to balance two engines whose minimal thrust was 8 tons, and which usually operated at around 30 tons thrust. Hence the two main helium rocket engines had to be almost completely balanced by the hydraulic system for the front engine to be able to finetune the system into perfect balance.

In order to achieve this precision, the bearings were custom ordered from SKF, an American bearings manufacturer specializing in the design of super precise bearings. The order arrived at a factory in Johnson, Tennessee. But mistakes were made in the translation of the metric system used in Israel to American inches. Thus, the entire order had to be repeated, resulting in a massive delay.

The hydraulic system itself was ordered in Israel, but any connection between the guarantee of the manufacturer who won the tender to complete supply within two months and the actual supply time was quite coincidental. Since the order and the tender specifically warned that failure to meet the delivery date would result in substantial fines, IAI informed the manufacturer that these fines would be implemented. In retaliation, the manufacturer halted work on the project and informed IAI he was taking them to court.

The courtroom in Tel Aviv was a rather dim room, with metal legged wooden benches and a raised platform for the judge, which did rather a bad job of concealing the wretchedness of the chair and computer cables under the desk of the court typist. It was clearly an Israeli rather than an American court, and as such, the judge seemed to think he was getting paid to mediate a settlement rather than make a definitive ruling. And indeed, the court offered a settlement, as is the wont of Israeli courts, according to which IAI would not activate fines against the manufacturer in return for the manufacturer delivering the systems around two months following the date to which he had committed — for a total of twice the original delivery time. To the surprise of all present, the manufacturer refused the settlement, claiming he needed at least four more months.

"So why did you commit to two months, if you knew you could not meet the delivery date required by the tender?" the judge asked the manufacturer's lawyer.

"If we had not committed to two months, we would have lost the tender. No one actually meets these deadlines, and no reasonable person expects manufacturers to meet them," the manufacturer's lawyer exclaimed.

The judge found this argument both logical and persuasive, but before he ruled in favor of the manufacturer, Yossi Turgeman, Director of the Flight Division, who was seated in the audience, burst out: "This delay will result in IAI losing a project worth hundreds of millions of dollars. The project will be relocated to the United States and hundreds of Israeli workers will lose their jobs."

"That is an internal matter of IAI, not my client's business, or the matter under deliberation in this court," the manufacturer's lawyer responded.

The judge mulled doing the unthinkable and actually requiring the manufacturer to pony up and pay the fines he had agreed to in the contract he signed with IAI should he fail to meet his obligations, but then Yossi offered his own compromise — the manufacturer would undertake to provide a hydraulic system for one plane in another two months, and for the other plane in four months. This was agreeable to the manufacturer, and hence to the judge as well, who was well pleased with concluding yet another trial successfully. The judge did not, of course, see himself as contributing to the inability of Israeli industry to meet mutually agreed timetables.

By April, the six helium rocket engines were ready. All of the engines were tested and calibrated in Mitzpe Ramon. However, the planes lacked the support systems necessary for the engine installation. Nonetheless, the four engines slated for the two yet unready planes were duly transferred to IAI. The inventory keeper who received the engines did not understand why four iron rings arrived with such heavy security, and why the division director ordered 24/7 security to be placed on the warehouse where these rings were stored.

In the meantime, Joel, Adam and Nadav tried to figure out how to open the engine after its initial activation and the welding of the engine lid to the chassis by the massive magnetic forces it generated. Drilling the six-centimeter-thick steel turned out to be impossible, for these massive magnetic forces not only welded the lid and the chassis into a single iron lump, but it also transformed the lump into a super-powerful magnet. Any attempt to drill was stymied by this magnetism, which captured the drill as soon as it penetrated the steel, preventing it from rotating. Laser cutting also failed, since as soon as the beam penetrated past a certain threshold, the magnetism would cause the hole to collapse upon itself, effectively re-welding the material together. All of their attempts to overcome this seemingly trivial problem came to nothing.

Nadav offered a new, surprising approach.

"Since we have been stymied by this problem for months," Nadav suggested, "let us leverage the problem into a solution. Since the only way to open up the ring is by subjecting the steel to 1200 degrees Celsius, clearly all of the substrates and intersections of the superconductors would be destroyed by such attempts throughout the entire ring — not merely at the welding point. That means our secrets are safe. We can give the ring to whomever we want without needing to worry they might steal our technology and produce an engine on their own. No one else will ever be able to peek under the hood of our engine and understand its internal structure. Do you get it? We knew we would eventually have to share these engines with the United States, China and the other great powers. But now we can do so without worrying about losing control of the use of our technology."

"Yes, but they will still be able to use the engines we provide them in whatever way they see fit," Adam said.

Joel stood up and thought this over.

"Well... yes and no" he said thoughtfully. "We could implant an electronic fail-safe within the ring. A component capable of deactivating the engine, which would have to receive a unique, predetermined, weekly code from us to avoid doing so. That way they could only use the engine for a week until we transferred them next week's code. This would let us keep control of the engines that way, even when we do not physically hold them — and nothing in the world could change that."

Nadav and Adam loved the idea.

Now, however, a new problem emerged. They had initially thought they could conceal their project from the political echelon for a year or so. Only at that point, after they were spaceborne, did they intend to involve the American NASA, and the Chinese CNSA. But, by April, it turned out that their plans were incompatible with reality.

One of the ten engineers they had briefed on the technology had blabbed to his mother, in complete confidentiality of course, the fact that they were building a space shuttle for IAI. She talked with the Minister of Defense's office manager, a childhood friend. Her friend had always insinuated that she was exposed to incredible secrets in her position. To even the score, the engineer's mother casually mentioned IAI's space shuttle program in one of their conversations, just to show that she was also in the know. The mother assumed that her friend already knew, but the surprised friend decided to raise the matter with Barry. Barry, who assumed she was querying him on behalf of the defense minister, was forced to admit that they were working as a subcontractor for the Rakefet Company, who were constructing a space shuttle. Barry immediately notified Shlomo that the defense minister now knew, giving him the opportunity to report to the Defense Minister himself and try to heed off the political shitstorm which was sure to come. The defense minister was sure to assume that the prime minister was aware of the project and had cut him, the minister responsible for such matters, out of the loop. Barry, of course, assumed the same thing, as Shlomo had insinuated as much, and it was unthinkable that the prime minister should not be aware of Rakefet's activities. Shlomo, accordingly, rushed to schedule a meeting with both the prime and the defense ministers, assuming this would buy him a few more months until their schedules synchronized. Much to his surprise, he was summoned for a meeting within two weeks, as the 'Israeli Space Shuttle' issue began to bounce between the Prime Minister's Office and the Defense Minister's Office like a hot potato.

Rakefet's founders, left with only two weeks to prepare, scrambled to line up their ducks. Their greatest fear was that so long as the technology remained confined to Israel, the defense minister could pass an ordinance forbidding its removal from the country. The temptation for the Israeli government to weaponize the technology on the one hand, and to leverage it to improve Israel's relative economic position on the other, while sidelining the goal of saving humanity from the unfolding environmental catastrophe, would be overwhelming once they assumed control of the technology. Indeed, removal of technology from the country was generally forbidden whenever a startup company received funding from Israel's Chief Scientist Office.[16] That was why Shlomo had veered away from any national science-supporting funding opportunity.

In this case, Rakefet did not truly want, at this stage, to take the technology overseas. But it did want to create the impression that the technology had already spread to the various great powers, so that no single state could seek to exploit the technology for narrow national interests, rather than the general interests of mankind.

Given the impenetrable nature of the post-activation engine, the solution they settled on was to transfer the welded engine to another country. This would generate the impression that the

16. The Israel Chief Scientist is an institution providing government support to startup companies.

chickens were out of the coop, without actually giving another country a chance to replicate the technology.

"I think we should transfer the technology, that is, the engine, to China rather than the United States," said Adam at a meeting with the board of directors, "if we transfer the engine to the United States we will have accomplished nothing — Israel is in any event a 'wholly owned subsidiary' of the United States, so whether the engine stays here, or is moved to America, U.S. pressure on Israeli decision makers will ensure they have control... and you can be sure this will include defense ministry ordinances against technology transfer to any country but the United States. But, if the Americans know the engine is already in China, they will have to play ball."

"I'm not sure about this," said Shlomo, who had already heard all this from Nadav and Adam in their initial presentation. "I know the Americans and know how to work with them. I don't know the Chinese, and there is no predicting in what way Chinese interests will align."

"Philosophically speaking," Galit intervened, "we decided from the outset that we are rejecting Athenian democracy and open debate and were putting ourselves in the position of Plato's benevolent philosopher kings. That is exactly the operational principle of the Chinese Communist Party ever since they ditched doctrine Marxism a generation ago. Say what you may about their system — it delivers results, and you can't argue with success."

Galit's arguments turned Shlomo around eventually, and the next day she boarded a plane to Beijing, which just happened to be hosting a conference on the philosophy of ethics that week. A surprising number of intelligence service retirees from around the world, be it the Israel's Mossad and General Intelligence Service (GIS), the American CIA and NSA, or the Chinese MSS., had chosen to take up academic studies dealing with the philosophy of ethics and were attending the conference. Actually, Galit mulled, perhaps this was not so surprising.

Galit set up a meeting with Professor Chou Wang, one of the conference organizers. Professor Wang was a former senior MSS operative. They both knew each other by name, face and reputation, though they had never met or communicated.

6.

When Galit landed in China, a car was waiting to take her directly to a meeting with the professor. Wang was the name of an old Chinese scholar-gentry clan. During China's Cultural Revolution, the Red Guards had murdered Chou's parents, who were also in academia,[17] and Chou was subjected to what they termed as 'reeducation.' However, following the death of Mao, the Chinese Communist leader, persecution of 'class enemy' families such as Chou's, ended.

Three people were seated in the small, functional meeting room that Galit entered. The conference room was in an office building, and not a particularly opulent one, but certainly modern, orderly, and very clean. Professor Chou was a short, rotund and jovial man, nothing like what his profile picture suggested. Chou began with introductory pleasantries, in English of course, and offered tea. Only after Galit sipped from the teacup did Chou get down to business.

"Galit and I have known each other for years, back from when I was responsible for the Middle East Desk at the MSS, and Galit was responsible for North America Desk in the Mossad," Chou explained to the three others in the room. "It has been years since Galit left the Mossad and joined the academia," he went on to explain. "Today, Galit comes here as the Chair of the Board of Directors of the Rakefet Company, which is of great interest of our comrades[18] in China."

This introduction somewhat surprised Galit. First, her intelligence role had never been presented to any forum outside the Mossad. Second, this confirmed that the MSS were tracking Rakefet, as she and Shlomo had suspected. Finally, this made clear to her that this conversation would be very purposeful,

17. Many people belonging to the Chinese intelligentsia were murdered by Mao's Red Guards during the Cultural Revolution.

18. The term comrade refers to the governing institutions in Communist China.

with no beating around the bush. This was precisely what Chou had intended. Chou went on to introduce the other three people in the room: two engineers and an operations manager[19] at the MSS Technological Division.

"Well, since you came to us — the stage is yours," Chou said. In fact, Chou was 'playing ping pong' and he had just delivered her a fast, spinning serve meant to throw her off balance.

To strike the iron while hot, as well as a counterstroke to Chou's surprise, Galit hit back just as fiercely, delivering the ping-pong into Chou's court with four decisive sentences, each sufficient on its own.

"Rakefet is building a spacecraft powered by nuclear fusion engines, which generate thrust by propelling helium particles at near light speed. The immediate goal is to mine Lunar Helium 3 and bring it back to Earth. The first Helium 3 shipment is projected to arrive in a little under a year. The long-term goal is to solve humanity's energy problems and reduce the existential danger posed by global warming."

Galit's words left the operational manager unmoved, but she had succeeded in shocking the two engineers. She assumed, correctly, that the manager simply did not understand the significance of what she had said. Accordingly, she decided taking a restroom break would give the two technicians a chance to explain to the suit exactly what was at stake here, so she politely excused herself.

Upon returning, she concluded from the poleaxed expression of the operational manager that he was now up to speed as well.

"Rakefet has subsidiaries in Hong Kong," she picked up immediately, "New York, Brussels, Moscow, Tokyo and Delhi. Eventually, Rakefet will be run by a board of directors, whose operational aspects will be managed by eight members. One

---

19. Operational Manager is the equivalent of a Station Chief in the CIA.

from Israel, a representative of the founders, one from China, one from the United States, one from the European Union, one from Russia, one from Japan and one from India. The eighth member, and the chair of the board of directors, will be a representative of the global academia."

"At this initial stage, our board of directors is purely Israeli, and I am its chair, representing academia. Over the next two weeks, you and the Americans can select your own representative, and the others will soon follow."

"Our spaceship will take off from Earth from a standard airstrip, just like a run-of-the-mill commercial jet. Right now, that is set to be Ben Gurion Airport, Tel Aviv. The spaceplane will also land back in the airport, like a regular commercial jet.

"To enable the CNSA to examine our claims we will provide both training on the engine, and about the engine itself, to our subsidiary in Hong Kong, which will provide the engine and the instructor for CNSA inspection in Beijing. There is a container ship by the name of Red Waves of the Chinese Merchant Fleet in Athens right now, which is supposed to set off tomorrow for Haifa and will arrive in Alexandria over the weekend. We are interested in loading a container with one engine to this ship, for shipping to Hong Kong. The problem is that this is an extremely sensitive shipment, and it must not fall into the hands of any other party, particularly pirates or terrorists of any sort. We want China to undertake responsibility for securing the cargo; that means, I expect armed MSS personnel onboard. Moreover, should China want to expedite things by flying the engine to Beijing, we are certainly in favor. However, you would have to arrange a flight from Cairo, for the engine weighs over 11 tons, and there is no available cargo space in planes leaving Israel for China this week. I leave the matter at your discretion."

Galit sipped from her tea as her audience took in the information, and then continued in an even tone, "As you no doubt understand, Shlomo the CEO of Rakefet LTD is in Washington right now, holding the same conversation with the Americans." The operations manager nodded to Chou in confirmation, confirming to Galit that the Chinese were indeed following Rakefet's personnel.

"There are two differences, right now, between you and the Americans as far as Rakefet is concerned," Galit added. "The first is that frankly, we need the Americans more at the moment, because they have specific technology that we require. NASA has developed a form of concrete, or more accurately epoxy glue, which can be sprayed over a radius of two hundred meters to enable our rocket to land on the moon without our rocket engines raising dust clouds which will interfere with the landing. Although dust will rapidly fall back down without an atmosphere, such a heavy plane will constantly generate dust particles — enough to get in our way. "However," she emphasized, "the Americans will not be receiving, at this stage, an engine for inspection."

"We expect that the transfer of the engine for inspection will allay any concerns you may have about being excluded. And now, until the flight tomorrow to Tel Aviv, beyond the time dedicated to your questions, I also want to provide you with a short presentation which will explain why we are in such a rush with implementing this new technology in space — or more accurately, why all of mankind needs us to hurry up as much as humanly possible. I have prepared a presentation that outlines the milestones required to establish regular Helium 3 supply lines, which presents precisely where we are right now. I can also provide general explanations about the engine and how it is incorporated in the Boeing 767 turned spaceship. But more in-depth technical explanations will have to wait for the instructor, who will fly here as soon as the engine reaches Beijing."

When Shlomo returned from Washington, he immediately headed out to meet the prime minister. Shlomo asked and received authorization to bring the chief scientist from the ministry of economy and industry with him. Joel had met with the chief scientist the previous day and updated him on Rakefet's plans, up to the importation of Helium 3 from the Moon, so that senior officialdom and the decision makers in Israel, the United States and China were all in the loop. In all three countries, Rakefet implored the officials and decision makers to maintain secrecy until the moon mission was complete — a milestone which was to be met by September.

Maintaining secrecy for three months was trivial for the Chinese government, not too complicated in the United States, but almost impossible in Israel. The only thing which prevented Israeli politicians from running to the media was the explicit threat by Rakefet Ltd. to transfer their base of operations from Israel to the United States, and openly blame the blabbing politician for this. Since Rakefet Ltd. was a private company, it was certainly entitled to do so, and the politician lacked any leverage against it at this point. This did not prevent both the defense and prime minister from carrying out a thorough investigation on Rakefet. Israel's GIS, like the American NSA and the Chinese MSS, swiftly identified Hadas, Adam's wife, as the weakest link in Rakefet. The phone conversations between Adam and Hadas made clear that she knew who the secret holders were in the company, and perhaps other things as well. Moreover, character profiles prepared by these agencies also indicated that Hadas had a major gratification deferral problem, and that she would be susceptible to outside pressure. Nonetheless, the prime minister did not authorize such pressure for now, as he did not want to irritate Rakefet's founders before the constraints of this situation became clear.

The defense minister, for his part, was incensed with the fact that Ismail, an Arab with absolutely no security clearance, was in the thick of things.

"Yes, I opposed this as well," Shlomo said, "but it was Galit's decision."

"Who is Galit?" the defense minister demanded.

"The board of directors chair," Shlomo replied. "Galit is the ultimate authority in Rakefet, and I defer to her, certainly in matters of ethics. She is a Professor for the Philosophy of Ethics. She is in Delhi at the moment, trying to get the Indians onboard with the program," Shlomo added. "The more you delve into our project, the more you will understand why ethical questions are a central issue in it. So, before you make demands of Galit, you had best arm yourself with coherent ethical arguments or you will not make much headway."

As soon as Shlomo left, the defense minister began fuming, but the prime minister shook his head ruefully. "Let it go, Saul," he said. "They have us by the short hairs. All we can do is try to leverage Rakefet's position in Israel to best benefit the country — and to us."

The defense minister, though still incensed at the thought of explaining himself to a civilian who was not a top-level government decision maker, decided, as most politicians would, not to pick a fight he could not win.

A month after the meeting with the prime minister, many journalists knew, or at least thought they knew, large parts of Rakefet's plans. The only thing that prevented them from reporting what they knew was a gag order. In Israel, the courts still habitually cooperated with almost any request by the Ministry of Defense to issue such orders — just as Israeli reporters habitually evaded such orders by informing overseas colleagues about the censored material, and then reporting on "overseas coverage" of the matter, seconds after the overseas publication.

7.

In June, the first flight was undertaken. All the critical parts were in place: the two rocket engines in the wings, connected via the requisite hydraulics, the small engine in the lower front portion of the plane, and ten tons of the new engine ignition batteries. The hydraulic system for the second plane was still not expected to arrive for two more months — assuming no additional delays by the suppliers. Other than the installation of the batteries, the systems were as yet unconnected. The batteries electric connections were incomplete, as was the linkage of the computers and control systems to the rocket engines. Structurally, however, all was in place, and so it was decided to take the plane out for a spin.

The plane was painted in a golden color in order to reflect the radiation of the sun, preventing heating of the plane, which would not be shielded by the atmosphere once it passed the Kármán Line. Hence, any regular paint, which would absorb solar radiation rather than reflecting it, would reach melting temperature and cause the plane to melt like a piece of chocolate exposed to an open flame.

There were several reasons NASA used a real gold coating. First — gold does not rust. Even aluminum foil rusts, albeit slowly, resulting in reduced radiation reflection. The second reason was the high malleability of gold, and in particular the ability to flatten it to a greatly reduced thickness than that of aluminum or silver, thus reducing the excess weight on the plane.

A gold-colored airplane would be certain to attract the eyes of the curious. Hence, the plane was removed from its hanger at 1:00 am in the morning, and all the lights at Ben Gurion Airport were turned off for the takeoff to be performed without any lights on the runway.

Rotem piloted the craft during takeoff, with Noa as her copilot. There were also three engineers, whose role was limited to inspecting the usual system performance of the 767, for the new, special systems were not yet operational. Noa and Rotem wore night vision equipment during both takeoff and landing. They had often practiced such a take-off in the Air Force. In fact, the take-off was more convenient than their military training, for they were permitted to turn on the plan front lights, which did not illuminate the golden exterior of the plane. The flight plan was to head off towards the Mediterranean, rise up to a cruising height of 13 kilometers, and then return. The flight was completely unremarkable. The engineers who examined the plane systems remarked that, for such an old plane, it functioned quite reasonably, with no deviations from accepted parameters.

Over the following week, a large crew worked to connect the batteries to the electric systems, and the computer systems to the rocket engines. After a general inspection, the plane left for another round, this time, in order to test the ignition of the rocket engine.

Rotem and Noa switched positions on this flight. In addition to the three engineers, Nadav and Adam also boarded the flight this time. They wanted to inspect the rocket engine systems firsthand during and after the ignition. Unlike Noa, who had run into Nadav twice on her way to the restroom, Rotem had never met either Nadav or Noam.

"Who are you?" Rotem asked.

"I am Nadav, this is Adam. We work at Rakefet," Nadav responded underwhelmingly.

"Noa and Rotem," Rotem introduced, adding, somewhat defiantly, "and we work at Rakefet as well."

Nadav noticed the tone and smiled. He did not know whether Rotem thought she was senior to them at Rakefet and hence took a superior tone, or whether she knew he and Adam were senior executives and was expressing her criticism at them not being introduced to the other Rakefet employees. In fact, Shlomo and Ismail were the only Rakefet representatives they had encountered. All the other employees they met were IAI Flight Division Workers.

When they reached a cruising height of 13 kilometers, Rotem made sure with the TLV flight control tower that there were no planes in the air space between them and TLV. Noa double checked the Radar to ensure there were no nearby planes as well. And then, with great excitement, they went through the initiation sequence to ignite the rocket engines.

But nothing happened.

"I must have done something wrong," Noa said.

But Adam checked and saw that a current was sent from the batteries to ignition for under a millisecond rather than the necessary ten seconds. Immediately after that short current, all the batteries died.

"No point in continuing," Adam told Noa, "we have a technical malfunction. We need to return and land."

Rotem and Noa felt great disappointment. As they had learned, they expected the ignition to push the plane forward and that the sensation would be like take-off in terms of the forces acting on the body, just at a height of 13 kilometers, rather than the runway. Something perhaps similar to the feeling of G forces in a fighter jet. Deflated, they plotted a course back to the airport and proceeded to carry out a smooth landing.

When the plane entered the Hanger, Nadav and Adam opened up the batteries and began inspecting them. The hanger opening was veiled by a massive curtain which was meant to prevent curious passersby from examining the plane. The curtain alone weighted over a ton and could only be opened and closed with special engines. Only after the curtain dropped behind the plane did the hanger lights switch on.

"Can we stay here and watch or help?" Noa asked. Adam thought it was inappropriate and began to say as much, but

Nadav surprised him with an indifferent "why not." A few minutes later Joel joined their debugging brainstorming session.

After half an hour, Adam released a guffaw.

"The batteries' fuses are all burnt out," he said.

"A standard battery is designed to release a 100-ampere current, 300 under extreme conditions. That is why they are installed with standard fuses, capable of channeling up to 500 amperes. Our system required each battery to provide a 10,000-ampere current. We tested them and found them capable of withstanding 13,000 ampere for a ten-second period without being damaged. But it seems one of the Flight Division engineers, who was not familiar with our calculations and special requirements, exercised initiative and added standard protection to the batteries with 500 ampere fuses. Obviously, they all burnt out."

"Adding some protection to the batteries may not be a bad idea," noted Joel.

"Maybe we really should add the appropriate 13,000 ampere fuses." This time Nadav was the one who laughed.

"A 13,000-ampere fuse is not a small device. Maybe we can ask NASA to later design such a particularly tiny fuse for us — but this is not something we can add to the design at this point. We simply need to remove the fuses. Nadav left to call the technicians to start the work.

"Batteries without fuses is hardly safe," Rotem half asked, half noted.

"We aren't here for the safety," Adam answered brusquely. He was exhausted and frustrated. Rotem and Noa exchanged glances. They did not like his response.

"I am not here to commit aerial suicide," Rotem said.

"You are right," Adam, who was truly sorry for his words, even before he had finished saying them. "That was stupid of me to say. We performed all the necessary calculations, and the batteries are just fine as they are. Adding a fuse to them was a foolish and incorrect move. We paid almost $100,000 more for these specific batteries, because they are safer and do not burn out, even under extreme conditions." Rotem did not find this answer at all acceptable, but there was no point in continuing the argument after Adam apologized.

"I think we had better stick close to Adam and Nadav, because they seem to be the people who mess around with the decisions which determine whether or not we live till middle age," Rotem later told Noa. "And, in general, I think we should be more aware of the dangers at this project."

"All right," Noa said, "I will take Nadav, and you will stick to Adam." She deliberately chose Nadav. He seemed to her shy and introverted, her exact opposite, and this intrigued her.

By morning, the batteries were connected in accordance with the original specifications and the plane was ready for another rocket engine ignition test.

8.

They left on another test flight the following night. They were all more worried and irritated this time around. Once again it was Noa's turn to be captain and Rotem's turn to be co-pilot. Once again, they reached their 13-kilometer ceiling and thoroughly checked there were no planes behind them.

"Can I perform the ignition sequence?" Noa asked Nadav.

"Remember what we learned," he said, "you need to close the throttle of the regular engine down to minimum, let the plane glide, and remember that, following ignition, in addition to accelerating as if it were taking off, the plane will likely begin veering sideways, and probably turn over as well, because the engine's will not yet be balanced. You need to stabilize the plane with the wings and the other aerodynamic systems until the engines are balanced," Nadav turned to Rotem. "If you feel you are not managing to do this, you must immediately turn off the rocket engines. But if you can maintain a more or less straight line, Adam and I will try to balance the engines. If we succeed — then we can call it a day for this mission. The next time we fly, all the engine balancing parameters will be embedded in the engine systems, and much less, if any, finetuning will be required."

Noa initiated the ignition sequence.

Ten seconds after ignition, they could definitely feel the engines working — unlike during the previous takeoff. The acceleration forward pinned them to their chairs. Rotem and Noa went into action, Rotem trying to prevent the plane from spinning, maintaining a straight course forward, and Noa trying to stop the huge aircraft from rolling over like a fighter jet.

Rotem more or less managed to keep flying in a straight line, but Noa, who seemed at first to be able to keep the plane balanced, lost control after about five seconds, and the plane began rolling. Only after it had rolled over 180 degrees was Noa able to stabilize it. Adam and the three engineers threw their dinner up all over themselves; only Nadav was able to keep the contents of his stomach inside.

Nadav, having balanced the horizontal thrust of the engines, and having eliminated the tailspin, turned to balance their vertical thrust as well, once he realized Adam was incapacitated. The more Nadav reduced the rolling generated by the lack of vertical sync between the engines, the more Noa was able to regain control of the plane. Eventually, she was able to return the plane to a more or less level flight.

Noa reminded herself she was not in a jet plane, and that, should the plane pass the speed of sound at a relatively low altitude — it would break apart. To slow down the plane, or at least reduce its acceleration, Noa reduced the thrust of the rocket engines to 16 tons, their absolute minimum, and aimed the plane to climb at the highest possible angle possible for a 767 in the atmosphere; 45 degrees. At 13 kilometers altitude, gravity was more than strong enough to counter the acceleration generated by this 'low' thrust. The plane stopped accelerating, and even began slowing down slightly. Three minutes passed, during which the plane to climb. When she had begun the climb, the plane was already at 0.8 Mach[20] and it was now near 2 Mach and still climbing. At regular cruising height, the plane would have begun breaking up the moment it had passed Mach 1. But at their current altitude, the air was so thin that passing the sound barrier generated no supersonic boom — indeed, they had barely noticed it.

"Why did you not turn off the engines?" Adam, who had regained consciousness, asked.

"We are not here for your convenience," Rotem answered sarcastically.

---

20. The speed of sound in 1 Earth atmosphere pressure.

"You are right, and I see Nadav has managed to balance the engines," Adam, who understood her reference, responded.

The minutes passed with the crew hardly noticing. Flying at over 2 Mach's at a 45-degree climb meant the plane, though no longer accelerating, was still climbing at over 300 meters every second, and was now 15 kilometers above its cruising altitude.

The plane was now 28 kilometers high, an altitude only space shuttles and spaceships were capable of. The air was already very thin, and the aerodynamic properties of the plane had changed. Stabilization at this altitude or higher was designed to be performed by changing the angles of the engines with the hydraulic system, but the activation of the hydraulic system was only planned for next week.

"You have to turn off the rocket engine, or we won't be able to return back to the surface," Nadav yelled at Noa and Rotem.

Rotem immediately switched off the engines, and only then turned to verify their altitude.

The plane now required quite complex flying skills. The thin air at this altitude could no longer suspend the plane, and it began to rapidly lose height. The regular jet engines were still operating and Noa pushed the throttle to maximum to give them more power. However, even on full throttle, the engine still had very little power, given the thin air. Accordingly, she once again pulled the nose of the plane upwards, assuming that, at such rapid, supersonic speed, the plane, even while losing altitude in thin air, would not stall.

Noa continued like this until the plane descended down to an altitude of twenty kilometers. At this height, the air was sufficiently dense enough to enable it to return to more or less regular behavior for a plane, and in a slow process of gliding, after about forty minutes, return to a cruising height of around 14 kilometers.

At this point, the plane popped up again on the radar screen of the flight monitors around the Mediterranean. Since the plane had already reached Italy's airspace, the Sicilian flight monitor contacted them. In heavily accented English, he demanded to know where the hell they had popped up on his radar from. Rotem explained that they had had a malfunction in their communications systems and radar signaler and told him they were heading back to Ben Gurion Airport to repair it.

When they arrived at Ben Gurion, the three engineers reported the roll, and the Chief Engineer of the Flight Division decided that, because such an elderly plane had undergone such an ordeal, it had to undergo a safety inspection — which would take an entire week. Rotem asked the Aerodynamics and Structural Engineer to also add a layer of composite layer below the wing, as in air force transport jets — which meant from the edge of one wing to the end of the other. This layering was standard for transport planes on the Israeli Air Force 767 planes.

"This is an addition of over three hundred kilos," the engineer said, "I need Adam's authorization for this." Adam, who had already gotten on Rotem's bad side once, immediately authorized her request.

When Shlomo returned from his meeting with the prime minister, he immediately convened all the secret holders in Rakefet and IAI.

"After the flight in which the rocket engines were operated," he stated, "the secrecy level of 'Little Oaks;' the plan to bring Helium 3 from the Moon to Earth, has been badly compromised. Hence, there is no longer a need to maintain absolute confidentiality regarding your activities. This means that each and every one of you, at your discretion, can share the plan with a single first degree relative; someone of their choosing who can keep this a secret."

Murmurs of excitement rose from the crowd and Shlomo continued.

"In addition, the plan is now to ascend to the Kármán Line a week from today as soon as the engines are activated and tested. During this flight, we intend to circumvent the earth three times. Should this flight go smoothly, then the very next day we will perform an identical flight with three additional flight crews, so that they will be able to see how things work firsthand, and then, gradually, will begin to practice on the second plane. One team will be composed of veteran IAI test pilots, a second will be American, and a third will be Chinese. One month later a Japanese, Russian, European and Indian flight crew will join us, and by that point, IAI personnel will take over the instruction from Rakefet."

Early in the morning, when Rotem returned home, after she showered and prepared herself an impromptu meal, she waited at the dining table for her husband, Nimrod, to wake up.

"I want to talk to you about a significant development at my job," she told him when he entered the kitchen.

"I need to head off to work," a bleary-eyed Nimrod answered, puzzled.

"Call in late today, and take an hour to hear me out," she asked, "this is important to me."

"I flew 28 kilometers high tonight," she started, "and it is only thanks to Noa's extraordinary flying skills that we were able to return to the surface."

Nimrod didn't get it.

"28 kilometers? No plane can fly that high. What were you flying? A spaceship?" he asked jokingly.

"Yes, that's exactly right," Rotem replied, staring him straight in the yes. Nimrod thought she was joking at first, but gradually realized she was dead serious. He paused, taking it in.

"So... you are an astronaut?" he asked after a moment.

"That's right," she answered evenly, still dead serious.

Their children began to stir, and they had to cut the conversation shot.

"I can't talk about this with the children around. Can we carry this on in the evening after we put them to bed?" Rotem asked.

Nimrod, however, could not stand the suspense.

"Hell no! This isn't 'one thousand and one nights.' Let's send them off to school and then you tell me the rest of it."

Usually, one of them would prepare the children for school and kindergarten. This morning, their children got some quality time with both parents.

"I don't think I will go to work today," Nimrod said after they got back from putting their children at school. "I want to understand what is going on here."

Rotem thought that was a good idea. She took their cellphones, turned them off, and secreted them in the bedroom. Then she returned to the living room, drew the curtains closed, and sat down with Nimrod, who asked no questions about her unusual precautions.

"So, it's like this," she began, "while my place of employment is IAI in Lod, I am actually drawing my salary from Rakefet Ltd. Rakefet is a top secret, multinational company, with offices in the United States, China, Europe and elsewhere. Its goal is to mine Helium 3 on the Moon and bring it down to Earth."

Nimrod stared at her skeptically. "All right... go on," he said, as evenly as he could.

"I won't get into all the physics right now, but with Helium 3 you can, in the greenest, cleanest possible way, relatively easily produce electricity — a lot of electricity. Enough to meet humanity's energy needs for the foreseeable future. Enough to reduce, even stop, global warming."

"Global warming is of less interest to me right now," Nimrod said. "How many astronauts do Rakefet currently employ?"

"At the moment just two — Noa and myself," Rotem responded. "Last night, which is early this morning, we performed our first flight over the regular cruising altitude of a regular 767 plane."

"The Americans and the Chinese are all counting on you and Noa?" Nimrod asked incredulously.

"That's right," she replied, "because at the moment they don't have any other choice. But there will be other flight crews later on. This week I won't have any more flights because the plane is undergoing a checkup, but if all goes well, I will have two flights next week. And on the second flight I will be breaching the Kármán Line."

"What's the Kármán Line?" asked Nimrod.

"The Kármán Line is another way of saying I will be a hundred kilometers from Earth. This is also the height considered by many people to be the end of Earth's atmosphere and the beginning of space. At this height, the air is so thin that it does not impact the plane, the plane's wings have no lift, and they do not influence the flight."

"But if you could barely return from a 28-kilometer altitude, how will you return from a 100-kilometer altitude?" Nimrod asked.

"We only reached 28 kilometers because of a juxtaposition of our error with an engineering error. We never should have reached that point. The hydraulic system balancing the engines had not yet been properly tested. This is the system which will enable us to steer the plane at such altitudes — and beyond."

"What do you mean 'beyond?' Isn't a hundred kilometers dangerous enough for you?"

"The next week we are planning to reach six hundred kilometers, the cruising altitude of space shuttles."

"So, at this altitude you will be floating inside your airplane the way astronauts do in the movies?" Nimrod asked.

"Yes, but that will happen at the Kármán Line, because our horizontal speed, which is the speed of the rotation of the plane around the planet, is so high, that a centrifugal force will be generated that will cancel out gravity, resulting in a floating effect."

"I don't get it," said Nimrod. "you sometimes talk about a plane, and sometimes refer to it as a spacecraft. Which is it?"

"The plane is the Boeing 767, which, as you know, I have been flying for years. But this plane has been upgraded with rocket engines, and all sorts of other effects, which enable it to function as a spaceship, much like a space shuttle, but far more sophisticated."

"Isn't re-entry back into atmosphere very dangerous? I still remember how Ilan Ramon died during re-entry," Nimrod asked, referring to Israel's first, and until now only, astronaut.

"In our case, re-entry is far less dangerous," Rotem soothed him. "Our plane has an effectively infinite energy supply. In contrast to a space shuttle, which expends almost all of its energy in order to leave Earth, we have plenty of energy to slow down our re-entry as well. When a regular space shuttle makes re-entry, it essentially absorbs all the kinetic energy it generated when leaving the surface. Without enough fuel to slow down, it essentially depends on friction with the atmosphere, which generates massive amounts of heat, to slow down its descent. We have sufficient energy to slow down before re-entry, down to the flight speed of a regular plane in atmosphere. Hence, there is no such heat during our re-entry. We will land just like any other plane does down on the runway."

"So, I go to sleep every night with an astronaut without having even known," Nimrod said with a slightly irritated smile.

"I was not an astronaut until this morning, and I told you as soon as it happened," Rotem said, without noticing his irritation.

"I drew the curtains closed and put away our cellphones, because we have to assume the Americans, like the Chinese, are listening in to everything I say," she added.

"The satellite can pick up anything we say in any room with an outward facing window and hence it is better not to speak there and, in any event, to draw the curtains."

"But didn't you just say they were partners?" Nimrod asked.

"Yes, but the partners also want to make sure they aren't being screwed."

"Well, now that I think about it," Nimrod noted in a deliberately casual tone, "it is much more intimate here, in the living room, than in the bedroom."

"True, I have had the same idea ever since I learned about the spy satellites," Rotem, who immediately understood where he was going, while glancing at the huge oak tree concealing the view from outside their living room window.

Since Nimrod was no longer going in to work, and because Rotem had the entire day off, they decided to celebrate her return to Earth in their living room. What Rotem did not know was that the American satellite could listen in even through the living room window curtains and oak tree beyond. True, they interfered somewhat with the quality of the surveillance, but the NSA operative listening on both on their conversation and subsequent celebration was easily able to fill in the blanks with a little imagination.

9.

Nadav attended a series of lectures on the Earth's atmosphere Daniela gave at the Hebrew University at IAI. By the second lecture, he began to think that the lecturer was quite attractive, despite her being a decade older than him. He was flattered by her attention, and Daniela herself was genuinely attracted to the brilliant, albeit awkward, inventor. She was also excited to play the Bond girl, something she had never done in all her years as a covert agent. It was not too long before they found themselves in bed together. Indeed, Nadav was suddenly the focus of more feminine attention than he had ever experienced.

As Noa and Rotem agreed, Noa stuck close to Nadav. At first, Nadav found this very odd. Noa followed him around like a puppy everywhere. Nadav was not aware of Noa's and Rotem's decision to stick close to him and Adam in order to better understand dangers they might be exposed to, and such blatant female interest was not something he was used to. Nadav was not particularly handsome or tall, and he had an odd-looking gait due to his childhood injuries. True, when he taught in college, there were some female students who sought to improve their grades by displaying interest in the awkward lecturer, but such efforts were transparent to him. But now he was being stalked by Noa, a mature, stunning head-turner, for no apparent reason. His social awkwardness led him at first to suspect that Noa was mocking him, in retaliation for how he embarrassed her on their first meeting. But he soon realized Noa was near impossible to unsettle or embarrass. When her behavior continued, he did not know what to think. This attention, and his newfound popularity with the fairer sex, was very strange to him.

"Why are you constantly next to me?" he finally asked her.

"I want to learn. Is it bothering you? She answered and giggled. The answer, and the question, surprised him.

"I am not bothered, I am flattered," he answered jokingly.

In fact, Noa was actually learning a great deal from being around Nadav. First of all, she realized he was really high-up in Rakefet's murky hierarchy. His exact position was never made explicit, but engineers kept on coming to him with questions, which he usually answered on the spot. When he did not have the answer, Nadav conferred with Adam or Joel and then responded. She therefore concluded that Joel, Adam and Nadav were the technical triumvirate leading Rakefet — and that Shlomo and Ismail were not a part of this group. Noa's conclusion was that the company had three managerial layers. Galit Cohen, who was a category unto her own, Shlomo and Ismail's layer, and then Joel, Adam and Nadav. Seemingly, Galit was at the apex of the pyramid and the chair of the board of directors; Shlomo was the CEO representing the middle, executive layer; and Nadav's layer was technical implementation at the bottom. But sometimes she got the impression that the 'worker' layer was the one calling the shots and that the others were only there to assist them.

Another thing which became clear to her was that Nadav was an extraordinarily shy fellow in a way she could not even begin to understand. At first, this really bothered her. In one case, when one engineer raised an issue with Nadav one-on-one, Nadav solved it on the spot and briefed the engineer on how to handle similar issues in the future. But when the same issue was raised in a different forum, where there were many people and the question was not directly addressed to Nadav, he remained mute. Noa could see Nadav wanted to answer the question, but the crowd seemed to throw him off balance. Noa assumed he would eventually get over it, but as time went by and they continued discussing the problem, she could see Nadav had lowered his eyes to the ground and seemed to be just waiting for an opportunity to leave the room. This really bothered and irritated her, although she didn't understand why.

"Nadav already solved this problem," Noa broke into the discussion and provided Nadav's answer.

This only embarrassed Nadav more, and he stormed out.

Noa went after him.

"Yes, I find it difficult to talk to a large audience, and you are only making things more difficult for me," he told her.

"You should not run away when things get tough," she told him.

"Perhaps, but you are not my mother," he barked at her.

"You are right," Noa grabbed his hand and said, "but when I see something I want, I do my best to get it, and never back down." Noa did not intend to sound like she was so blatantly hitting on him. But that is what burst out of her subconscious in the heat of the moment. Nadav certainly understood at that point that Noa was hitting on him. Her hand was still gripping his. Fortunately, or perhaps unfortunately, Adam passed by.

"Coming for lunch?" he asked. Somewhat surprised at how Noa was gripping Nadav, he added: "Why don't you join us? Rotem is coming as well." Rotem was sticking close to him, just as Noa was to Nadav, though with less considerably fission and awkwardness.

"We are coming," Noa told Adam, and added pointedly to Nadav, "See? I don't run away."

And so it happened that Nadav, the shy "nerd" who had never had any romantic relationships, found himself simultaneously developing a serious relationship with Noa while simultaneously maintaining a torrid affair with an older woman.

10.

Rotem piloted the first flight to the Kármán Line. Everything went smoothly. With the engines already calibrated, igniting the rocket engines at a cruising altitude of thirteen kilometers proved to be trivial. Stabilizing the plane via the hydraulic system modifying the engine angels was also easily accomplished, with the engine computer automatically identifying the required angle. Furthermore, the finetuning of the engine's balance was performed via the standard non-nuclear fusion front rocket. In fact, the primary job of the pilot was to input the desired angle towards Earth's horizon and the plane's course up into the heavens. As the plane ascended and the atmosphere thinned, the view of the sky from the cockpit turned black. This transition was something even experienced astronauts had never encountered, for the strain of launching up through the atmosphere at an acceleration of over 3 Gs naturally precluded any appreciation of the scenery.

The most significant complication during the flight occurred when the plane passed over the Pacific Ocean, and communications with the control tower in Lod became really bad. For around half an hour, it was almost impossible to understand each other.

The speed they reached was over 15,000 kilometers an hour, over five times the speed of sound. At such speeds, centrifugal forces roughly balance out gravity. They felt the 'floating' effect, but not perfectly, because the engines remained active throughout the flight, generating acceleration and hence a sensation of gravity.

In order to maintain the same altitude while orbiting Earth, it is generally necessary to turn off rocket engines, as this would result in constant increase in speed and, thereby, in altitude as well. However, in this case, the greatest danger was that they would not be able to re-ignite the engine once they turned it off. This could end up being a major problem. Although ten tons worth of batteries had been installed in the plane, they only had enough energy for two ignition attempts, three at the most. Failure to ignite meant the plane would remain in space as a satellite, without any ability to return to the surface. Friction with residual atmosphere would eventually lead the plane to lose altitude and plummet to the surface, but this would take years, and the passengers in the airplane would be long dead.

They therefore made the decision not to turn the engines off, instead choosing to turn the plane around every few minutes by reducing thrust from one engine. The plane would turn in the direction dictated by the thrust of the stronger engine until it faced backwards, at which point the engines would be rebalanced, generating "reverse acceleration" countering the planes existing momentum. The process would be repeated every 10 minutes, with the "strong" and "weak" engines alternating in every cycle to maintain an average speed and course deviation.

The average speed would be 5 Mach's, and the average altitude would be a bit over the Kármán Line. For the passengers, this was a less than pleasant experience, since although gravity for them was consistently to the rear of the plane, at every turn they were alternately pulled to either the left or the right, leaving some of them quite queasy.

This maneuver was, of course, only possible over the Kármán Line, where the atmosphere was negligible. Any plane attempting such a stunt in the atmosphere would break apart upon presenting its tail forward. This maneuver was nothing new — space shuttles had performed this maneuver even back in the 1980s in order to slow down. Where Rakefet was treading new ground was in their use of the maneuver to achieve near zero speed relative to the Earth, and by turning the helium rocket engines downwards at full blast — to nearly nullify the pull of gravity. In later flights, there would be stages in which they would have to turn off their engines in order to preserve their fuel, which was water, but by then there would be at least one plane which they would be able launch to help extract the other plane, should it fail to register.

At this speed, it took them around two hours and forty minutes to circumnavigate the planet, which they did twice. Together with the ascent and descent, total flight time was around six hours and twenty minutes. There were communication issues with the control tower when the plane was on the other side of the planet. To overcome them, they used Inmarsat satellite phones.

A week before the flight to the Kármán Line, after the engines were activated in Noa's plane, secrecy was taken down a notch. The Space Division of IAI was also brought into the picture. They were deeply offended. They, the profitable division, the "crown jewels" — they were compartmentalized out of the project? While the Flight Division, made up of graying engineers still pining for the Lavi Jet, were the ones who basked in the glory?!

Barry's explanations that this was not even his decision, but the "demand of Rakefet, who are calling the shots here," availed nothing. Still, it was clear to the Space division that the upgrade of the 767 was the Flight Division's business. The Space Division, however, eventually got over their grievances and allowed it; they had far better communication solutions, and that they could, within a month, guarantee clear broadband communications with planes positioned on the other side of the planet.

"Great," said Barry, "you have one week."

"What? Impossible. We need at least two weeks," they said.

"Tell me," Barry asked them, "are you planning to sleep during these two weeks? Are you planning to work Fridays and Saturdays? Because in the Flight Division, they have not slept in six months already, and some of them have forgotten that there is such a thing as a weekend."

"We will try to get it done in a week," they answered begrudgingly.

They did not meet their objective in a week. But by the following flight, the one carrying the additional Israeli, Chinese and American flight crews, at least they had communications backup from the Space Division.

The new Israeli flight crew, made up of two highly experienced test pilots, had already undergone a week of instruction by Ismail. The Chinese team had landed the previous day, and the American team landed at dawn.

The two Chinese pilots belonged to the Technological Division of the MSS, the Chinese intelligence agency, rather than to the CNSA, the space agency. This made no difference to anyone because they were experienced 767 pilots and very nice people. The American team were NASA personnel. They were more standoffish and, given the American law forbidding entry of Chinese citizens to NASA facilities, were far more suspicious and ill at ease.

The intelligence agencies were engaged in a fierce rivalry to secure Rakefet's technology. When America dropped a bomb on Hiroshima in 1945, it took the Soviet Union four years, utilizing spies and sympathizers within the American research community, to replicate the apocalyptic weapon. In the 2020's, however, one did not need human spies and sympathizers to steal technology, and surveillance technology was sufficiently advanced that maintaining technological secrets for even four years would be nothing short of a miracle.

Nonetheless, Rakefet's security measures were sufficient to stymie American technological intelligence gathering for now. Hence the hopes pinned on Daniela by her operators. It soon became clear, however, that Nadav's tendency to keep silent, especially regarding anything to do with Rakefet, even in bed, was an unbreachable barrier. Hence, Daniela's operators redirected her efforts to another target, one closer to home and thought to be even more vulnerable to the attentions of an attractive woman — Joel.

"Our main advantage is that the number of people who know the secret is very small," Shlomo said. In fact, even Galit thought that it was Shlomo and Joel who were the secret holders, and that each knew the entirety of the secret. Only the four founders: Shlomo, Joel, Adam and Nadav knew that Adam and Nadav were the secret holders, and that even they only held half the secret each. "In the Manhattan Project," Shlomo continued, "thousands of people were involved. So maybe we have more time than I thought before the beans get spilled. If we can keep the technology secret and preserve a competitive advantage for only five to ten years, then we might just be able to convert the world to green energy."

Galit's idea was to induce shock in the foreign flight crews by immediately boarding them on the plane for the test flight the very night of their arrival. The Chinese flight crew, which had arrived a day early, had a chance to meet with the Israeli test pilot crew and get a good night's sleep in the hotel before boarding the plane. The American team was chivvied directly to the plane, where all the flight crews assembled to hear Rotem and Ismail speak.

"Tonight, you are flying with me and Noa over the Kármán Line to perform two circumnavigations of the planet," Rotem began. "You have no doubt been appraised by your respective agencies that last night we performed such a flight with no issues, and we are hoping for a smooth and comfortable flight today as well. We are leaving at 10:30 pm and are planning to be back by 4:30 amam, local time. Your role on this flight is that of passengers and nothing else, so that you may get a chance to feel the plane. Later on, we will begin training. Fairly soon, I imagine within less than two weeks, you will be able to fly such a plane yourselves. The flights will for now depart from Ben Gurion Airport, so you had better prepare for a long stay in Israel."

The American and Chinese teams had planned on a six-month stay in Israel. But they had thought they would only get to fly towards the end of this stay. Taking off on the very night of their arrival excited them.

"This is Ismail," Rotem introduced him, "during the day he will provide you with a six-hour instruction. You will then have a long recess before the flight, and at 7:00 pm you will be collected from your hotel back to Ben Gurion Airport. At 9:30 pm you will board the plane and at 10:30 pm we will take off to the Kármán Line and perform two circumnavigations of the planet."

The foreign crews were then given the presentation outlining the state of global warming and the reason for the tight schedules and were quite surprised. Up to this point, the material provided to them by Rakefet's instructors in China and the United States was purely technical: the operation of the helium rocket engine, the associated physics matters and the aeronautical issues specific to the 767 that fulfilled the functions of both a space shuttle and a spaceship. But up to this point, they had never been told why everything was being rushed in a manner so uncharacteristic of the usual mode of operations of both NASA and CNSA. At the end of the lectures, they returned to the hotel and each flight crew called up their respective agencies and reported excitedly that they were embarking on a flight that very night.

For Rotem and Noa the flight had already become almost routine, but it was a unique experience for the new crews. The cockpit of the upgraded plane was no longer cramped, since its rear bulkhead was removed and replaced with a sort of curtain that blocked noise and light from the passenger compartment. This curtain was located towards the rear of the plane, and so there was plenty of space. The passenger compartment had also undergone renovation, with the packed rows of seats replaced with about twenty couches which could be unfolded into beds. This design was intended to give pilots and passengers alike a comfortably flight to the moon, a flight which would take over fifteen hours — twenty-four hours if one included reaching Earth's orbit and the Lunar circumnavigation.

The curtain separating the cockpit and the passenger compartment was open on this flight, to enable flight crews sitting in the first row behind the cockpit to observe Rotem and Noa's actions. Nadav was seated next to Noa, running several more tests on the Helium Rocket Engines, as was an IAI Flight Division engineer who was performing checkup on the front steerage rocket engine.

The crews seated in the back could see all the activity in the cockpit as if they were watching a play at the theater. Most of the conversation in the cockpit took place in English, for the benefit of the foreign crews. The spectators, beyond the pedagogic advantages of observing the pilots, also enjoyed watching the dynamics between the people in the cockpit. One of the things they particularly enjoyed watching was the great interest Nadav and Noa showed in each other. Indeed, it seemed they were more interested in each other than the flight.

After breaching the Kármán Line, one of the engineers pointed out to Rotem — in Hebrew — that she had forgotten to open the valve which channeled the oxygen discharged from the rocket engines, into the crew's oxygen tanks.

"You're right, I did forget," she admitted.

"You realize that on a longer flight we would eventually have begun experiencing an oxygen shortage and, in our befuddled state, we may not have realized that the valve was closed. We could have all ended up dead, with salvation within grasp," he chided her.

160

Mark, the junior American pilot, was a Jewish American. He knew enough Hebrew to grasp the gist of the conversation. Mark also had a good grasp at just how amateurish and perfunctory Israelis could be. The realization that his life now depended on amateurish Levantine engineers troubled him.

When the plane landed, at 4:30 in the morning, the flight crews lined up on the stairs of the plane, without the engineers, for a photo. In accordance with the agreement between the United States, China and Israel, a statement to the press was released, accompanied by this photo. Since it was 9:30 pm in the United States when the plane landed, the White House speaker immediately released a statement following the publication of the image, followed by an immediate media blitz. In China, it was early afternoon, and the communist party also immediately released its own statement.

In Israel, however, it was 4:30 am and everyone was still sound asleep. Soon however, Israeli reporters in the United States began calling up their contacts in the Israeli government, demanding an official response to the news. Due to the gag order, reporters in Israel, who were well aware of the rumors surrounding Rakefet, could not respond. At 5:30 am, Israel's Haaretz newspaper submitted a motion to nullify the Defense Ministry's gag order. The defense minister's lawyer, sleepy and ill-informed, did not know what this was all about and asked for an hour to catch up. The judge told him he had ten minutes because the news had already been published all over the world. Since the lawyer was unable to get a hold of the defense minister during those ten minutes, the judge nullified the gag order. By 6:00 am, all the Israeli newscasts led with the Rakefet story, but their reports were confused, incoherent and partially false, far too based on the rumors which had accumulated around the company.

Part D: The second plane

1.

Mark, the junior pilot on the American team, spoke with Ismail and raised his concerns at the less than meticulous design and procedures that were revealed by the conversation he overheard between Rotem and the flight engineer.

Ismail listened patiently. When Mark finished venting, Ismail responded simply: "that is precisely why you, the Americans and the Chinese, are here."

"I don't see the connection," Mark said.

"Look, from my perspective, Israel is an immigrant state, much like the United States, but on steroids." Ismail explained. "My own ancestors immigrated from Arabia to what is now Israel during the great Islamic conquest of the Middle East, 1400 years ago, while the Crusaders migrated here 900 years ago. And some 150 years ago, European Jews began fleeing here from antisemitism in Europe. Seventy years ago, the Israeli government helped Middle Eastern Jews flee antisemitism in Muslim countries and arrive here. All in all, over 90 percent of Israel's Jewish population are immigrants or the descendants of immigrants."

"Sorry, I still don't see how this is relevant" Mark said impatiently.

"Religiously, about 80% of our population are Jews, and around 20% are Muslim," Ismail explained. "A small majority of the Jews are of Middle Eastern, primarily Arab, heritage, and fewer than half are of European heritage. This fusion of European and Middle Eastern cultures has made us Israelis good at thinking outside the box, skipping forward, improvising — but not so good at planning or the meticulous execution of plans. Our organizational culture is a fusion of the imaginative and visionary nature of Oriental culture, which tends to neglect the small details, with European, particularly Germanic culture and its meticulous nature which disdains human frailty and over-imagination. You are here to complete us and fill in our weak spots. That is what the all-human effort in this project is all about."

In fact, Nadav and Adam knew from the start that Israeli teams would not be able to plan, construct and fly such a complex system without critical, and even fatal, malfunctions. They were afraid that they would not meet their goal. Their solution was to manufacture two planes that could back each other up. The problem was that the second plane was not ready at the same time as the first plane, because of the delay in the supply of the second hydraulic system. The system was now finally due to arrive. Therefore, it was decided to wait to install the system on the second plane before ascending substantially beyond the Kármán Line.

In other words, they had two weeks of waiting ahead of them. They used those two weeks to pound some learning into their new crews. Lessons began at 7:00 am in the morning every day and ended at 7:30 in the evening. In the middle of the day, lectures were interspersed with coffee breaks, lunch and also some time to work out in the gym. The American and Chinse crews were both impressed with the meticulous order of the training, in contrast to their expectations that everything would be chaotic. They assumed that the timetable would be mercly a recommendation and that the lectures would be confused, among various other Israelism's they'd been prepared for, in accordance with the briefings they received before arrival. "In Israel, like elsewhere in the Levant, everything is always a mess," they were told.

But the lessons were given at the Interdisciplinary Center in Herzliya, which was fanatical with upholding Western standards. The well-equipped classroom had been rented from the center at an exorbitant price. Ismail managed roughly one third of the lectures, another third were given by IAI engineers who had worked on the project, and the final third were provided by Rotem and Noa. The lessons took place with meticulous order, and the cleanliness, care, computerized teaching aids and advanced projection systems of the place were in complete contradiction to the American and Chinese expectations.

A week later, the Chinese and American flight crews were joined by their engineer counterparts. The agreements with their respective governments had determined nine Chinese engineers and nine American engineers would be present in the classroom. NASA did indeed send precisely nine engineers — but the CNSA sent over a hundred! It turned out that the CNSA had leased its own classrooms in the Interdisciplinary Center. The nine Chinese engineers who studied in the Rakefet classroom for 12 hours each day, split up into three teams of three instructors, who spent the evening hours in four-hour shifts instructing classes composed of thirty-three of their countrymen.

At the conclusion of the two weeks, practical training for the pilots began. During the training they boarded the plane and embarked to the Kármán Line several times. Since they had almost completely discarded secrecy, flights were now launched in the daytime, with crowds of journalists photographing the golden plane from every possible angle, though at a distance, for they were not allowed to come near.

None of the foreign crews had yet to perform the ignition of the rocket engines.

At the end of these two weeks, the second plane was driven out of the hanger next to the first one. The two golden planes made quite a spectacle, stationed next to one another.

The international media was besides itself in excitement. The appearance of another space plane two weeks after the press release announcing the first ignited journalists' imagination. The media frenzy also caused the stock valuation of Rakefet to skyrocket to nearly a thousand dollars per share, up from around one dollar in the first investor round — not that anyone was selling.

After a slight delay, the American and Chinese representatives joined Rakefet's Board of Directors. Actually, the Chinese representative had been ready earlier, but they wanted to see who the American representative would be first. The American representative was Faina Marvel, the deputy President of NASA, with a MSc from MIT.

The Chinese representative was, surprisingly, Chou. They decided that other than the initial meeting which they physically attended and in which they received a detailed situation report and were fully briefed on upcoming developments, they would hold future meetings by Zoom.

The second plane launched its inaugural flight the day following its appearance on the runway. It, too, at first performed a regular flight, without the ignition of the rocket engines.

This time, learning from the inaugural flight of the first plane, the hydraulic system was activated and tested prior to the ignition and calibration of the rocket engines. The identity of the crew on the initial ignition and calibration of the rocket engines was a matter of some debate. It was clear to all that the inaugural blastoff was a dangerous stage — perhaps too dangerous. On the one hand, how were the new flight crews to learn how to perform the initial ignition if they did not see it? On the other hand, what purpose would be served by jeopardizing more people than strictly necessary? Moreover, who would fly the first plane should the ignition fail, and all the qualified personnel perish?

Finally, Galit decided to limit the flight to a crew comprising of only Rotem, Noa, Nadav, as well as a lone IAI engineer to inspect the equipment and offer another pair of hands in an emergency. In order to improve the instruction process, ten video cameras were installed on the plane to record the event from every possible angle. This time around, everyone appeared more stressed than excited prior to the ignition. Rotem was piloting with Noa as her co-pilot this time around. Rotem was scared, given her earlier experience, but did not want to give up flying the plane on this mission. Noa sat closer to Nadav and instinctively clung to him before the ignition.

But this time, perhaps because they were better prepared, or perhaps because the systems were better calibrated and balanced, it was much easier to take control of the plane after ignition. The plane did not turn over, and Nadav, who also flinched before the ignition sequence was launched, was able to rapidly calibrate the rolling of the plane. Nadav moved on to the horizontal engine deviance calibration monitor. This time around, the plane was tilting leftwards rather than rightward. Noa took charge of the steering wheel and, at first, easily held the course steady. But then Nadav made an error. Having prepared himself to correct a rightwards tilt, as he did the previous time, he initially performed a reverse correction, worsening the leftward tilt.

This error put quite a bit of pressure on Noa, who forcefully sought to compensate for the error. Eventually, out of frustration, she took her hand off the stick[21] and slapped Nadav's leg.

---

21. The helm.

In a certain respect this was fortunate because it snapped him out of his fixation, and he understood he was performing an ass-backwards correction. But he was also greatly offended. Noa, who realized his feelings were hurt, hugged him with one arm.

"I promise not to hit you again," she told him. Nadav blushed, and she snuck him a kiss to the back of the neck when she thought the cameras were not recording them. She was mistaken.

"It's a good thing they are not on the same team or have subordinate-superior relations," Galit told Shlomo. "Otherwise, their relationship could be a real problem."

Shlomo, who was slow on the uptake in such matters, did not fully comprehend what Galit was talking about.

At the end of the day, they completed the rocket engine calibration in under two minutes. They did not reach a tremendous altitude (less than twenty kilometers) and they had a hydraulic system to change the direction of the thrust, so that descent proved a piece of cake, more so than the Kármán Line descent which all of the teams, even the Chinese and the Americans, had practiced repeatedly over the past two weeks.

Once they landed and de-boarded, Noa gave Nadav a ride home.

"You know," she told him, "I divorced my husband because of a lighter blow than what I gave you today. I am really sorry."

"It's all right. It's just, I don't really know how... I mean I had girlfriends before, but I was never... intimate," Nadav stuttered. Noa decided this situation required rectification. She had known Nadav was introverted, but only now realized just how much. Luckily, she took life relatively easily. Yet, he confused her by the way he was able to speak to her so directly and forthrightly on the one hand but fell silent as soon as he was in company on the other. Her initial amorous forays ran into a wall. Noa understood she would have to operate more slowly and get to know him better before she could progress.

That very same week they flew up to a height of six hundred kilometers, once with the first plane, and then with the second. A week later, all the crews had already completed their solo flight on the second plane. It was decided for the time being to reserve the first plane exclusively for Rotem and Noa.

2.

A month later, they decided to take the planes up to 36,000 kilometers, the height of stationary satellites such as communications satellites which appear, from the vantage point of the earthbound observer, to be fixated on a single point in the heavens. In fact, these satellites revolve around the planet, but at the precise speed the Earth spins around its axis, meaning that they complete an orbit around the equator every 24 hours. This occurs at an altitude of 36,000 kilometers, about a tenth of the distance to the moon.

Rotem was to be the pilot, and Noa the co-pilot. They were to be accompanied by an American and Chinese representative of the international crews. They embarked on a circumnavigation of the planet from Ben-Gurion Airport, flying southwestwards towards South America. Unlike communications satellites, they did not fly directly over the equator — on the contrary, the last thing they wanted was to blast these satellites with the Helium jet, which would slice through them like a laser beam. Flying beneath them was not an option either, for this might interfere with its broadcasts. NASA did ask at first that they repair a communications satellite over the Pacific Ocean, but they were eventually brought around to accept that this might delay their primary mission — importing Helium 3.

This time they decided to try to activate the helium rocket engines at full power for a relatively long period. In addition, they decided that on the way back, flying one hundred kilometers high, they would try to turn off the engines and reignite.

In fact, flying at 36 kilometers was simpler than maintaining altitude at the Kármán Line, or at an altitude of six hundred kilometers. To maintain an even altitude without turning off the engines the plane had to turn around every few minutes. So, when rising to an altitude of 36,000 kilometers, they simply accelerated until they reached the required height, and only then turned around using the rocket engine thrust to slow down and thereby gradually descend.

Once Rotem and Noa reached 36,000 kilometers, the additional Israeli crew remained on standby with the second plane, just in case of a problem. This time, the flight was followed by the world's various space agencies and the media received a connection to the cameras in real time from the Rakefet spokesperson. The flight passed without incident.

The next day, the Chinese flight crew took the second plane up to 36,000 kilometers. Rotem and Noa were on standby in the first plane to render assistance in case of a malfunction. The second plane also performed an attempted engine turn-off and reignition at 100-kilometer altitude.

It was decided that over the next two weeks every flight crew would perform a solo ascension from between 36 to 40,000 kilometers and would practice the turnoff and reignition of the engine during the flight. As aforementioned, this would be a necessary step on longer flights. In addition, the oxygen tanks for the flight crew, and a number of other systems were inspected and calibrated.

It was further determined that the American and the Chinese governments would each contribute a 787 plane, the more advanced model of the 767. Though the Chinese lacked an advanced plane-manufacturing industry, they possessed a well-developed plane upgrading and modification commerce. Hence, they modified one of their 787 planes in accordance with Rakefet's requirements, and transferred it to IAI to install the engines and complete the upgrade.

However, supervision of all work and specifications would be American in regard to the exterior and flight capabilities, whereas internal structure and adaptation would be Chinese supervised. This was ill received by the Israeli engineers who were demoted from masters of their own house to the underlings of foreign supervisors, forced to watch the corridors of the Flight Division trod by hordes of foreign colleagues.

Rotem asked to take a two-week vacation; she wanted to take her family on a trip down the West Coast of the United States, after visiting the Big Apple, of course. As the plan for the upcoming two weeks was in any case for the flight crews to train flying within the 36-kilometer envelope, Shlomo authorized her vacation.

Rotem and her family landed in New York's Kennedy Airport. At passport control, she was approached by a man who presented himself as an FBI agent. He explained that he was responsible for her family's security and ushered them through a passage which bypassed passport control to the VIP entry hall.

"I received your itinerary from the travel agency," he said. "We changed your hotels to venues where we could properly secure your stay — I hope you don't mind." They followed him.

"By the way, we had to cancel your leased vehicle. You will drive an FBI vehicle which is both armored and has room for your security detail," the agent went on as they walked. "Unfortunately, you will have to give up your camping trip, but you will be hosted in a nearby hotel, so you won't miss out on almost anything from the trip you had planned."

When Rotem went over the list of the five-star hotels that were reserved for them in lieu of those they had booked from Israel, she grew quite stressed and immediately called Shlomo to find out what the hell was going on.

"Don't worry," Shlomo reassured her, "Rakefet will bear any additional costs should they materialize. The Americans contacted me about your security in the United States while you were already in flight — what else could I do?"

The FBI agent explained to them that the administration had decided to treat the senior executives of Rakefet, including Rotem, like foreign ministers in terms of security and rolling out the red carpet — and so she had best get used to some royal, albeit confining, pampering.

Rotem's children were in fact delighted, for they now had a new friend, an FBI security woman who provided them with explanations for every question, treated them nicely and was simply an altogether positive person. Rotem and Nimrod's security guard was not quite as nice, but eventually everyone got used to the strange situation.

Nimrod and Rotem were somewhat disappointed because they were looking forward to an unfiltered overseas experience — which, for Israelis in the United States, meant calmly driving in unclogged and endless wide highways, enjoying pervasive courtesy, and the everyday astoundment of watching how people entering a building ahead of them would hold the door open, while the person behind them made no effort to shove them aside in a scramble for the door. Being surrounded by security who opened the door for them, drove their car, and generally screened them from any unfiltered interaction with locals rather spoiled the whole concept.

"It seems," Nimrod told Rotem one evening as they got ready for bed, when they finally had a moment of privacy from their security detail, "that I am no Bibi."[22]

"What do you mean?" Rotem asked with a smile.

"When Bibi took his vacation, he did it on the private island of one of his billionaire friends, who made sure he would not have to suffer from an interaction with the locals or be forced to do his shopping like a normal human being. But I do not enjoy being surrounded with security who keep me from interacting with the local population. On the contrary, this was the experience I was looking forward to on this trip, and I really missed out on that."

---

22. "Bibi" is the nickname of Israeli Prime Minister Benjamin Netanyahu.

3.

About a week into their vacation, while they were staying in San Francisco, Rotem's phone rang — it was Noa on the line.

"I am above the United States right now — 40,000 kilometers above to be exact. So, I'm actually further away from the United States than any point on earth."

One might have interpreted Noa's words as no more than small talk, but Rotem knew that Noa was supposed to stay in Israel as an emergency backup. If Noa was in space, then something must have happened. Besides, Rotem knew Noa and immediately understood from her tone of voice that she was distressed. She excused herself and stepped out of the room to continue the conversation in private.

"What's happening?" Rotem asked in a businesslike tone.

"I am currently five meters away from plane number 2," Noa said. "I left on a rescue mission because Plane 2 shut off its engines and we were unable to reignite them. The Israeli team with Avi as pilot, and the Chinese team are on it, currently."

Their protocol for performing the extraction was to first transfer the crew members from the malfunctioning plane to the extraction plane, and then to return to Earth. Only after that were they to head back up with a technical team to try to resolve the malfunction. After all, the malfunctioning plane could stably orbit Earth for months, even years.

The crew was supposed to be extracted via a portal in the ceiling, slightly behind the cockpits of the plane, which was specifically designed by the Flight Division. For the crew to pass between the planes, they had to align with each other, ceiling to ceiling, with only a few meters separating them. In zero gravity, of course, up and down meant nothing.

Once aligned, the ceiling portal of one plane would open, and a foldable, flexible sleeve eight meters long was extended to the other to latch onto its counterpart's portal with a magnetic clamp. The clamp was capable of directing the foldable sleeve to the correct position with a precision of 0.1 millimeters, provided it was brought within 50 centimeters of the final position. Once the sleeve was locked into place between the planes it would be pumped full of air, the other portal opened, and the crew of the malfunctioning plane could then easily make their way out to the extraction plane.

"So, what's the problem?" Rotem asked.

"It turns out that we have a design engineer who liked to show excessive initiative. He seems to have deemed the steel ring around the ceiling portal unnecessary, thinking the portal strong enough on its own to withstand forces involved in the procedure. So he removed it from the design entirely. But now the magnetic couplings on the terminus of the foldable sleeve have no way of guiding it to its precise coupling position on the other portal.[23] I've spent several hours here already, and it's totally useless without the magnet. I was able to bring it up to five centimeters within the alignment position, but I need a precision of half a millimeter to achieve coupling. I just can't do it without the magnet."

"How are the crew in Plane 2?" Rotem asked.

They have enough oxygen for one more day. After that — they're dead. I don't know what to do and I've wasted too much time on these fruitless attempts," Noa responded.

"In the meantime, Shlomo has talked to the Americans at NASA," continued Noa, "they are right now collecting a team of four astronauts with experience in spacewalking. We don't even have spacesuits, let alone people trained in their use, or who have actual spacewalking experience. In any event, they will be ready to head out to Israel in another six hours with all the necessary equipment."

---

23. Magnets are attracted to the iron, but not to the aluminum of the plane.

"But another four hours plus flight time to Israel — that's ten hours, and then another four to return to Plane 2, and then another six of spacewalking to complete the extraction — Plane 2 crew will die!" Rotem exclaimed.

"True," said Noa, "But there are two other possibilities: the first is that I land in the United States in another four hours and take off from there with the astronauts and their flight suits. The other option is to put the astronauts on five NASA F15 planes (yes, it turns out NASA has those as well), rather than a commercial flight. They would fly at an extremely high altitude at 2.1 Mach, and that will get them to Israel within three and a half hours, allowing for aerial refueling over Europe. Why do we need five planes? One plane and one pilot to taxi each astronaut, because while they can fly such planes themselves, they will be in no condition to spacewalk after the flight. The fifth plane will carry the equipment. The second option, with the F15s, is what will probably be implemented. The Americans convinced Shlomo they are unprepared for having me take off from an American airfield. The whole issue of keeping an air-traffic free space behind our planes because of the helium jet is very problematic in the United States' crowded airspace." Noa paused briefly before continuing.

"Let me get to the point; the real reason that I called. I want you to return right now to Israel and join me in the rescue mission."

"But how?" Rotem asked.

"You are in San Francisco now, right?"

"That's right," Rotem replied.

"In less than half an hour, a United States aircraft, probably an F16, will be waiting for you at San Francisco Airport with a pilot. It will take the shortest possible route to Ben Gurion Airport, over the North Pole. Which means we will see each other in about six hours."

"So, I take it this is not a request but an order?" Rotem asked sardonically.

"That's right," Noa replied, "but not my order — this comes directly from Faina Marvel, the Deputy Director of NASA, and as you know, now also a Rakefet Director."

4.

As soon as the conversation ended, Rotem's security detail scrambled into action. Obviously, they had been appraised of the new instructions. Rotem began to fill Nimrod in, but before she got through her second sentence, her burly security guard more or less dragged her out to the waiting vehicle.

"Tell the children there is an emergency in Israel... I mean in space," she was able to shout out to Nimrod, "I will call them once I am in the air."

The security detail sounded the siren, and the drive to San Francisco Airport took only ten minutes rather than the usual hour. On the way, Rotem called Nimrod and explained the situation to him.

"I just don't understand how you are supposed to reach Israel within six hours," he said.

"I have no time to explain. I promise that when I reach Israel, I will call you and we will decide what to do, alright?"

The Airport security opened a gate especially for Rotem's FBI escorts and they entered the airport through it. When they arrived, Rotem caught a glimpse of an F16 landing. Rotem was far from the only one to take note, for the San Francisco Airport was a civilian facility from which military aircraft did not regularly make an appearance.

The plane halted and the security guards brought her right up to the aircraft. As the airport was not prepared for a combat plane to land there was no purpose-built ladder. Instead, the airport operational crew had brought over a passenger jet stairwell, which, even at its lowest position, was a meter too high. Nonetheless, Rotem climbed the stairs, the pilot opened the cockpit, and Rotem climbed, or rather jumped, down into the co-pilot chair. It was all very surreal, for Rotem was still dressed in the cocktail dress and high heels she was wearing for the play she and Nimrod had planned on seeing before Noa's call came in. A local journalist immortalized the iconic image of her leaping, high heels in hand, from the civilian jet stairs onto the F16 cockpit.

The F16 took off within less than five minutes, only to land a few minutes later in a nearby military airfield. They never left the plane — the plane was just there to refuel on the runway, as well as be equipped with detachable fuel tanks.

After topping off, they took off once more.

"Well, since I am also a navigator, why don't I help you navigate?" Rotem told the pilot.

"No need, thanks. Everything is all computerized here in any event. But I will fill you in that a refueling plane has just taken off from Norway and will meet us over the North Pole. Another refueling plane will take off from the Spangdahlem Air base and meet us over Germany. I estimate that the American taxpayer will be forking out over $300,000 to bring one pretty lady to Israel. Can't rightly see the how and why of it."

"I am supposed to help rescue a Chinese astronaut crew," she said, deliberately leaving out the Israeli crewmembers.

"You are an astronaut in the new Israeli American Chinese space shuttles?" he asked, astounded.

When she replied affirmatively, his entire demeanor shifted from dismissive to deeply respectful. She was no longer the little lady in the cocktail dress, high heeled shoes in hand, who leaped into the copilot chair so gracefully. She was an astronaut!

"So, if my navigational skills aren't needed," she told him, "I'll just doze off. I have plenty of work ahead of me once we land."

"Yes, no problem, ma'am" he answered, awe struck.

Rotem was still asleep when they refueled over the North Pole, but when refueling over Germany she awoke, deeply impressed.

"Wow, I've never experienced aerial refueling before," she said. "I think you pulled it off perfectly."

The pilot was glad for the compliment, and they chatted for a while before she dozed off again, waking up when they landed at Ben-Gurion Airport.

She called Nimrod in the United States straight away to update him, but found out the media had beat her to it. Her picture leaping into the F16 copilot seat, high heels in hand, had already been published in outlets all over the world.

Once her picture had been published, Faina and Shlomo decided that Faina should make a statement to the press. Faina, as the Deputy Director of NASA, duly called a press conference.

"There is a malfunction on Shuttle 2," she explained, "and in order to rescue the Chinese crew onboard, we have sent American astronauts with special equipment to Israel to take the first shuttle up to extract them. The fastest way to get them to the shuttle was with supersonic jets. That is why five planes left Edwards Air Base with the astronauts. Another plane left San Francisco with our most experienced shuttle pilot, Rotem, who was on a family vacation in the United States. This was the picture that was published." Faina also left out the Israeli crew on the malfunctioning shuttle, in order to emphasize the angle of Americans coming to the rescue of the Chinese crew — all in the spirit of international cooperation.

Faina and Shlomo had also agreed that this was their chance to go public with their mission to mine Helium 3. Thus, Faina added as follows:

"Such accidents can occur, and were taken into account, in the fulfillment of Rakefet's mission. Rakefet was founded with the aim of solving the global warming generated by the burning of fossil fuels. To do so, it has set out to import a clean substitute to Earth — the so-called Lunar Helium 3. Global warming is the reason for the great urgency of this project. This is the reason we constructed our two shuttles, and I am pleased to announce that they will soon be joined by two additional shuttles: a European

Russian funded shuttle and a Japanese Indian funded shuttle. Once this roster is completed, Rakefet's board of directors will be expanded to host a Japanese, Indian, Russian, and European representative. At present, Rakefet's board of directors is composed of our chair, representative of academia Professor Galit Cohen, entrepreneur Shlomo Grossman, a representative from China and myself, the American representative who also represents the UK, Canada, Australia and New Zealand.

When she concluded, the NASA spokesperson took the microphone.

"Thank you, Faina. Faina must leave now, but I will try to answer any questions to the best of my ability." In fact, he knew little, or very little, and was not able to satisfy the journalist's frenzied attempts to extract new information.

Initially, when Rotem's picture was published, she was recognized as the pilot of the plane-shuttle who had appeared in the group photo following the Kármán Line mission. This spawned a rumor mill about a major disaster in Rakefet, leading to a precipitous drop in Rakefet's stock valuation.

Following Faina's press conference and the outing of the Helium 3 goal, Rakefet's stock valuation leaped to totally unreasonable levels.

5.

Rotem rushed to her room in IAI Flight Division. Noa was waiting for her there with a change of clothes. "The American extraction team has arrived in Israel and is sitting down with the Flight Division engineers," said Noa.

"The Flight Division is currently installing a pressure lock for spacewalking missions on the front right doorway of Plane 1. That means it will be a sealed room within the plane, right by the portal, with another opening into the plane. The room will have two valves, one of which will enable the release of air from within the room into the space when the inner door is closed, and then open the outer door and exit the roomlet into space. Another valve is set to insert air from the plane into the roomlet after it is entered from space and the outer door is closed. The valve will also equalize the pressure, and then the plane itself can be entered."

"When do we need to leave?" Rotem asked.

"The crew in Plane 2 has enough air for another eight hours," Noa said. "It takes four hours to reach them, and another two hours for the extraction process, so we need to take off within no more than two hours. The problem is that the roomlet is not yet complete. Nor is the procedure that will be defined for the rescue clear yet."

"Why?" Rotem asked.

"There are several problems: the first is how the astronaut who is floating in space will cling to the second plane. One engineer from the Flight Division offered a plunger, as one used when installing glass, but Nadav pointed out that a plunger only worked on Earth because of air pressure and would be totally useless in space."

"He's right!" said Rotem.

"The Americans thought of a rope which would encircle the plane, and that the rescuing Astronaut would grip onto it like a bull rider at a rodeo."

Rotem laughed.

"Ismail suggested a screwdriver that would be used to attach a handle to the plane fuselage. The Americans were horrified at the idea of drilling "like barbarians" into the fuselage of an airship as if they were pounding on an old tractor but Ismail insisted that one of the rescuing astronauts could enter the sleeve himself and use the drilled handle to pull the sleeve into place instead of the magnet."

"Can't this be done from outside the sleeve?" Rotem asked.

"The circumference of the foldable sleeve is two and a half meters," Noa responded, "so a human being cannot grasp it, certainly not while wearing a spacesuit. In any event, the Americans actually liked Ismail's idea."

At the end of the day, Shlomo decided that three astronauts would leave the plane. Since they could leave the sealed roomlet one after the other, the first two would go around Plane 2 with a rope, creating a lasso. Using the lasso, a third astronaut would hold on to Plane 2, drill into the portal and connect an external handle to it. They would then remove the lasso, and the third astronaut would enter the sleeve and drag both himself and the sleeve into position manually, using the handle. The sleeve would then be locked in place, as originally planned, fill the sleeve with air, and transfer the crew into the extraction plane.

Now all they needed was to bring a handle and screws, which no one at IAI knew how to find at midnight.

"I suggest Ismail and I take heavy equipment and a police car, and we will drive to Lod and break into the nearest hardware store," Adam said.

"My uncle lives in Lod," Ismail said, "I'll talk to him, maybe he knows a store we can get what we need without breaking and entering."

On route in the police car, they rendezvoused with Ismail's uncle and his friend, a hardware store owner. They entered the store and gathered several sets of screws, handles and electric screwdrivers.

"We need the older electric screwdrivers, not the new impact types," said Ismail. So, they took all types just to be sure.

When they got back, the exit roomlet was still unprepared, but time was ticking away and they had to leave.

"All of the workers currently working on the exit room," said Shlomo, "Will continue to work on it during the flight. You have four hours of flight before you reach Plane 2."

"You had better take epoxy glue as well," said Ismail, "so that if there are any air leaks from the roomlet you will be able to glue them up."

"Leave on the flight as well," Shlomo told Ismail, "Together with Adam and Nadav."

And so, they left with the plane on the runway: Rotem as pilot, about a dozen IAI workers who were still putting the finishing touches on the roomlet, four NASA astronauts, Noa, Nadav, Adam, Ismail, and a doctor with medical equipment.

The doctor was a last-minute addition. A police car was sent to Beilenson Hospital to bring a pulmonary specialist. However, no one at the Beilenson understood what they were talking about. In the end, after moderate physical pressure by the police and a phone call from the minister of health, they sent a local pulmonary doctor who had still not completed his residency. He brought a few resuscitation kits with him, intended to revive people who had almost drowned in swimming pools and had not drawn breath for a few minutes.

It was, in short, a typical Israeli jury-rigged improvisation, much to the growing dismay of Faina Marvel and NASA.

Meanwhile, Noa worked together with IAI Flight Division workers on the roomlet.

"Shouldn't we sit down and buckle up for takeoff?" one of the workers asked.

"Never mind that," Noa told him, "Keep working. Only those not working right now should buckle up. Those who are working — grab onto something to stabilize yourself when the plane starts accelerating on the runway."

The NASA astronauts were shocked. They expected a lengthy simulation exercise on a model of the rescue process. They simply could not believe the level of casual, off the cuff improvisation. After takeoff, it turned out that there was a Lufthansa plane in sky behind them. The control tower had to get it out of the way before they could ignite the rocket engines. That wasted another ten minutes they simply did not have to waste.

About two hours after takeoff, the Flight Division completed the preparation of the roomlet. The difficult part was the completion, in which they had to work in near zero-gravity. They were not used to this and were unable to function. Thus, two NASA astronauts and Noa had to perform the finishing touches and IAI Flight Division only told them what to do.

Ismail wanted to examine the roomlet and therefore inserted an air tank into it, shut the door, and opened the tank to raise the air pressure within the roomlet and check for leaks. Within seconds he could hear the tell-tale sound of escaping air and located an unsealed point between the fuselage and the roomlet. Ismail removed his epoxy glue.

"That is not very good glue," said the engineer, "for it takes it an hour to harden and four hours for full strength to be achieved. We need a quick, ten-minute hardening glue."

"All right," said Ismail, "So bring me the quick-hardening glue," the engineer said, "I don't have it."

"So why are you wasting time?" Ismail said angrily and began to apply the epoxy. "This is what we have, and this is what we need to work with," he concluded.

The NASA astronaut watched their interaction in bewilderment. He asked Noa what was going on, and after she explained, he sat down in his chair and grabbed his head in denial of the amateur operation he was involved in.

When they reached the environs of Plane 2, Noa took over the pilot seat from Rotem, as she had already performed the approach to Plane 2 once before. And indeed, she carried it out more smoothly this time around.

By the time the maneuver was completed, however, Plane 2 had only two hours of air remaining — one air tank for each of the four crew members. By this point they were breathing exclusively from the emergency balloons, because the oxygen in the plane had long been exhausted. They decided the two pilots, the Chinese and the Israeli, had to be kept alert during the rescue and it would not be terrible if the other two were to lose consciousness as they could always be revived after the rescue. Thus, the pilots used three of the air tanks, leaving only one for the other two crew members.

Noa reached within ten meters of Plane 2, and the moment of truth was upon them. The astronauts donned their spacesuits and organized their equipment. The first astronaut entered the roomlet with spacewalking equipment, including small rocket engines enabling movement in space. The astronaut also took a rope with him to secure himself to Plane 1, and another long rope to lasso Plane 2. When he opened the air valve to depressurize, it turned out that the process was much slower than they thought. It took nearly half an hour to remove the air from the roomlet and reach a state enabling the outer door to open.

"It has to be this way," one of the engineers explained, "doing this any quicker could damage the fuselage."

"Then it is another half an hour to pressurize as well," Rotem said, "which means it takes an hour to get an astronaut out on a spacewalk. Since we need three astronauts to work outside this will take three hours, which means the crew on Plane 2 will die, for they already have less than two hours of air."

Since the intercom systems of the two planes were connected via Wi-Fi, the crew on Plane 2 heard her as well, and the Israeli crew understood, as she spoke in Hebrew.

"Look," Avi the pilot told his Chinese colleague, "One of us has to stay conscious until they come to get us. It will probably take longer than we thought."

"How do you know?" the Chinese captain asked him.

"Trust me. I just heard them talking," Avi responded. "You are physically smaller than me and so use up less air. I will share one air tank with our copilots, leaving you three air tanks. Agreed?"

This conversation was overheard in Rakefet's control room on Earth. Galit, considering Avi's words, informed both planes via intercom that it was the right call and had to be carried out. The Chinese pilot began to argue, but then Chou stepped in and backed Galit, ending the discussion.

"Perhaps we should have the second astronaut exit right now with the electric screwdriver, screws and handle," said Rotem. "That way, once they complete tightening the lasso around Plane 2, by the time the third astronaut exits they can begin connecting the door handle."

Last minute changes in procedures were very hard for the Americans to accept, but Faina from NASA, who was also online, said she agreed with Rotem, and that is what they did.

When the third astronaut exited their plane, everything was already prepared. He entered the sleeve, grabbed the handle the second astronaut prepared, and maneuvered the foldable sleeve into position within a few minutes. The entire procedure took two and a half hours — 30 minutes over the point they initially assessed that Plane 2 crew would run out of air. Only thanks to the fact that three of the crew had deliberately chosen to pass out did the Chinese pilot have enough air to function. The pilot locked the foldable sleeve in place and duly opened Plane 2's emergency hatch.

At the same time, Rotem was opening the portal on Plane 1 and air began to flow from Plane 1 to Plane 2. The two astronauts who were left outside the foldable sleeve began to make their way back to the plane's entrance.

Rotem made her way through the foldable sleeve to Plane 2 to help the third NASA astronaut to transfer the passed-out crew members to Plane 1. That was not at all simple. Each had to be grabbed by the head and legs and pulled from one side while being pushed from the other.

"This is a lot like forceps delivery," said the doctor, who watched Rotem manhandling the Chinese copilot through the round emergency hatch, "only with a slightly larger baby."

As soon as Rotem and the third astronaut exited the foldable sleeve, Ismail and the fourth astronaut, who had been held in reserve up to that point, entered. They extracted the Israeli co-pilot, who duly underwent the same forceps birth. Each was immediately transferred to the care of the doctor, who did not seem excessively concerned with their condition.

Rotem and the third astronaut returned to the foldable sleeve and brought Avi the Israeli pilot, and finally the Chinese pilot made his own way to their plane.

The doctor, who had been unperturbed when examining the copilots, nearly descended into hysteria when he saw Avi. He quickly intubated him and began undertaking resuscitation procedures which proved extraordinarily complex to perform in zero gravity. The doctor was unable to put his weight into applying pressure to Avi's chest, and so Rotem sat on him and grabbed the chair to create a counter pressure.

"He is not in good condition," the doctor said. "Although he was oxygen deprived for less time, his condition is critical. We need to return to Earth as soon as possible."

"I can't move until the two NASA astronauts complete their re-entry," Noa said in frustration from the pilot's chair. "One is already in the airlock, but as you know it will take an hour for the other one to be able to enter."

In the meantime, one of IAI Flight Division engineers replaced Rotem, but no one knew enough to relieve the doctor. The doctor said resuscitation had to be maintained throughout the entire flight time, until they reached the hospital. It was in fact a combined activity of a respiration machine, with an oxygen tube inserted into the lungs, while alternating pressure was placed on the chest to simulate respiration. In the meantime, the Israeli copilot woke up.

"Avi took almost no oxygen from our tank," the Israeli pilot said, "I was sure he was already dead."

The Chinese copilot regained consciousness after about another half hour. Noa did not even wait for the second astronaut to finish closing the outer door. Noa ignited the engines, and they began circumventing the Earth, heading back to Ben-Gurion Airport.

"Take it easy with the speed," Nadav told her. "We don't want to burn up on reentry."

"If I take it any slower it will be too late for Avi," she responded.

Before penetrating the atmosphere, Noa turned the plane to face away from Earth, engines at full blast to achieve maximal speed reduction. Noa then turned the plane back towards the Earth and glided downwards at a truly outrageous speed into the atmosphere. Noa reach Tel Aviv from the sea at a height of 40,000 feet (thirteen kilometers) and then performed a fighter jet style dive towards the Jerusalem Hills.

"You are cutting it too fine," Rotem whispered to her in alarm. A few seconds later, Noa dove into a wadi winding between the hills no more than a hundred meters from the ground, barely managing to level the plane while making a turn, the mountains of Jerusalem towering to either side of the plane's wingtips. Emerging from the wadi, still flying at well above appropriate landing speed, the plane aligned itself for a landing on Strip 30 at Ben Gurion Airport. The plane's wings creaked in protest at the extreme forces they were subjected to. The NASA astronaut seated in the back stared aghast at the wingtip, which reached its maximal flexibility, bent upwards way past the Boeing design parameters. It was not, after all, a fighter jet, even if Noa was flying it like it was. The plane straightened above a traffic jam on Route 6, nearly scraping the high-power lines flanking the road. The sight of the golden plane nearly crashing into the road, the sound of the jet engines firing at full blast, and finally the bone chilling screech of the straightening wing, brought the snail-paced traffic to a complete halt. The straightening of the wing, much like the wing movement of a bird, was performed with the aid of the layered material Rotem demanded be added to the bottom of the wing. This wing movement pushed the plane some fifty meters upwards. Noa rushed in behind a small EasyJet plane, which was already in its final landing stages, almost touching the runway. Although the control tower had ordered the little plane to abort its landing, the confused pilot did not respond in time. The control tower now instructed the pilot to proceed to the end of the runway, because a large plane was landing right behind him. The EasyJet pilot understood that instruction just fine. Fortunately, the Air France pilot, who was preparing to land after the EasyJet plane, was a veteran pilot. When he saw the golden space-plane emerge out of the Adlib streambed beneath it and cut beneath its approach vector to hit the runway only a few hundred meters below, he did not lose his cool and asked for instructions from the Lod control tower. The tower instructed him to turn north, rise, and perform another turn.

Noa's landing on the ground was perfect, almost imperceptible to the passengers. This was quite by chance — she did not always have such perfect landings. The NASA astronauts were completely befuddled. They had never experienced such a flight, which took the modified 767 to the edge of its performance envelope and beyond, so flawlessly executed and completed.

"She flies like an eagle," one of them told Nadav in admiration.

"You are not the first to say that" Nadav responded. Noa reached Ben Gurion Airport from orbit in less than two hours. A chopper was waiting at the airport to transport Avi. Within less than twenty minutes, Avi was on the landing pad above the Davidson building at the Hadassah Ein Karem Medical Center.

"Thanks for the composite layers in the wing," Noa told Rotem while Avi was being manhandled onto the chopper, "if you hadn't insisted on it, they would have needed to scrape us off the streambed of the Jerusalem Mountains."

"Anytime," Noa coolly responded.

"I'll sleep at your place tonight, alright?" Noa told Nadav.

It was not their first time, but something in the air felt different.

"Sure," he replied.

On the way , Noa drove while Nadav sat beside her, and then, in a moment of inexplicable courage, his mouth opened, and the words seemed to speak themselves.

"Will you marry me?"

Noa pulled over by the side of the road and turned off the car engine. She looked at him and smiled.

"First of all — yes!" she said, "but we aren't even an official couple yet. We've slept together a few times, but we haven't even had a chance to get to know each other. We haven't even had a proper date."

"So, what does that mean?" Nadav asked, staring at his feet in embarrassment.

"I'm with you, but we need to talk about how we will get to know each other, before and after the wedding, irrespective of the wedding itself, alright?"

Nadav nodded.

"And now I really need to get some sleep," she said and started the car up again.

As both the NSA and the MSS were listening in on their conversation, Chou and Faina were the first to know about their upcoming nuptials.

6.

During the directors meeting, Faina raised a motion to suspend Noa from flights. "Due to reckless flying which endangered both the crew and the irreplaceable plane on the return of the rescue mission to Earth," Faina argued, "any professional and ethical dilemma Rakefet employees face must be weighed by them against the salvation of humanity. Saving a single individual, in this case Avi, cannot justify risking the entire mission. We don't even know if his life has been saved, and if it has, we don't know whether landing in Ben Gurion within two hours instead of four made much of a difference. We do know that if Noa would have crashed the plane everyone on it would have died — and with Plane 2 still stuck in orbit, the mission would have been set back for several months at the very least. I know that you are worried about how Nadav will react to her suspension, especially with their upcoming nuptials, but surely, he of all people understands that the risk she put the project in outweighs any marginal benefits to the survival of a single individual," she said.

"I must correct you and say that while we would have faced delays had Noa crashed the plane," said Shlomo, "we have a backup in place for every Rakefet employee, so the project definitely would not have ground to a halt. That said, I do think Noa's suspension is called for." Shlomo cleared his throat and added, seemingly as an afterthought, "by the way, how do you know about Noa's nuptial plans?"

Chou rushed in to rescue Faina from an awkward moment. Chou knew, of course how Faina knew Noa and Nadav were planning to get married — Chinese intelligence had been listening in on the same conversation in Nadav's car.

"What do you mean? Everyone knows they are getting married," he said. "I understand Faina's concern, but I think that, at the moment, such a suspension will harm the morale of our flight crews — and not only them. Noa is currently viewed as a hero by the team. Certainly, she is the most talented pilot we have. Rotem is probably the better pilot, when you take into consideration her judgment, experience and moderation — but Noa's raw flying talent is unparalleled."

Galit supported Chou, "while cold calculation favors suspension," said Galit, "crew morale has considerable influence on how fast the project can progress. And as Faina noted, that is our paramount concern."

And so, absent the as-yet unappointed representatives of the EU, India, Japan and Russia, they had a tie. Faina and Shlomo favored suspension, whereas Galit and Chou opposed it.

"To the best of my recollection," Shlomo said, "the Rakefet articles of incorporation state that in a case of a tie among the board, the chair casts the deciding vote." They therefore decided to pass the matter over to Joel, who would investigate the matter and provide his conclusions within a week.

In the meantime, Galit summoned Noa for a reprimand.

"Saving Avi did not justify your hell-bent descent. Even Rotem said as much to you, which means her judgement was better than yours."

Noa was silent.

"I decided to fine you 10,000 New Israeli Shekels. I know that I have no legal authority to do so, but we need to emphasize the severity of your actions. I expect you to contribute these funds to "Yad Sara Charity' — by tomorrow morning I want to see a receipt from them on my desk."

And indeed, a duly signed receipt from Yad Sarah was on her desk. To it, a note was attached, reading: "In retrospect, I understand I acted irrationally. The importance of what we are doing for mankind is greater than any one individual among us. I promise to make every effort in the future to do the rational thing. But I won't lie to you, or to myself. Given that we made it back safely, I am glad Avi still has a chance."

Joel analyzed the incident and uncovered a continuum of mistakes, failures and malfunctions. First, the Israeli crew on Plane 2 did not turn on the battery charging system or the oxygen filling system, since they thought there was an automatic mechanism that switched them on after ignition. True, this system had been installed on Plane 1 but had yet to be installed on Plane 2. That was why there was so little oxygen on Plane 2; an error which nearly killed the entire crew and might yet kill Avi. In addition, the measurement system of the batteries showed that they were fully charged. They really were nearly full, but as they had to supply a massive burst of energy during the ten seconds of the ignition, they could only do so when they were over 80% full. The battery charge indicator screen was standard and was not adapted to Rakefet's requirements due to lack of time — it displayed a green light for a battery charge of over 40% and hence no one noticed the battery charge was low. When the battery was at 100% capacity, it could withstand three ignitions. Each ignition drained the battery by 9%, leaving 91% after the first ignition, 82% after the second ignition and 73% after the third ignition, which is what happened in this case. But although each ignition only took 9% of the charge, the charge of the battery had to be very high, over 80% of the battery's capacity, to ignite the helium rocket engine.

Another foul-up emerged. Every plane had a tank intended to provide 96 hours of oxygen to a crew numbering twenty people. For a four-man crew, the air should have lasted at least two weeks. But the tank was empty — it had not been filled since the connector of the filling tube was defective and had not been fixed.

When Joel presented his inquiry to the board, Faina and Chou called to replace the IAI quality control team who inspect the plane before take offs, as well as the team inspecting each and every plane upgrade. Ultimately, they agreed to have a team from China perform inspections before every takeoff and team from the US to oversee inspections after every upgrade made. IAI offered only weak protests — they realized the screwup was too big to do anything but accept the penalty.

7.

After the meeting of the board of directors, which took place on Zoom, concluded, Faina stayed in the chat and asked Shlomo to stay as well. She cut straight to the chase. "I want to come to the wedding, together with the American ambassador to Israel," she said. Shlomo hesitated, "I don't know Faina, I'll talk to Nadav," he finally responded.

"Why do you want to talk to Nadav about Ismail's wedding?" she asked, wrinkling her brow. "I want to check this sort of thing with Nadav," he ruled.

Shlomo actually had no idea what Faina was talking about and was determined not to reveal his ignorance about the goings-on at his own home base.

Thoughts were frenziedly running through his head: He did not know Noa and Nadav were going to get married, he only found out by chance when Faina brought it up. Now, he finds out that Ismail is about to get married, and again, he knows nothing. He tasted bitter bile in his mouth.

Immediately after signing off of Zoom, Shlomo went to speak with Ismail. Ismail was seated in a spotlessly organized room in the training area allocated to Rakefet at IAI. The wooden door had a metal letterhead on it with the words: "Training Department Manager" inscribed on it in Hebrew, English, Chinese, Russian and Arabic. Up until about a month ago, the room was completely empty because Ismail had no time to sit in an office — he was running around between trainee groups. Shlomo reprimanded him and explained that Ismail was the company's face to the trainees. They could not present a disheveled, frenetic appearance. Ismail duly, but perhaps somewhat challengingly, had human resources prepare the letterhead and organized a spit-spot office.

Ismail seemed surprised at the question.

"Why yes, Shlomo, I am actually planning to get married in another two months, but I haven't told anyone other than my parents and the parents of my future wife, of course. How do you even know?"

"I think the NSA was working extra hours here," Shlomo said with a smile.

"Look, the wedding will be huge, and because my mother is considered Bedouin nobility, the heads of the various clans will each be gravely offended if they are not invited," Ismail answered with a smile. "You need to understand that when Bedouin clans are offended it eventually ends in a blood feud. In any event, the wedding will be huge come what may. But what does the American director want with my wedding?" Ismail asked.

"I think that the intelligence agencies are trying to put their hands on Rakefet's technology," Shlomo said. "They believe that we have secret holders who possess various keys to the technology. They think that the secret keepers are Joel, Adam, Nadav, and us two. And we are therefore considered to be geostrategic linchpins." Ismail stared at Shlomo with a confused expression. "If Faina arrives," Shlomo continued, "she will of course arrive with Chou, and then the Russians and the Europeans will come, and then, before you realize it, our government, our prime minister included, will show up too. And if any of them are offended, your inter-clan blood feuds will seem like mere child's play."

Ismail shifted his eyes to the window and gazed out on the scenery, thoughtful.

"That is why," said Shlomo, "I suggest Rakefet pay for the wedding. We will handle the international politics surrounding it, and I will ask Nadav to coordinate everything versus your internal politics. What do you say?"

"Nadav will have to talk with my grandfather on my mother's side," Ismail said.

"Why with him?" asked Shlomo.

"Because my grandfather is the head of the Huzail Tribe," Ismail answered.

"I may be Tarabin, because of my father, but it is my mother's lineage which matters."

"I thought your mother was a dentist. How does that work?" Shlomo asked.

"She is an oral and jaw surgeon, mostly dealing with aspects of pharyngal cancer. She is also a dentist. At the same time, my mother also comes from a very distinguished family."

Shlomo did not realize quite how distinguished it was until the wedding itself.

The wedding was attended by ambassadors from most Western countries, as well as Russia and China, and also all of Rakefet's Board of Directors members, quite a few IAI executives including the CEO, and also Israel's prime and defense ministers. The Chief of Police for the South District also had to come, for this was a golden opportunity to end several ongoing blood feuds between rival families.

The wedding took place in a huge hanger in Mitzpe Ramon, to which quite a few Bedouin tents were attached. Because of all the VIP arrivals, they needed both police and General Security Service (GSS) security, which maintained several complex perimeters around the area. Most of the Bedouin guests invited to Ismail's wedding were model citizens — but some were leaders of criminal organizations, and a few were suspected of links to terrorism.

In addition to all these complexities, the guests also included two special ambassadors. One was Jordan's ambassador to Israel, who was a relative of Jordan's king. The Hashemite monarch was also Bedouin and held a trump card — he was a direct descendent of the Prophet Muhamad and with a verified family tree to prove it. The Bedouin tribes in the Transjordan bordered the tribes of the Negev and the Northern Sinai — but their borders had nothing to do with state borders between Israel and Jordan. Some portions of the Huzail Tribe physically resided in the State of Jordan, and so "belonged" to Maira, and vice versa. For the same reason, the wedding also had a special envoy of the King of Saudi Arabia.

Ismail's grandfather was delighted. Maira was his only daughter. Though she was considered Bedouin Princess of the Negev, the succession wars between his brothers and nephews over his position as leader were already heating up. The whole Rakefet issue did not really interest him. As far as he was concerned, the ambassadors of the various countries were there to honor his daughter marrying off her son — and to recognize her, as his only child, as the legal heir of Sheikh Salman Al Huzail. While traditional Bedouin society did not accept women as leaders, even Bedouin society had to move forward. As far as he was concerned, this wedding was about making a queen out of his princess daughter, Maira Salman.

Faina booked a room at the Bereshit Hotel in Mitzpe Ramon, where she was briefed by the NSA prior to the wedding. They explained to her that Ismail's mother, Maira Salman, was a Bedouin Princess, but that, as a woman, she lacked any status and had no authority. In practice, Faina saw how Maira stood and received the guests, moving on to small talk with the important guests. She casually passed by the heads of certain families who were discussing affairs in hushed tones with the police chief of the South District. "After over 15 years," she said, "I would be happy if you would honor this marriage by ending the feud."

Maira's character fascinated Faina. Faina tracked her with her eyes and knew her for the strong woman she was. The body language of the men surrounding her, she noticed, was that of men who saw her as their superior. Faina was all too familiar with those gestures from the men around her. She too, as the deputy chair of NASA, was an aggressive woman, always surrounded by subordinates. In addition to her bodyguard, the embassy also gave her a translator in case she had to talk with Arabic or Hebrew speakers. The translator was a Bedouin who worked at the embassy.

Faina now asked the translator what Maira was saying. The translator told Faina that Maira had said that she would be happy if the feud between the two families ended that day.

"Actually," the translator added, "it was more of an order than a request."

"Why was that an order?" Faina asked.

"It's like the Emperor of Japan asking a Japanese citizen to do something," the translator explained. "The citizen doesn't have to honor the request — the emperor has no formal power in the Japanese constitution. But it would be disgraceful to refuse — even if acceding to his request cost him his life — just as Fukushima nuclear reactor employees entered irradiated zones during 2011, motivated by his exhortations to do all that was necessary to contain the leak.

And indeed, those were the gestures Faina noticed most amongst Maira's audience. Maira's power derived precisely from her contradictions. She was a feminist and a world-renowned researcher and doctor who was careful to toe the line set out by the traditional Bedouin code. She was not involved in either national or tribal politics in any formal way. Some of her children served in the Israeli Army, whereas others did not. Faina understood that the NSA had no idea of the significance of the goings-on in this wedding and did not realize that it was possible for a Bedouin woman to exercise such authority.

What Faina did not realize was that what she was seeing, in real time, was nothing short of a revolution in Bedouin society, a revolution which would echo throughout Muslim society in Israel and beyond — just as Ismail's grandfather intended.

Maira passed by Faina, together with Ismail and his new wife, and Ismail introduced everyone to one another, including Faina to his mother. Maira chatted with Faina and the two powerful women soon established rapport between each other.

"You know," Maira told Faina in a moment of honesty, "I never expected Ismail to amount for much in his life. All of his brothers are doctors, and Ismail, who is not a doctor, ended up surprising me."

Faina, who was nibbling on a pastry suddenly bit down on something hard and gasped, as a sharp pain pierced her mouth.

"Oh," Faina said and raised her hand to her mouth, "I think I just cracked my tooth."

Maira looked over Faina in concern. "I'm an oral doctor and a dentist," she said, "come with me to the adjoining tent and I'll look you over properly."

Once they had some privacy, Maira used her iPhone to shine light into Faina's mouth and she carefully examined her tooth and oral cavity. After a few seconds she stepped back.

"Well, you didn't break a tooth," she told Faina, "But I want to see you tomorrow at my pharyngal department in Soroka at 8:00 am sharp." Faina began to protest, but Maira cut her off authoritatively.

"No, this can't wait, not even to tomorrow afternoon," she told her, "If you would rather go to another medical center, I can make reservation for you for tomorrow morning in any hospital in Israel, but it has to be tomorrow morning."

Maira's tone and insistence alarmed Faina and she showed up the next morning at Soroka at 8:00 am. An embassy security guard escorted her to the Pharyngal department. Maira had not yet arrived, but the nurse, who had been informed of her arrival, prepared her. When Professor Maira Salman entered, Faina was already seated on the dentist's chair, lamps shining at her mouth. The security guard stood right beside her.

"Are you a relative?" Maira asked him briskly.

"No, doctor," he responded.

"Then please clear the room. You can wait outside." Maira's authoritative tone had him moving before he even noticed Faina nodding her consent. She smiled at his back — Maira was certainly a unique character, she thought.

After a short examination, Maira sat down, facing Faina and spoke to her directly.

"You have a tumor in your mouth. I need to perform a biopsy to see whether it is malignant," she said.

Faina stared at her, speechless.

"So, what now?" she asked after a few seconds.

"The secretary will take care of everything," Maira told her, "Don't worry — I work both in Israel and in the United States and the medical services in Israel are as good or better than the American norm. Israelis also have a longer life expectancy than the Americans.

"We will know for sure what type of tumor you have only after we analyze the results of the biopsy. We will analyze the results; both preliminary results, however, indicate a strong possibility it is malignant. My worry is that it may have already metastasized. We will just have to wait in hope. If this is a non-metastatic tumor, you will have to undergo an operation. If there are tumors, it is a more complex procedure," she finished.

Faina got on the phone as soon as she left Soroka. After a series of consultations with expert oncologists in the United States, who examined the results of the biopsy, the CT-PET, and Faina's oral cavity, a consensus was reached by all: her best bet was to make sure Professor Maira Salman be the one to operate on her. She was the leading surgeon for pharyngal cancers, and it was rare for her to perform such relatively simple surgeries.

This was how Faina's and Maira's relationship began. They spoke with each other by phone on a near weekly basis and would usually meet every month or two. Maira would consult with Faina on matters related to the politics of the Bedouin in the Middle East, while Faina would consult with Maira on matters related to Rakefet. Shlomo and Galit remained unaware of this communication channel, which the NSA effectively ran, defining Maira, whom Faina thought of as a bosom friend, as an agent of influence.

Part E: The Moon

1.

The NSA had a small but significant advantage over the other intelligence agencies, since they controlled the communications channel between Faina and Maira, Ismail's mother. The information they acquired through this channel enabled them to decipher several riddles. First and foremost, they identified Joel, Nadav and Adam as the secret keepers. Ismail himself thought Joel was the senior secret keeper, because academically, Joel was clearly the most senior. Moreover, he was oftentimes presented in professional discussions of the three. In these discussions Joel was clearly the senior individual of whom Adam and Nadav listened to and respected.

Joel, who was divorced and content to be single for many years, did not at first understand what Daniela wanted from him, but her tenaciousness paid off. Daniela was able to secure Joel's detailed report on the Plane 2 malfunction and rescue, but its salient points had already long since been transferred via Faina. The Israeli GSS, which constantly monitored all of Rakefet's senior executives, easily noticed the NSA's machinations, but knew, through their compromise of Hadas, Adam's wife, that Joel was not one of the core secret keepers. Furthermore, the GSS was quite satisfied to have the NSA fruitlessly bark up the wrong tree. On the other hand, they made great efforts with Hadas, developing a strong friendship between her and Irit, an experienced GSS agent. Still, they were encouraged by the NSA's success with Joel, which proved that perseverance would eventually triumph.

By the next directors meeting, there were already four new directors. Dr. Badai, the Indian representative, was the youngest board member. Then there was Charles, the European Union representative, a tall and mustached French space engineer, and Evgeny, a Russian engineer who moonlighted for the FSB. Lastly, Matsushima was the Japanese representative. A fighter plane pilot from the Japanese SDF, a petite woman whose small appearance belied a tenacious disposition. Galit remarked acidly that at least on the board, women were equally represented. During that meeting they determined to create a separate multinational team for each mission. Each would be headed by an engineer selected by one of the directors. The team chief would report directly to Rakefet's management.

On the technical side that engineer would be subordinate to Joel, Rakefet's CTO. Administrative issues could be directed by the engineer to Shlomo, the CEO.

The moon flight and landing plan team was assigned to NASA (the Americans).

The Lunar settlement and life design team was the responsibility of the CNSA (the Chinese).

The Helium 3 mining design team was assigned to the Russians and the Japanese (in fact, the Japanese were assigned to make sure the Russians, who had much experience in mining in difficult conditions, but less experience in meticulous planning and avoiding catastrophic accidents, did not screw the pooch).

The Mars flight plan team was the responsibility of the Israelis (this would be the first time IAI's Space Division was given an essential part to play).

The Mars settlement and life plan was assigned to the Europeans and Indians.

In addition, two new 787 Dreamliner planes, not the old 767's, were flown into Ben Gurion Airport. These planes were repurposed into spaceships with all of the hard learned lessons they had acquired over the past few years. One had been prepared in China, and one in the United States, and two more were slated Airbus A350 to arrive in the upcoming months from Japan and Germany.

IAI now needed only to install the helium rocket engines, and all of the associated systems, in all of these planes. The American army designated a site near the Buchholz Air base in the Pacific Ocean's Marshall Islands where the engines could be activated on the ground. An area where NASA would ensure no people would be present in a range of twenty kilometers — a place previously used to test atomic bombs. Once the nuclear rocket engines were installed on the planes, together with their hydraulic system, they were directly flown to Buchholz Air Base. There, they were installed in the special ground testing systems designed and prepared in NASA. Only then were the rocket engines activated and calibrated on the ground, without risking the plane flipping over.

And so, the new planes stood, calibrated and ready for action, on the runway of Ben Gurion Airport. They now had more planes than flight crews, for Avi had yet to regain consciousness. The company chose to train an Indian pilot to take Avi's place as soon as possible, and to bring the complement of each nation represented by the board to two flight crews - one more American and Chinese crews, and two new European, Indian, Russian, and Japanese flight crews.

Helium 3 mining

The source of the helium 3 isotope was from the core of the sun, where fusion of hydrogen to helium occurs, resulting in the heat and radiance which makes life on Earth possible. Part of that helium was emitted from the sun as helium 3. This helium, together with other charged particles, made up the phenomena knows as solar wind. This wind, emitted from the upper layers of the sun, move at a speed of over 250 kilometers per second, to every direction in space. The solar wind is emitted from the sun at that speed, which means that the solar wind also reaches planet Earth. Fortunately, the Earth's atmosphere and magnetic field prevented wind from reaching the surface. In their absence, Earth would be sterilized of life. And yet, the impact of solar winds on our planet does leave a trace noticed by mankind since ancient times — the polar lights, or Auroras. These lights are generated by the impact of the solar wind on the Earth's magnetic field, but the charged particles within it do not reach the surface.

In contrast, the solar wind does impact the lunar surface directly, for the moon lacks both magnetic field and atmosphere. Thus, the solar wind and its helium 3 particles have bombarded the moon over billions of years, leaving its sand suffused with Helium 3 to the depth of about one meter. Heating the lunar sand to six hundred degrees Celsius releases the helium 3 as a gas — and then all that is required is to pump the gas into storage tanks.

All that was needed to set up a sustainable helium 3 mining operation was large electric tractors capable of working on the lunar surface. They would gather moon dust, deposit it in large electric kilns and then, after the dust was heated to remove the helium 3, deposit the depleted dust back in place.

The Japanese and the Russians were asked to build electric tractors and kilns that could be broken down into parts that would fit into the plane. Both had to be able to plug in to the electric grid that would be constructed on the moon by the Chinese, who were responsible for life support and infrastructure on the moon.

Life infrastructure on the moon

For long-term habitation on the moon, there is no alternative to living underground, where humans would be protected from the solar radiation. Fortunately, both Moon and Mars were suffused with underground lava tunnels.[24] Though both celestial bodies are now cold and geologically inactive, when they cooled down, massive tunnels, hundreds of kilometers long and hundreds of meters wide, were left behind. The plan was to render those tunnels habitable and capable of supporting life.

There were several locations on the moon, and Mars as well, where these tunnels opened up to the surface. The moon landing had to be performed near such a portal, which would of course have to be blocked by a wall impermeable to air, and with another two walls about a kilometer apart, to close the tunnel off from the rest of the tunnel system. This space, a kilometer in length and up to three hundred meters in width, could then be gradually pumped full of air and rendered habitable. Helium 3 reactors would be used to light the space. With lighting and air, agriculture would become possible. Indeed, the pressurized cavern would constitute a complete ecological system which could exist for an almost unlimited period of time, without any connection to planet Earth. Every such tunnel would be titled an "alternate world."

The plan was to construct three such alternate worlds on the Moon and three more on Mars, so that there would be a backup habitat in case of a malfunction on one or more alternate worlds. They would be named World 1, World 2 and World 3.

It would take many years to construct such a world through conservative design and planning. Accordingly, the Chinese government were put in charge because they knew how to carry out projects which would take years in the West, in mere months.

---

24. Molten liquid stone.

2.

Matters began to move along quickly now that they had a surplus of space planes. The American team circumvented the Moon. On the Apollo flights, when the spaceship faced the dark side of the Moon, there was no communication with the spaceship from Earth, and everyone was tense, waiting to see if the spaceship would emerge from the other side of the Moon or not.

This time, the size of the spaceplanes enabled a much larger cargo, including five orbital transponders which were seeded when the plane entered orbit around the moon. These satellites orbited the moon, each observing and communicating with the next satellite over the horizon, both ahead and behind it in orbit. This enabled them to communicate both with each other and with Earth on the one hand, and with the plane on the other. In this manner, a continuous communication was maintained with the planes, even when they were on the dark side of the Moon.

During the flight, two revolutions around the Earth were to be performed at a height of 40,000 kilometers. It took around four hours to reach this altitude, rising up in a spiral from the Kármán Line at minimal throttle from the plane.

Once an altitude of 40,000 kilometers was reached, all systems were examined to ensure no malfunctions developed, the thrust of the engines was increased to around half the throttle, and acceleration continued to a speed of 80,000 kilometers per hour (a bit more than twenty kilometers per second). This speed was reached at the halfway point to the Moon. At this point, the throttle remained roughly the same, with the same thrust in the engines, but the plane was turned around so that the thrust would decelerate the plane as it approached the Moon. The flight to the Moon therefore took place at an average speed of 40,000 kilometers per hour. Since the distance to the

Moon is around 360,000 kilometers, this part of the flight to the Moon lasted around nine hours.

The plane then entered an orbit around the moon. The first moon mission remained in orbit for three days and performed a large number of missions. It distributed the relay satellites, photographed the intended landing sites and the openings of the tunnels. The flight was crewed by the American pilot and co-pilot, but also included Japanese engineers that examined the areas where Lunar dust was to be gathered for Helium 3, as well as Chinese engineers who identified sites to establish nuclear power stations. The decision to ensure a triple back-up for each part of the infrastructure meant that each world required three energy sources, which meant nuclear power stations located seven and a half kilometers from the entrance to the habitat's entrance tunnel, in a triangle formation. The infrastructure requirements dictated by this distance and duplication were considerable but viewed as unavoidable in order to safeguard against a potential point failure.

Since there was no air on the moon, the transmission cables could be very thin and still carry over ten million volts. With no wind and a much lower gravity, the high voltage pillars could also be far less massive. All this was very important, for every component had to be brought on the planes from Earth.

In the return flight, a long-foreseen problem came to be. Because the speed of the plane reached over twenty kilometers per second — twenty times the speed of a rifle bullet — any asteroid, or even a debris fragment less than a millimeter in diameter, that collided with the plane would penetrate it easily, smashing through the plane until it emerged on the other side, destroying all in its path — including crew members. To reduce such a danger, they upgraded the radar installed at the nose of the plane to a more sophisticated one capable of identifying such particles a hundred kilometers away from the plane.

The radar was directly connected to the flight computer, and as soon as it identified such an obstacle, performed a very rapid course correction. It had to be extremely rapid indeed, since at twenty kilometers per second it only had five seconds to correct the course before running into an obstacle a hundred kilometers away. There was no possibility of halting, and even if there was, the deceleration would have killed the passengers. Of course, even a course correction that would prevent a collision would generate considerable acceleration. As misfortune would have it, the radar identified a two-centimeter sized particle on one return flight from the Moon.

The correction performed by the flight computer pasted the entire crew to the ceiling. Quite by chance, Rotem and Noa were the pilots, and were, thanks to force of habit, strapped into their seats. But the rest of the crew were all injured, to a greater or lesser extent. One of the engineers broke his hand, and another cracked two ribs. But none were in critical condition, and they landed at Ben Gurion Airport in accordance with the flight plan.

Adam was tasked with improving the system so that it would be able to perform the maneuver without killing the crew, even at a speed of two hundred kilometers per second — the planned speed for the Mars flight. Shlomo lauded Rotem and Noa for wearing their belts on the flight and added the requirement for pilots to be buckled up at all times to the growing procedure list.

On the next flight, there were ten passengers and three pilots, including the lone remaining Israeli pilot. They split shifts throughout the five days of the flight, one day heading up, three days orbiting the Moon, and another to return. The business class chairs installed for the crew and passengers on all the planes proved themselves, as the crew was able to sleep properly, as were the engineers, who kept busy photographing and mapping the various planned landing sites, world-habitats, power stations, and their alternates.

The next day, a Sunday, another flight embarked with the Chinese flight crew, but this time it orbited the moon for less than six hours, about three low altitude circumnavigations, so they were back by Tuesday night.

The Moon, unlike the Earth, does not rotate around its axis. The Earth's gravity applies such a powerful influence on the moon that it prevents rotation. The Moon, therefore, always shows the Earth on the same side, so that the observable portion of the Moon remains the same to an earthside observer. When the Earth facing side of the Moon is fully illuminated by the sun, it appears full.[25] When the Moon is dark to earthside observers, it's "Dark Side" is actually being illuminated.

The flight carrying the Chinese crew left during the New Moon, so that they could see the dark side of the Moon during their Lunar Circumnavigation. The images were amazing and quite different from the view of the Moon they had grown up seeing in the heavens. The crew decided that Noa and Rotem would perform their first Moon landing, given their more extensive experience. However, it was neither Rotem nor Noa who first stepped on the Lunar surface, but the four American astronauts they carried. Faina, at the behest of her political leaders, had insisted upon that.

In order to simulate the landing, the Americans constructed a new program to mimic the 767 flight. In addition, all sorts of hydraulic parts which looked like adjustable legs were meant to support the plane on the uneven surface of the Moon. The assembly program for the stands included three days for assembly and three weeks for ensuring soundness. This was a new requirement in Rakefet's operations. Until that point, the lion's share of the time was invested in construction and installation, whereas inspections and quality control were neglected. Now,

---

25. When we look exactly from the same direction there is a lunar eclipse.

with the Americans and Chinese running things, priorities were reversed.

On Wednesday, upon the return of the Chinese crew, Rotem and Noa also embarked on Lunar circumnavigation, to ensure that they would be fully experienced in all stages of the journey in preparation for the Moon landing. On Sunday, they left for the United States to train on the new simulator, a program which had been designed to last an entire month of intensive training.

3.

Prior to the Moon landing, Galit, Chair of the Board of Directors, decided to hold a symposium in which they would each make presentations reflecting their areas of expertise. Galit opened with a detailed explanation of the concept of a "philosopher king," while Chou followed with "the Dark Forest" and Faina concluded with the "CAT rules."

Philosopher King

Determining the control mechanism of any given organization is important in order to understand the function of an organization, those within it, and its motivation. The organization can be a military unit, a state - or a commercial company."

Galit began: "While Rakefet is neither a state nor an army, its influence is greater than that of most countries. It is therefore important for you, those who control the company, to understand the mechanism of control. The Rakefet articles state that the purpose of the company is to work towards the preservation of life on Earth — and particularly, the survival of human life. Thus, each member of the Board of Directors must exercise his or her personal judgement, regardless of the country which appointed them, in service of human survival."

"I don't see the problem" said Charles, the European representative, out of his square on Zoom.

"Companies, and particularly multinational companies, have immense strength," Galit explained. "Consider the political and economic power of Google, Amazon, Microsoft and other mega corporations. Each has a yearly cycle greater than that of most countries in the world. In other words, their political power is far from negligible. Their goal is to increase their bottom line as much as possible for the benefit of their shareholders. There have been overpowerful corporations in the past, such as Bell Corporation.[26] But the federal government rightfully broke it up into many small companies in order to limit its power. The contemporary Federal government cannot, and does not want, to break up Google, for this would sharply curtail the power of the United States and enable foreign companies to compete in the markets Google currently dominates."

Galit paused, considered the boredom on the faces of the others through the Zoom screen, and continued on regardless.

"Rakefet may well dominate the majority of the world's energy production within three years. This alone will make it immeasurably more powerful, economically and politically, than Google. In addition, Rakefet will control the ability to freely move within the Solar system. Rakefet will generate new horizons for humanity on the one hand, but on the other, it will also generate growing understanding, by both states and individuals, that the survival of humanity depends on Rakefet's success. This cannot but undermine the legitimacy, and hence the power, of governments when compared to the might of Rakefet."

"If we examine different forms of government, we will see that Socrates and Plato did not consider democratic rule to be good. And this was at a time when government was truly democratic. Every essential issue was brought to a vote by all of the citizens of Athens. Control, even of the army, was rotated between the representatives of the different quarters of the city. The famous battle in Marathon in which the Persians were expelled from Greece for a time, took place on a day the military commander had been switched. The new commander, who woke up on the wrong side of bed, decided to bellicosely assault the Persians with a small handful of Athenian warriors, most not from his quarter. To everyone's surprise the Athenians

---

26. An American phone company.

defeated the Persians, who could not believe the Greeks were really attacking them. Until the very last moment, the Persians maintained most of their forces as a reserve, since it was clear to them that this assault by the small Athenian force was a mere ruse. Once they realized their mistake, it was already too late. Panic had spread and the battle was lost."

The other directors showed marginally more interest at the unfamiliar retelling of the story behind the famous Greek victory. "Plato and Socrates were probably the first to raise the concept of a philosopher king as a desired form of government. Many philosophers, to this day and age, elaborated on their model, considering it to be an optimal form of government — provided, of course, a reliable method to produce an enlightened philosopher king could be developed. It is worth noting, however, that this model has, and is, implemented far more widely than you might think — because it was developed in contrast to direct Athenian democracy, not our representative democracy. Indeed, representative democracy reflects an integration, at varying dosages, between the principles of enlightened kingship and Athenian democracy. Governance in the United States, for example, is run by a president, not so different from a king, except elected directly by the body of citizens to be their enlightened philosopher king for a period of four years, with an option for another four. The limitation of his term for a period of eight years is part of a complex system of checks and balances, including separation of power, limitations on authority and so forth. In Israel and in other parliamentary democracies, it is the parliament which, via a different system of checks and balances, elects a prime minister to act as our enlightened philosopher king."

"The definition 'enlightened' is not simple. In many cases one can rely on the definition of its opposite to get a better idea of what enlightened means. A certain degree of wisdom, to be sure, but superlative wisdom, even wisdom such as beholden by King Solomon, is not enlightenment. Corruption represents the opposite of enlightenment, which cherishes honesty and integrity. Concern solely for oneself and one's immediate friends and relations is not enlightenment — an enlightened king must show concern for all humanity. For those familiar with the value scale in Lawrence Kohlberg's developmental theory, an enlightened king's values must match the sixth level, that of the "Universal Ethical Principles.

"But let us return to our own dilemma. In the upcoming period, we may well discover that we are humanity's philosopher kings. We are not a regular commercial company who seek nothing more than expanding our profit margin. Rather, we wish to be an enlightened king. The way we sought to manufacture this enlightened king, to the best of our ability, is to establish a board from which to control Rakefet's abilities. Our directors have no shareholder representation, other than those of its founders. The board, all of you present, are representatives of the enlightened and powerful world. Moreover, you will read in the company's fine print that, once the valuation of the company exceeds one billion dollars — which we have long since achieve — the company may no longer allocate dividends at values greater than its yearly inflation, relative to the stock valuation. In other words, the stock has become a type of government bond. All this was done in order to keep Rakefet focused on human survival and steer it away from being a profit-oriented company."

"Further note," she continued, "that the articles limit each representative on the board to an eight-year term, much like the president of the United States. The international academy has a single representative, the chair. The founders chose me to serve as the representative of academia, but the two hundred leading institutes in the world will have to prepare a mechanism to select my replacement after my four-year term is up.

"In addition, there is a representative of the founders, who currently serves of the CEO of Rakefet. Shlomo fills this term currently, but his term shall end within eight years."

"The remaining representatives are you, the representatives of China, the United States and the UK, the EU, Japan, Russia and India. Your term shall be no less than two years, but no more than eight. You have been appointed by the government who sent you, but once you have been appointed, your priority is the survival of humanity, not the country that sent you. In addition, your commitment to secrecy is absolute, which means you may not transfer any confidential Rakefet information, not even to the governments which appointed you. These details are known both by you and by your governments, who have signed these provisions — as did you, personally.

"It is very important to me to provide you with a comprehensive explanation about the concept of the enlightened king," said Galit, "as it is all too easy to slip from a position of king, to ruthless dictator. The danger is twice as great when the tasks we face are so essential, such as saving humanity. Tasks in which the ends justify the means."

"The darkest tyrants of the 20th century enjoyed the support of an overwhelming majority of the citizens. Indeed, Hitler was voted into office. Most likely, Stalin and Franco in the USSR and Spain respectively would likely have won a free election, had they chosen to hold one."

Galit looked around the table and concluded: "That is why the importance of absolute integrity in the decisions we make here as Rakefet's board of directors is so great; much greater than that of any government. Any indictment served in any country against any of our members for anything involving corruption will result in immediate suspension of that member from our board."

The Dark Forest

"Following my review of the weight of duty as I see it, I would like Professor Chou to explain the 'Dark Forest' theory," Galit continued and sat down, making way for Professor Chou.

Professor Chou had hitherto always appeared on Zoom with his face alone. This time, he presented his full body; a short, rotund Asian man. He seemed set to play the evil villain in a Bond film, with Sean Connery as Bond. But when he stood up to polish his glasses, he clearly found it difficult to break into his monologue. Indeed, he seemed to find speaking to a crowd difficult — which made him seem like an affable uncle to the other board members. Galit suspected that the effect was quite deliberate.

Directing his gaze at the camera and his audience, he hesitantly began: "It is commonly accepted that life forms wherever conditions are suitable for its development within a period ranging from several million to three hundred million years. In our galaxy alone, there are hundreds of billions of stars. In recent years it has become apparent that many, apparently most, have planets orbiting them. Moreover, a significant number have planets in the "Goldilocks zone" that is suitable for the development of life — not too close to the sun (too hot) or too far away (too cold). Spectral analyses have revealed that these locations have both water and carbon compounds; the building blocks of earth-based life. Their worlds coalesced into their present form billions of years ago — so they must contain life!"

"Scientific development teaches us that whenever we thought ourselves to be unique, we turned out to be wrong. When we thought the Earth was the center of the universe — we were wrong. When we thought the location of our sun in the galaxy was unique — we were wrong. When we though our galaxy was unique — we were wrong. There are billions of galaxies similar in shape to the Milky way, and we are neither particularly large nor particularly small. Moreover, we are projected to collide with the Andromeda galaxy within a few billion years, just like galaxies all over the universe collide with one another."

"Today, given all the knowledge we have accumulated, it is sheer nonsense to believe life is unique to our planet and solar system. Given that statistical certainty, why can't we detect signs of life on radio waves coming in from the myriad stars of our galaxy? There are several possible explanations. First, we have generated artificial radio waves for less than 200 years. This is only a tiny fraction of our 4.5 billion long planetary history. In other words, should humanity destroy itself in the upcoming years, which it likely will, it is unlikely that our alien counterparts will pick up our radio waves in the brief interval when our broadcasts reach their planet — because they will likely either be too technologically unadvanced to do so, or will be in the aftermath of their own extinction event apocalypse. On the other hand, an intelligent race, perhaps even us, may well recognize the danger of self-destruction in time, and hence develop technologies or social-political institutions which will forestall self-destruction. But even if only a tiny percentage of the Galaxy's species should survive, we should be able to pick up millions of such worlds — and we can't. There are none to be found.

"And this is where the 'Dark Forest' theory comes in. There is a hunter in the dark forest. The hunter sees anyone who lights a lantern to see, and he will kill it. That is why the only animals to survive in the forest, by a process of Darwinian selection, are the animals who learned not to light a lantern. In other words, a hunter civilization will eliminate any civilization that reveals itself. The hunter strategy of eliminating anyone lighting a lantern is also a survival strategy. When two civilizations meet, one almost inevitably enslaves or exterminates the other. This is what happened less than 50,000 years ago, when Homo sapiens became the sole survivor of dozens of archaic human species. This is what happened during the age of discovery, when Europeans encountered Native Americans and Sub-Saharan Africans.

The encounter between Neanderthal man and Homo sapiens also demonstrated another important issue in the old argument between the relative importance, or rather dominance, of realistic-mathematical men, and humanistic-literary men. In the modern age it is often wrongly assumed that the realistic type dominates the verbal type. And yet, it was Neanderthal man, with its huge well-developed brain, that was conquered and utterly exterminated by modern Homo sapiens, whose realistic brain was inferior, but whose baruka region[27] was more developed. The Homo sapiens' abilities enabled them to function as a group and push out the Neanderthals. It was more important for any military commander or corporate executive to know what made his subordinates, colleagues, superiors, allies and rivals tick, than to be able to solve differential equations. So, what mattered more to group survival was humanistic rather than realistic capabilities."

"But let us return to the problem of the hunter," said Chou. "If I, a sentient species on some alien world, see artificial radio waves coming from some other world, and I have the technology to destroy that other world, then I should very much do so. Otherwise, that world will destroy mine once they spot me. You might think it is only worthwhile for me to destroy worlds at my technological level or higher, but you would be wrong.

"You would be wrong because I have no idea what the technological progress speed is on the other world. It may be that the world I see is far less developed than mine, but its techno-

27. A region in the brain responsible for verbal communication and the ability to interact in groups.

logical progress rate is greater than that of my own world. At the moment that world might be less developed than my own, but the world that I see is dozens of light years away from me, and the balance of power may change by the time we reach each other. Thus, instead of being ripe for subjugation, the other world might subjugate mine. Therefore, if I can destroy the other world — I should. My Darwinian chances of survival are higher if I do — which means the surviving advanced worlds are likely to either be aggressive hunters, or very quiet.

"It follows that lighting a lantern in a dark forest is a very dangerous thing to do," Galit stepped in. "We know that both Chinese and American satellites picked up on the unique electro-magnetic radiation that the helium rocket engine emits. At first, they did not know what it was. This engine will enable our civilization to move freely within the Solar System — and probably, eventually, beyond. If I were a hunter in the Dark Forest of our galaxy, then I would be prowling for that unique radiation which would mark out a civilization worth destroying."

"Moreover" Chou added, "the philosophy of astronomy divides civilizations into several ranks."

"How can you rank a civilization you don't even know exists?" Charles asked.

"Well," Chou replied, "you don't need to see a black hole in order to measure it, know the circumference of its event horizon and hence, figure out its mass or other parameters. As in Alice in Wonderland, you cannot see the cat, only its smile. By the same measure, you don't need to see a hypothetical civilization in order to rank it." Chou paused and took a measured sip of his tea before dropping the bombshell. "The lowest rank of civilization, rank 0, is defined as a sentient species that can only exploit the resources of his own planet."

"So, we are at the exact same level as prehistoric man?" Charles, who was not very tactful, burst out again.

Chou smiled, though Galit was not sure if it was at Charles' outburst or his deduction.

"Yes, in terms of an astronomic scale of billions of years, the evolutionary difference between you and prehistoric man 300,000 years ago, is negligible," Chou said sedately before continuing, like a teacher explaining the world to little children. "A civilization capable of exploiting the resources of its native Solar System, such as our goal of mining Helium 3 from the moon, is considered to be a rank 1 civilization. A rank 2 civilization can exploit the resources of its surrounding star cluster."

"The moment we ascend to rank 1," noted Galit, "the neighboring hunters have a much greater interest in taking us down."

Chou, who always enjoyed virtual ping pong, did not miss the opening.

"When we bring in gold from Mars, it will upgrade us to a rank 1 civilization" he said, examining Faina's face.

The issue of Martian gold had always been the elephant in the room. Everyone, other than Charles, knew that the Americans had already discovered Mars had vast quantities of easy-to-mine gold. Faina did not fall for Chou's trap, however.

"If and when," Faina said with a smile. She did not even notice she was on mute.

Cat 5

"I will now give the floor to Faina, so she can give us some idea of the problems life faces in the Solar system," said Chou.

Faina began speaking, and only then understood her Zoom was on mute. She sheepishly switched on her microphone and repeated her opening sentence.

"There is a non-negligible possibility that life exists, at least in the form of micro-organisms, in the Solar System. I mean micro-organisms such as bacteria. Such bacteria may be dangerous to life on Earth, and, conversely, the bacteria we carry might be equally harmful to whatever life exists on the planets we visit. The advanced civilizations of the Western Hemisphere, such as the Inca, Aztecs, Maya and others did not collapse due to the conquest of the Spanish soldiers, but by the plagues they brought with them. The Spaniards inadvertently brought bacteria and viruses with them to which the Native Americans had no resistance, resulting in the death of nine out of every Native Americans exposed to them."

"NASA has done extensive work to survey the chance of encountering extraterrestrial microorganisms in our Solar System. Our mapping includes five categories ranging from category 1, where the chances for life are negligible, to category 5, where a significant, though still small, chance exists for microorganisms to be found. There are four locations in the Solar System which reach category 5: the Enceladus Moon of Planet Saturn, the Europa Moon of Planet Jupiter, Mars, and our own Moon."

"We have no plans at the moment of colonizing Enceladus," Galit noted in summary, "but we certainly do plan on setting up outposts on the other two planetary bodies. That is why we are preparing a decontamination system which will ensure no bacteria shall be either imported or exported."

4.

When Rotem and Noa returned from their month-long training on the American simulator, the plane was already ready, having undergone a thorough post-upgrade checkup by the American team, and the pre-flight inspection of the Chinese team. Rotem returned home to Nimrod and her children and informed them that she would be with them for the long weekend, but would have to leave on Sunday morning for the long-awaited moon-landing. The flight was planned for five full days, which meant she would be back by Friday afternoon. They would fly with a relatively large crew — the American and European team, which included the German Dr. Schmidt and the French Mary Givernet, also trained on the simulator, and they would observe them during the landing stage. The flight would also include four Israeli trainees who had already been equipped with spacesuits and begun training on space and lunar operations. None of them would leave the plane at any point, barring malfunctions. Nadav, alongside two engineers, would also accompany the crew in order to supervise the landing process itself, as well as the four American astronauts who knew how to work with space suits outside the plane. They would be required for three stages. In the first stage, while they orbited the moon, two astronauts would leave the pressure chamber, equipped with particularly strong decontaminants to eliminate any bacteria that might latch onto the fuselage. They would spray the fuselage from outside — including the plane wheels and its hydraulic system to keep them from contaminating the lunar surface. In the second stage, they would leave and operate the plane unloading system. There were fifty tons of equipment which needed to be unloaded on the Moon, and this would take place gradually, in various stages. The final stage, would see the American astronauts — once they took off from the Moon and reentered orbit — decontaminate the plane's exterior.

"Why were no decontamination procedures performed on the Apollo flights from the Moon?" Rotem asked.

"On re-entry to Earth the temperature on the exterior of a space shuttle is over a thousand degrees Celsius," Nadav explained, "so they underwent a far more thorough sterilization process than our space planes. As far as infecting the lunar surface was concerned, there was no awareness of this possibility back then."

On Sunday morning they took off. Amazingly, no media leaks occurred and hence there was no particular coverage of this flight beyond the usual crowd of photographers lurking at the perimeter of Ben Gurion Airport to catch a shot of the golden planes.

The flight to the moon, with the requisite Earth orbit, took some 15 hours before they entered lunar orbit. The American astronaut crew entered space and performed decontamination of the plane from outside. The airlock underwent a significant upgrade, enabling them to pressurize and depressurize within ten minutes rather than half an hour. The airlock could now contain two people at once, with all of their equipment, enabling the four astronauts to enter and leave the plane within 25 minutes. The decontamination procedure on the exterior of the plane took around four hours. They practiced the procedure several times first while still in the United States, otherwise it would have taken them over ten hours. Generally, they performed many simulations in each stage of their operations, enabling smooth work.

Rotem and Noa used the time to rest prior to the landing itself. Noa entered Nadav's chambers, which were only separated by a thin curtain, and they immediately fell asleep. Rotem was somewhat jealous of Noa, who did not need to be apart from her partner. The American crew, who were there primarily to observe and study the landing procedure, were at the helm of the plane.

"The landing procedure begins when we are 25 kilometers over the lunar surface flying at a speed of nearly 4,000 kilometers an hour," Nadav explained to them earlier. "But we are orbiting the Moon like a satellite — our energy expenditure during the circumnavigation of the Moon balances out its gravity. This can be performed at a very low altitude, thanks to the moon's weak gravity and lack of atmosphere. Thus, it is possible, even at an altitude of 15 kilometers, to fly at very high speeds. However, the moment you slow down — you fall down. Which means every reduction in speed results in reduced altitude."

"In order to reduce our speed, we will need to fly opposite to our current velocity. And in order to avoid losing altitude we will need to change the orientation of the helium rocket engines at the same time. We can change the wing-engine orientation with the hydraulic system. So, as we approach landing, flying at a horizontal speed but steadily descending speed and altitude, the engines will transition into 90-degree orientation versus the wings. Actually, when the plane touches the ground, the engines will be a bit past the 90 degrees point, because most of the plane's weight is in the front, and we want to balance it out while using as little of the oxygen-hydrogen combustion engine as possible. Since the pilot cockpit is up-front, when the pilot flies backwards he is backing up — as you would if you put your car in reverse. But unlike a car, the plane has no rear-view mirror or rear window, so the pilot must observe the monitor, which is much like the rear camera in newer vehicles — except that he is not backing up carefully at a few kilometers per hour, but at Mach 3."

Rotem performed the process of lowering the plane's altitude from 25 kilometers at a speed of 3,800 kilometers per hour to a bit below a kilometer at a horizontal speed of zero, a total stop, hovering over the lunar surface like a helicopter.

At this point Noa assumed control. Noa slightly changed the direction of the engines via the hydraulic system and enabled the plane to slowly glide forward. The change in direction, together with the advance forward, lowered the nose of the plane. The lowering of the nose exposed the lunar surface from the front windows of the plane, a surface which hitherto had only been visible from the monitors and side windows. As the plane glided forward the lunarscape seemed as if it were taken from a science fiction movie. The drapes behind the cockpit were open, and it was not merely the American team who leaned forward attentively taking in the landing maneuvers, but all 17 passengers — who had spent the entire flight chattering in multiple languages — who now held their breath. They all knew the landing site, which was close to a huge lava tube slated to house the World 2 habitat. World 2 was the Chinese habitat, which, since the Chinese were responsible for constructing all the lunar infrastructure, was first in the construction queue. All of the passengers had seen aerial photographs and simulations of the site from different heights. However now, in real time, it was quite literally breath taking.

As they glided and spun forward, Noa descended to the landing zone. At an altitude of fifty meters, about two hundred meters from the landing point, Noa halted. The helium rocket engines raised massive dust clouds which completely obscured the surface. Noa descended another thirty meters without seeing a thing, relying solely on the ground radar installed in the belly of the plane, even though she knew it would be extremely imprecise within the dust cloud. Now she resumed her slow glide forward, leaving the cloud in its wake. It was now apparent that, though the radar had indicated a twenty-meter altitude, they were actually less than five meters above the surface. Indeed, the belly of the plane nearly brushed the ground. Noa raised the nose of the plane slightly and glided the remaining two hundred meters. When she reached the landing point, she halted. The dust was obscuring everything once again.

Noa activated the tripod mechanism NASA had prepared. The mechanism was much like the hydraulic legs made to stabilize crane operating trucks, balancing the crane by gripping the road. However, in this case, each of the three tripods were able to extend for a length ranging between one and seven meters, so that the plane was capable of standing even on extremely uneven surfaces. On this occasion, the forward leg descended about a meter and a half, the right extended by about four meters, and the left descended some five and a half meters.

When the legs locked in place and the plane was completely level, Noa switched off the engines. As if by magic, the dust cloud disappeared. Unlike on Earth, where the presence of air slows down the descent of dust and keeps it suspended for many minutes, on the Moon, dust falls to the ground immediately. The moment dust ceased to be generated by the rocket engine, it immediately dropped down to provide perfect, clear sight. Once again, the view that was revealed to them was breathtaking, with the lunar surface below sharply contrasting with the blue disc of Planet Earth hanging above them. A palpable sigh of relief washed over the control room, a sigh that was audible in the plane as well. It was early in the morning in Israel, about 24 hours after they had taken off. Shlomo's voice boomed as he congratulated the entire crew.

With the helium rocket engine in operation, there was no oxygen problem. On the contrary, the engine had filled up the empty tanks. But as soon as the engine shut down, all of their oxygen came from the contents of those tanks — enough to supply all 19 people for 25 days.

The Chinese crew was on emergency standby in Ben Gurion Airport in case they failed to perform the ignition. In that case, the team from China would have enough time to fly to the moon and back again twice over before any significant oxygen problems.

The Chinese crew, however, had yet to train on the NASA simulator due to the American Law which had yet to be amended.
The law which forbade Chinese citizens from entering NASA
facilities. CNSA, the Chinese Space Agency, had decided to
develop their own landing simulator, but it was a week out from
completion.

The focus of the mission was now on the American astronaut crew to work outside the plane. According to the plan,
they were to sleep seven hours prior to being certified to exit
the plane in order to begin the nine hour task of unloading
equipment. The rest of the crew had also gone to sleep. The
other crew members now had three days of almost no work
to look forward to, with the exception of the Israeli trainee
team, whose task was to observe, study and remotely assist
the American team.

"And I implore you," Shlomo warned them in advance, "avoid
chatting with the Americans and offering them solutions and
ideas they do not ask for unless you identify a clear and present
danger. Is that understood? That kind of interference may be
acceptable in our culture, but it is not in theirs."

The group dynamics over those three days of enforced indo-
lence was somewhat challenging. While the conditions were
good overall (they each had their own space, better than business class on a regular plane, including a curtain which provided them with a certain level of privacy), without stewards, they
had to prepare their own meals in the plane kitchen. They all
brought along books to read for those three days, but for how
long can one read? They all had laptops, and they all had work
to complete, but they were still left with more time than they
knew how to use.

After completing the flight, Noa and Rotem took up the political argument that had begun between Nadav and the engineers. The non-Israelis on the plane did not understand what

they were shouting about, but they understood the topic was political.

The American crew watched the argument unfold with much perplexity. The loud culture of bellowing arguments in which no one seemed to listen to the other was very odd to them — and at times, hilarious.

"What's so funny," Rotem belligerently demanded.

"We have no idea what your argument is about other than politics," one of the Americans languidly replied, "but it just seems funny when watching it from the sidelines."

This somewhat insulted the Israelis but did not lead them to halt their argument.

"It is more of an ideological argument than a political one," Rotem told them.

"If I could have," Yoav Heller, a yarmulke-wearing engineer continued, "I would have studied just Torah in *yeshiva*[28] and not served in the IDF or studied engineering."

This statement infuriated Nadav. "Those who call themselves ultra-orthodox are nothing more than idolators," he said.

Yoav, the religious fellow, almost lost it there and then but tried to control his anger.

"Why do you say that?" he demanded, voice rising.

"Look, I understand that this infuriates you," Nadav replied, "but your statement makes me angry as well. Secular Jews are always being told they must be considerate of religious Jews, but ultra-orthodox and religious Jews show no consideration for secular people. If you wish, and if you are capable of listening to my arguments, I will explain it to you, but perhaps we had better drop the topic, so that we do not grow angry at one another."

"Religious Jews constantly have to compromise and show consideration to secular citizens," Yoav said from the aisle next

28. A yeshiva is a traditional Jewish educational institution focused on the study of Rabbinic literature.

to an empty seat. "After all, we live in Israel, which is a secular state. For example, the billboards that display near-naked women are not to my liking and I have to look away, just as I must do when walking the streets of Tel Aviv in order to avoid seeing abominations. I do not complain, it is fine, and I do it lovingly, out of consideration for secular people."

Nadav laughed, both to reduce the tension and because Yoav's argument truly amused him.

"In practice, you have taken over the education system, to the point where Darwin's evolutionary theory is no longer even taught in secular schools. Scientifically, in terms of the development of Israel's high-tech industry, not teaching evolution is just as bad as not teaching physics. The technology of the future, from brain science to medicine and any other agricultural or biological development, is based on understanding evolution. The problem, as far as I am concerned, is that liberal secular Jews are not fighting this fundamentalist takeover tooth and nail, because liberal values are not compatible with total investment in such an ideological struggle. That is the 'liberal problem' — by failing to take the offensive and showing how fundamentalist values are harmful to humanity, they are surrendering the field to the fundamentalist, which blames humanity's problems on liberal values. They are exploiting liberal society to undermine and attack it. This is a problem not merely in Israel, but throughout the world. The various fundamentalist movements, Muslim, Jewish and Christian, are grabbing more and more power across the world. But there is no point in continuing this argument — this is not something we will solve here."

Nadav's arguments surprised and saddened Yoav. He shook his head and went to the kitchen to prepare himself a cup of tea.

The unloading crew, which included the four American astronauts, completed their seven-hour rest, donned their spacesuits and left the plane to unload the equipment.

Within nine hours they had unloaded a ton of equipment, amounting to about 160 kilos in lunar gravity. Unloading 160 kilograms on Earth would not, of course, take four highly skilled professionals nine hours, particularly if they had spent much time practicing the unloading in various simulations. Half an hour, tops, and the equipment would be unloaded. But on the Moon, operating in clumsy spacesuits, everything was more complicated. Utilizing various monitors and communication equipment, the American teams had examined the surface from Earth deciding what would go where. Their first target was to unload and assemble the components of a crane which was specifically constructed to help unload the rest of the equipment in a more efficient manner.

They finished unloading everything within the nine hours and returned to the plane. They were supposed to eat and rest, but they weren't all that tired, so they joined the dynamics of the other 'loafers' on the plane. On the eve of their second day on the Moon, they all slept. There was constant light outside, but the crew had made their own day and night by closing the window shutters. The Israeli trainee crew stayed awake in shifts in the cockpit in order to maintain an open line of communication with Earth, so the curtain separating the cockpit and the passenger compartment was closed to enable the other crew to sleep in peace. Cycles of light and dark on every spot on the Moon lasted for 28 days: 14 days of alternating day and night — precisely the same as the lunar orbit around the Earth.

In the morning the unloading crew was roused, and they left the plane (spending thirty minutes depressurizing during exit and pressurizing when they entered anew). It was the third day of the mission, and the task of the unloading crew was to assemble the crane whose components they had unpacked the previous day. This time, they were able to complete the task in half of their allotted time.

"You don't have to return to the plane," Noa told them, "You can get started on unloading the rest of the equipment rather than waiting for the next day."

The crew, while gung-ho to carry on, found the concept of going off-plan at a moment's notice difficult. They consulted with Faina, who also found it hard to cope with the last-minute change in plan, but after consulting with Shlomo, she signed off on continuing the unloading for the remainder of the nine-hour window.

Utilizing the crane, they had to unload another 49 tons of equipment. It included two types of robots. One was a kind of electric Bobcat controlled by a monitor back on Earth. Since there was a communication lag of three seconds from the Earth to the Moon, it was not fully remote controlled — many of its activities were performed autonomically. The second type of robot were paint distribution robots. Indeed, most of the equipment, some 35 tons, was special epoxy paint. The idea was that once the equipment was unloaded, the bobcats would construct runways and landing pads, and the painting bots would coat the entire landing zone with the epoxy, thereby preventing dust from rising up in future flights. A very thin layer of paint was sufficient to prevent the dust from rising.

The unloading crew also assembled a charging station, run on a hydrogen fuel battery, which would enable the robots to charge up until the Chinese crew arrived with the small nuclear reactor. The reactor allowed for charging of heavy equipment which would also arrive.

As soon as they unloaded the first Bobcat, it was put to work. First, it began gathering earth and bringing it to the unloading crane. This enabled the crane to unload equipment and to return helium-3 rich lunar soil to the plane in a single motion.

The second Bobcat they unloaded began preparing paths for the paint-bots. They then unloaded a paint-bot which immediately followed the Bobcat, coating its path with paint. To those observing from the plane windows, this hectic activity looked like a busy anthill, each ant focused on its task in perfect synchronization with one another, dancing to the tune of the hidden queen. After nine hours, around the time of Earth's evening, most the activity was completed. All that remained was to reposition the crane so as not to interfere with the takeoff of the plane.

"I suggest we wrap everything up now," Noa said, "just another half an hour of work and we can fly back."

But Shlomo and Faina both vetoed this, saying the unloading team must return to the plane to eat and sleep.

And so, it was. They entered, rested, ate, and then went to sleep. Surprisingly, the activity of the Bobcats and paint-bots outside made noise that disturbed their rest a little, in spite of the absence of air to carry sound. The Bobcat's were making such a din that the lunar surface shook, transmitting the noise through the plane legs into the fuselage and from there, into the air of the plane and the ears of those within it — but it was a weak and vague noise. After ten hours of rest and recreation, the crews reemerged to wrap up their work on the landing zone. They operated one of the Bobcats to reposition the unloading crane to a location where it could help deliver the next planes without interfering with their takeoff.

The remotely operated bobcats were also assigned to prepare a level landing pad for the next planes and to install a radio transceiver near it that would enable them to land autonomously, without the need for human judgement. The computer on the plane would receive the radio signal and perform the landing on it in an independent manner.

About ten minutes after the unloading crew re-entered the plane, Noa and Rotem were already in their seats in the cockpit, requesting authorization for takeoff. After a brief hesitation from the control room, they were granted it, and they ignited the engines to launch back to Earth. Thanks to the new paint on the landing zone, there was almost no dust during takeoff.

The passengers, peeking out of the windows, saw the crew of ants continue to work, not even feeling that the plane took off and left them on the Moon.

Noa and Rotem brought the plane into orbit around the Moon and handed over control to the Indian crew. The Indian crew was the least experienced. Therefore, in order to gain experience, they performed the entire flight to Earth under the supervision of the American crew. The unloading team once again left to perform decontamination from the outside.

Since the Indian crew flew the plane, and the American team supervised the Indian team, the Americans and Indian were kept far busier than the Israelis — who had already had plenty of idle time on the Moon already.

"Well, I am calm now and really want to hear your arguments," Yoav told Nadav.

"Look," said Nadav, "I am not a religious man, but there are religious people whom I admire for their faith, such as the late Prof. Leibowitz for example. Leibowitz said that when ten people make a minyan and pray in a dirty and smelly market, the place they pray in becomes holy while they pray, just like the burning bush, which returns, at the conclusion of the prayer, to what it was — no more than a bush. In contrast, Leibowitz referred to the Western Wall as a "disco wall" and called to transform the courtyard of the Western Wall into a discotheque." At this point, the Israelis gathered around them, because they had nothing better to do, and Nadav, who did not notice the audience, continued, "there are many spheres that have nothing to do with a physical space. For example, I love Noa. This is an absolute and very tangible truth to me, but there is no physical way to measure my love. I cannot prove that my love for Noa is greater than your love to your partner, and you cannot prove the opposite. By the same measure, the religious sphere is not a physical space. When you mix up the religious spiritual space with the physical space, which is the material space, as in the case of the Golden Calf — that is idolatry."

"The Ultra-Orthodox do not make any golden calves," Yoav said defensively.

"Fundamentalists of all religions, Christians, Muslims and Ultra-Orthodox Jews do precisely that when they seek to subordinate the public sphere to their fundamentalist interpretations. In fact, they function in practice as a single religion, but since they never pause for self-reflection, they focus on differences which are almost entirely cosmetic." By now, Nadav had already taken notice of the crowd of Israelis and others listening in, but he was able to continue speaking as he was on a roll, vocalizing his long-held truth.

"In Israel, fundamentalists who insist on the absolute physical-historical veracity of biblical stories are Messianic fanatics who are actually quite similar to the Medieval Christian Crusaders. The Crusader Kingdoms did not survive for long, and neither will the State of Israel if Messianism gains traction. I believe the Bible, and Judaism, is filled with universal values and principles, from the Ten Commandments through to various rules and norms, some of which may be based on older codices from other cultures, such as the Code of Hammurabi. The State of Israel, based on these values, can be our national Jewish home and endure for many generations to come. Provided, of course, that humanity as a whole survives its self-destructive urges..."

"So long as we all pull together and apply our collective energy and talent to solving our common problems. What

Yeshiva students do is the exact opposite — in unprecedented numbers, greater than the combined number of Yeshiva students in all previous generations, they turn their native talents to idle churning and regurgitation of legalistic interpretations, enforcing narrow anti-science limitations on those who are struggling to contend with the real-world challenges we face, while at the same time, having great multitudes of children whom they cannot support, further burdening the limited resources of the planet." Nadav finally fell silent, breathless, and Yoav and their audience were quiet as well, taking in his words. Noa pressed close to him.

"I liked how your love, a true love, is tangible," she told him with a smile and whispered in his ear: "I love even more that you spoke out like that, before an audience."

After the procedure played out back on home base, an English engineer suggested that the decontamination material be released as a cloud behind the plane. The cloud would then travel in space at exactly the same speed as the plane. As the plane decelerated, the decontamination cloud would scour it back to the front. Acceleration would sterilize it, front to rear.

Most of the people dozed off during the flight back to earth, but everyone woke up for the landing.

About five minutes before the landing, Galit made an announcement on their communication system.

"There are many journalists waiting for you, so be ready to be photographed and recorded from the moment the plane lands," she warned. This did not suit Noa, Rotem, or the French Marie, for they were after almost five days without a shower, with unkempt hair and no makeup.

"Don't worry," Galit told them, "The plane will land, and a sleeve will be attached to the entrance, so they will not see you when you actually exit the plane. I reserved a shower and a professional makeup team for each of you, so that you will only see the journalists 45 minutes later. During your make-over you will also undergo a medical examination."

It turned out that, prior to landing on the Moon, Rakefet had begun transferring video from the plane to various news agencies. Since there were around thirty cameras on the plane, including cameras in the space suits, and about the same number of microphones which picked up the sounds in the plane, a studio was set up to transfer the films, each time from a separate camera. The video was broadcast with a twenty-minute delay, so that the editors at Rakefet could edit out problematic segments. This feed, which was covered by CNN and every other news outlet in the world, enjoyed sky-high ratings. The entire crew were celebrities, and when the segment where Noa and Rotem landed the plane on the moon was released, they became global super-stars. Neither of them had ever been treated to a professional makeup artist make-over. Undergoing the treatment prior to the press conference at Ben-Gurion Airport, they felt somewhat ambivalent. While they enjoyed the upgrade in their appearance, they felt silly with all the frenzy around their make-up and 'look.' It looked good on the cameras anyway.

"So what was it like to walk on the Moon?" the journalists asked. "Actually, we never left the plane," they answered, "only the unloading crew left and actually worked on the lunar surface." That was the truth, but it was a disappointment for the journalists.

Hadas, Adam's wife, was frustrated, since it seemed to her that Adam, who, at first was the central mover and shaker of the company, seemed to now be shunted aside. He wasn't even on the first flight to the Moon. Financially they were doing much better — Hadas had long since become a millionaire. Before entering the second round of investments, Shlomo had allocated ten million dollars to each founding partner. But Hadas never appreciated money. Her concern was that Adam was not being given the credit he was due. She shared those feelings with Irit, a GSS agent planted precisely to capitalize on her resentments. At first, the GSS and the Mossad had fought over who would have jurisdiction in gathering the information, but since this was collection of information within Israel, and as the GSS pointed out Galit's contacts within the Mossad might leak information to her, the prime minister decided to let the GSS take the lead.

Irit certainly knew how to exploit the crumbs of information she received. Hadas, who was aware of the limitations of secrecy, never exposed details or data, and always spoke only about her feelings, experiences and personal frustrations. But Irit knew how to ask 'around' what Hadas shared, without going into names or obviously identifying details, to secure the information she was looking for. Irit soon figured out, and reported, that the real secret keepers were Adam and Nadav. What Irit did not know was that the GSS, unlike the Mossad, had conference rooms with windows — which meant all of the discussions held by the GSS were effectively shared with both the American NSA and the Chinese MSS, whose spy satellites maintained constant laser surveillance of those windows.

The Americans did not buy Hadas's insistence that Adam was the secret keeper. They believed it was her jealousy and resentment talking and held on to their thesis that Joel was the central axis. The Chinese, in contrast, accepted that Adam and Nadav alone were the secret keepers. Additional intelligence gathering revealed that Nadav and his associates had purchased nearly a dozen special substances in Jenin, as well as another seven substances purchased by Adam's associates. These findings, however, merely led the Americans to reject the possibility that Nadav and Adam played a central role in Rakefet, as the idea that Rakefet's central secret keepers relied on this slapdash procurement method was incomprehensible to them.

It was clear to everyone that the core of Rakefet's innovative technology was the superconductor formed by the interface between two crystals. But the number of possible permutations, even after screening out the unlikely ones, was between one and two million.

The Chinese were not deterred. They established a dozen huge institutes, each of which examined around two hundred such variations a week. According to their calculations, that pace was sufficient to provide them with the correct combination within five to ten years. Perhaps, with a little luck, even less than that.

Part F: The Moon Worlds

1.

A "moon world" was actually a volcanic tunnel many kilometers in length, between one hundred and three hundred meters wide, and fifty to one hundred meter high. As aforementioned, they were created from lava tunnels; molten rock, which flowed around a billion years ago on the Moon. The lava cooled and shrunk, generating these underground tunnels. These locations were natural hideouts for human beings who could not survive for long, exposed to solar radiation and meteors showers. Even a tiny meteor, under 0.1 grams in weight, moving at a speed of twenty kilometers per second (and thousands such collided with the Moon every day), could penetrate a space suit and slay an individual without overhead shelter. Such a tunnel, when sealed and filled with air, is a perfect habitat for human, plant and animal life on the Moon.

Three tunnels were selected to establish the American World 1, the Chinese World 2 and the Russian World 3. The Europeans, Indians and Japanese would establish Worlds 4-6 on Mars, but that would only happen a year down the line. Each world would of course house workers from many different countries, but the world would be managed by the Rakefet Board of Directors representative for the respective country.

The country affiliation of each world would define many of its operating parameters, chief amongst them time. The time each world operated under would be that of the managing country. Still, human beings cannot operate according to lunar time, where each day and every night lasts 360 hours. Human beings need a 24-hour cycle to function in a reasonable manner. While the tunnels were completely isolated from the sun, the lighting system would be able to provide residents with a 12-hour day and a 12-hour night, with a gradual transition between the two. The timing, however, of the day and night, would be synchronized with the time used by each country back on Earth. To maintain law and order, they decided to use the legal system of each country in their respective habitats. In the event a true court would be required — the trial would be held in an Earth courtroom via Zoom — in spite of the three second communication lag.

Each country would be entitled to establish research facilities, as well as lease out land for commercial companies.

Each world was obligated to reserve space for at least one hundred Rakefet employees. Furthermore, while each state was permitted to staff up to 1,000 workers in each world in the initial stage, the world was required to possess the capability of providing living conditions for an unlimited period of time for 3,000 people — for all of the residents of all the Moon habitats, as an emergency backup. In this way, each lunar world would constitute a guarantee of survival to all the others. In addition, the world had to maintain means of transporting all of its residents to another lunar world should it become necessary.

Sustainable life needs agriculture. Each world had to allocate sufficient space to agriculture in order to feed 3,000 people. Diversity was critical to survivability, for the appearance of pests or disease in a single agricultural crop on which the habitat depended might easily result in famine similar to the Irish Potato Famine of 1846.

Agriculture not only generated food for the residents of the world, but also involved photosynthesis and the recycling of oxygen from carbon dioxide emitted by human respiration. Agriculture required water, which would at first be imported via the planes. Later on, water would be brought in from the lunar polar regions, where craters hidden from the light of the sun contained massive ice deposits. Elsewhere, the temperature generated by the solar rays unfiltered by an atmosphere, resulted in daytime temperatures over a hundred degrees Celsius, immediately vaporizing water into space. Conversely, during the lunar night, temperatures dropped to minus a hundred and fifty degrees Celsius, freezing water solid.

On Earth, the prospect of agriculture dependent on polar, or even extraplanar water imports, appeared daunting. But given the sealed and self-contained nature of the lunar habitats, long-term, large-scale importation of water would not be necessary, as any water brought into the system would remain within it, rather than evaporating away. Thus, each sealed tunnel was much like earth — the distribution of water in the system changed, but its total amount remained constant over time. On Earth, vaporized water condensed into rain. In the lunar worlds, large condensation machines restored water vapor into water for agriculture and human consumption.

To grow and perform photosynthesis, plants need energy in the form of light. This energy was supplied from two sources. First, from the energy infrastructure constructed for each world by the Chinese based on three helium 3 fueled nuclear fusion plants. Each such power plant was intended to be sufficient in and of itself in order to supply all the energy required by each world. The other two power plants were solely for backup. To ensure they were all working properly, the power plant supplying energy to the world would be changed every day. In addition, each world was equipped with plentiful solar panels, far more productive on the atmosphere-free lunar surface. Such panels could not, of course, provide energy during the lunar night.

Therefore, a stable and reliable energy supply was of the utmost importance. Any interruption of the energy supply might result in the death of all the residents in the world — 1,000 people.

The lighting system within the world-tunnel was based on LED-type semi-conductors. Some, particularly those utilized in the agricultural regions, emitted ultraviolet light, to allow plants to thrive.

In each of the worlds, Rakefet employees were to be in charge of the energy infrastructure. They would also be responsible for the world's airports and the transportation of residents to and from the world. This, in addition to their primary mission — collecting lunar soil, extracting Helium 3 from it, and shipping concentrated Helium 3 to earth. Activity over the next few weeks was divided into several work cycles. Each cycle included a flight to the moon, several days of lunar work, and a flight back. The bobcats, the paint bots, the digger bots and the sealing tarp layer bots remained on the moon and were operated remotely by Earth based teleoperators. The operators worked in shifts cycling between centers in Israel, the United States and Japan, so the various bots were worked for 24 hours straight around the clock.

All the initial work was concentrated on the construction of the Chinese "World 2," so as to provide a stable base for the construction of lunar infrastructure by the Chinese. The American World 1 was intended to house a massive research complex, whereas the Russian World 3, located in a tunnel adjacent to a South Pole crater, would be dedicated to ice mining and water production for all the worlds.

2.

The first lunar work cycle was undertaken by the crew sent by China. Upon completion of training on the simulator they constructed, they took off to the Moon. Rotem, as substitute pilot should a problem arise, Adam and Hadas, Joel and Daniela — whom Joel awkwardly, and belatedly, introduced to his amused colleagues — were all on the flight. Rotem found it very convenient to have a group of Israelis along for the ride. Nadav was thankfully absent from this flight, as he was badly embarrassed by Daniela's transition to Joel. He did not raise the issue with the older scientist, as he did not want to admit, even to himself, that he was sleeping with Daniela even as he and Noa had begun their relationship.

Adam enjoyed the view and the thrill of the flight to the Moon but was simultaneously irritated at the waste of time and idleness. Unlike Nadav, he found it difficult to isolate himself from distractions and work wherever he was. On the other hand, he was glad to see Hadas in high spirits. Hadas formed a connection with Daniela the geologist, who provided in-depth explanations of any piece of lunar rock they brought to anyone prepared to listen. Hadas and Rotem enjoyed both her explanations and her company, and the connection between the three strengthened during the days spent together in enforced proximity during the flight and their lunar stay.

On the flight itself there were no problems, and the dust-free landing was performed on autopilot on a completely level surface prepared by the bobcats and paint bots. Every time a plane landed or took off, the bobcats and paint bots scurried to repair the level landing field and repaint the surface wherever the helium rocket jet sliced through the previous coat of paint. Given the tiny diameter of the jet, only a minute amount of paint and a few minutes work by the bobcats were required to return it to pristine condition.

The plane transported twenty bobcats this time, various types of diggers, and additional hydrogen batteries meant to recharge them until the nuclear fusion reactor arrived — an event slated to occur only next month. The Chinese crew also brought a large number of Chinese space suits with them. In addition, they also brought a pressurized container meant to serve as a shelter for the crew working outside the plane where they could rest without re-entering the plane. The Chinese spacesuits were lighter than their American equivalents and hence easier to work with, but they had a far shorter operational time limit. The American suits had enough oxygen and electricity for thirty hours, while the Chinese suits only had enough for ten hours. Thus, the workers had to take a 30-minute break in the container as their suits recharged. These suits were utilized by five Chinese and the two Israelis who were the trainee crew on the previous flight. There were also two IAI engineers who served as backup in case of a malfunction. The plane bound crew was relatively small this time around, including the two Chinese pilots, Rotem and the engineers — and the three passengers all in all, mostly Israelis. The lunar surface crew included two Israelis and five Chinese people.

Three of the Chinese astronauts occupied themselves with unloading the plane's cargo with the crane left on the lunar surface from the previous flight. First, they lowered a bobcat fixed with a wagon with room for passengers. One member of the Chinese crew took the driver's seat, another Chinese member and two of the Israelis joined as passengers as the bobcat duly drove off into a tunnel, whose entry way was some two hundred meters away from the landing site. As soon as they unloaded additional diggers, they raced after the first bobcat and passed it. They drove far more quickly because they had no cart, and they were not afraid to roll over because they had no people in them. When such a digger rolled over, another digger could easily come to assist in righting it. The small diggers weighed less than four hundred kilos on Earth, which meant they weighed only sixty kilos on the Moon, so that even an unaided man in a spacesuit could roll them over and feel like a superman while doing so.

After a few minutes, the astronauts reached the entrance to the tunnel. The diggers were already busy preparing the way so that the digger with the cart full of people could enter.

Before entry, the crew dismounted and took measurements of the entrance to the tunnel with cameras and laser measuring devices. They saw the opening was similar to a pit in the lunar surface. The opening had collapsed, making it accessible to descend into the pit over the piled-up earth. The pit was a few dozen meters deep, but several hundred meters wide — too wide to place a seal over it. They returned to the cart and began traveling on the path that the diggers had prepared for them. After about another fifty meters, they paused and photographed the tunnel again. They saw the lights from the diggers ahead of them frenziedly clearing the way ahead. These diggers were capable of lifting 2.5 tons, but on the moon, they could lift up to 15 tons — the equivalent of a heavy-duty truck. Thus, to the external observer, the diggers seemed to be on steroids, lifting massive rocks that were larger than the digger itself, with their operations wondrously synchronized. Of course, their earthside teleoperators were highly trained teams who had undergone countless simulations in preparation for this day. The autonomous functions of the diggers enabled the operators to limit their intervention to showing the digger which rocks they should move, and where to. When necessary, the program was capable of using two synchronized diggers to perform a single task. The performance efficiency of the designated operations was also massively more efficient with the aid of the autonomous program. In the meantime, other diggers dragged the rest in a container which had been unloaded from the plane into the tunnel. The crew entered the container, examined its oxygen pressurization and electrical functions, then rested for half an hour. They did not bother removing their space suits to avoid wasting time depressurizing and repressurizing the container. The container did have a pressurization capability, but it was intended as a backup for cases in which a crew member was injured and required immediate pressurization so his spacesuit could be removed and his wounds treated. The great advantage of placing the container within the lava tunnel was that it would be protected from meteor impact under the lunar rock.

At the entrance to the tunnel, they placed a transponder. It picked up broadcasts from within the tunnel and transmitted them to one of the communication satellites that was orbiting the moon. In this way, direct contact could be maintained — video feed and control included — between the diggers' teleoperators and their machines, even once the diggers were deployed dozens of kilometers down inside the tunnel. The tunnel itself acted as a Faraday Gaussian layer which maintained the strength of the broadcast signal. Thus, even a milliwatt home Wi-Fi transmitter could easily penetrate a few kilometers inside the tunnel.

Rakefet put the video feed from every digger online with a twenty-minute delay, during which it was edited at Rakefet's studios. Online viewers did not know of the delay and assumed they were seeing things unfold in real time. Certain outlets, such as Netflix, in collaboration with CNN, edited in real time, adding explanations, thus presenting the most interesting video at any given moment. The feed had an even greater rating than the Apollo 11 moon landing. It was fascinating and suspenseful. Sometimes a bobcat could be seen flipping over with other bobcats helping it return on its wheels or tracks. But even simply watching it drive into the lava tunnel, knowing that no-one, absolutely no-one, had ever seen that tunnel before, and that no-one knew what would happen next, was fascinating.

Thus, the entire world, be it in an ultra-modern Western home, or in a Tuareg tent in the Sahara Desert, watched the robots explore and build the Chinese World's lava tube.

3.

The nuclear fusion reactors to be constructed on the Moon were intended to supply energy to the newly established lunar habitat worlds. That energy would sustain life on the Moon, which meant they were life support systems and had to meet rigorous standards. The representatives of NASA, CNSA and Shlomo, Rakefet's CEO, agreed from the very first that all life support systems on extraplanetary sites that were set to sustain over fifty people, would have a triple backup.[29] The Moon suffers from rather frequent moonquakes, generated primarily by the tidal forces of Earth's oceans. As these moonquakes are not generated by lava flows, they are weaker and usually more predictable than terrestrial earthquakes. The standard for backups on Earth define that the substitutes must be at least forty kilometers from each other, so that an earthquake whose hypocenter is adjacent to the primary site would not destroy the backup. On the Moon, fifteen kilometers between the backups were sufficient to meet these same standards. That was why the American World (World 1), and the Chinese World (World 2) were sited fifteen kilometers apart. The Russian World (World 3), however, would be five hundred miles away, close enough to the Lunar South Pole to be able to mine ice and produce water from the nearby crater.

Thus, in order to provide a triple backup to World 1 and World 2, it would suffice to provide each with two power stations, each seven and a half kilometers from the opening into the tunnel's entrance, so that they would be the requisite fifteen kilometers apart. Power lines would be laid down between the reactors and the world. Given the absence of atmosphere, they could run millions of volts through wires, for spark generation vacuums required four times as much voltage in Earth's atmo-

---

29. Three separate systems, each independent, each capable of providing all the necessary power in case the other two fail.

sphere. By the same measure, the lines could be ultra-thin, and the distance between the suspension pylons could reach seven hundred meters in the low lunar gravity.

A 15 kilometer power line between World 1 and World 2 would provide an additional power back up for each world. Thus, four reactors provided triple backup to the two worlds.

In contrast, the Russian world would need three independent nuclear reactors.

It was clearly imperative to prepare reactors which would perform a nuclear fusion of Helium 3. It was both safe and environmentally sound. Preserving a clean environment on the Moon was important both in and of itself and as a symbol for the rest of earthbound humanity.

The simplest method to produce electricity from Helium 3 fusion was to fuse the substance with Deuterium, a hydrogen isotope containing a neutron as well as a proton and an electron. Deuterium was twice as heavy as normal hydrogen, which was why water containing the isotope were known as 'heavy water.' It is fairly simple to manufacture such water, and dozens of factories annually manufacture hundreds of tons of deuterium on Earth for a variety of purposes. The same planes loading up on Lunar Helium 3 before returning to Earth would unload Terran Deuterium when landing on the Moon. When Helium 3 is fused with Deuterium, a fascinating product results: regular Helium and a positive Ion that travel at incredible speed. That ion contains 70% of the fusion reaction energy, with only 30% released as heat. The electric charge of this kinetic energy actually constitutes electric energy. There was a massive advantage to having the nuclear energy being directly transformed into completely green electrical energy. In normal nuclear reactors, the energy contains a great element of danger and contamination, and the process is complicated. The usual process begins as heat, which transforms water into steam which drives steam engines, which rotates generators, which end up generating electricity. Skipping all those stages reduces energy wastage and also enables a much smaller system.

The Chinese had already prepared a system which could be loaded into ten large standard containers and would be assembled on the Moon into a full nuclear fusion capable of producing ten gigawatt, about the power required to operate a city with some 100,000 Western residents back on Earth. On the moon, that was only enough to support around 3,000 people, for the energy must also support lighting for agriculture, the manufacture of oxygen and for the operation of many vital systems which were not needed on earth. The reactor constituted, in effect, an 'alternative sun' — the source of all sustainable life in the lunar habitats.

Accordingly, the first reactor midway between World 1 and World 2 was assembled, and later relocated to its permanent position in World 2.

As there were now five active planes, and each such plane could perform two round Moon flights a week, the containers necessary to assemble the reactor could be delivered within two weeks. Although the plane was capable of performing two flights a week,[30] its crew was only cleared to perform one such flight a week. And indeed, everyone except the Israeli crew, of whom Avi still lay unconscious in Hadassah hospital in Jerusalem, had two crews ready.

---

30. Based here on the transatlantic flight protocols, which are similar, in some respect, to lunar flights.

4.

Friday night dinner at the Dagan household was always a drawing together of hearts and minds. When Noa was in Israel, she never missed Friday night dinner. For Noa's mother, her arrival was a slight compensation for her girl moving out and living alone. When they gathered around the table, she surprised everyone by announcing, half in pride and half in embarrassment, her intention to marry Nadav. Her sister drew in her breath in amazement, and her mother nearly dropped the salad. Oded, Noa's first husband, visited and had dined with them for years before the wedding. But this was the first they had ever heard of Nadav.

"Where is the fellow from?" asked her father, who recovered first.

"He is from work," she answered briefly.

"So how long have you known each other and where did you keep him hidden away?" her sister asked.

"First of all, I did not hide him away. Secondly, I have known him for less than a year. Nadav is a senior executive at Rakefet, but because of how secret everything in this job is, I don't know what his formal position is. We were never an official couple, but he proposed, and I accepted."

"Do you love him?" her mother asked, concerned.

"I think so, but I can't know for sure," Noa responded. "I thought I loved Oded before the wedding. Perhaps now, the second time around, it will last longer."

Nadav and Noa's wedding was funded by Rakefet, to prevent the appearance of discrimination. But it cost less than $200,000, in contrast to Ismail's wedding which cost over two million dollars.

One of the main reasons it was so much cheaper was because Nadav and Noa only invited four hundred people, not 2,000. Invitees included Rakefet's directors as well as their respective ambassadors in Israel, but not representatives from across the Arab world. Still, the Israeli Air Force sent a respectable delegation. Security was certainly simpler, as were the politics.

Joel arrived with Daniela. Though Faina and Daniela knew about each other, they exchanged neither word nor glance.

In fact, Daniela was beginning to treat her relationship with Joel as more than a job. Not only did the relationship suit her, but she was falling in love with him.

This complicated her mission somewhat, but in another way made things easier because it relieved her of the burden of pretending Joel mattered to her and that she loved him. In that respect it was simpler.

Nadav and Noa had never discussed previous partners. Nadav knew that other than her ex-husband, Noa had been sexually active, even promiscuous, in high school, but had never asked for details, for which she was grateful and appreciative of his sensitivity. Noa assumed that Nadav never had a girlfriend before, which was true enough — if one disregarded Daniela, which he studiously did.

The happy surprise wedding guest was Avi, who arrived in a wheelchair from the hospital. It marked the first time that Avi had left the hospital and he still could not walk, and his speech was slow and labored. In fact, no one in Rakefet had known he had woken up from the coma. He had decided to surprise and arrive at Noa's wedding because his wife, who had been invited, told him that it was only thanks to Noa that he was even alive.

Avi immediately made a beeline to Noa and embraced her, tears running down his cheeks. Noa replied in kind, and her own eyes welled up for the first time in many years. The last time Noa cried was when she was seven years old, when she found out about the murder of her biological father.

The wedding ceremony began. Noa in her bridal dress, surrounded by her parents, and Nadav and his parents on the other side. Nadav was frozen, unable to say the words, unable to even breathe. His face was beginning to turn blue for lack of oxygen — this was the worst possible moment for his social anxiety to rear its ugly head.

Noa did not know Nadav very well for a woman entering into a lifelong commitment with him. But the second time they made love, Noa saw the long scar down his leg. Nadav told her the story behind it, and how he pissed himself before his entire class in second grade, and how he lost his voice during school. Noa immediately understood what she had to do.

She halted the Rabbi performing the ceremony and approached Nadav.

"I am your wife now," she whispered to him, "you don't need to say anything."

This opened up the blockage and Nadav was able to speak again.

"You know," he told her later when they were alone, "in evolution, difficulties often generate developments."

"What do you mean?" Noa asked.

"Life that does not require couples," he explained, "are less developed than paired life. Bacteria, for example, can reproduce by fission, requiring no male and female bacteria. Since they never experienced the difficulties inherent in male-female couplings, they remain a primitive life form."

"Wonderful, so needing you makes me more developed than a bacterium," Noa laughed.

"Yes," Nadav answered, "but human evolution contains another complication. There is a psychological theory named the Imago Method, invented in the 1980s by Dr. Harwell Hendrix. Hendrix did not address the evolutionary side of things, but I have already made the connection for you. The theory explains that for more advanced evolutionary-cognitive development, every individual has another person who serves as a key for certain cognitive zones. These zones can be primarily emotional, as in with me, or in other ways. This evening, during our marriage ceremony, I realized that you, Noa, are my key."

Noa was moved to tears by his words. Later, they made love for the third time.

During high school Noa was both chubby and sexually active. Her classmates referred to her as a "sex-bunny." Any other girl might have been offended by this, but Noa's denial and suppression enabled her to shrug it off, and she seemed not to care. Noa herself used this nickname, but the rejection and disparagement of the girls who were envious of her left its mark. After graduating flight school and combat flight training, Noa developed sufficient self-confidence that she lost the need for positive reinforcement via sex. She also lost a lot of weight. Noa still found sex to be pleasant, but not much more than that. But when she made love to Nadav this time, her sexual experience was completely different. Noa understood that Nadav was her key as well.

The next morning, they remained in bed and talked.

"I want to take one of the spacesuit classes, either with the Americans or the Chinese. It's a month-long course where you can also spacewalk and perform minor missions, which seems pretty cool," she said.

"I'll go with you," Nadav said, "but perhaps we can go to China and make it our honeymoon?"

"But they only speak Chinese, we will not understand what to do," Noa protested.

"Two things," Nadav said and sat down in bed. "First — rank hath its privileges. We are sufficiently senior to pull rank and ensure they perform one course in English especially for us. Second — since we will only be able to hold small talk with each other — this will be a chance to get to know each other."

"I would like that," Noa smiled.

"And we can also toss in a tour of China for a few days," Nadav added.

"Yes! Rotem isn't the only one who can take a vacation abroad," Noa agreed.

5.

That month, five more planes arrived from China, the United States, Russia, Japan and India respectively. With them came another twenty spaceflight crews, who created a lot of extra work for Ismail, being responsible for collective training. The increased number of spaceflights generated great pressure on Ben Gurion Airport, which had to ground all of its flights prior to every rocket engine flight, due to the dangers inherent in the helium rocket jet. Every spaceflight grounded the airport to a halt for an entire hour, and times in which three or four flights occurred in one day constituted a very real problem. Hence, Rakefet took the decision to launch flights out of both China and the United States. Following consultation with the FAA, Faina decided Hawaii would be the base for such flights, just as Chou and the CAAC decided their flights would launch out of Woody Island in the Paracel Island Chain three hundred kilometers south of mainland China. This left only one flight a day from Ben Gurion Airport.

The first nuclear fusion reactor was established as a temporary measure at the very entrance to the Chinese World tunnel. The idea was to minimize the wait period for habitation of the first world by waiving need to place the power plant far from the habitat, thereby saving them the requirement of immediately laying down seven and a half kilometers of high-power lines. By the end of the month the world was powered up.

The provision of limitless electrical power enabled them to bring over a hundred robots into the world. Operating them required two hundred earth-based teleoperators on duty at any given time, around the clock. Most teleoperators were Chinese, for they were the only ones able to provide a significant amount of skilled employees in such a short time period.

The rate of work now was very quick. The bobcats cleared five kilometers of the lava tunnel, even though the initial stage to build the foundations of the world called for only 370 meters, and even the second stage required only three kilometers. There were simply so many diggers over such a small area that they got in each other's way. To avoid either inefficiency or idleness, they were sent down the tunnel. Four barriers were built in the cleared tunnel: the first, almost at the opening of the tunnel, the second 120 meters down, the third after another 250 meters, and the fourth, 500 meters later. The preliminary 120 meters were titled "Zone 1," the next 250 meters "Zone 2," and so forth.

The floor of each section was cleared and then work was carried out on the ceilings and walls. The work there required the installation of special systems on the bobcats which enabled them to cling to the walls and ceiling. These systems were actually drills that drilled holes in the walls and ceiling into which the bobcat screwed in screws. The bobcat tread clung to these screws, enabling the bobcats and other robots to maneuver on the walls and ceiling, applying the entire interior of the tunnel with the special epoxy glue developed by NASA to seal it off from any air leakage. After each section was blocked off and sealed, it was filled with a low concentration fluorescently marked gas. Special sensors tracked the movement of the fluorescent gas, all the remaining leakage points which were then duly sealed.

Airlocks connecting the sealed habitats to the lunar environment were installed, enabling entry and exit in a manner similar to that of the airlock on an airplane. Special airlocks were installed to enable lunar vehicles, bobcat-like constructs capable of carrying up to eight people without equipment, to enter the tunnel. As the vehicle matched airlocks fit the dimensions of the vehicles almost completely, only ten liters of air were required to fill the space between the vehicle and the airlock walls — a process which could be performed in under a second.

The opening, closing and passage system in the airlock room was completely automatic, and so the time the vehicle needed to pause within the airlock was less than a second and a half. Prior to entry, the vehicle was placed in a fully autonomous state, so the entire passage in and out of the world took place in an almost unbroken drive, with the vehicle pausing for no longer than an earthside vehicle would take to stop by a stop sign. In addition, there were air locks which enabled transportation of a standard 40 container into the world,[31] allowing for the transfer of containers from the plane into the tunnel without unloading it outside. All of the containers being shipped to the Moon were now standardized 40 containers, but they were constructed of aluminum in order to reduce thrust requirements for the plane, and since the mechanical strength of aluminum was sufficient under lunar gravity conditions.

As soon as a container was transported inside the lunar habitat, dedicated robots began transforming it into a residential unit. Each such container had 25 square meters of floor space and required relatively little work to transform it into a room — merely an entrance door, two windows, and a special emergency airlock-equipped door, as well as connections to the world's water and electricity infrastructure. In emergency situations the regular door and windows would be automatically locked and sealed, leaving the airlocked door as the only entry and exit point. Thus, should the world's seals be breached, it would still be possible to live and work within the residential and office units. Every such unit also contained emergency supplies, oxygen tanks and batteries which were sufficient to maintain life over four days.

In this manner, several types of residential and office buildings were constructed. The most basic type was intended to

---

31. 40 container – a 12-meter-long, 2.3-meter-wide, and 2.5-meter-high container.

house six people, specifically, temporary two-week employees. Due to the precise planning the rooms were quite comfortable in spite of their small space. 'Luxury' suites were made by attaching two containers together. Three room apartments intended to comfortably suit a couple was mostly made for demonstration purposes, as no one thought it would actually be in use in the initial year of operations. The containers were placed on top of one another, with external staircases, and painted so as to appear like an apartment building on Earth. These 'apartment buildings' were spaced out so as to give the impression of a residential neighborhood.

Initially, only Zone 1, at the entrance to the tunnel (maintenance), and Zone 2 immediately thereafter (residential), were active. Though Zone 2 was defined as a residential, rather than agricultural zone, the area between the 'apartment buildings' was designated to be filled with field crops such as potatoes, tomatoes, lettuce and cucumbers, as well as fruit trees. Gardening was performed by a dedicated robots which were able to extract quite a bit of produce from the relatively small 250x150 meter (7.5 acres) tunnel segment.

This produce was not negligible — it was sufficient to provide food for over fifty people, far beyond earthside yields. But earthside fields did not benefit from the work of dedicated autonomous robots who provided each sapling and seedling with customized care.

An airfield was prepared adjacent to the entry to the world, with two sites for planes to land. As the helium rocket-equipped planes landed on the Moon much like helicopters, vertically, these sites resembled a helicopter pad, albeit large, rather than a landing strip. Parking spots for five additional planes were also prepared. One plane was on the landing pad at any given point to enable emergency evacuation. Since a single plane could only contain sixty people, provided comfort was no object, it was decided to limit the size of the crew in the world to fifty people during the construction phase. For the same reason, a standing air crew was also required. Entry into the world was made simple and rapid thanks to a dedicated lunar vehicle constructed in Germany. It was connected to the plane, much like a sleeve in the airport, transferring the people through the barriers and their airlocks directly to Zone 2 and the residential and office buildings, all within a few minutes — less than the time required to board the plane in Ben-Gurion Airport.

The staff required at this point was, at least primarily, a limited setup crew. All of the tools, bobcats, robots and computer systems were controlled from Earth by teleoperators in the control centers. The actions which required human intervention were actually quite limited. Some of the people worked in the large garage in Zone 1, repairing the bobcats and various robots. Others worked in advanced software workshops debugging computer malfunctions in the Zone 2 offices. Only five Chinese crewmen were needed to handle malfunctions on the lunar surface, as such malfunctions were quite rare. Thus, most of the crew had a very light workload, particularly the spaceflight crew who idled away their time preparing for an emergency evacuation which never materialized.

6.

As the moon base was taking shape, the environmental crisis on Earth worsened. The Polar melting progressed faster than even the most pessimistic projections. It was already quite clear that by the 2070s, no ice would remain on the poles. Flooding of the coastal cities had begun, not in the massive waves seen in horror movies, but with the simple rise of sea level. At first the crisis was dealt with utilizing the reclamation methods perfected by the Dutch. Massive earthen dikes were built in many coastal cities at the initiative of mayors and municipal governments. In giant cities such as Manhattan, dock-like concrete barriers were constructed. Simple calculations, however, were sufficient for engineers to demonstrate the futility of such measures. It would soon be cheaper to relocate these cities inland, away from the rising tide, then to surround them with massive dikes.

Many scientists from different disciplines reached similar conclusions: it was necessary to place a massive mirror in space to refract some of the sunlight that reached Earth, away from the surface. This seemed somewhat silly at first — how would the mirror be kept in place for so long in a fixed position between the Earth and the Sun? And, surely a massive mirror would be required to have any effect on the global temperature?[32]

One option was to set up the mirror in a LaGrange point.[33] NASA had already exploited the properties of these points to place two satellites there.[34] This was the only position where

32. If the sun was a point light source, it would have been possible to place even a tiny mirror next to the sun in order to generate a permanent solar eclipse. But the sun is actually huge – its diameter is a hundred-fold that of Earth, necessitating mirror placement nearer to Earth.

33. The LaGrange point is the equilibrium point between the Earth's gravitational pull and that of the Sun satellites placed in this position, which revolve around the Sun at the same rate as they revolve around the Earth, which means they remain stationary between the Earth and the Sun.

34. SOHO for solar observations and DSCOVR for weather predictions.

a satellite would maintain a fixed location between the Earth and the Sun. But these points were 1.5 million kilometers from Earth, too far to shade the Sun way from the radiation that was reaching it.

A second possibility, seemingly impractical, was a helium-filled airship whose upper portion was a reflective mirror. It turned out that even IAI, as well as numerous other aerospace entities, had looked into the use of such airships at altitudes over 25 kilometers as a possible means for solar relay stations. NASA's concept was to utilize a rigid air balloon shaped like a massive sea mattress. The helium balloon, or rather helium mattress, was originally supposed to float at an altitude of twenty-five kilometers. But the plan was now to bring the helium mattress to an altitude of sixty-five kilometers, where the thin atmosphere would enable the high cruising speed required to maintain a fixed position between the Earth and the Sun. However, rising up or maintaining altitude at this thin atmosphere was quite difficult, albeit possible given the light weight of the helium mattress. The mattress itself was built in the shape of a huge wing, capable of maintaining lift even at the miniscule air pressure at a 65-kilometer altitude. The wing-mattress was towed by the Bismuth engine at a speed which maintained a consistent cruising height of 65 kilometers.

After rising, all that it needed to do was maintain an altitude and shield the surface of the Earth from the sun. The upper portion of the mattress would also contain solar panels which would supply electricity to the motors. These motors would enable navigation of the mattress to the position required to place the mirror between the Sun and the Earth. But the essential problem was the required size of the mirror. To reduce solar radiation by only 0.01%, the area of the mirror had to be 5,000 square kilometers. Even if it were constructed of only 3-micron thick aluminum it would still be a truly massive amount of aluminum. Moreover, in order to survive for over a year in the Sun and be truly capable of reflecting solar radiation into space, the sun-facing side of the mattress had to be coated with pure gold. A thin, 0.1-micron coating would suffice, but 0.1 microns times by 5,000 square kilometers still comes out to over a hundred times more than the world's annual production of gold.

Mars, however, had been identified as containing massive amounts of relatively accessible gold. Specifically, the seven-kilometer-deep Mariner Canyon on the Red Planet was identified by NASA astronomers as containing, at a depth of five kilometers, more gold than all of the accessible deposits on planet Earth.

Up to this point, plans to bring this gold to Earth had been made for purely economic reasons. But Rakefet's Board of Directors was focused on the survival of the human race, shaping the two decisions it made when the polar ice melt acceleration became apparent: First, to move forward the Mars flights and colonization.

Second, that any importation of gold from Mars to Earth would be made solely for the purpose of NASA's mirror. The gold would not even land on the Earth's surface but would be kept in orbit — or at least at a sixty-kilometer altitude. Thus, it would have no impact on the world's gold reserves or the global economy. These decisions greatly advanced the completion of humanity's transition from a Rank 0 civilization to a Rank 1 civilization, according to the ranking system Chou had explained.

China and the United States had already begun designing and constructing massive desalinization systems as an alternative to the rapidly drying up rivers, including the Yellow River and the Yangtse in China and the Colorado and Mississippi rivers in the United States. Nadav contacted Chou and they raised the idea of making the restoration of the Sahara into a green zone with plentiful water and vegetation into a global project with the board of directors and various other international forums. Success would help ameliorate the greenhouse effect by locking up more carbon in the resultant vegetation, as well as reducing solar absorbance, which is particularly high in the desert. As an added bonus, Chou discreetly noted to his European audiences that reversing desertification in the Sahel and North Africa would do much to reduce the flood of migrants from Africa northwards. The idea was to return the Sahara to the state it existed prior to the prior Ice Age, 50,000 years ago. The idea was to direct a massive infusion of desalinated water, made possible by the Helium 3 power generation technology.

Various green organizations arose to oppose the plan, claiming, quite correctly, that greening the Sahara would eliminate the native species unique to the desert. Following a public debate, global forces decided to preserve at least 5% of the desert in order to protect native species. Given the massive tracts of the Sahara planes, and the massive efforts which would be required to irrigate and fertilize it enough to sustain forests and grasslands, this obligation was not particularly onerous.

The Sahara Desert contains East-West Mountain ranges starting with the Tibesti Mountains in the east, 3,000 meters tall, the Tassili n'Ajjer Mountains, 2,000 meters tall, and the Atlas Mountains in the west, 4,000 meters tall. Everything north of these mountain chains drained into the Mediterranean Sea, and all south of them flowed through West Africa into the Atlantic Ocean.[35]

Chou's idea was to construct four massive desalinization plants, similar to those China was constructing to replace the

---

35. These Mountain chains are the African equivalents of the European Alps. They were formed by the same forces – movement of Arica's tectonic plate northwards and the European tectonic plate southward, thrusting up the Alps in Europe and the Tassili n'Ajjer Mountain in the Sahara.

parched-out Yangtze and Yellow rivers. Each such station would desalinate twice as much water as was desalinated in the entire world in the pre-Hydrogen 3 era, nearly half the water capacity of the river Nile — nearly 1,500 cubic meters per second. These desalinization plants would, naturally, require massive amounts of energy, as well as gigantic pipes and pumps to transfer the desalinated water to release points along the watershed line formed by the Sahara Mountain chains. The total length of pipes would amount to nearly 10,000 kilometers. The water would spill into rivers which would flow mostly to the Mediterranean Sea, but about a third would end up flowing into West Africa as well. Two desalinization plants would be built in the Mediterranean — one in Libya and one and Algeria. Another station would be built in Morocco and pump desalinized water from the Atlantic Ocean towards the East Atlas Mountain. The final station would be built in Nigeria and pump water from the Bight of Benin. The Nigerian station would transfer the water to the Tassili n'Ajjer Mountains, into Iherir Wadi, where water currently flowed seasonally.

Pumping water from the Mediterranean Sea might reduce the water in the inland sea and thereby increase the current passing through the straits of Gibraltar. However, since the majority of the water generated by the desalination plants would flow into the Mediterranean, although half would derive from the Atlantic, the sea-level would remain stable.

Rakefet undertook the task of implementing the high-altitude mirror project, intending to complete it within fifteen years.

As for the Green Sahara project, China would construct two of the desalinization plants, piping included, and the United States would construct the other plants. The Rakefet Company would supply them with all the Hydrogen 3 required for both the desalinization plants and the pumps.

The Chinese immediately announced they would begin work, planning to complete the project within a decade. But in the United States, the Green Sahara project sparked an immediate political struggle. The Democratic party wanted to start and finish the project within 15 years, while the Republican Party completely opposed the effort. Once the American political imbroglio became clear, the Chinese pounced, announcing that they were prepared to establish the entire project, including the four desalination plants, on their own, without any American involvement.

As soon as the Chinese statement entered the news cycle, the Republican leadership made an about-face, and declared it supported the project and, moreover, wished to complete it within only eight years, aiming to finish well before the Chinese. And so, the desalinization race between China and the United States kicked off. Each desalinization plant was composed of several smaller plants, built in sequence. So it was that the first Chinese desalinization plant began pumping desalinating water, as well as transporting it a relatively short distance of around 150 kilometers within less than a year. This situation enabled Libyan farmers to begin growing crops in the small river delta that was formed by the resultant river. The Chinese speed of completion frustrated the Americans, who were only then beginning to complete the design phase, but enflamed public opinion and support for the race on both sides of the Pacific.

7.

After the spacesuit course and a week of hiking and touring China, Noa suggested to Nadav that they take up residence on the Moon for a period of time.

"It would have several implications," she said. "First of all, it would be a literal 'honeymoon.' Also, since we are doing the whole 'love at first sight' thing, it will give us a better chance to get to know each other. Earthside, we have very little time without the scrutiny of journalists or Rakefet's management."

"Yes," Nadav agreed with a smile. "As it is, there are all sorts of two-bit shrinks analyzing every gesture we make on the morning shows, to the point where it becomes the entire show."

"I can be part of the mandatory standby space crew, and you can work from anywhere."

"Alright," Nadav agreed, "I don't have anything urgent to do in the next two weeks anyway."

"That's not what I meant," said Noa. "I want us to live on the Moon for the next six months or so."

Nadav was surprised. At first this idea really did not seem right to him. "I need to think about this," he said. "I will talk it over with Shlomo."

"You are like a little boy, needing Shlomo to sign off on everything," she teased him, but Noa acknowledged, inwardly, the difference between them. She was spontaneous, uninhibited, and as such tended to deny rejection. Nadav was the opposite. Any rejection he encountered injured him further, and hence, Nadav was cautious and careful.

This contrast between them created their mutual completion and love. As Nadav said, they were the key to one another.

Shlomo actually thought lunar relocation was a good idea when they met to discuss it in the windowless Kinneret room.

"I am thinking about how we can confuse the competing intelligence agencies," he told Nadav. "I need them to misdirect them away from the identity of the primary secret keepers. Muddy up the waters enough to keep them from deciphering our real secrets. If you relocate to the moon for an extended period, you will drop off their radar — they won't view it as credible that a secret keeper could do something like that."

And so it became that Noa and Nadav left for the Moon to become its first long-term colonists.

In spite of what it may seem, it did not mean that they cut themselves off from Earth. Firstly, there were online communications (with a three second lag). Secondly, during this period there were between one and three flights to the Moon and back every day, so it was easy to take an occasional earthside vacation.

Nadav took several Rakefet bulbs with him. The flight also carried thirty chicks. Veterinarians went over all the chicks, feather by feather, to ensure they were not carrying fleas, ticks, or any other diseases.

There had already been several attempts to transfer beehives, but that turned out to be complicated, because the bees had to get used to the lunar gravity — something only one beehive was able to do, and even those bees barely survived. Bees were critical to the pollination of fruit, vegetables, and trees in the lunar habitat. Without bees, robot gardeners had to painstakingly pollinate every single flower manually — a task which would require many more robots than they sought to support.

Robot gardeners looked like a lawn mower crossed with a vacuum cleaner, except equipped with cameras and numerous arms with various tools such as a shovel, pruning shears, a hammer, a brush and various manipulators capable of tying various wires.

Special weights were prepared for the lunar crew to prevent their muscles from deteriorating, and to help them maintain balance in the reduced gravity.[36] Soon, however, most of the crew removed the weights for much of the day, because the reduced weight was both pleasant and liberating.

As the only couple planning to stay on the moon for more than a month, Nadav and Noa were awarded the deluxe 50-square-meter, two-container apartment. It really was a deluxe apartment with a spacious living room that had a large window, a small bedroom, and a tiny study — also equipped with windows. They even had a real bath and lavatory, as well as another small water closet. The apartment was on the fourth floor, over three other container-apartment floors, but running up four flights of stairs in low lunar gravity was no big deal.

Nadav began working on the solar shade project from their little study. Noa was effectively idle, for her role as the standby evacuation pilot left her with nothing to do. Noa found herself an occupation in Zone 1 in the robot repair workshop, but they too had little left to do, let alone extra work to give her, so she was occupied for less than an hour every day. They began taking walks outside. Noa could only leave the compound when there were other pilots at World 2. However, at the current frequency of flights, there was almost always another spaceflight crew or

---

36. A small individual who weighs sixty kilos on Earth (containing a sixty-kilo mass) would weigh ten kilos on the Moon. To keep their muscles from atrophying on the Moon, they would need to carry an additional fifty kilos of weight. In other words, they would need to carry an additional three-hundred kilos of mass. On Earth, this weight would prevent an individual from standing up. But on the Moon, they would feel much as they would on Earth. Every individual on World 2 was fitted with personally adapted lead weights. They were coated with a special cloth and attached to their ankles, knees, hands, belt, and a vest that looked much like a bulletproof vest. But even with all this weight, leaping was much easier, because the spring of the leg muscles would bring the leaper up to the exact same speed with which they would spring on earth, but that speed would bring them to a much greater height in the lower gravity, before they fell back to the earth – or rather, back to the Moon.

more at World 2. She was therefore effectively free to travel as she chose.

They had two options for an outing — the first was to take a pressurized lunar vehicle, the second to walk the moon in a spacesuit. They both preferred the Chinese spacesuits they had trained on, both because of their familiarity with them and because they were far less cumbersome than the American equivalents. They therefore usually travelled in the pressurized vehicles, wearing spacesuits but with the helmets off. When they wanted to leave to walk the lunar surface, they donned the helmets and took a walk on the Moon.

At first, they wandered around the aircraft landing pad and the environs of the World opening. Then they headed out to observe the nuclear reactor and the Helium 3 factory constructed by the Chinese. From afar, the factory looked like a quarry. Large diggers and small trucks brought huge lunar rocks, some the size of a small house, to the refinery. These rocks could be picked up and moved because their weight on the Moon was relatively small. They were loaded up on a conveyor belt that brought them into a machine which crushed them into dust. The dust was conveyed into a system of kilns which heated it to a temperature of around seven hundred degrees. In that temperature, the Helium was vaporized out of the dust and compressed into steel balloons. This compression took place in the shade, where the temperature was around minus one hundred degrees. While Helium remained gaseous until near absolute zero degrees, the combination of the low temperature and the pressure applied enabled storage of quite a bit of Helium 3 in the steel containers. On Earth, of course, the temperature would be much higher — an issue that was resolved by maintaining the containers within isolating arrays. Once the containers arrived on Earth, the Helium would be immediately transferred into larger containers at the airport, where the pressure would be much lower, before they had a chance to warm up. Once the temperature rose over minus 90 degrees Celsius, emergency valves would vent excess helium, though that would represent a very significant loss. Still, venting would not result in any environmental damage, for helium is an environmentally friendly gas.

Noa and Nadav also travelled to the tunnel opening of World 1, fifteen kilometers away from the entrance to World 2. The Bobcats had, by this stage, begun to construct World 1. However, in comparison to World 2, World 1 was only just starting out. It had no fusion reactor to provide electricity, but its landing pad had been completed. They had begun to install its nuclear reactor, which had been brought by plane directly from Earth, rather than through World 2. The moment the reactor would be completed it would be possible to bring in a large number of Robots who would work on the construction of World 1 at a more rapid pace.

Two weeks later, an issue arose with the chicks; they had all flown the coop, or more accurately, hopped over the fence which had imprisoned them, a feat they had accomplished easily in the low lunar gravity.

Worse was to come — while adult chickens could not fly on Earth, on the Moon, the low gravity enabled them to take wing, getting everywhere in the habitat, pecking and devouring all the crops. The robot gardeners sought to protect the plants and capture the chickens, attempts which met with some initial success, with half of the runaway chickens being captured and caged. The other chickens, however, adapted their behavior to avoid the capture attempts of the robot gardeners. They sat on the robots and covered their cameras with their bodies, preventing it from functioning autonomously or capturing them, and preventing remote teleoperators from effectively operating the robot. Only a local operator who could literally see the chicken seated on the robot could debug the problem.

Since so much of the activity on the Moon world was broadcast live on Earth, the issue soon became a matter for public discussion. Some kid in Japan suggested operating drones to capture the flighty chickens. The suggestion was taken up, and two drones specifically adapted for lunar gravity flight were brought up to capture the chickens and the standby pilots were duly assigned the duty of bringing them to heel.

The next week, Noa piloted the chicken hunting drone. The drone would hover over the chicken and release a net that would entangle it, preventing it from flying away. In short order, the flighty chickens were captured, but that did not solve the problem of the problematic birds. On Earth, chickens could be relied upon to lay one egg every day, producing plenty of delicious omelets for their human keepers. But on the Moon, the chickens flew like eagles, behaved like eagles, and apparently thought like eagles. They saw no reason to idly sit and lay an egg every 24 hours.

The *rakefet* flowers, in contrast, were a stunning success. They were planted in pots inside Noa and Nadav's apartment, as well as in the ground surrounding the apartment. Their adaptation was rapid, and the rakefet leaves grew to about twice their earthside size. The flower itself, however, stayed about the same size. The *Rakefet flower* growing inside the apartment developed normally, but outside the apartment, some animal would occasionally eat one of the leaves in its entirety. This was problematic less on account of the rakefet, but more because there weren't supposed to be any unaccounted-for animals in the lunar habitat. The crew therefore took the decision to station a robot-gardener at a safe distance, so that the rogue animal would not be scared away, and then to capture a picture of the rakefet-leaf eater. For an entire week, the robot gardener lay in wait and photographed nothing before it was returned to its regular duties. That very day, the leaf thief devoured several more rakefet leaves, from various different plants. A robot was therefore assigned to track the rakafot full time from a carefully concealed position. The very next day, the devouring beast was found. It was Mung, one of the one-week Chinese employees. Mung was summoned for questioning, which Nadav attended. Mung was rather frightened, but it eventually turned out that Mung, and the employee he replaced, came from the coastal Guangdong Province, adjacent to Hong Kong, where rakafot were common and widely used for cooking. The prior employee had told Mung during his orientation that there were massive rakafot plants on the Moon that grew to a size he had never seen on Earth. Moreover, they were uncommonly juicy and delicious.

"What do you mean, delicious?" Nadav asked.

Mung was surprised at the question.

"When you prepare rice rolls, wrapped in Xiankelai leaves..." Mung stuttered.

"You mean rakefet leaves? You eat the rakefet leaves?" Nadav asked.

"Sure," Mung replied, "they are delicious, I did not know this were forbidden here."

"It is not that it is forbidden," Nadav said, "but I simply did not know they were edible."

"The tuber may be poisonous," Mung said, "but the leaves are soaked in boiling water, and then you can roll rice up in them. It is best where you use the type of rakafot with an odor, which is rare on Earth. Here, however, rakafot has a wondrous odor."

"The name rakefet was selected as the company name, precisely because we thought rakafot was in existence simply for its beauty and was not practical for use," Nadav explained.

"That they can be eaten is fascinating, because this proves that everything in nature has a role to play, even when you think something is neither useful nor contributes to the cycle of life — you are mistaken," he summarized.

The rate of Helium 3 importation from the Moon grew at a rapid pace. Every nation on Earth raced to construct Helium 3 reactors, with China and France supplying most of the reactors ordered by developing countries. The Japanese specialized in building miniature reactors used to fuel ships. Fossil fuel prices plummeted, but over 50% of the world's energy consumption was still derived from fossil fuels — coal, oil and gas. Rakefet's updated projections were that it would take ten to fifteen years.

But this success came at a cost. Accusations were raised that Rakefet's policy was racist, discriminating against countries with a high population growth. The incitement against Rakefet on social media was wild, and supported, in Israel, by the Ultra-Orthodox rabbis who were joined, as in many cases in recent years, by fundamentalist Evangelist ministers, reactionary Catholic priests, and fanatical Muslim imams.

An even greater problem was that, in spite of the reduction in carbon emissions, it became increasingly apparent that global warming had passed the point of no return. The rate of polar icecap melting, though it slowed down, continued progressing, and this was a self-sustaining process — the smaller the icecaps, the less solar radiation would be reflected into space, resulting in greater warming which would accelerate the melting of the icecaps. More and more scientists concluded that the only hope for the planet was in the solar reflector project.

Part G: Mars

1.

Daniella's and Joel's relationship grew closer, and they began speaking about the possibility of getting married. Her NSA controllers thought, quite rightly, that their relationship had exhausted any intelligence gathering potential, and that Daniella could not extract any more relevant information, regardless of how hard she tried. Daniella wanted to tell Joel that she was an NSA agent, but was afraid that, just as in the movies, the revelation that the origins of their relationship was not romantic but interests-based would create a rupture in their relationship, leading to inevitable separation. Still, she was, at the end of a day, an American, and Americans strongly believed in the myth of redemptive truth. Daniela could not to go into a marriage without telling Joel the truth. That was why, with great trepidation, she ended up confessing.

Daniella was astonished at his response.

"This is a second marriage for both of us" he said, nodding. "We are both a bit long in the tooth and more worldly than the average bride and groom. The reasons for our relationship beginning — don't matter too much. I am happy that you are an ideological person, who values putting yourself at the service of great goals. I personally think that Rakefet's path, in which technology is entrusted in the hands of the 'enlightened,' is better for humanity, including the United States, than entrusting it to any single government, but I have no magic mirror to prove to me that I am right. I may well be wrong," he said. "But whoever is right and whoever is wrong, we won't split up over it." Though Daniela confessed to Joel that she was an CIA agent, she had never told him, and he never asked, about her relationships with other men, including her torrid affair with Nadav.

"This is the third wedding of a senior Rakefet executive" Shlomo said. "I can open a matchmaking service." Rakefet assumed the costs of the wedding this time as well, with two hundred guests in attendance. While the five Rakefet directors arrived with ambassadors, the groom had barely a hundred guests, and the bride less than twenty. The cost this time was around $50,000, and Shlomo said that, at this rate, they would be able to fund the next wedding from the petty cash box designated to pay for the office coffee.

The Rakefet board of directors' decision to bring forward the flights to Mars in order to import gold for the mirror project was not secret. On the one hand, the entire world understood the massive importance of reaching Mars. At the back of everyone's mind was the increasingly violent weather tornados that had become routine all over the world, ravaging everything in their path like the Kansas storm that blew away Dorothy's house to the Land of Oz. The need for a mirror which would help ameliorate global warming had become an established consensus in the scientific community, though less so for the general public. The existence of massive gold deposits in the Mariner Canyon on Mars had also become general knowledge. These deposits were formed by a similar geologic process to those which formed the Californian deposits that sparked the 19th Century gold rush. However, the Martian gold deposits were located five kilometers beneath the rim of the canyon and were nearly a hundred-fold larger than the Californian gold deposits.

The sudden accessibility of these deposits to the new technology generated countless political difficulties. Many countries and corporations wanted the gold for themselves, regardless of Rakefet's plans to use the gold to coat the floating mirror to ameliorate global warming.

Once it became clear that Rakefet would be able to mine extraterrestrial gold and bring it to earth at a negligible cost, the world gold prices crashed. The price crash resulted in serious instability in the financial markets, including a fall in the value of the dollar and other gold-backed currencies. Once the Rakefet decision to utilize the gold solely to coat the floating mirror and not allow the importation of gold to the world's surface was enacted, markets stabilized. Any importation of extraterrestrial gold via pre-Rakefet technology was uneconomical, for gold was $60,000 per kilo, whereas fuel and associated costs required to bring it as payload down to earth was around $400,000 dollars per kilo.

Thus, in parallel to the frenetic work of preparing the lunar habitats and the importation of Helium 3 from the surface of the Moon, the world in general and Rakefet in particular began to ponder the specifics of a mission to Mars. In a lecture given by Galit at MIT, she explained that, prior to Rakefet's establishment, sociologists estimated that the population of the world would peak at nine billion in around 2065. But terrestrial resources could not support such a massive population. Rakefet's efforts to import resources of Lunar Helium 3 and Martian gold from across the solar system to support this population was therefore a natural, even inevitable development. The paradigm of the transition from a Level 0 to a Level 1 civilization was increasingly accepted throughout the world, pushing the valuation of Rakefet ever upwards. However, one of their energy-saving solutions resulted in new problems.

Rakefet's energy allocation policies taxed reproduction, limiting birth-rate beyond replacement level.

This policy was harshly criticized, not least in Israel. Rakefet's founders went from national heroes to enemies of the people. The company found the hostility unpleasant, but they were prepared for it. Funds were allocated to public relations outreach, which helped keep the backlash contained. Their focus, still, was on preparing for the Mars Mission.

The distance to Mars depended on the orbits of both Earth and the Red Planet. Mars was farther from the Sun than Earth, and it took it nearly two years to orbit Sol, which meant their positions relative to each other varied considerably. The greatest distance between them was at 350 million kilometers, when the planets were on opposite sides of the Sun. When they lined up on the same side, they were "only" 50 million kilometers apart. In practical terms, over the next decade, the distance would range between 100 million kilometers and 300 million kilometers over most of the year. The maximum speed of the spaceplane was around two hundred kilometers per second.

Though 200 kilometers per second was less than a thousandth of the speed of light, the protons rotating at near light speed within the ring would, as a result of the movement of the spaceship, be traveling 200 kilometers per second faster on one side of the ring, and 200 kilometers per second on the other side. This was an insignificant issue according to Newtonian mechanics, but in relativistic physics, accelerating these near light-speed particles would require a huge energy input.

Beyond 200 kilometers per second the investment in fuel was simply not worth the extra boost in speed. Thus, at maximal speed it would take one week to reach Mars at a distance of 100 million kilometers, plus an additional day for acceleration and an additional day for deceleration. With Mars at its furthest distance, 360 million kilometers, it would take about three weeks. This was a completely different ballgame from a moon landing which involved a distance of only 360,000 kilometers, less than a thousandth of the farthest distance between Mars and Earth — and with far fewer navigational complications.

Social media was aflame with controversy over which nation would have the honor of piloting the first Mars mission. Naturally, both the Americans and the Chinese demanded the honor, and in the heat of the argument Chinese leaders went so far as to declare that, should they not be given prime place, they would nationalize any planes in their possession and prepare them for an independent Mars flight.

Galit thought this was a good chance to demonstrate to the world that Rakefet, and Rakefet alone, controlled the technology. As every rocket engine required a weekly password update to be activated, and the magnetic welding caused by its activation prevented physical bypassing of the password, engines simply could not work without Rakefet's active intervention.

"What do you think, Shlomo?" Galit asked.

"I'm with you," he agreed. "I also think that we can get a majority on this decision among our board. China will vote against us, perhaps with Russian support, but even if the EU fearfully abstains, you and I, as well as the United States, will support this step. I think India and Japan will as well. Not that we need a majority — you are the deciding vote in case of a tie, and China cannot gain a majority against a shut-down."

Galit duly raised the proposal to deactivate any aircraft confiscated by Beijing in the next meeting of the board of directors and received surprising support.

"I favor this proposal," Chou said bluntly. "True, if I am outed as supporting this decision I will be executed, but I think that if every country follows my homeland's lead in nationalizing Rakefet vessels, then our entire project will be endangered, and humanity's very existence will be imperiled. This is more important than my own life. And nonetheless, I would be grateful if you could conceal my support for this proposal against the government of the People's Republic of China, for which I would gladly offer my life — under any other circumstances."

"I support Chou's request," Galit said.

"I think the practical solution is to have Rotem and Noa perform the first Mars flight, and for Noa, our best pilot, to perform the landing. We have detailed records of all the flights by all the pilots to back this up," she continued and explained her assertion: "We performed a computer analysis of all our pilots. Then we normalized the results to award 100 to the best pilot and the rest in accordance with that score. Noa is at 100, followed by French Marie with 75, then Rotem with 73, then the senior American and Chinese pilots with 72 each, followed by everyone else. The lowest rank is 66 — one French and one Israeli pilot. But I ask this information remains confidential to this forum alone. Does anyone oppose this motion?" As no-one replied, Galit concluded the meeting.

The Chinese engines automatically shut down without a new password supplied by Rakefet. The next day, the Chinese government announced its support for Noa as the pilot responsible for the Mars landing, ending the immediate crisis and saving face for all. Nonetheless, Galit's message that it was not possible for any government to bypass Rakefet was heard loud and clear.

Chou's support for the shutdown of the Chinese rocket engine turned out to be part of a far more complex political machination than the principled stand of one man. The statement by the Chinese government that it would nationalize Rakefet's spaceplane was not fully coordinated with all the stakeholders in the Chinese government and Communist party, and it triggered much debate and controversy within the inner circle of both. Quite a few of the stakeholders foresaw Rakefet's countermeasures and understood they had no chance of carrying the day in Rakefet's Board of Directors. The only question was how Chou should respond to the projected backlash. Some stakeholders suggested the idea of Chou voting in favor of the resolution against China. As outlandish as this notion seemed at first, in depth examination revealed that this would best serve China's long-term position on the board of directors. In this manner, other states — including America — would understand the situation and avoid attempting to bypass Rakefet. This would increase humanity's chance of survival, and also enable China to act against the United States on the board of directors — if and when it should prove necessary. The board therefore decided to enable Chou to act in whatever way he saw necessary.

In retrospect, given Chou's speed of response, and their familiarity with his ping-pong diplomacy style, Galit understood that Chou was actually operating in accordance with the policy determined by at least a faction of the ruling circles in Beijing, rather than in opposition to his government. She shared her insight with Shlomo, but neither of them raised the matter to Chou.

Rakefet decided to send two space planes on the Mars mission, which would serve as each other's backup — especially given that they knew of the many malfunctions in the Israeli system. Most of the space plane's electronics were still based on Israeli methods which had not yet undergone full reconfiguration by the Chinese or Americans. One would be manned by Noa, Rotem and the American crew, and the other to be piloted by Marie, the second-best pilot, and a mixed French Chinese crew. The goal of the flight was to prepare an airfield near a Martian tunnel entrance (Mars, much like the Moon, was crisscrossed by long-dormant volcanic tunnels) and begin constructing the European Mars 1 World. Accordingly, Noa was recalled from the Moon and began training for the Mars mission.

2.

The design of the floating mattress intended to save the planet from a runaway greenhouse effect faced several challenges. First, the mattress had to soar at an altitude of sixty-five kilometers on an imaginary plane connecting the center of the Sun with the center of the Earth, always facing the sun's rays wherever they impacted the zenith of the Earth. That meant facing the southern hemisphere during winter, and the northern hemisphere during summer, between the Tropic of Cancer and the Tropic of Capricorn. The mattress would hover far above the altitudes reached by either civilian or military aircraft. One problem was that occasionally the mattress would pass below the broadcasting area of satellites. In order to solve this problem, the mattress was equipped with reception plates in its upper part that were connected to a transmission antenna in its lower part. These systems operated without any need for additional energy, since they merely cancelled the disruption in transmission that the mattress generated in its passing. The final design was for a mattress stretching over 5,000 square kilometers, with an average width of ten kilometers, and an average length of 500 kilometers. It was the shape of a thin, long and flat pencil. The mattress had to be capable of cruising along the stratosphere at a speed of 1,700 kilometers per hour. Air pressure at such an altitude is less than a millionth of the air pressure at sea level — indeed, air pressure is so low that the 1,700 kilometers per hour is well below the speed of sound at this altitude.

Because of the low air density, flight has very different aerodynamic properties at this altitude. Maintaining high speed did not require investment of particularly large amounts of energy — what was required could be provided by solar panels. Indeed, this altitude was selected precisely because of the fact that not much force was needed to accelerate the mattress to a high speed and maintain the momentum, else the thin mattress walls be ripped asunder. The mattress walls could not be any thicker without being much heavier, and thereby unable to be elevated to the necessary height. Each mattress was constructed out of various different cells, so they had the appearance of packing nylon filled with bubbles. Should a single bubble be punctured by, for example, a meteorite, the function of the mirror would not be impaired.

The upper layer of the mattress was made with ultra-thin gold leaf coating. Although the density of gold was very high, it could be applied at a much more uniform thickness than any other metal, so that the weight of the coating per surface area was significantly lower than aluminum.

In any event, the complicated part was raising the mattress to the required height. In the early 2000s, when the idea of using floating mattresses to place cellular relay stations at an altitude of twenty-five kilometers first arose, a timeframe of three months was scheduled; from the moment the mattress began to be pumped full of gas to the moment it was stabilized in the required position. In this case, the required altitude, nearly three times as high, and the necessary stabilization in such a thin atmosphere area, was much more difficult. A type of helicopter capable of assisting in lifting and stabilization of the mattress was required. Once the mattress was already stabilized, engines were required to pull it along at the necessary speed.

Nadav worked on constructing such engines. As aforementioned, the mattress had to move very fast to follow the Sun.

Helium fusion rocket engines, such as the space-plane engines, were too strong and would rip the mattress apart. Nadav's solution was an ionic engine.[37] Such an engine was

_____

37. Appendix C "Ionic Engines."

used by satellites to modulate their position. Nadav used a Bismuth element and the Rakefet superconductor, thereby significantly improving the existing engine.

NASA decided to build a single prototype of the helium mattress which would be brought up to the required altitude. To do so they required two things: to design and construct a helicopter capable of reaching a height of sixty-five kilometers (a regular helicopter could not reach an altitude of eight kilometers, due to the low air density,)

and gold, a lot of gold. In order to move the analysis process along, they chose to use a 14 karat gold paint, rather than full 24 karat gold coating for the prototype mattress. The mattress with the weakened gold coating was only expected to survive for a few months at an altitude of sixty-five kilometers but would enable validation of the concept. Adam took upon himself to design the helicopter. Adam decided to use the Sikorski King Stallion platform. It would be equipped with two helium rocket engines and a small hydrogen rocket engine in the exact configuration in which the engines were installed on the Rakefet company planes. As the helicopter was much lighter, these engines were powerful enough to enable it to float in place. The problem then was that the helium stream would be pointed downwards, which meant they could only take off from above the Pacific Ocean, in areas that the United States military could completely clear any potentially disruptive ships or flights. After passing an altitude of thirty kilometers they would be able to operate anywhere in the world, because planes fly at a height of around ten kilometers, so the helicopter would be flying twenty kilometers higher than any regular plane, which was more than safe enough.

Accordingly, two engines were sent to the Sikorsky Company to be installed on the chopper.

The upgraded helicopter was set to be operational and waiting for them in the American Military base in the Pacific Ocean in another four months. This base was the intended recipient of the prototype mattress and Nadav's first Bismuth engine. Nadav was therefore placed under considerable pressure to promote the completion of his engine design.

The structure and weight of the mattress required an engine for every half-square kilometer of mattress. Since the total area of the planned full-scale mirror-mattress was 5,000 square kilometers, around 10,000 Bismuth engines were required.

By this point there were almost no scientists who denied that the rate of the depletion of ice in the poles was exponential, so it was clear to everyone that in the absence of the mattress, the ice would disappear by the end of the century — even if the greenhouse gas emission should be massively decreased. There simply wasn't any other option other than the solar reflection mattress at hand.

3.

The Mars flight plan included two planes. Both had to perform the exact same flight plan, and fly at a relatively close distance of ten kilometers from one another.

The flight was supposed to last for twenty days, with each day meticulously planned for missions that needed to be performed. During the first day of the flight, the two planes were scheduled to accelerate for 24 hours to a speed of around 200 kilometers per second. This was the highest speed any man-made vehicle had ever reached. The closest was 150 kilometers per second by the space probe Parker, but this was when it passed Mercury and fell towards the sun.

On the ninth day, Noa would perform the Mars landing. After the landing, the American crew, who took the first steps on the Moon from the Rakefet aircraft, would step out with Rotem to install the lever with which they would unload the bobcats on the tenth day. Rotem needed to be the first person to set foot on Mars, simply to avoid a situation in which the Americans would be the first, which would gravely offend the Chinse. They would then have another week heading back, returning to Earth on Day 20.

Since on this voyage they had to accelerate and decelerate twice, to and from a speed of two hundred kilometers per second, they would be consuming massive amounts of fuel. The fuel was water, and, in addition to the amounts calculated for the flight, the plane was topped off with an additional 20% for safety margins.

The communication lag between Earth and Mars was far more significant than that between Earth and the Moon: radio waves travelled at the speed of light, that's 300,000 kilometers per second, so it would take about eight minutes for radio waves to traverse the 180 million kilometers which would separate Earth and Mars during this mission. Any query sent from the plane to Earth would only be answered after twice as much time: twenty minutes.

Noa, Rotem and Marie travelled to the United States to train on the NASA simulator. After a week of training, they travelled to China to repeat the drills on the Chinese simulator. As the Chinese were forbidden by law from training at NASA (a law American legislators seemed determined to uphold even in the face of global extinction), the Chinese likewise decided to forbid Americans from training on their simulator. The other pilots found it less important to train on both simulators and were content to train on only one or the other. Nadav intended to travel with Noa to Mars, and hence accompanied her to the United States, but not to China. Nadav had to return to Rakefet's headquarters and attend to the calculations dealing with engine behavior at high speeds. In theory, one could see that fuel consumption rose markedly after passing the two hundred kilometers per second mark due to relativistic effects. That was why Nadav wanted to limit the maximal speed to around one hundred and eighty kilometers per second.

Noa and Rotem's visit to the United States raised much media interest given the dramatic conclusion of Rotem's previous visit, and the image of her hopping into the F-16 cockpit in a cocktail dress and high heels was once again circulated widely.

Eventually, the Mars flight passed smoothly, just like the first Apollo 11 flight to the Moon. Since the flight took a little over a week both ways, the pilot crews rotated around the clock. Rotem was the pilot when deceleration began, and she synchronized the maneuver with the pilot in the second plane. Unfortunately, Marie was not on shift at the time, and the young pilot who was, did not see that the pilot on the previous shift had already turned the plane around to enable him to begin a slow deceleration with minimum power, as was done in Rotem's plane as well. In deep space you really need to know your stars. Therefore, instead of decelerating, he accelerated, turning the plane back towards Mars, and activating the engine at full speed. Within seconds the gap between the two planes grew and Rotem was unable to contact him, for the communications system between the planes was only effective to a range of five hundred kilometers. It took Rotem several minutes to contact ground control on Earth for them to relay her warning. What followed was an extremely frustrating twenty-minute time-lag in communication, where ground control tried to sort out who was right and who was wrong.

Two hours later, ground control ordered both planes to reduce thrust to a minimum to give them time to figure out where the error was and how to correct it.

On a conventional spacecraft, control was meticulously maintained remotely from Earth. But on the Rakefet planes, the pilot had full control. The pilot saw where the plane was flying and controlled the thrust accordingly.

By the time everyone grasped the situation, half a day of flight at two hundred kilometers per second had already passed. Not only was Mars easily visible through the portside window, but it was also clear to both pilots and passengers that they were rapidly passing it by.

"We now have two options," said Noa. "Either I continue advancing towards the other plane to rendezvous with it, or I decelerate, enter the orbit around Mars, and meet Plane 2 later on, once it reverses course and enters Mars' orbit. Which do you prefer?" she asked Marie, who assumed the helm of the other plane.

"I would rather rendezvous in orbit, because we never trained for a rendezvous in space," Marie responded. "How would we even see each other? It's like looking for an ant on a soccer field. Besides, we would be flying in each other's direction and risk running into each other's helium jet stream and no doubt other problems we have not considered which I can't even think of right now."

Noa, though she had not overshot Mars as badly as Marie's plane, still had to reverse course to enter orbit. Marie, who was much farther along, took over a day. The problem was meeting when they could only coordinate via Earth, which meant a twenty-minute communication lag in relaying messages, and a forty-minute time lag in receiving responses.

The original flight plan was to land on the Tharsis plain near the Mariner Canyon, adjacent to an opening to a Lava tunnel which was to serve as the Mars World 1 habitat. The Tharsis Plain was a massive 5,000 kilometer wide plain which covered nearly a quarter of the Martian surface. It was formed by volcanic activity over three billion years ago which spread lava across the plain. The 4,000 kilometer long, 7-kilometer-deep Mariner Canyon, the deepest canyon in the Solar System, bisected the Tharsis Plain, roughly at the Martian equator.

Noa relayed a message to Marie that at 14:00 (2:00 pm) Jerusalem time she would be orbiting Mars, north to south, thirty kilometers above the landing point, and that she expected Mary to orbit mars east to west, forty kilometers above the surface, to reach the same point at that time so they would be able to communicate directly and synchronize their operations. Jerusalem time was the accepted time in Rakefet flights as a compromise between competing American and Chinese demands, and as a legacy of Rakefet's Israeli origins.

Marie informed Noa she would arrive at the rendezvous, but there was no need for Noa to wait for her. Marie's plane had five communication satellites, relay transponders that she was supposed to scatter around Mars to generate a continuous communication capability with Earth. But it seemed it was now more important to generate continuous communications capability between the two planes. Once the communication satellites were deployed, communications with Earth might be continuous, but would still suffer from a ten-minute communication lag in either direction. The communication lag between their planes would be less than a second once the transponders were deployed, no more than a regular phone conversation. Noa relayed that, in that case, she was commencing landing.

4.

Landing on the Tharsis plain was far simpler than their initial Moon landing. First, Noa was more experienced. Second, the volcanic smooth rock of the Tharsis plain did not rise into dust clouds at the impact of the thruster jets as it did on the Moon. Mars also had an atmosphere, albeit a thin one. It inhibited dust from rising, although it also kept it from settling. An additional advantage in landing next to the Mariner Canyon was that any dust clouds raised by the native Martian wind currents tended to sweep any dust on the plain into the canyon.

The landing excited considerable attention in international media, as did the first step taken by humankind, as represented by Rotem, on the Moon.

"I hope that the journey of humanity in the Solar System brings prosperity to mankind, without any damage to the extraterrestrial environments," she said, extensively quoted by every media platform.

The American team followed her onto the Martian surface and began assembling the crane that would help unload the space-plane's cargo.

Mars, similar to Earth, revolves around its axis, with a slightly longer cycle of 24.5 hours — making for a similar night and day cycle.

It's temperature, however, was much lower. The maximum temperature was slightly over 0 degrees Celsius, but the minimum temperature dropped below minus 100 degrees Celsius, so that in the absence of insulating spacesuits, it was not possible to spend even a few seconds in the Martian night. Here, too, life would have to be limited to the worlds constructed inside frozen lava underground tunnels.

Assembling the crane took the now experienced team only two hours, in contrast to the entire day it took them to assemble the crane for the first time on the lunar surface. Not only were they more experienced now, but the level plain was also easier to work on, and Rotem lent them a hand as well. After assembling the crane, a bobcat capable of carrying three people was unloaded, as well as paint-bots and robots dedicated to preparing the tunnel for habitation.

At the same time, Marie entered orbit over Mars and began scattering the communication satellites over the equator in a stationary orbit. As Mars, unlike Earth, does not maintain a uniform axis of rotation, the satellites, though stationary, seemed to wobble North and South from the perspective of the Mars-bound humans. In any event, the satellites enabled restoration of direct contact between the planes.

They began, of course, with a whole slew of jokes concerning the ability of Plane 2's crew to differentiate between their own front and rear. After a few minutes of light banter, Nadav turned serious and asked: "Do you know how much water you have?"

Since every tank was connected to its own status gauge, and the additional tanks they added had no automatic status gauges attached, they could not answer this basic question.

"I'll check it out and get back to you," said Marie.

5.

The next day, as soon as the sun rose, Noa, Nadav and the American pilot Bill, took the bobcat to the Mariner Canyon, five kilometers from the landing site. Although the terrain was as flat as a pancake, the drive took an hour. They did not want to deplete the bobcat's battery and so they drove sedately, more or less at walking pace.

In the last five minutes, towards the end of the drive, they began to see the Mariner Canyon. In fact, they observed the South Bank of the Canyon which at that particular spot was slightly higher than their own Northern Bank.

At the same time the Rakefet studios, which was sharing camera transmissions from Mars — with a one-hour delay — to news networks, broadcast the bobcat's latest viewpoint. The transmission grabbed everyone's attention, as the world was looking forward to seeing the view from the rim of the Mariner Canyon. It was common knowledge that the Mariner Canyon was much larger than the Grand Canyon, the largest canyon on Earth. But this abstract knowledge did nothing to prepare them from the otherworldly scenery picked up by the bobcat's camera from fifty meters away from the rim of the canyon.

The Sun was nearing the zenith, and they walked by foot towards the edge of the cliff that overlooked the canyon. The view of the near-vertical seven kilometer drop to the bottom was breathtaking — quite literally. Visibility, though not always perfect on Mars, was absolutely clear that day — which was the cause of the mishap which was to follow.

Bill approached the edge of the cliff and glanced back towards them for a moment. Suddenly, without any of them comprehending what was happening, an invisible hand appeared to fling him upwards from the ground, tossing him up in the air before smashing him down into the ground. Fortunately, since the Martian gravity was only a third of that on Earth, Bill was not badly injured. His helmet visor, however, was completely smashed.

With the wisdom of hindsight, they understood that the winds exiting the canyon when it warmed up in the sun, climbing from a depth of seven kilometers, reached a speed of over four hundred kilometers per hours. Since it was a day of perfect visibility, without any dust, those winds, which seemingly sucked Bill inside them,[38] were effectively invisible.

Fortunately for Bill, it was 15:00 (3:00 pm) Tharsis Plain Standard Time, which was the warmest hour. The temperature outside was only minus 55 degrees Celsius. Had it been colder outside at the time, Bill would have perished instantly. As it was, he faced a near certain death, for Martian atmosphere was all at once too thin to breathe, extremely poor in oxygen and filled with carbon dioxide — all factors which would lead to certain suffocation even had the atmosphere been thick and oxygen rich enough to subsist upon.[39]

At the moment though, it was the cold which was the immediate threat — Bill could feel his face literally freezing off. Noa ran to help him, whereas Nadav instinctively ran in the opposite direction, towards the bobcat, seemingly running away in panic, and hiding inside the tractor. Noa, disappointed in Nadav, could not help but wonder if she knew him as well as she thought.

But Nadav did not huddle helplessly once he got inside the bobcat. Instead, he purposefully ripped out the padding from the driver's seat and ran back to Bill. Bill was shielding his face with his hands, but the fierce cold was still penetrating. Noa

38. The Venturi effect, which is a special case of the Bernoulli Effect, generates a sucking phenomenon.

39. A feeling of suffocation is not generated, as is commonly thought, by the absence of oxygen, but by a high concentration of carbon dioxide.

was unable to do anything for him aside from helping him to cover his face, which shielded him somewhat from the cold, but did absolutely nothing to prevent him from passing out from oxygen deprivation.

Nadav arrived and pushed her aside, shoving the padding he ripped out of the bobcat onto to Bill's face and tightening it to his helmet as much as he could. Bill couldn't see anything with the padding over his eyes, but his oxygen system was now isolated from the thin Martian atmosphere, and he was able to breathe. While thermal isolation was not perfect, his face was at least not freezing anymore.

Noa immediately grasped she needed to drive the bobcat to Bill. She rushed to the tractor, put it in manual driving mode, and headed towards the two men. Bill had recovered sufficiently enough to hold the padding to his face on his own, and Nadav was merely supporting him. They entered the tractor and made their way hastily back to the landing site, taking less than five minutes to reach the airlock they asked the plane to prepare for them. Within ten minutes they were back on the plane, much to Bill's relief.

Analysis of their photos showed that Nadav ran to the bobcat as soon as he saw the hole in Bill's mask — faster than any conceivable human instinct. Moreover, he did so after already thinking of using the padding of the driver's seat to seal Bill's mask. It was quite impossible.

Noa once again concluded that she did not really know Nadav. Her conclusion this time, however, was that she needed to trust him and his decisions.

It was morning in Israel, and the near disaster and Nadav's heroics were broadcast on every news channel across the world. Rakefet decided not to filter any of the events. Although it was only 03:00 am in Washington, NASA decided to wake Faina up to help craft their public response.

Meanwhile on the plane, Rotem began treating Bill's frostbite. Fortunately, Rotem had always been interested in medicine and had extensive medical knowledge — in high school she volunteered for the Red Star of David, and when she enlisted in the IDF she marked medic as her second choice should she not be accepted into the pilot program. Once she became a pilot, she asked to be sent to a medic course, and this request was granted, though she never completed the training, being recalled to her squadron on the last week. Now, all her interest and accumulated knowledge came in handy. Rotem shot down any suggestion of applying ointments to Bill's face — she knew the big problem would be the infections that would later develop. The frostbite was not too severe — though his face had turned blue, there were no black spots.

"Close your eyes," she said and poured iodine over his face before bandaging it tightly.

"You will probably need to keep the bandages on until we return to Earth," Rotem told him, "But we are being filmed right now, and I will likely receive new instructions within 20 minutes."

Faina, who was listening to their conversation, immediately picked up the phone and called Maira.

"Which doctor should we turn to, Maira?" she asked.

"You had best contact Dr. Lisa Mor from the Fairfax hospital in Washington D.C," Maira responded.

When the police banged on her door at 03:00 am, the last thing she imagined was that she was needed by NASA. As an Afro-American, she had frequently encountered discriminatory behavior by police officers and disturbing childhood memories emerged when her husband opened the door to the cops. To her surprise, the policemen addressed her respectfully, even deferentially.

"We have been sent here by NASA," they said. "We don't need you to leave your house, just contact a conference call with the

Mars Mission, as a dermatologist with facial specialization is required."

She stared at them in befuddlement.

"We don't know all the details yet, but you will be informed during the conversation. We will wait outside until the conversation is over, so we can assist should anything be required, or drive you to wherever you need to go, alright? Please inform us when the conversation is over, and we are no longer required."

"You can wait in the living room," her husband said, "I will brew you a pot of coffee."

Lisa had seen the transmission of Rotem bandaging Bill and was briefed by NASA about previous events.

"You need to understand that you are watching events unfold with a delay of about ten minutes, and by the time your instructions reach Rotem it will take another ten minutes," Faina explained. "So do not be hasty and carefully consider before you provide instructions, because this is not an interactive conversation."

"How long will it be before they reach a hospital on Earth?" Lisa asked.

"At least a week," Faina responded.

"The frostbite does not, at first glance, seem to be too serious," said Lisa after examining the photos and videos.

"Exposure to minus 55 degrees for a few minutes should not result in too much damage. Rotem's treatment also seems reasonable to me, she will just need to change the bandages twice a day."

As Bill was being treated, the American construction crew working outside the landing zone was wrapping up the unloading of the plane. By the time Lisa was done examining her patient, they had boarded the plane and were preparing for take-off.

Then Marie called from Plane 2.

"We double and triple checked," she said, "But as it currently appears, we only have a quarter of the water, which is fuel, with which we left."

"This is what I was afraid of," said Nadav.

When Plane 2 overshot Mars and continued accelerating, it had passed the two hundred kilometer per second threshold. Continuing their acceleration for two hours past their point, and then decelerating while they were traveling faster than two hundred kilometers per hour, expended massive amounts of fuel. They now didn't have enough fuel to get back to Earth.

"So, what should our flight plan on the way back be?" Noa asked.

"According to my calculations," Nadav replied, "so long as we don't pass the 100 kilometers per second threshold, they should have enough fuel to make it back. We will both travel at this speed. If they run out of fuel, we will have to link up and transfer their crew to our plane. Either way, it will now take about two weeks, instead of one week, to return. Nothing to worry about, we have plenty of oxygen and food."

"What if your calculations are wrong?" someone shot out.

"It would be bad, but not a disaster," Nadav explained: "Because another plane with large reserves of water, and means to transport it to our fuel tanks, is being prepared right now. If we find out we don't have enough fuel to make a controlled descent to Earth, we will enter Earth's orbit to be refueled there. Such a scenario would take some 20 days, rather than two weeks, to make it back.

"Tell me," Noa asked Nadav quietly when they were alone. "How did you realize so quickly that Bill's helmet needed to be sealed with the driver seat padding from the bobcat?"

"On the contrary, Nadav replied, "I did what I did because I am relatively slow."

Noa did not understand, and he explained.

"When I saw Bill flying through the air, I understood that he would need to be evacuated in the bobcat and ran towards it. By the time I began running I already saw him falling and you running towards him. Then I saw his helmet visor was smashed. I continued running to the Bobcat, thinking only about the need to evacuate him to the plane. Only once I got there did I realize it would take time to shift the Bobcat from automatic to manual drive. At that point I saw the padding on the seat, and I understood that ripping it out and running back to Bill would take less time than switching to manual control and driving to him." Nadav paused and smiled at her. "In the video it looked as if I was swift of thought and that I planned out everything in advance, but it was the exact opposite."

"My slowpoke," Noa whispered, kissing him before falling asleep. Her ability to fall asleep in any situation always astounded him anew. Nadav thought it was part of her ability to suppress anything, including fear.

While the return to Earth did indeed take 14 days to complete, there were no additional mishaps. The Chinese crew were disappointed they did not get to land on Mars, and it's government even more so, but everyone understood that this would be made good in the next Mars Mission.

Everyone was relieved when Lisa, the dermatologist who oversaw Bill's treatment, examined Bill in person and released him of his bandages with a clean bill of health.

6.

By this point there were already 14 active planes. Most were occupied by Helium 3 runs from the Moon and back. The helium importation was proceeding relatively slowly due to the fact that the Lunar Helium 3 mining systems were not yet operating at capacity, with less than a hundred kilograms of Helium 3 imported every month. Earthside, construction of the Helium 3 fuel electrical generation reactors were also lagging, so that meager stream of Helium 3 was sufficient to fuel the few reactors already built. Governments had begun to realize just how inexpensive electrical power generation from these new reactors really was, nearly free in comparison to fossil fuel power stations, and less than half the cost of nuclear fission or water-power power generation. Hence, they began investing in the construction of the new reactors.

'Fake News' pundits immediately began to spuriously claim that the new reactors would inflict infertility on those living nearby, and all sorts of other nonsense which was only spurred on by the big oil companies and religious fundamentalists.

The IAI only installed the rocket engines for these planes — all the other systems were installed in the United States for the 787 Boeing, and in Europe for the A350. Europe was upgrading a plane every three weeks, including preparing wing space for the rocket engine, the heat reflective gold coating and the interior systems which included business class seats for a crew of up to twenty-five people, oxygen systems, a sophisticated baggage compartment suitable for being unloaded under difficult conditions and a system of efficient airlocks.

Boeing 787s were upgraded at roughly the same rate, so the IAI had to install new rocket engines for three planes every month. The final inspections of the planes were performed by NASA. Every malfunction found by the inspection team resulted in a one million dollar fine for the company responsible for the malfunction — IAI, Airbus or Boeing. A fundamental malfunction resulted in a fine of ten million dollars. To prevent the responsible party from settling their way out of the fine in court, as commonly occurs in Israeli courts, the jurisdiction in case of malfunctions was determined to be the Chinese.

The first time IAI was fined for one million dollars, it appealed to the Chinese court in Beijing. The court lasted for less than 90 minutes and the ruling was to raise the fine to a million and a half dollars. The judge wrote in his ruling that Chinese law mandated a double fine for spurious appeals to the court, but as IAI was not yet familiar with the Chinese legal system, he would be lenient and set the fine at only one and a half million rather than two million. IAI's legal department was drily informed that, in such unambiguous cases, no appeal was possible.

Airbus ended being fined twice for one million dollars, Boeing three times, and IAI was fined six times for one million dollars and once for ten million dollars on account of a fundamental malfunction.

As Shlomo foresaw, the fines deterred everyone. After a few months, the malfunctions found in the final inspections were so rare and negligible that NASA decided there was no point in levying fines for them.

At this stage, the Rakefet board decided to place greater emphasis on Mars. Control of robots from Earth, in spite of the autonomy they were programmed with, was very complicated and slow. It took ten minutes to relay new orders to Mars, and another ten minutes to see the feedback from the Red Planet. Mars-bound operators were clearly necessary in a way that they were not on the Moon, which made the preparation of World 1 all the more necessary.

The concept of survivability, a cornerstone of Rakefet's thinking, was to ensure that the Lunar and Martian habitats could serve as a safety net for human survival in case humanity suffered extinction on Terra, and for however many centuries it may take for Earth to be recolonized. Sustainable Martian habitats, far away from any conflict which may erupt should humanity fall into a violent spiral under the pressure of a collapsing eco-system and depleted resources, would greatly increase human-ity's chances of survival.

In the meantime, a dramatic development took place. Chi-nese efforts at cracking the secret of the ultimate superconduc-tor finally bore fruit. After screening over 100,000 substances, they identified one with extraordinary superconductor proper-ties. The Chinese substance was superior to Adam and Nadav's substance in its temperature tolerance — it remained a super-conductor even at 125 Celsius degrees, above the boiling point of water. Where it was not equal to Rakefet's superconductor was in its high-capacity currents transmission. The Chinese immediately introduced their substrate into MRI and electric train systems, undermining Rakefet's dominance of this hun-dred-billion-dollar market. While this came as a blow to the company, it was not yet a threat to their monopoly over the rocket engine, nor of the global energy market.

7.

As soon as the first mission from Mars returned, two additional planes were sent there, this time with the purpose of setting up a permanent human presence. Residential containers were brought in to enable robot operators to work from Mars rather than from Earth.

This time the flights were careful not to pass the one hundred and seventy kilometers per hour threshold, leading to a flight time of ten days to Mars and ten days for the return to Earth. This time, there were no fuel problems.

Leaving a permanent ground crew on Mars required maintaining regular flights there. It was therefore determined that a two-plane Mars flight would be performed twice a month. Given that the flight, unloading and return took around three weeks, there were four planes: two 787's and two A350s enroute at any given time. In any event, the board of directors at Rakefet decided to stockpile sufficient supplies to last the Mars-based crew six months in the case of an emergency. Thus, the size of the ground crew was limited at first, until a sufficient quantity of supplies was stockpiled.

The size of the crew also determined the number of bobcat operators and hence the pace of the work.

Engineers in France built a miniature nuclear reactor capable of fitting within a single container. Though unable to produce as much electricity as the Chinese reactors, it was more than enough for a small world with a few hundred robots and several dozen crew members. The nuclear reactor arrived and was installed on Mars on the third flight.

Immediately after the reactor arrived, they began to install a cable car down to the lower levels of the Mariner Canyon, where frozen water could be found. This water was used as a source of oxygen generation to fill the tunnel in which the world was constructed. The other components of the world's atmosphere could be concentrated from the existing components of Martian atmosphere.

To mine the ice, it was necessary to saw it into one-meter square cubes and then bring it up by cable car. A single square meter had a mass of about a ton, which weighed about three hundred kilos on Mars. This was weight that a cable car could handle without requiring an overly thick cable.

One great advantage of the Martian atmosphere was that it enabled the use of choppers. True, the atmosphere was very thin compared to Earth, but gravity was also much weaker. Martian choppers had different design constraints than those of earthside choppers. They had to be electric, for gasoline-based engines would not work without oxygen. In addition, the rotors turning had to be much faster, therefore the blades themselves were larger, and the angle greater as well. The Sikorsky Company in the United States had assumed the mission the previous year, and they had prepared a dozen Martian Choppers, each capable of bearing four people and a little luggage, a load of around two hundred kilos on Earth, but on Mars, a little over six hundred kilo mass. The choppers could work remotely via an operator on the Martian surface (no earthside operator could manage a chopper with a twenty-minute delay, of course) or it could be manually operated by a pilot in the cockpit.

Three American astronauts were trained to fly the Martian choppers. The decision was also taken to train Noa to operate them, hence as soon as the initial Mars Mission returned, Noa left for a month-long training course in the United States.

Nadav did not join her this time around and she really missed him. The feeling of missing Nadav was foreign to her. Noa thought that this must be what her reserve pilot comrades felt when they were called up for their annual 30-day service. Nadav stayed to complete the inspections of the Bismuth fueled Ionic engine. In the meantime, many scientists pinned their hopes on the Solar reflection mirror scheduled to be emplaced between the Earth and the Sun.

8.

Within a relatively short period of time, the Boeing Company was able to assemble the first primary unit around which the three 787 planes would need to revolve. The Airbus would take several more months to complete the central unit around which the A350 planes would revolve.

The central unit was constructed out of four parts. Each component was brought up into orbit separately to be assembled on the space planes, as they were too large to all fit in a single plane. The assembly required several flights of technicians and engineers who operated robots and oversaw the astronauts performing the tasks requiring manual human input.

Once the unit was completed, it began orbiting earth as a satellite. Three planes were to be simultaneously sent up to enter orbit, together with the central unit and dock and berth. Rotem was sent to the unit as the Israeli pilot alongside an American, Russian and Japanese crew. No Chinese or Europeans were sent as the European teams were occupied in manning the Mars flights and the Chinese were busy constructing the lunar worlds.

Rotem and her crew practiced docking and berthing the three planes to the central unit and dismantling them. On each flight they performed four berthings and four separations of the three planes.

From the second flight onwards, every time they performed the docking and berthing, they also performed the yawing maneuver, so that the three planes performed a rotation around the central unit. When the yawing was performed, the central unit was left without any gravity, but on the plane itself, a centrifugal force was generated which gave the feeling of gravity. Not earth-level gravity, but somewhat higher than on the Moon. This was very convenient for the crew because objects no longer floated in space and it was possible to eat, drink and go to the bathroom in a regular manner.

By the third flight they were already operating the central unit, including Rotem's cockpit. A single pilot could control the flight of the entire three-plane formation through the cockpit. A crew from each plane could transfer to the central unit via the foldable sleeve and manage the flight from the unit's cockpit. In addition, in emergencies it would be possible to transfer the entire crew of a malfunctioning or damaged plane to a functional plane via the central unit.

Thus, after a month of tests and inspections, a triple flight to Mars was approved. This flight was characterized by far greater comfort than the usual missions. First, all of the crews enjoyed gravity throughout. Second, the pilot crew performed only a third of the shifts, although they were in zero gravity when piloting the triple flight from the central unit.

The flight began when three different planes took off simultaneously from Ben Gurion Airport, Hawaii and China. They were all teams who had trained over the past month in the triple docking maneuver and flight. Noa had returned from her chopper training in the United States but was not familiar with the connection to the Central Unit, while Noa and Nadav had only just joined the Mars flight as passengers. They were supposed to stay on Mars for two months, during which Noa was set to fly the helicopters as well as serve as a back-up emergency evacuation pilot.

Given this, the Israeli plane carried a single Chinese pilot who had also trained in the triple flight. Once they docked and began rotating, Noa and Nadav felt right at home. The gravity on each plane was only slightly higher than that of the Moon, and they had already adopted the moon as their home. Each plane had only two pilots, plus the five passengers and cargo. The planes were constructed so as to hold five pilots and twenty-five passengers comfortably in business class conditions, or five pilots and a hundred passengers in more crowded conditions such as during an emergency. With only five passengers, it was very comfortable indeed, similar to travelling first class on a luxury airlines — including a shower every two days for each passenger and an office-like cubby with a desk, screen and so forth included for every passenger. This enabled them to work productively during the twenty-day round-trip.

Nadav was comfortable enough, for he had plenty of work, but Noa found the trip rather boring. She decided to inspect all of the planes and the central unit. Each plane was carrying two new choppers to Mars, as well as an electric lines system intended to transfer electricity between the Mariner Canyon to the Mars 1 World.

Electricity was required in order to activate the cable car engines and the station at the bottom of the Mariner Canyon. Therefore, a nuclear fusion power station had already been assembled on Mars and enough Helium 3 brought to it directly from the moon to last many years to come.

What was needed now was water to be extracted from the lower Mariner Canyon so that oxygen could be produced for the Martian World 1. Obviously, the electrical and cable car infrastructure required to extract the water would be more expensive the lower they went into the canyon, which is precisely why they selected the highest accessible ice deposit in the Mariner Canyon — "only" 4.5 kilometers deep. No road would be built to connect the water deposit to World-1: all infrastructure would be laid down via helicopter.

The tunnel selected to house Martian World-1 was thirty kilometers long with an average diameter of around 150 meters. Ultimately, the plan was to pressurize 13 to 15 kilometers, with a partition every 500 meters on average. Due to the proximity of water to the world, filling it with oxygen could be accomplished relatively rapidly. Nitrogen, which makes up 80% of Earth's atmosphere but only 3% of the atmosphere on Mars, was to be extracted through pumping Martian air, separating and condensing the nitrogen and venting the filtered nitrogen into the sealed tunnel. This, too, was a relatively simple and rapid mission.

It was therefore possible to build much larger worlds on Mars than on the Moon. The completion of all of World-1's 15 kilometers on Mars was slated for conclusion far before the Moon worlds, even though they were both smaller and had begun to be constructed prior to the Martian worlds.

The larger Martian worlds could house and sustain 10,000 human beings, but the plan was to restrict population to no more than 1,000 during the first two years. The Martian worlds would also house farm animals, chickens, and everything else that would be required for a small colony to be self-sustaining.

Prior to landing, the triple flight entered orbit around Mars. The three planes terminated their yawing and detached themselves from the central unit. The termination of the yawing generated chaos on the Israeli plane, for there were quite a few items that the Israelis had forgotten to fasten down and they began to float around inside the plane. Noa, who had not flown for a long while, returned to the cockpit and asked to be given the helm to land in World-1, near the Mariner Canyon.

"I'd love to," the Chinese pilot told her. By this point, no-one thought it was a particular honor to land a plane on Mars since the procedure had been repeated enough times so as to become routine.

The central unit remained in orbit around Mars, waiting for the planes to dock and berth to it for the return voyage. Noa was the last of the three to arrive at the landing pad. The majestic Martian scenery astounded all of her passengers, who had a clear view ahead with the curtain separating the cockpit and passenger compartment open. This time, Noa arrived from the direction of the massive Mariner Canyon. Before she completed her descent, everyone was treated to a view of the twenty-six-kilometer-tall Mount Olympus, the highest mountain in the solar system, its base ringed by six kilometer high cliffs which were visible on the horizon.

It took several hours to unload all three planes from the two helicopters with the cables intended for the cable car. It would require another five three-plane flights over the next two and a half months to deliver all the cables.

After being unloaded, the planes immediately prepared for takeoff to return to orbit where they docked and berthed with the central unit to begin their ten-day flight back to Earth.

Prior to returning home, Rotem bid farewell to Noa and Nadav.

"It is just like when we said goodbye on the Moon when we stayed there," Noa said.

"I envy you," Rotem told her, "because you are inseparable, while I have to say goodbye to Nimrod and my children before every flight. Now with the flights to Mars, each goodbye means twenty days or more of separation, which is a very long time."

The Martian World-1 was beginning to take shape and form, with the first two partitions containing Zone 1 and Zone 2 having been constructed already. Zone 1 was just 120 meters long, in contrast to the other 500-meter-long zones. It would later be used as a maintenance area and for entry/exit to and from the rest of the complex but was currently serving as the world's sole residential area. Although several residential containers had been placed within it, only the containers were pressurized. Once a regular supply of water from the Mariner canyon was established, Zone 1 would begin to be pressurized. In the meantime, it had been filled with nitrogen so as to ensure it would be ready to absorb oxygen and become breathable with air for human beings. At the moment the world only had fifty workers, thirty of whom were teleoperators of the bobcat tractors and other robots. Given that each operator could only pull an 8 hour shift a day, this meant only ten robots could be simultaneously operated throughout the day. Still, the operators were not granted days off as they only stayed on Mars for a month before returning to Earth for a month-long vacation. Nadav and Noa once again received a high-status residence. This time Noa took this special treatment for granted, only casually musing on how easy it was for leaders to slide down the slippery slope of corruption.

9.

The day-to-day operations on Mars World-1 were completely different from what Noa and Nadav were used back on the Lunar Worlds. The Moon World was operated, in practice, from Earth, so that the Moon employees were almost completely idle, while Robots scurried around them 24/7, each operated by two earthbound teleoperators at any given time. Here on Mars, the exact opposite seemed to be true. While everyone worked 24/7 operating the robots, given that there weren't enough people on Mars to operate all the robots around the clock, the robots appeared half-idle. Unlike on the Moon, where earth-based teleoperators could manage their robots with only a three second communication-lag, the twenty-minute communication lag made this quite impossible on Mars. The robots were programmed to perform autonomously only a very limited range of actions during these twenty minutes, such as driving from one location to another or performing repetitive actions. Most construction and tunneling activities did not meet these parameters, hence requiring a local operator to manage the robots. Given the manpower shortage, each robot was assigned only one operator, who could not work around the clock — given the basic needs of human beings to have lunch, visit the restroom and take the occasional break. Accordingly, on Mars, one could occasionally see a robot idling, something which simply did not happen on the Moon.

Once the choppers were assembled, they looked nothing like the helicopters we know on Earth. While the fuselage was not too different, the rotors of the choppers looked more like fan blades than a helicopter propeller. They were extremely wide compared to regular planes, due to the very thin Martian atmosphere which required a greater surface area to generate lift.

The chopper could lift a mass of four hundred kilos on Earth and could fly up to 185 kilometers per hour for about an hour and a half under battery power. On Mars, it was capable of lifting over a ton, equivalent to one cubic meter of ice. Deeper in the canyon, where the atmosphere was much thicker, the chopper could lift around two tons.

This time around, Noa had plenty of work to do and it was Nadav who was "unemployed" and lazed about at home. Nadav still had plenty of work to do, for the flying mattress design was a massive task, but he did his part from the tiny office in their apartment.

The first day Noa only trained and familiarized herself with the chopper as it was a new aircraft for her. Also, she figured, flying a simulator is never like flying in real life — and flying on Mars is not like flying on Earth.

Noa was weary of approaching the cliffs of Mariner Canyon at the edge of the Tharsis Plain. She well remembered the wind that rushed up from the bottom of the canyon, flinging Bill upwards the moment he approached the edge. The engineers made their calculations and came to the conclusion that while approaching the edge of the cliff by foot was exceedingly dangerous, flying over it with a helicopter was safe, provided an altitude of two hundred meters — four hundred meters to keep a safety margin — was maintained.

On the evening of the first day, Noa rose to an altitude of six hundred meters and passed over the cliff face. The passage was far from smooth. While the helicopter made it across the threshold, it took quite a buffet. As soon as the passage was completed, the flight felt normal again. Measurement devices inside the helicopter tracked the strength of the winds and the tremors it went through. Sikorsky engineers who analyzed their readings said that while the winds were very powerful indeed, the plane was capable of absorbing much more powerful blows. Since they were cautious American engineers rather than fast and loose Israelis, Noa was inclined to believe them.

In any event, Noa identified a location about ten kilometers north of her point of passage in which the descent to the bottom of the canyon was less steep and hence the winds rising from the bottom of the canyon could be expected to be less powerful. She resolved to attempt the passage over the cliff edge at that point next time around.

The greatest danger to helicopters on Mars were the dust storms. Those storms, science fiction descriptions aside, presented no danger to human beings on the surface, as the thin atmosphere meant that even a hundred kilometer per hour tempest would feel to an individual on the surface like no more than a fifteen kilometer per hour breeze on Earth. It would take a super powerful gale, like the four-hundred-kilometer per hour wind emerging out of the Mariner Canyon and into poor Bill, to pummel a human being — and even that was only an issue because the low Martian gravity did not anchor humans quite as firmly to the ground as Terran gravity.

Helicopters with rotors the size of windsails was something else entirely — they were far more sensitive to winds. Small regional sandstorms developed on Mars several times each year. Once every several years a global sandstorm would develop which covered all of Mars with a cloud of dust. The first such storm to be observed by telescopes from Earth was recorded in 1909. Such storms contain foci with winds hundreds of kilometers per hour strong which cover the entire Martian surface for a period ranging between a few days to several months. During this period winds at a minimum speed of seventy kilometers per hour (the speed required to raise dust) swept across Mars. With the exception of the high velocity winds at the foci of these storms, the only problem this global dust storm would present for human beings on the surface was reduced visibility. For choppers and systems dependent of solar panels or their energy, however, such storms were extremely problematic.

The Chinese achievement in developing and marketing superior superconductors led the Americans to redouble their own efforts and investigate new directions. Specifically, they decided (quite typically) to 'think bigger.' Their idea was to construct a science fiction style spaceship the size of an actual ocean liner or aircraft carrier. This ship would contain a large nuclear reactor (or two, for backup). Thrust would be provided by Bismuth engines, like the one Nadav developed.

Nadav had solved several differential equations enabling the concentration of thrust power even at very high energies, whereas the American researchers did not yet have a solution for these such issues.

Soon, the experts at NSA and their ability to cross reference tiny pieces of information and leverage personal connections came into play. They began to work Ismail by utilizing the relationship between Faina and Maira. The Bismuth engine was not a classified secret for Rakefet, hence Ismail did not consider it to be a secret. The NSA arranged for him to be invited to various conferences and, following urgings by her colleagues in Mount Sinai hospital, Ismail's mother pressured him to participate and make a name for himself. At those conferences, Ismail met with scientists and engineers informally in between presentations, and when the subject of the Bismuth engine came up, seemingly naturally, he provided them with the explanations which were to enable American researchers to solve the equations.

10.

The day after her inaugural flight, Noa began working hard. That first flight was primarily meant to photograph the contours of the area in which the cable car would pass. Noa flew along the entire line, surveying the points where the cable car pylons would be erected, until she reached the ice mining site. She used a special electric saw to carve out samples from the ice. It was incredibly easy to saw through the ice with, so, rather than contenting herself with a small sample, she stuffed the chopper full with several hundred kilo mass pieces of ice. Then she began flying up to World-1. On her way up, she examined the massive cliff, several kilometers high. No such cliffs existed on Earth, where gravity, rain and tectonic activity combined to wear them down. Peering upwards, she could not even see the upper edge of the canyon.

However Noa was not just there to sample ice and survey the proposed cable car route. She had been assigned a secret mission by Rakefet, and her photos and videos for this mission were only transferred on to the company. That was the reason she was not assigned a copilot. Already on her flight back up Noa observed a shining golden layer on one of the rock formations. Noa mused that this was the gold needed for NASA's mirror. The layer was truly glittering in the sun after the sandstorms of Mars had polished it.

Yet the gold mining plan was not where the surface deposit was exposed. It was slightly to the north, where geologists believed they would be able to rapidly access thick veins of gold. Rakefet did not want this activity to be recorded and exposed to the public, as any activity associated with large amounts of gold attracted criminal attention. Thus, the less information was made available to the public, the less danger there would be.

In any event, the crews first needed to secure a water supply that would enable the expansion of Mars World-1, which would enable the establishment of a gold mining operation. The gold was not a goal in and of itself, rather a means by which to regulate Earth's climate and turn humanity back from the slippery slope towards extinction.

Their instructions were to plan their flights so that their batteries would still have half their charge by the time they returned to World-1. In practice, Noa saw her batteries were three quarters full when she returned from her first flight into the canyon. So, it was on the second mission when she begun ferrying pylon components to the planned site of the final cable-car stop. When she returned from that second mission it was already early evening, and she was exhausted. She fell asleep the moment she got home, and Nadav had to carry her into bed — not too difficult for him even on Earth, let alone on Mars. During the Martian night, the analysis of the ice she had mined was completed — it was found to contain excellent quality water.

The explanation for the relatively slow depletion of the battery seemed to be, according to the Sikorsky engineers, that flight through the lower portions of the canyon required far less energy due to the denser atmosphere, as well as the updraft from the bottom of the canyon.

The next day, Noa performed three missions, each including about half an hour of flight and a further hour and a half of loading and unloading equipment, including sawing off chunks of ice. No one drank the ice water, at least not before the biology specialist, the Ukrainian Sergei, ensured it did not contain any Martian viruses or bacteria. Sergei only knew basic English, and his homeland was not represented on Rakefet's board of directors, but he was still brought in in spite of Russian opposition, because he was second to none in his field.

"Well, the water contains fascinating viruses," Sergei declared after a week of review.

"We need to get the water to Earth for a more thorough analysis. However, all of viruses are actually fossilized. They "lived" on Mars over ten million years ago, but there is no life in the water now — it is perfectly safe to drink," Sergei summarized and as proof of the fact, he poured a full glass of water and drained it down his throat.

"As delicious as spring water," he said, smacking his lips.

As everything was being recorded, soon the video of Sergei drinking Martian water was broadcast on Earth. Galit, who was in China at the time, also saw the unsanctioned consumption of the Martian water. Galit immediately ordered Sergei into isolation, but he refused. This generated an immediate legal quandary. Since World-1 was under European administration, a European court had legal jurisdiction. The legal counsel of Rakefet's European Branch was on vacation in Venice at the time, and so the judge on duty received an urgent motion to enforce compulsory isolation on a Ukrainian citizen on Mars.

The judge did not understand what this had to do with the jurisdiction of his court, and his initial inclination was to rule that the court had no dominion to discuss the matter. But then he was told that because Mars World-1 was under European jurisdiction, any legal dispute on such a locale could be tried in court, specifically, the first court to which the case was submitted — his court.

Furthermore, should the judge fail to rule in favor of an immediate isolation, this might lead to the outbreak of a pandemic which would make COVID-19, which killed 150,000 Italians, look like a minor winter flu. Indeed, unchecked exposure of Terran populations to extraterrestrial viruses might end up being worse than the Black Plague, which killed a third of all Europeans. The judge may have dismissed the Black Plague as ancient history, but memory of the COVID-19 pandemic was still fresh in his mind. Accordingly, once he learned the facts of the case, he ruled in favor of immediate isolation in accordance with the Italian Public Health Ordinance.

"But even so," wondered the judge, "How did this case end up in Italy? And in Venice of all places?"

When he heard that the reason was that their legal consultant was vacationing in the Danieli Hotel in Venice, he shook his head, smiled, and muttered in Italian: "Wondrous are the ways of God," before signing the verdict.

After ten days of isolation passed with Sergei displaying no symptoms, the experts reached a consensus that there really was no need to keep the Ukrainian engineer in quarantine, and that the Martian water was safe to drink. And indeed, some of the World-1 crew decided to try the water, and they all agreed it tasted quite wonderful. It took two more months for everyone to feel comfortable enough to drink the local water. Some even flouted regulations, bringing a few bottles back to Earth and selling them to luxury restaurants for over a hundred dollars per small bottle.

In the following days, Noa grew increasingly efficient, performing five to six missions a day. She unloaded a robot at the site of the final cable car station. The robot duly began to assemble the cable car pylon from the components she had dropped off earlier. She was managing to complete the transfer of components and a robot to one pylon site every day. Since the cable car required 27 pylons, the completion of the transfer was projected to require a month. In the meantime, the other chopper, headed by a Norwegian pilot, began its own work. Norway had belatedly joined the EU after a combination of falling gas prices and rising sea levels brought the vulnerability of the fjord dotted land home to its government, and once it became clear that the only way to gain influence over Rakefet's decision-making was to join the regional block.

The Norwegian pilot took charge of dropping off supplies and robots for the power stations and their requisite high voltage cables and pylons. The geologists said that on Mars, the three power stations needed to provide backup to Mars World-1 need to be twenty kilometers apart.

Once the robot and its teleoperator on World-1 completed assembling the lowest pylon of the cable car, they were tasked with slicing out blocks of ice from the frozen lake. The robot duly began stacking up piles of half a cubic meter sized ice blocks. At the conclusion of every mission, Noa would load two ice blocks from the lower pylon and deposit one of them at pylon number 10, about a kilometer below the level of the Tharsis plain. Up to pylon 10, the atmosphere was sufficiently thick to easily lift a cubic meter of ice. Once she deposited half her load at pylon 10, Noa ferried the remaining block to World 1 — to a total of about three cubic meters per day. As the internal temperature in World-1 was around 22 degrees, the ice rapidly melted, and Zone 1 looked like a Thai fishing village. The residential containers were surrounded by water and connected by bridges the robots had built to keep people from muddying their feet. The robots had begun to plant vegetation in an effort to generate enough oxygen that people would be able to breathe outside of the containers.

Zone 1 contained atmosphere that was pumped in and condensed from the thin Martian atmosphere, saturated with carbon dioxide which the plants eagerly broke down, generating oxygen as a byproduct. For the plants, the carbon dioxide and water-saturated environment created optimal conditions, and they rapidly grew.

Within 100 days, the atmosphere inside Zone 1 reached 10% oxygen — half the concentration of Earth. It was now possible to breathe outside the residential compartment, albeit with some difficulty and discomfort, less because of the low oxygen concentration and more because of the high carbon dioxide concentration. Many people gave up wearing a spacesuit for short walks, instead rushing from one container to another, trying to breathe as little as possible along the way.

Nadav would occasionally join Noa in the chopper just to get outside the container and enjoy a change in scenery. The view was incredible, and they would fly along the canyon for their pleasure as well as on missions.

Rakefet eventually chose to share the pictures they took of the canyon's gold layers, for they did not contain the location where mining would actually be initiated, and they drove earthside audiences wild.

Within two months since the construction work began, the lower pylons of the cable car had been assembled in place and Noa's ice runs targeted the stockpile of ice blocks she had accumulated at the pylon 10 site.

In addition, Noa covertly unloaded another robot on the site intended for the gold mining. A highly experienced, dedicated teleoperator crew, who had their own separate container to work from, was responsible for the operations of the so-called gold robot. Everyone who was not in on the secret was sure that the Indian crew was operating robots that were working on the preparation of deeper zones of World-1 for habitation purposes.

11.

Rotem finally arrived on Mars with Nimrod and her children. No children had ever been on any Rakefet flights, and their arrival was obviously preceded by quite a few arguments.

During the Rakefet board meeting preceding the flight, the Russians, Europeans and Japanese opposed the notion of permitting children to fly to Mars, whereas the Americans, Chinese and Galit supported it. The Indians and Shlomo abstained, and so Rotem was authorized to take her family with her.

The family spaceflight turned out to be a smash hit on every television channel. The children passed from plane to plane through the foldable sleeves so they could be seen passing from yaw-induced gravity on one plane, to zero gravity on the central unit, only to return to gravity on the second plane. People on Earth had gotten used to the frequent spaceflights and the inclusion of children reignited their interest.

During Rotem's landing, she noted dust storms at the bottom of the canyon. After landing, she was told that Noa had descended to the bottom of the canyon to bring new batteries to the robot mining ice at the bottom of the canyon. Because of the electro-static charge formed by the dust storm, they had lost contact with her. Noa should have returned by now, but no one had heard from her.

While inside the canyon, Noa had been unloading the new battery for the "gold robot" when the dust storm hit her. A moment before, Noa had picked up a gold nugget the size of a fist and placed it in the chopper. I wonder what Daniela would say about this nugget, she thought. What she probably needed to do was to leave the chopper and tie it down to stakes pounded into the ground.

But Noa did not know how long the storm would last, and if it lasted for more than a few days, she would die of starvation in the canyon.

Therefore, in spite of the storm, she tried to fly back to World 1. That turned out to be a grave mistake. The moment she took off, the storm intensified.

Noa would have had no trouble withstanding the Martian winds on the surface in spite of their rapid speed — the thinness of the Martian wind reduced their impact. But the massive rotors of the chopper were deliberately designed to harness thin air on the Tharsis plain for lift. But, at a depth of over four kilometers below the plain, air density was nearly twice as high. The wind therefore impacted the chopper with far greater strength than the chopper was designed to withstand. As soon as the chopper left the ground, the wind tossed it around like a piece of paper. After a few minutes in which it swept the chopper down the canyon at four hundred kilometers per hour, the storm turned it over and shattered its rotors. The chopper immediately dropped to the ground from a height of ten meters. Such a fall would have killed Noa on Earth, but with Martian gravity only a third that of Earth, the blow was not quite as severe. The wind continued rolling the chopper down the canyon until it fell down a sand slide. Sand continued to pour down on the chopper, burying it completely.

Above, the wind continued to howl. Noa was nearly knocked senseless by the blows she took during the crash and rolling of the chopper, and lost consciousness when the chopper fell down the sand slide. Her China-made spacesuit was only designed to provide five hours of oxygen, with an emergency reserve for another hour. Noa had already used up about an hours' worth of the oxygen supply on her flight to the gold robot mining site. When Noa was able to rouse herself back to consciousness, she did so to the sound of the warning alarm, indicating her emergency reserve oxygen supply had been activated.

She had less than an hour worth of oxygen left. The warning was originally in Chinese, but since Noa had been paired with this suit during her training in China, they had translated the warning and other audio notices into English — though not any English recognizable as such by any native speaker.

Regardless, Noa understood the warning loud and clear. She knew her time for a rescue was very limited. When she realized the chopper was buried and upside down, she was unable to maintain consciousness. It was though a determined anesthesiologist insisted on shutting down her brain as she fell back into merciful unconsciousness.

While she slept, someone she could not see spoke to her.

"You will soon wake up," the voice informed her, "and you need to perform several tasks in the order I tell you, alright?

First of all, you need to release yourself from the pilot's harness. But since the chopper is upside down, you need to hold on to the ceiling with one hand as you release the harness in the other, directing the direction of your subsequent fall to the left.

After you do that, you should find, right next to your legs, the rapid connection to the choppers' oxygen supply. You need to connect your spacesuit oxygen tank to this rapid connection. Do you hear me? Good. Since the cable is not long enough, you need to lie on your back and perform the connection with both hands behind your back, without seeing what your hands are doing, relying exclusively on your sense of touch."

Even in her dream, this seemed completely insane. With all due respect to ones sense of touch, to pull off such a stunt she would need to be an octopus — and preferably not in a spacesuit. As if in response to her unspoken reservations, the instructing voice seemed to pause. Noa felt the speaker was smiling, as if she had told it a good joke.

"Alright. Move yourself slightly towards the center of the helicopter, lie down on your right side so you can see your left hand, and use your right hand to support yourself. Then lean on the rapid coupler to keep it from moving."

This maneuver seemed very problematic to her as well, but this time she did not argue.

"You need to lie that way for half an hour in order to fill the oxygen tanks of your suit. Once this is done, uncouple the hose — there won't be much oxygen left there in any event."

"The helicopter is completely buried in the sand," the voice continued. "You need to operate your communication device to contact Mars World-1 and let them know where you are. They won't be able to see the chopper from above because the sand conceals it completely."

"So how do you know the helicopter is covered in sand?" she asked.

"Stop arguing about everything!" the voice barked back at her.

Noa shut up and listened to the rest of the instructions.

"The helicopter antenna is broken," the voice told her. "So, you need to take the communications device out. It has a coaxial cable[40] in the rear which stretches out towards the antenna. You need to pull out as much of this cable as you can and peel off its end with your teeth. Peel it and leave about forty exposed centimeters from the inner wire. That is about a quarter the wavelength of the communication device and can serve as an ersatz antenna. You need to push this antenna out of the dust covering the helicopter.

"To get out of the helicopter, you need to shatter the front windshield, and to do that you need the hammer left there, below the pilot's chair."

Nadav once told her that his experience in the IDF's Armored Corps was that any technical problem could be solved with a one-kilo hammer — except for problems which could only be solved with a five-kilo hammer. That was why he kept a ham-

---

40. An electric cable composed of a mesh or conductive cylinder which coats an isolating layer through which another conductive wire passes. Such a cable is used to transmit high frequency signals.

mer beneath his chair when he flew with Noa — and sure enough, he forgot to remove it when he left.

"How do you know there is a hammer beneath the chair next to the pilot's seat?" Noa asked her guide.

"Because you are in my head," she answered together with the voice.

Then, Noa began to stir. She found it very difficult to wake up, much like being roused after being put under anesthesia in hospital. Blurrily, she heard the Chinese spaceship system inform her that she only had ten minutes of oxygen remaining. Noa was still blurry and unable to move her hands. She was angry at herself for wasting precious time on dreams. By the time she was able to move her hands, the overhead voice was telling her that she was completely out of oxygen.

During their training in China they were told: This is the final stage where you die. Noa could certainly feel the terrible suffocation from an inability to draw in oxygen.

But her hands were rock-steady now, obedient to her will, and mechanically followed the instructions of her inner voice, one step after the other.

Within thirty seconds she was lying on her side, her right hand stabilizing her and not allowing the oxygen coupler to move, while with the left she grabbed her suit's hose and tried to connect it to the coupler. Noa thought to herself that when she planned this in her head it was much easier, both because the coupler was not so stubborn, and because in her dream she had air, whereas now she had no air and as she suffocated her vision faded away to darkness. The voice in her head was right in one respect: it was only thanks to her sense of touch that she was able to connect herself to the helicopter's oxygen supply. But now she had to open the oxygen tap and this was beyond her physical capabilities while she was suffocating. Noa made one last effort to reach the handle and passed out again.

After a few more minutes Noa regained consciousness. She felt that she had air to breathe. Noa did not remember managing to open the oxygen handle, but the fact was that it was now open. Noa continued to lie there for another half an hour, until the oxygen tank in her suit filled up and the helicopter balloon emptied out. All according to plan.

After half an hour, Noa decided it was really stupid to rip out the communications device from its position in the chopper. She decided to first try to leave the chopper and realized that her internal voice was right — everything was buried under the dust, and there was no possibility of getting out.

Then, Noa remembered the hammer. She had to smash the front windshield with all her might to crack the glass.

It took her another half hour of repeated blows to the crack before the glass around it truly cleared.

This energetic effort may have only taken half an hour, but it burned up over two of the five hours she had left.

Having broken the glass, the sand simply poured into the chopper. Noa could see the sunlight, but only vaguely, through the spilling sand. It was now clear beyond a shadow of a doubt that the communications device could not operate without an antenna.

Noa remembered her original plan and scrambled to extract the communications device, but it was covered with sand that had spilled in through the shattered windshield. Noa ruefully recalled that the original plan was to first extract the communication device and only then break down the window. She was now sorry she did not stick to the program but told herself with a smile that there was no point crying over spilled sand.

Noa began searching for the chopper's communication device beneath the sand that was piled upon it. When she found it and pulled it out, she was careful not to disconnect the power cables connected to the device. She identified the coaxial cable at the rear of the device via touch, extracted as much of it as she could, and was left with two meters. She used her teeth to peel the final forty centimeters of the cable in order to keep a quarter of the communication device's wavelength. She did not remember the one quarter wavelength requirement for an antenna until her inner voice reminded her of the Technion lesson where her professor explained it to the class. Noa thought with a smile about the serious Prof. MacGyver.

Now the only remaining problem was figuring out how to shove the jury-rigged antenna out of the sand in which the helicopter was buried. Noa grabbed the one-meter-long pole she usually used to grab the end of the cable attached to the cargo she was supposed to transport. The pole had a small hook on one end, which was very useful in grabbing the cargo cable without too much futzing around. She now attached the jury-rigged antenna to this hook. She pushed the pole through the broken window straight up but had no idea whether it had broken through the sand.

Noa decided to try to broadcast a distress call.

"This is Noa, on the emergency channel. Can anyone hear me?"

Incredibly, she got an immediate reply: "This is Rotem, where the hell are you?"

"I'm stuck at the bottom of the canyon, probably several kilometers east of the lowest cable car pylon," she replied. "The helicopter is buried in sand and may not be visible from the above. I have around two hours' worth of oxygen left."

Hushed silence fell on the other side of the line.

"I imagine the best way to track me down will be to trace the source of my signal," she added.

"We're on it," Rotem responded.

Half an hour later she heard Chopper 2 above her, and half an hour after that, Noa was already speaking to Nadav who was digging through the sand in order to extract her. Watching her oxygen dial down as Nadav labored to uncover the chopper enough to pull her out was nerve wracking, but it did not take too long for them to be able to clasp hands through the hole, and more importantly, to push an oxygen hose through. An hour later she was out and headed back to Mars World-1.

Noa was moved to see Rotem, Nimrod and their children, all of whom were waiting tensely for her return.

Everything was, of course, filmed from every possible angle, including Noa's bodycam. After the video footage from the helicopter were connected to the system, her roll-over videos were broadcast all over the world and watched as if it were an action thriller movie. Experts described Noa's actions as masterful survival craft under extreme conditions. Few other people would have been able to make the right call and carry out the necessary actions with such precision and perfection.

12.

After returning to Mars World-1, Noa realized she had no real reason to stay, given that her helicopter was completely trashed. It would take at least two months to bring in a replacement helicopter. Rakefet elected to bring Noa and Nadav home on the very next flight, alongside Rotem, Nimrod and their children.

The flight back seemed more like a family vacation where they relaxed, read books and watched movies, though the twenty-minute communication lag when streaming movies on Netflix was a source of irritation for the children.

Noa did not need to pilot the plane the entire flight, because she was not part of the roster.

"I am happy I don't need to fly the plane this time," she told Nadav.

"Why are you happy?" he wondered out loud. "Usually, you love logging your flight hours, no?"

"Yes, but since the chopper accident I have a bit of a problem," she replied.

"What do you mean?" Nadav gently asked.

"Do you remember how I told you that I first lost consciousness when the chopper crashed, regained consciousness, and then lost it again? You can see it on the video footage," she said.

"Yes..." Nadav replied, not sure where she was going.

"So, the second time I woke up, it was more like a dream where I was thinking about what was required from me. A dream in which my inner voice was planning the required actions with me."

"Yes," he urged her on.

"So that inner voice was problematic," said Noa.

"Problematic how?" Nadav asked.

"When I began waking up, the voice drained me of my inner peace," she replied.

"How do you mean?" Nadav asked.

"I'm not quite sure," Noa replied in frustration. "Think of it like a big bath, filled with seemingly placid water which cover sharp rocks and reefs of unresolved issues and memories. The rock representing the murder of my father is huge. But there are others. In high school, everyone mocked me as a fat slut, the girls to my face and the boys behind my back. Flight school, during the combat course when I brought the plane to the edge of its technical capabilities — which is professional jargon for nearly crashing and burning. The tub is filled with countless other rocks. We talked about this; I am the queen of denial. When people tell me they are afraid, I understand them and know what they mean — but only intellectually. I do not feel fear, and I can't remember experiencing fear, ever since I was young." Noa paused for a moment and Nadav stroked her hand.

"When the voice in my dream woke me up, it also drained the water in the tub. The rocks are now exposed over the water. I am scared shitless of flying the plane now."

Nadav hugged her tightly. He did not know what to say.

When Noa returned home, she asked for a meeting with Galit and shared her fears with her.

"First of all, you have time now to rest and relax," Galit told her. "Secondly, I recommend getting CBT therapy for your anxiety. Such treatments are very effective in helping overcome anxiety in the short term. In any event, you are probably going to stay on Earth for the next three months, without any flights."

"I suggest that you visit a social worker or educational consultant who works with CBT. If you go to a psychologist, it will be registered in your Air Force reserve duty personal record," she added. "We will cover the cost, just go — we need you."

Galit recommended a counselor proficient in CBT therapy who treated both children and adults.

"This counselor saved my son," Galit said.

In the days following their return to Earth, Noa avoided leaving the house and stayed closed to Nadav, her parents and her sister. Nadav was badly troubled by this. He was also troubled when he discovered a gold nugget the size of his fist scattered amongst her things — gold she had obviously not reported or handed over to Rakefet.

"I think you really do need to visit Galit's counselor," Nadav abruptly told her after his discovery.

They went to the first meeting together.

Noa began with two meetings a week. After several meetings, Noa told the counselor she felt as if a popular Israeli song by Rachel Shapira was playing in her head.

"What do you mean?" the counselor asked.

"I mean the song, "Be still," Noa replied.

"Which means, don't be frightened. Those words: 'As if vulnerability itself is a sort of strength. As if serenity is the shoreline of fear.'

As if my high school vulnerability was supposed to give me strength? As if my bathwater is the shoreline of fear. But I want my bathwater back, you see?

'It is not hell and certainly not heaven. It is the world we have and there is no other world... As if air is your protection.' I don't want air to be my protection, I want the water. I don't want this hell, I want the other world, the one I lost. I want my ability to deny. I want it back.

'Even the suffocation will loosen its grasp.' Yes, in the chopper when I was running out of air, I was supposed to die. I was only able to connect the oxygen hose after I had already run out of time, out of air, after my last moment had passed. The voice in my dream took away my water and left me in a state of terror."

"Yes, that is one way to interpret the event," said the counselor. "But you can also look at that same event from a different perspective. Perhaps it was the voice in the dream which filled you with fear that saved your life back there?"

Once Nadav felt Noa was doing better, he decided to confront her about the gold nugget. He had already presented it to Shlomo and asked to pay for it according to the current market value. Shlomo understood there was a good reason for the unusual request and chose not to ask too many questions. Nadav duly deposited, according to the previously established "Noa slipups" protocol, $150,000 with the 'Yad Sarah' charity organization.

When confronted on the gold nugget, Noa blushed. This was the first and only time Nadav would see Noa blush.

"It is so hard to live with your righteousness," she responded, "You never taste grapes in the supermarket, you run off to tattletale to "Father Shlomo" over every little thing. Grow up and start living as an independent man."

Nadav was insulted but smiled.

"Yes, I don't sample the wares in the supermarket," he replied, "and yes, I certainly value the opinion of certain people, like Shlomo, as well as the opinion of my wife, the woman who is forced to live with my childishness and righteousness."

Inwardly, however, Nadav mused over the story of Adam and Eve, and the temptation of the apple — in this case, the golden apple. It was the most misogynist thought he had ever had, but he now wondered just how grounded in reality the cultural stereotype reflected in the story was. Or perhaps, the stereotype was a sort of self-fulfilling prophecy.

After three months and over twenty sessions with the counselor, Galit met Noa again.

"How are you doing, Noa?" she asked her.

"Still afraid, but less terrified," she said.

"Fear will sharpen you," Galit told her. "The mongoose hunting the cobra is afraid, but it relies on dexterity and instinctive speed to capture the snake. We need your mongoose instincts. But as for the fear, we are better off with it than without it."

Eventually, Noa got back in the saddle with an "easy" flight — just a "routine" Helium 3 run to the Moon.

Rotem, aware of Noa's new anxiety, was just as stressed before the flight as Noa was — perhaps more so.

Prior to takeoff, Noa sat down in the cockpit, felt the helm with her mongoose paws, bared her claws and brushed off a piece of dirt. Then she opened the throttle and took off.

Part H: The Golden State

1.

About a year after Noa's crash landing on Mars, the Chinese already had two desalination plants transferring about one hundred cubic meters a second each to a distance of two hundred kilometers inland into the Sahara Desert. One was in Libya, to the shores of the Mediterranean Sea, and the second in Morocco, on the shore of the Atlantic Ocean. The Americans had only one operational station in Algeria, and its pipeline was only eighty kilometers long. But the single American was already generating one hundred and eighty cubic meters a second, almost as much as both Chinese stations combined.

It is incredible how rapidly vegetation and grass grow in the desert when massive amounts of freshwater flow over the sands. When Noa returned from the Moon, she told Nadav that she could see three green spots in the Sahara from space. Nadav smiled shyly and Noa easily noticed his sense of pride. His and Chou's idea had formed flesh and form. True, Nadav was focused on the flying mattress and was not a partner of the Green Sahara Project, even the idea of sparking a desalination race between the United States and China was Galit's, but the basic idea was his.

After a relatively small number of mishaps, utilizing the rapid-lift chopper Adam designed, the floating mattress prototype was set up at the required location, sixty-five kilometers over the planet, on the exact line connecting the Earth with the Sun. The maneuver was based on the mattress being capable of rising to a five-kilometer altitude on its own, with nothing but the lift provided by the helium. The Bismuth engine is then activated to take it to a height of thirty kilometers. That took another five days. Slow progress was necessary to avoid rips in the helium mattress. The chopper then lifted the helium mattress to a height of sixty kilometers over the next twelve hours. Once the flying mattress reached a suitable altitude, it took another month of fine tuning to stabilize it to the precise altitude. Most of the steps required to launch the mattresses could be performed with many mattresses simultaneously, but lifting the helium mattress from thirty kilometers to sixty-five kilometers was a chokepoint that could only be performed by the helium rocket powered helicopter. An ordinary helicopter could barely reach a height of eight kilometers.[41] As there was, at present, only one single helium rocket powered helicopter, even should it be capable of fully automatic operations and the chopper never broke down or had to land — simply ferrying up to 10,000 helium mattresses (and that was the number that was required to reverse global warming) would take fourteen years. The powers that be therefore decided to construct another two helium rocket helicopters immediately.

About two weeks later, the first gold run from Mars arrived. Its cargo was thirty tons of pure gold, valued at two billion dollars. A huge haul — but only a tiny fraction of the thousands of tons which would be required to manufacture the 10,000 mirrors, each 100 times the size of the Hindenburg, necessary to save humanity.

------

41. At a height of over eight kilometers, the air grew too thin to provide sufficient lift to the chopper propellers, for the lift power to overcome the weight of the chopper.

The Gold flight landed in an American air base in the Pacific Ocean. In this manner, the security problems of transferring the gold were made much simpler

Chinese officers and soldiers from the MSS, as well as FBI agents, were to be responsible for the gold's security. Naturally, the transportation of thousands of tons of gold resulted in significant security issues. Placing MSS officers inside an American military base was quite impossible. Hence, the base was to allocate a zone that would belong to the Rakefet Company. In this zone there was a factory that soldered the gold plating to the upper portion of the flying mattress. It was also the base from which the flying mattresses were to be launched.

In this manner, it was easier to safeguard the gold because it did not leave the base. The gold arrived to the base from outer space and returned to outer space from the base. Well, not quite outer space, but 'only' to a sixty-five-kilometer altitude — still far beyond the bounds of the terrestrial sphere.

The Americans codenamed the Rakefet compound "The Golden State," California's nickname. The mattresses were launched from the base at a rate of one per day, with the intention being to increase the pace to two a day when the additional choppers arrived.

By this point in time, North America and Europe had suffered four consecutive years of harsh winters, whereas Australia had suffered a plague of wildfires. The unstable and increasingly extreme climate was responsible for the death of tens of thousands of people in the West, and far more in the developing world.

2.

Despite the climatic mayhem, scientists cautiously projected that the various steps being taken, albeit belatedly, would be sufficient to halt, and even reverse, global warming — if, and this was a big if — population growth was brought to a halt. The Helium 3 reactors had almost completely replaced the fossil fuel-based electricity generation. Gasoline based vehicles had been banned throughout the world, and almost everyone had transitioned to batteries. The Green Sahara and Sunshield projects offered a tangible, if elusive, hope for improvement. Some experts were even so optimistic as to suggest that the Polar ice melt might be halted by 2050, leaving 20% of the existing glaciers in Greenland, and 10% of the glaciers in Antarctica. Such remnants, however paltry, would serve as germ seeds for the recovery of the Polar glaciers by the end of the century.

The desalination plants and the agricultural production they supported removed the threat of global hunger. Of course, fundamentalists of all religions, fake news producers and science deniers continued to rabidly attack Rakefet, claiming that "if the winters are freezing cold and stormy today more than ever before, just imagine how terrible things will be when Rakefet's hellish workers hide away the sun with their satanic mirrors."

Polls held in the United States showed 40% of the population to be opposed to Rakefet's environmental activities, with 45% in support, in contrast to Europe where 25% opposed and 49% were supportive.

In China, only 7% of those polled voiced opposition with 85% approval, but polls in China were less than reliable — they tended to mirror the official party position. Although so did the genuine opinions of Chinese citizens.

The United States proceeded apace with the construction of their own spaceships — massive vessels with two nuclear reactors and Bismuth engines. These ships could not land or take off from the planet surface, because their thrust was much lower than Terran gravity, but they could orbit a planet and travel between different planets in the solar system. The first such spaceship was intended to serve as a shuttle between Earth and Mars, taking three months to complete its journey. Cargo would be loaded and unloaded while it was in orbit. Internal gravity would be maintained via rotation around its axis. The cargo capacity of these mammoth ships was far greater than that of Rakefet's spaceplanes, justifying the relatively low speed of the voyage — up to 30,000 tons, and hundreds of passengers could be delivered on each run.

The stated intention was for Rakefet planes to perform the loading and unloading. But there was a fallback option. The Chinese built rocket engines with their own superconductor. Although they were not as efficient as Rakefet's engines, they could be used to load and unload the American spaceship, thereby enabling the two superpowers to work around Rakefet — provided they were able to work together.

In an interview on CNN, Galit stated again that the best demographic forecasts were that the population of Earth would reach a peak of nine billion human beings in 2065. She warned against ever surpassing this number.

Galit said that as a liberal woman, it was clear to her that it was up to each individual to determine how many children they wanted. However, liberalism, like democracy, had a right and duty to defend itself. Just as democracy was committed to "undemocratic" rules to safeguard democracy, liberalism also had to safeguard human existence. People with more than two children, who are responsible for human population growth beyond replacement, or sustainability, endanger human existence. They cannot expect society to support them economically, socially or morally.

About 70,000 years ago, the human race suffered a catastrophe which reduced its population to several hundred individuals.[42] From that moment, until about a century ago, the literal fulfillment of the commandment "be fruitful and multiply" was required to strengthen human existence, which was the essential meaning of the commandment. But in this day and age, upholding the true intention of the commandment, preserving human existence, required each individual to have no more than two children. Should humanity fail to adapt to this change, it would not survive the changed circumstances. Galit concluded optimistically: "I am certain that we, the only sapient race, will understand, adapt, and survive the change."

---

42. One can trace the female ancestors of every individual via mitochondrial DNA. Research has revealed that 70,000 years ago, all human beings had a very small number of female ancestors (as in the biblical "begats," but tens of thousands of years ago, not thousands of years ago as the Bible suggests).

Afterword

On the eve of the Jewish New Year, Nadav purchased pome-granates, symbolizing the promise of things to come. Noa's parents were on vacation, and his own parents had invited them to spend the holiday with them. Before heading out, he peeled the pomegranates and the red juice stained his white shirt. Standing on his parent's balcony, leaning on the metal railing and gazing out at the Mediterranean Sea, its rising waters barely restrained from flooding the Port's docks and beachfront neighborhoods, he suddenly noticed the stain. He could smell the holiday cooking from the apartment below and vaguely hear the sound of prayers rising from the nearby synagogue. The pomegranate, the smell and the background chanting recalled a childhood memory of when his father had taken him to synagogue to listen to the New Year prayers. It was the only time prior to his Bar Mitzva that he had visited the small synagogue beneath their home. At that time, he did not realize the significance of the *Unetane Tokef* prayer, popularized by Leonard Cohen's "Who by Fire," written in the aftermath of the Yom Kippur War, but he could feel its power. Now, standing on the balcony, he really did feel that God was about to pass judgement on all of mankind. Would they live, or would they go extinct and make way for God's next grand experiment at a sapient, moral creation? Nadav's mind idly mused in freeform association about the delicate balance which both safeguarded the world and paralyzed humanity from taking effective action. The tension between tradition to religious fanaticism. The polarization between Republicans and Democrats in the United States, between Right and Left in Israel and Europe, each entrenching their positions ever deeper. These fierce divisions, each attracting roughly half of the citizen body, seemed to Nadav to be meaningless conflicts which only held up progress towards sustainability. It was like a high school equation that needed to be solved. It could be solved by reduction to either the right or the left of the equation, but the paralyzing balance kept everyone standing in place, going nowhere...

Noa touched his shoulder, bringing him back to reality for a moment before his thoughts began wandering again. Things were better now than they were the previous year — absolutely terrific, in fact, in spite of the climatic turmoil and the erosion of Rakefet's monopoly on the technology which could be humanity's salvation. There was now hope for a better future, for a world in which his own children might form nostalgic memories with him, Noa and their grandparents. He wondered whether enlightened politicians would arise to fulfill this future, or whether the technological potential he and Adam had uncovered would be wasted away on fulfilling populist promises to those still mired in the past.

Appendix A – scientific background

Nuclear energy
When two nuclei hydrogen (protons), the first element on the periodic table, collide, they merge into Helium, the second element on the periodic table.

When one element is transmuted into another, this is not a chemical but a nuclear phenomenon which generates nuclear energy.

Nuclear fission occurs when a large atom splits into two smaller atoms. A nuclear fission generated via a Uranium nuclear bomb, or nuclear reactors to generate electricity, is a polluting process, generating very hazardous byproducts. In contrast, the fusion of hydrogen into helium is a clean, green process. The central problem is that, as of 2023, there is no technology capable of performing this feat.

Protons carry a positive electric charge, and hence they repel each other with a force which grows inversely to the distance between them. Hence it requires extraordinary circumstances to cause them to collide — such as those that exist in the core of the sun, where the massive gravity of the sun presses them together to fuse into helium. As they undergo fusion, they emit massive amounts of energy — energy which illuminates and warms our planet, sustaining all life on Earth.

To achieve this effect outside the solar core, hydrogen atoms need to be accelerated to near light speed and then brought to collide with another hydrogen atom, preferably one whose nucleus contains two neutrons as well as a proton — something which cannot yet be accomplished.

In contrast, fusing two helium atoms, both containing two protons and a single neutron, is quite achievable using present technology. This helium isotope is known as Helium 3. Unfortunately, this isotope is quite rare on Earth. The common form of helium on our planet contains two protons and two neutrons — hence Helium 4.

The Moon, however, is constantly bombarded with Helium 3 particles from the Sun. Hence, its surface is suffused with Helium 3, which can be easily extracted. Less than a hundred tons of Helium 3 would be enough to supply all of Earth's energy requirements for an entire year. Two-three Boeing 767/787 flights, or a single 747 flight, would be enough to transfer this amount to Earth — if only those planes could reach escape velocity and cross the void to the Moon.

Magnetism

When an electrically charged particle, such as a proton, travels in a straight line and then enters a fixed magnetic field, it begins to follow a curved path until it forms a complete circle. The diameter of the largest particle accelerator in the world, located in Geneva, where protons are accelerated to the highest velocity, is around nine kilometers.

These accelerators were developed from the cyclotron, a relatively small system developed in the 1930s. The newer systems, which take relativistic effects into account, are called Isochronous cyclotrons. They are also relatively small, and very limited, just as the ability to manufacture super strong magnets is limited.

The large accelerators obviously utilize the most powerful magnets in existence. Magnetism is measured in units of "Tesla," like the car, both named after the inventor Nicola Tesla. The most powerful magnet in the world in 2020 could generate around thirty Tesla, utilizing, of course, superconductors.

Superconductors

Every substance has a certain resistance to electricity. The most commonly utilized material for electric conductivity is copper; only silver conducts electricity slightly better. In both metals, resistance is fairly small, but exists, nonetheless. This causes the conductor to heat up when an electrical current runs through it. The greater the current, the greater the rise in temperature. To conduct high currents, thicker copper wires are required, where the resistance is lower and resulting in milder heating.

In 1911, superconductivity was discovered when temperatures approached -270 degrees Celsius, which approaches absolute zero. This is very difficult to achieve, even in a laboratory. Superconductivity is generated via a certain configuration of energy levels on the surface of the material. In a state of superconductivity, electrical resistance is 0. Not very small, not minimal, but actually 0. In other words, the material does not heat up at all when an electrical current runs through it. See Appendix B — "Ismail's technical lecture."

However, there is a limit to the electrical current which can be conducted via a given area of a superconductor. When you surpass this threshold, the superconductivity vanishes. In fact, there are two limitations to superconductors: they need to be very cold, and they can only transmit a given current per area unit.

Since 1911, superconductors have been improved to enable performance at higher and higher temperatures. In 2020 a superconductor at a temperature of over 0 degrees Celsius, that is to say the temperature of an airconditioned room, has been achieved. However, it required highly complex laboratory conditions.

Superconductors have been used to manufacture extremely powerful magnets. As aforementioned, by the 2020s superconductors were already widely used. MRI machines are designed on the basis of powerful electromagnets constructed out of superconductors. High-speed trains, such as those widely utilized in China, which surpass 400 KPH, avoid friction via superconductors — and there are many more uses both in industry and in research.

Rocket engines

Rocket engines operate by expelling mass, usually ignited fuel gases, backwards. The power the engine uses to push the mass backwards results in thrust on the engine forwards in accordance with Newton's third law. The greater the mass expelled backwards, and the greater its speed of expulsion, the greater the thrust generated.

Appendix B – Ismail's technical lecture

"Let's start with a short explanation about superconductivity," Ismail began. "So what actually generates electric resistance?" Ismail asked but did not wait for an answer.

"Let me explain in reductive terms. When an electron travels through a medium, such a metallic lattice of atoms, it repeatedly bumps into the atoms of the lattice. These collisions make it difficult for it to move forward and are termed as electric resistance of the substance. But as you have no doubt heard, particles can also be described in physics as a wave. So, for example, a light wave can also be described as the movement of particles called photons. Similarly, one can also describe electron as a wave. If the wavelength of the electron itself matches exactly the gaps in the lattice in a given direction of the electron movement, the electron will not bump into the atoms of the lattice. Quantically speaking, the electron and the atoms cannot occupy the same position. In other words, resistance to electric current will be equal to 0. Given this, why do we need to cool the material to achieve the desired effect?"

This was another rhetorical question and Ismail did not expect an answer. But this time, Rotem answered.

"Heat is random movement of particles, so while the atoms may be fixed in place in the lattice, the entire lattice is shaking since the electrons will collide with the atoms dancing in the lattice."

"That's right," said Ismail. "Below a certain temperature threshold, the quiver of the atoms is sufficiently small as to enable electrons as a wave to skip between the holes in the lattice without colliding with dancing atoms and forming electrical resistance." Here Ismail halted and said. "Now to the secret part, the one covered by the NDA you signed earlier." He paused for a moment and continued: "The superconductivity in our system occurs in the contact area between two different substances. At this contact area the atoms are no longer dancing randomly in every direction because there is a preferred direction — the direction of the second substance. Hence, our substance is not merely a superconductor — it is an incredibly improved superconductor. This is the information I can share with you at your classification level. We will now take a short recess and return to another physics class."

During recess, Noa laughed and told Rotem: "I did not know you were such a physics hot shot."

"Yeah," Rotem smiled at her, "there are still a few things you do not know about me." When they returned, Ismail was already in the room.

"As you no doubt remember from your high school physics classes," Ismail began, "a charged particle moving through a magnetic field develops a circular motion. The power, in this case an enormous power exercised by the magnetic field, requires no energy input, and so the system does not accumulate heat."

"I studied this in kindergarten of course," Barry quipped cynically, "but I would prefer you review the technology working under the assumption that the fellows here are not physics majors."

Ismail understood he might be speaking over the head of

his audience and shifted gears, trying to think of an example of force being applied without energy investment.

"Suppose that I take an iron pipe and grab it with a pair of clamps. The force applied on the pipe can be huge and I can keep the pipe in the clamps for an hour, or an entire day. Nonetheless, no heat will be generated, and no energy will be wasted. "Likewise," he continued, "the massive magnetic field exercises a massive force on the particles revolving inside the ring and does not generate any heat whatsoever. The particles we accelerate within the ring are protons which carry a positive electric charge, of course, and hence can be accelerated via an electric field. We accelerate the particles via an electric voltage we provide to small plates in which the protons pass through a narrow aperture. This action does require a great deal of energy because we are accelerating the protons to near light speed. However, due to the magnetic field, from our perspective outside the ring, they are actually revolving inside the ring. We order the protons in a group which races through the ring, accumulating more and more speed with every rotation, until it reaches the critical threshold speed, which we will soon discuss."

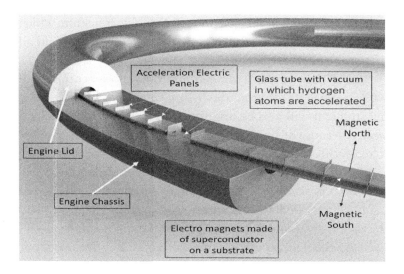

Schematic cross section image of the engine ring

"But let us return for a moment to Barry's kindergarten," Ismail said acerbically. "What are protons? I remind you that every substance in nature is composed of chemical elements. Every chemical element is composed of atoms, which are composed of low mass negatively charged electrons which rotate around the nucleus. The nucleus contains heavy weight, positively charged protons, and neutrons. The differential equations describe what actually occurs, and when there is no solution to an equation in a given state, which means this situation does not exist in nature. Situations which represent a solution of the equations are the quantic states which exist in nature, but we won't go into that today."

"In neutral atoms without either negative or positive charge, the quantity of negative electrons and positive protons is identical. If an electron is missing in the atom, it is called a positive ion. Elements in nature are arranged in the periodic table, which begins with the hydrogen atom, which has a single proton and a single electron. The next element in the table is helium, which has two protons and two electrons, and so forth throughout all of nature's elements."

"Going back to the hydrogen atom. As aforementioned, if we take away its electron, the hydrogen will be a positive ion, but in fact it will also be nothing more than a proton." Ismail smiled because he saw his audience really was making an effort to recall this high school level material.

"We have a very powerful particle accelerator," he added, "but it is also very small. What is our secret? Without delving into too many details, we have the ability to generate a magnetic field that is ten-thousand-fold more powerful than the most powerful magnetic field produced up to this point. But this is not our only technological innovation. We will touch on our other strong points later on. In contrast to the kilometer-diameter sized particle accelerator, such as the famous particle accelerator in Geneva, the diameter of our particle accelerator is only two meters — small enough to be installed in the wings of a 767 plane."

"But to return to our proton group, which are like a group of runners in a racing track. They are not randomly scattered across the track, but are a cohort running together, which means that if we examine a particular location on the track, sometimes there is an electrical current running through it — when the cohort is passing through. And sometimes there isn't. Once the cohort passes it, that section of the track remains empty. In practice, we have two cohorts running in order to balance the forces in the ring and prevent vibrations. However, as you must know, a current passing through a given location which sometimes has a current and sometimes does not, is called an alternating current. We will later understand that this alternating current is actually a generator operating the plane's systems."

"Let us return to our cohort of runners. At a certain stage they approach light speed. At this stage, every photon has enormous energy. Now we are "pulling a stunt on them" and tripping them up. What do I mean? We are adding additional hydrogen atoms, of which have no speed at all, just to get the speeding protons to collide with them. Well, what's the problem with that? Well, as you know, two positive charges repel one another, and the closer they are to the other, the more they repel each other. So, in principle they cannot collide, because at a certain stage they will be close enough for their repulsion to be sufficiently large enough to prevent the collision and keep them away from the other. But this is where the powerful force in the atomic nuclei comes into play. When the distance between the protons is smaller from the radius of the atoms nuclei, the strong force of the nucleus becomes much greater than electrical repulsion force. At that point, the two protons cling to each other and actually become the helium atom nucleus, an atom with two protons — the two protons which just collided. This is called nuclear fusion. The fusion is the moment the hydrogen atom (proton) becomes a two-proton nucleus, which is helium. This action generates massive nuclear energy."

Yossi Turgeman's face reddened. He was incensed with fury. "You want to put a nuclear reactor in my plane?" he asked with shocked outrage.

"Not one, but two nuclear reactors," Ismail answered. "That is not so bad. Aircraft carriers have a nuclear reactor as do nuclear submarines. Putting a nuclear reactor in a plane is simply the next step."

Yossi began to connect the dots in his mind.

"What happens here," continued Ismail, "is that the two protons which were once hydrogen become helium. In other words, the two lonely protons, which, up until now were called 'hydrogen,' collided and became single nucleus with two protons. A nucleus which has two protons is called, as aforementioned, 'helium.' We have transmuted one element into another. That is precisely what any high school chemistry teacher tells his students that can't be done or alternately only in a nuclear process.

"And indeed, the process I just explained is a nuclear fusion process. Our process is designed to emit most of the helium atoms from the emission aperture of the ring. Moreover, the equations themselves show that almost all of the collisions occur three meters outside the ring emission aperture. The heat and energy are sucked out, the ring itself only cools from the process. Our ability to solve these equations in this particular case is another of our relative advantages. The helium jet, whose particles move at near light-speed, generates the thrust for our helium rocket engine."

Yossi vaguely recollected his physics lessons from the Technion.

"That does not add up for me," he said, "because according to the law of the conservation of momentum, if one proton is at rest and the second collides with it, let us say at near light-speed, then once they fuse into a helium atom, its speed should be only half-light speed."

"Very good," Ismail said. "You are right, but your calculations which are based on Newton's law of conservation of momentum, are only true in non-relativistic speeds. When particle approaches light speed, Einstein's theory of relativity comes into play, and utilizing its calculations, the speed of the helium emitted from our engine are around 80% of the speed of light. However, the full explanation is beyond the scope of this introductory lecture."

"Luckily..." muttered Barry.

"Now, where do we get the hydrogen?" Ismail continued., "Our basic fuel is water. To return to Barry's kindergarten, I remind you that water is H_2O. That means that each water molecule is made up of two hydrogen atoms and a single oxygen atom. Do you remember the electric current generated by the generator of the cohort of runners in the ring? So, this current is used to electrolyze the water. What is electrolysis? In a small water bath, two electric wires are inserted. One is connected to a positive charge, and the second to a negative charge. The moment electricity is activated, water breaks into oxygen and hydrogen. Next to the positive wire, a stream of oxygen bubbles emerges, whereas hydrogen bubbles emerge from the negative wire. The oxygen is used to enable the plane passengers to breathe, whereas the hydrogen is transferred to the engine as fuel. The engine generates thrust by emitting helium particles backwards at incredible speeds, and electricity which is used to generate more oxygen and hydrogen." Ismail took a break and looked over his audience to assess the impression his words had made on them.

"Returning to our cohort of runners, some of the energy generated is used to get the hydrogen we push into the ring to generate another cohort of runners, who sprint in the same direction as the cohort of runners who generated them. The equations used to describe this system are similar to those governing the environment of a laser generator. The difference is that, in the case of the laser, the photon impacting excited photons generates a beam of photons travelling in the same direction as the original photon, whereas in our engine these are not weightless photons, but relatively heavy protons. The problem is that in the first stage, there are no collisions and no proton movement either. You need electrical energy to accelerate the protons to reach a critical speed approaching light speed, so that the collision will be powerful enough to generate helium from the colliding hydrogen particles. This stage is called engine ignition. The ignition takes around ten seconds but consumes quite a bit of electrical energy. To perform the ignition around ten tons of sparkling new batteries will be installed, and even that will only be enough for two ignitions, perhaps three. The batteries are recharged by the engine they ignite — it takes it around an hour to recharge them and permit another ignition."

"Let's talk about motion in space a little. So long as the plane is in the atmosphere, or to be more accurate, below the Kármán Line, we rely on the plane's aerodynamic structure to stabilize it. But above the Kármán Line the atmosphere is too thin to support the plane fuselage and affect its flight pattern. Let us suppose we have two engines, and they are thrusting in a single line precisely below the plane's center of gravity. If they are doing so then the plane will advance in a straight, steady line in the direction of the thrust. Now let us suppose that one of the passengers moves inside the plane. His movement has just shifted the center of gravity. Now the engines are no longer in a single straight line below the center of gravity. That means the plane will begin rolling, and since the engines are rolling together with the plane, the direction of flight will change. The roll will be slow but be uncontrolled by the pilots."

"In fact, it is much like a table," he continued"

"We need a similar finetuning mechanism in the plane. Let us suppose for a moment that the plane was attached to a hydraulic device that will enable the pilot to control the direction of the thrust. So long as we are below the Kármán Line, the thrust will be directed backwards, and the closer one approaches, and then passes, the more the thrust will be directed downwards. Control over the hydraulic system will have to come from a computerized system which will also be fed with data from the gyro systems in order to keep the plane from spinning. Control over the direction of the system will be in the hands of the pilots."

"Since that is also not enough to perfectly stabilize the plane, there will also be a regular rocket engine, not a nuclear engine, and a relatively small one at that which will combust normal hydrogen and oxygen to generate thrust, solely for the purposes of fine stabilization. All in all, this engine is supposed to generate less than 0.01% of the thrust energy of the helium rocket engine. This engine will be installed beneath the pilot cockpit, in the area of the front wheel of the plane and will serve as the third leg of the table."

Ismail examined the expressionless faces of his audience, realized that his technical explanation had not really delivered the take home message, and changed tack:

"The plane, equipped with all the systems I just reviewed, has to be ready to take off in April, precisely another six months."

Appendix C – A short explanation of Nadav's ionic engine

As of 2023, ionic engines are used by satellites to correct their position. Satellites have solar panels that power their ionic engine. An ionic engine emits a stream of ions that are accelerated by electric energy to generate thrust. Ionized Xenon is used in most of the current satellites, but new engines are being designed with ionized Bismuth.[43] Bismuth atoms are almost twice the mass and so offer better thrust for longer time. The ionized atoms are accelerated utilizing the Hall effect.[44]

The Hall effect requires a powerful magnet, which would normally be quite heavy. The Adam-Nadav superconductor, however, enabled the design of a super powerful, super-light magnet. Thus, Nadav's Bismuth ionic engine was perfectly suited to its task, generating thrust for over a decade.

----

43. Atomic number 83.

44. Physics Phenomena in which electric current is generated perpendicular to the direction of the current in the conductor when a magnetic field is applied to it.

Printed in Great Britain
by Amazon

34935802R00209